# Purpose and Passion

Foreword by Chad Pennington

# Purpose and Passion

## Bobby Pruett & the Marshall Years

BILL CHASTAIN

**MID-ATLANTIC HIGHLANDS**

A Grace Associates Book

ISBN:   0-9744785-8-X (Deluxe Edition)
        0-9744785-9-8 (Hardcover Edition)

Library of Congress Control Number: 2005936439

First Edition, First Printing
Printed in Canada

Cover Design and Illustration: Thom Marsh
Book and Additional Cover Design: Mark S. Phillips
Editorial Coordination: John Patrick Grace and Tim Stephens

Endleaves: Herd Quarterback Stan Hill evades hard-charging Ohio State linebacker A.J. Hawk and sails a pass downfield in Marshall's white-knuckle 24-21 loss to Ohio State in 2004. The Buckeyes needed a last-second 54-yard field goal for the win. *Courtesy Marshall University, photograph by Rick Haye.*

Additional Photo Credits:
Back cover, deluxe edition—*courtesy Marshall University, photograph by Marilyn Testerman-Haye.*
Dust jacket flap, hardcover edition—*courtesy Marshall University, photograph by Rick Haye.*

Mid-Atlantic Highlands
An Imprint of Publishers Place, Inc.
P.O. Box 2395
Huntington, WV 25724

www.publishersplace.org

# Acknowledgments

*Special thanks for help in putting this book project together go to Jim and Verna Gibson, Robert Hardwick of First Sentry Bank, Dave Wellman, Rick Haye, and Scott Morehouse of Marshall University, Frank Scatoni, literary agent to Bill Chastain, and Elsie Pruett, and all the sponsors listed on the closing page of* Purpose and Passion.

*In addition Coach Pruett expresses warm personal thanks to the following for their friendship and personal support during his coaching years at Marshall University: Athletic Director Kayo Marcum, former Athletic Directors Lee Moon and Lance West; former Marshall University President J. Wade Gilley, Ralph May, former head of the Big Green; Dr. Jose Ricard, team physician; chaplains, the late R.F. Smith, Bob Bondurant, and Allen Reasons; Edna Justice, his personal secretary, and all Marshall football coaches and players over his nine seasons.*

*Also to the following: Steve Ellis, president of the Quarterback Club, Charleston; and Mark George, president of the Quarterback Club, Huntington, Keith Morehouse of WSAZ-TV, who did the coach's show with him; Dan Shumaker, ESPN regional executive; Sheriff Kim Wolfe and Chuck Nuttercutt for police escorts;*

*Also to the following for their faithful support: Buck Harless, Bob Beymer, Tim Haymaker, Selby Wellman, Chris Cline, Charlie Carroll, Art Andrews, Marshall Reynolds, John Drinko, Bob Shell, Don Blankenship, Scott Hutchinson, Howard Beckner, Laurie Fox, Randy Dunfee, Rich DeHart, Alan Thacker, John Jones, David Hayden, Dan Egnor, Larry Tweel, Dale Manns, Jim Tartyu, Tom Wilkerson, Tom Wright, Carroll Justice, Jim Tarty, and John Montanez.*

# Contents

# Foreword

Coach Bobby Pruett has had a special impact on my life and on the lives of many, many others. Coach Pruett brought the philosophy of "We play for championships" to Marshall University, but that was much more than just a slogan and it extended well beyond the football field.

He insisted on our playing for championships in the classroom and in our personal and spiritual lives. He told us that if we worked hard and worked together, we would leave Marshall with a championship ring on one hand and a diploma in the other. We believed it and he was right. Coach Pruett is a man of his word.

I came to Marshall under Coach Jim Donnan, who did a great job of getting our program established at a higher level in the early 1990s. Coach Donnan built Marshall into an NCAA Division I-AA power. He brought in good players, sustained the program, built on what had been there before and set the foundation for success.

When Coach Pruett came in, he didn't try to take away from what Coach Donnan had done, but instead tried to add to it and build upon it. One look at Coach Pruett's record shows that he was highly successful in elevating Marshall to another level, a level that many could only dream of just a few years earlier. He took Marshall to heights it never had attained before.

Coach Pruett and Coach Donnan complemented one another. Both deserve credit for where the program is today. Each gives the other a great deal of credit. That says something about them. Each had his own style, but each style worked and worked very well.

I came to Marshall in 1995 and by the time I left after the 1999 season, we had won a lot of games, more than any other team in the 1990s. While I was at Marshall, we went 62-7. We won a lot of big games: division and conference championships, bowl games, games against some big-time powers.

Coach Pruett took the program to new heights. When I arrived in 1995, we were an NCAA Division I-AA team, competing with the strongest teams in that division, teams such as Furman, Georgia Southern, Montana and Appalachian State. When I left, we had beaten a whole different set of teams—Clemson, South Carolina, Brigham Young and others.

We never were intimidated by any of those teams. Coach Pruett's mantra that "We play for championships" instilled in us an expectation of winning. We expected to win each time we took the field, no matter who we were playing nor where we were playing. Fortunately for us, we usually did win. A key reason for that was the confidence Coach Pruett had in us and that we had in him. There was mutual respect there. Coach respected us as players and as individuals. He knew how to bring us together as a team.

Coach Pruett knows how to motivate a team. He knew when to get on us and when to ease off. He knew how to use his sense of humor to lighten the mood when that was needed. He knew when to be hands on and when to let us take responsibility upon ourselves.

Coach often told us before we went on the field, "We have better players, now let's be the better team." We had a lot of great players. We had a lot of individual talent. But having great individual players doesn't always mean having a great team. Coach Pruett made sure we were a great team. It never was about any one player. It wasn't Chad Pennington's team, nor Randy Moss' team, nor Byron Leftwich's team. It never even was Coach Pruett's team. It was Marshall's team. By that, Coach Pruett wanted the fans to feel like it was their team. He did an excellent job of conveying that message. It was the fans' team and it was a team they could be proud of.

I am very close to my father. For me, personally, Coach Pruett is like a second father. He's a great guy. He's fun to be around and he treats people the way he would want them to treat him. He goes out of his way to make sure that people have what they need. He's different from any other coach I've been around. Coach Pruett cared about the team, but he also cared about the individual. His door always was open.

As a player, I believed in Coach Pruett and in what he was trying to do. We combined with him as a coach and us as players to make the plan work. I owe Coach Pruett so much and I give him so much credit for how my college career turned out. We as players had a lot of faith in Coach Pruett and in what he was doing. I know he had a lot of faith in us. Personally, he gave me more and more responsibility and that helped me to improve as a quarterback and as a person. For that, I will be forever grateful.

Some of the decisions Coach Pruett made helped show me the right way to do things, as well as the right way to approach the game of football. He always had the best in mind for the football program, for his players, his coaches and the university. No one is a better ambassador for Marshall University than Coach Pruett.

A lot of people will remember Coach Pruett as a great coach. I'm fortunate to know him not only as a great coach, but as a great man.

— **Chad Pennington**
Syosset, L.I., New York

# Introduction

Byron Leftwich zips a touchdown pass to Josh Davis on the final play of the second overtime as Marshall remarkably comes back from 30 points down to defeat East Carolina 64-61 in the 2001 GMAC Bowl. ESPN instantly dubs the game a "Classic."

Classic. That's the word most fitting in describing Bobby Pruett. Not just his years at Marshall, but Pruett himself. The Man. The player. The coach. The husband. The jokester. The good ole boy from East Beckley, as Bobby might put it.

The man who directed the Golden Era of the green and white is much more than a coach. While Bobby Pruett's on-field success is what most fans remember, even more fascinating are the aspects that can't neatly be tucked away in the record books. The numbers—a 94-23 record, eighteen championships, five bowl victories, two undefeated seasons, one national title—tell merely part of the story. Like the bulky championship rings Pruett sports, the statistics are gaudy, glitzy. They make you take notice, gleaming symbols of victory as bright as the scoreboard at Joan C. Edwards Stadium.

Getting to know the Bobby Pruett outside the public eye, away from the cameras, off the sideline, is a journey teeming with anticipation and of marvelous revelation. Whether inside the locker room, where no outsider is permitted, or in the solitude of a hospital room of a critically ill fan, Bobby Pruett is the same. Steadying. Motivating. Comforting. Inspiring. Genuine.

In *Purpose and Passion*, Bobby Pruett allows us to delve into the personality of a coach who somehow combines brashness with humility in perfect parts to create a larger than life individual who deflects credit to everyone but himself. We see the inner workings behind the Xs and Os that were Chad Pennington and Randy Moss, but Pruett reveals the qualities that made his star players more than just familiar jersey numbers with identities hidden behind their facemasks.

*Purpose and Passion* is so much more than just a walk down memory lane. We revisit the glory of the Pruett years of Marshall football from a place few have been—from the inside. But we also trek to Pruett's formative years, to the time before he discovered his dream to be the head football coach at Marshall University. We glimpse into the life of a young coach who married his high school sweetheart and together raised three boys. We hear Bobby's wife, Elsie, remember what their lives were like when money was tight and the future uncertain then receive her take on the wonder of national rankings and Heisman Trophy ceremonies.

Coach Pruett and his players reveal what really took place at halftime of the East Carolina game. They tell us what they were thinking during the Thundering Herd's amazing rally to beat Western Michigan in the closing seconds of the 1999 Mid-American Conference championship game. We're privy to the inner workings that constituted the victories at Clemson, at South Carolina and at Kansas State. We learn how the 1999 Motor City Bowl matchup with BYU almost never took place.

Bobby Pruett tells us what he looked for in a player he recruited and exactly how he attracted Randy Moss, Byron Leftwich, Eric Kresser, Darius Watts and other stars to the Herd. We learn of the last minute decision to spurn Houston's multi-million dollar offer. We travel deeper into Coach Pruett's quest to schedule a series with West Virginia. We hear Pruett's former stars discuss their coach's passion, his sense of humor and his love for them.

Coach Pruett takes us onto the bus to hear the banter, into the locker room to understand the strategy and onto the sideline to see the game-changing decisions that made Marshall football what it is today. Coach Pruett invites us into the huddle, into the planning sessions, onto the practice field and into the very soul of the Thundering Herd. He allows us to experience the highs and lows, the lessons taught and the lessons learned. Coach Pruett gives us the opportunity to hoist the championship trophy over our heads and to cheer for him and with him once again.

In this book, we'll hear the thunderous chant "WE ARE...MARSHALL!" grow louder with the turn of each page, for *Purpose and Passion* is classic Bobby Pruett.

— **Tim Stephens**
  **Former Sportswriter, *The Huntington Herald-Dispatch***
  **Director, Fellowship of Christian Athletes**

# Purpose and Passion

# A HECTIC LIFE

## *Chapter one*

Hectic is the life of a college football coach.

Bobby Pruett's work schedule contained so many this ways and that ways that he barely had time to consider the job he had coveted most of his adult life: head football coach at Marshall University.

Located in the southwest portion of West Virginia in Huntington, Marshall held a special place in Pruett's soul. To the son of West Virginia, this little corner of the world was God's country and the place where he dreamed of returning some day. Only a journey had to be taken in order to find his way home.

Flash back to December 1995 to find Pruett working under Steve Spurrier at the University of Florida as the Gators' defensive coordinator. The team had a 12-0 mark after

**OFF THE FIELD —** As comfortable off the field as on, Bob used his position to further promote Marshall University in academics as well as athletics. *Courtesy Marshall University.*

*1*

A HECT

C LIFE

cruising through the regular season—including a 35-24 win over rival Florida State—before beating Arkansas 35-24 to become Southeastern Conference Champions.

Nebraska sat on the horizon. Florida had a Fiesta Bowl date with the Cornhuskers to settle which team could stake a claim to the No. 1 ranking. That left Pruett to spend hours each day plotting out how they could best combat legendary coach Tom Osborne's veer option attack.

X's and O's aside, Pruett had to think about filling the Gators' tank for the coming years by recruiting players capable of conquering an SEC schedule or going to Tallahassee and stopping FSU's always explosive offense.

Add to all of this activity the news that flashed in front of him. Kansas coach Glen Mason, who accepted the head coaching position at the University of Georgia, experienced a change of heart a week later. Some said his decision came because of a recent divorce settlement and child custody issues. Mason simply said the decision had been based strictly on the fact he couldn't leave Kansas. Whatever the case, Mason wasn't going to be the Bulldogs' coach and Pruett began to hear through the coaching grapevine that Marshall's coach, Jim Donnan, had become the leading candidate for the Georgia job.

"And this is a rumor, so I don't know how much fact it is," said Pruett chuckling at the memory. "But I had a lot on my plate right then, so I tucked it away because I had other things I had to do. You can't get distracted when you're about to play Nebraska for the National Championship."

Pruett had coveted the Marshall job since graduating from Marshall in 1965. Marshall was family, Marshall was home; Marshall would be the perfect fit—if he just got the chance.

"That was my dream job," Pruett said. "Becoming the Marshall coach was a dream and a goal I had had for as long as I had been a coach."

Pruett didn't have the luxury of fantasizing about landing his dream job. He had to figure out a way to stop Nebraska, and recruiting remained a priority. Meanwhile, other events continued to unfold.

Vince Dooley, Georgia's athletic director, put in a call to Donnan.

Donnan had an impressive resume including time spent as an Oklahoma assistant and there was the work he'd done at Marshall, where he had posted a 64-21 record in six seasons and had turned the Thundering Herd into a legitimate I-AA power.

Dooley offered Donnan the job and he accepted, leaving the Marshall position open. The news rocked Pruett like linebackers once did when he

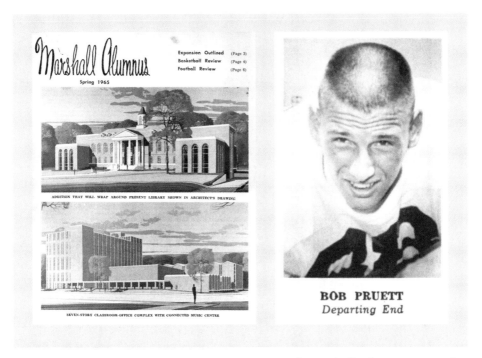

**DEPARTING SENIOR** — The Spring 1965 issue of *Marshall Alumnus* magazine featured photographs of the departing senior football players, including a crew-cut Bob Pruett. *Courtesy Bob Pruett.*

went across the middle to catch a pass while wearing the green and white of the Thundering Herd. Pruett could see himself standing on the sideline at Marshall Stadium coaching his university. The vision seemed preordained.

Pruett picked up the telephone and called Marshall athletic director Lee Moon to express his interest. Moon processed the information and told Pruett he would get back to him. Two days before the Fiesta Bowl on Jan. 2, 1996, Moon called Pruett in Phoenix to let him know they wanted to interview him for the job. Interview arranged, Pruett turned back to the business at hand, the Fiesta Bowl and the National Championship.

Spurrier's touted Fun 'N Gun offense scored points like a fast-breaking NBA team, leaving Pruett's defense only a quick breather before heading back onto the field to try and stop the other team's offense. While the Cornhuskers employed a different kind of offense than the Gators' they were formidable, scoring thirty-five or more points in every game while averaging just over two minutes for their eighty-two scoring drives during the season. The Cornhuskers had a physically dominant offensive line and a lot of speed coming out of the backfield.

Nebraska at 11-0 went into the game ranked No. 1 and Florida at 12-0 was No. 2, in what had been hyped as a scoring shootout where the last team with the ball would likely be the winner.

Instead, the Gators suffered one of the more embarrassing defeats in the history of bowl games getting humiliated 62-24 in front of 79,864 fans and a national television audience. The Cornhuskers had 629 yards of total offense, including 524 on the ground.

"That was a tough one," Pruett said. "Sometimes in bowls, the game gets away from you. The very next year, Florida plays Florida State in the National Championship game and Florida State had won their regular season game. Then the Seminoles are the ones who get get blown out in the National Championship game. You know, bowl games can get away from you, because the season's almost over and players start watching the clock. Particularly the seniors who think about how, 'I'm finished now and I don't want to get hurt.' We had some injuries and I just think that our energy level really dropped in that game. We were missing tackles and doing some things we shouldn't have been doing. You couldn't do those kinds of things against a team like Nebraska. That was a great, great football team."

Florida flew back to Gainesville licking their wounds, but Pruett had little time to mope about the defeat. Even though his defense had not played well, it had set a school record in 1994 on Pruett's watch by allowing just 84.6 rushing yards per game while holding opponents to 17.1 points. Pruett followed his successful year in 1995 with a defense that ranked among the top twenty-five teams in the country in scoring defense, pass efficiency defense, total defense, and rushing defense. And both teams played in major bowl games.

Yes, the Marshall job sat on the horizon, but given the fact there are no sure things, Pruett went about his business as if Florida would be his job for the next twenty years. That meant visiting recruits.

At the time of Donnan's resignation, the leading candidate to replace him was his defensive coordinator, Mickey Matthews, a fan favorite and the architect of a strong defensive unit. Matthews was a personable guy. Fans liked his rugged defense and his Texas drawl. Matthews wanted the job; Donnan would have liked Matthews to have it.

Marshall President J. Wade Gilley, though, wanted a Marshall man.

Marshall had become a program like a lot of schools its size—a stepping-stone to bigger jobs.

In 1985, Stan Parrish left after two years for Kansas State. He was replaced by George Chaump, who left after the 1989 season to become head coach at Navy. Now, Donnan had gone to Georgia.

Men's basketball was the same way. Dana Altman replaced Rick Huckabay in 1990 and left after one season for Creighton, his alma mater. And later, after Pruett was hired, the Herd's basketball coach, Billy Donovan, bolted for Florida. Tired of seeing coaches leave, Gilley looked for someone with loyalty to the school. He and Moon also looked for a coordinator from a major program with Marshall ties, which put Pruett on their radar screen.

The Gators' plane landed, Pruett changed his clothes and headed north to recruit players for the Gators' cupboard. Coinciding with the recruiting was the prearranged visit with Moon at a hotel at the Charlotte airport.

"Bob wanted to be a head coach, but we didn't know if it would ever happen," said Pruett's wife, Elsie. "There are so many coaches that you just think, 'Well, maybe he'll never get to be a head coach.' I remember driving around in the car and saying, 'Lord, I don't know if this is what you want and I don't know if it is the best, but all I can say is I know Bob would like to be a head coach someday, and only you would know whether that's right or not and there's just not that many jobs.' I had not prayed that before until then, never thought about it, him being a head coach. I knew if he ever was one I felt like he could go anywhere."

Marshall's basketball team happened to be playing Nevada in Las Vegas in an ESPN televised game at midnight, so Pruett headed over to visit Moon. They sat and visited while watching the game until 2 a.m.

"Then I got up the next morning, because I had no idea whether I was going to get the job or not," Pruett said. "So I got in my car about 4:30 in the morning and drove up to see a recruit, who we ended up getting at Florida, a big defensive lineman in North Carolina, a really good player; Chambers was his name. I came back to the hotel and interviewed with Lee at 10 a.m., then got in the car and drove to some town in North Carolina where I had a home visit with a fullback that we were recruiting. After that I drove back to Charlotte, caught a plane and flew to Norfolk and ended up meeting with a defensive back who did decide to come to Florida, I forget his name. Again, I don't know whether I'm getting the job or not, all I've done is interview for the job, so I've got to do my job, you know."

Despite a snowstorm, Pruett drove to Lynchburg, Virginia, the following day for a recruiting visit then flew back to Gainesville on a Friday. While Pruett was in the air, the Marshall contingent called Spurrier and Jeremy Foley, the Florida athletic director, for recommendations. Pruett received a call Friday night telling him he was going to be offered the Marshall job.

Pruett met with Spurrier at 9 o'clock the following morning. At the time Spurrier was in play as a candidate for the vacated head-coaching job of the NFL's Tampa Bay Buccaneers. They talked about that possibility and whether Pruett would be interested in going to Tampa if Spurrier became the Bucs' coach. Pruett told Spurrier the Marshall job was his dream. Around 10 o'clock, Pruett received a call from Gilley, who offered him the job. Pruett accepted.

Marshall intended to fly Pruett up for a big press conference over the weekend to announce his hiring, but a snowstorm covered West Virginia, making plane travel impossible. Never one to let his shirttail touch his rear end, Pruett got in his car and drove to New Orleans for the National Coaches Convention. Upon reaching the convention, Pruett found himself the focal point of the rumors he would be the new coach at Marshall. Behind the scenes he began to talk to coaches in confidence about the staff he planned to hire.

Once the snow in West Virginia began to clear, Pruett flew to Huntington where at age fifty-two he was introduced as the new coach of the Thundering Herd after signing a five-year deal.

Pruett was not the fans' first choice. They liked Matthews. Some liked the thought of Chaump returning and Chaump did explore that opportunity. No one else really caught their fancy. When Pruett was hired there were some who felt Gilley had hired a bumpkin who would risk letting a strong program fall apart.

Popular choice or not, the native of Beckley, West Virginia, had returned home.

**ONE OF THE BOYS** — A ten-year-old Bob Pruett (photo left) poses with older brothers John and Paul and his father, Roy Pruett. *Courtesy Bob Pruett.*

**TEAM PHOTO** — Bob's (front row, far right) ninth grade team. *Courtesy Bob Pruett.*

## *Chapter two*

Bobby Pruett grew up in Beckley, West Virginia, the fifth boy in a family of five.

Pruett's father, Roy, was a miner who would later die of black lung disease. Pruett watched his father and learned character lessons about the value of hard work and doing things the right way; his mother made sure he didn't step out of line.

"Well, I've said many times when I speak that I had a real drug problem when I was a kid," Pruett teased. "Mama drug me to Boy Scouts. She drug me to church. She drug me all over trying to make sure that I did the things that you need to do to have a good life. She did all that 'drugging' because I think Mom actually recognized the potential that I had to go to the dark side, as they put it in the Star Wars vernacular...I had a little mischief in me. Mother had her share of challenges

**PROPER TECHNIQUE** — Bob (28), while a senior at Woodrow Wilson High School, demonstrated how to wrap-up an opposing ball carrier. *Courtesy Bob Pruett.*

2

FROM PLAYE

R TO COACH

when she was raising me."

A passion for sports helped curb Pruett's tendency to find trouble. Sports lit him up inside. He enjoyed playing sports, and playing sports kept him busy. Initially he didn't have a favorite sport.

"When I was growing up, we'd go to the school yard, which was right up the street from me, and we would play football through football season, during basketball season, we'd play basketball; and then we'd play baseball," Pruett said. "And I didn't realize until I started running track in ninth grade—I had good track times—that I could outrun everybody."

Pruett's speed and size—six-foot, 195 pounds—eventually made football king with him.

"Football was the sport I played best," Pruett said. "I was sort of an aggressive guy, you know. As a kid, we all grew up in a time where, basically, part of growing up was going to the ball yard and playing and fighting. That was just normal for us."

When Pruett wasn't playing sports he worked as the custodian at the church he attended, St. Mary's Methodist Church. And he spent time with Elsie

Pruett and Elsie Riffe met in 1957, but did not actually begin to date until 1958. Elsie, who was from Crab Orchard just outside Beckley, was older than her boyfriend and, aside from the difference in their ages, some wondered what she saw in Pruett.

"Well, I think people were pretty shocked that I dated Bob," Elsie said.

Including Elsie's family.

One of Elsie's cousins, who lived near Pruett, expressed her concern and curiosity about Elsie dating him.

"Oh Lord, you're not dating *him,* are you? He's the meanest kid I've ever been around," Elsie's cousin told her. "He threw rocks at me."

A neighbor of Pruett's passed on a similar warning telling Elsie he had painted the side of their house.

Elsie did not heed the warnings.

"I remember thinking that I could envision him doing those things, but something told me that he was OK," Elsie said. "He was real sweet and shy. You tell that to some people and they might find it funny because they just don't see him as being shy. He's always had that wonderful sense of humor. That made him fun. People wanted to be around him."

The pair was smitten from the get-go. Elsie still remembers Bob dancing well. And like most couples they had "their" song—"Cupid."

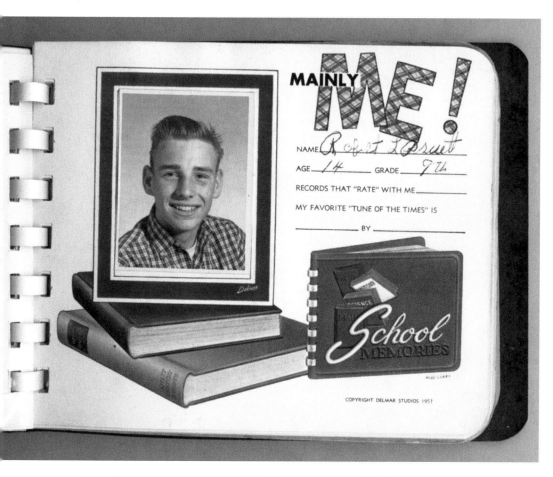

MAINLY **ME!**

NAME _Robert Pruett_

AGE _14_  GRADE _9th_

RECORDS THAT "RATE" WITH ME_____

MY FAVORITE "TUNE OF THE TIMES" IS

_____ BY _____

*School* MEMORIES

COPYRIGHT DELMAR STUDIOS 1957

**NINTH GRADE YEARBOOK** — A fourteen-year-old Bob Pruett smiles big for the camera. *Courtesy Bob Pruett.*

"Elsie and I started dating during the summer of my ninth grade year," Pruett said. "She was a much more mature than me and her wisdom spilled over onto me. You know, she sort of took me under her wing, and we dated through high school. I didn't date a lot of other girls, even when I was a junior and she had gone away to college. In my senior year we got back together."

Elsie graduated from Woodrow Wilson High School in Beckley in 1959 and Pruett, who played football, basketball, ran track and wrestled, graduated in 1961. Marshall coach Charlie Snyder liked what he saw in Pruett and offered him a football scholarship to play halfback for the Thundering Herd.

Pruett's standout high school career earned him other scholarship offers, but when Marshall made its bid, he couldn't refuse.

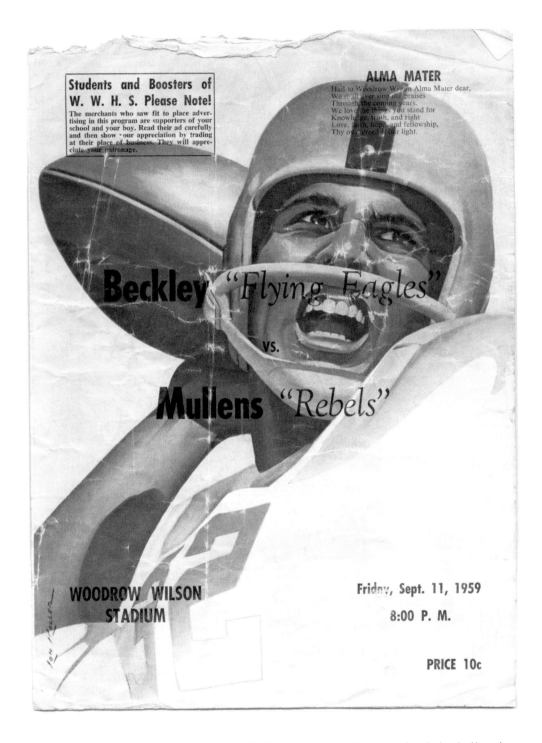

**FOOTBALL PROGRAM** — In 1959, Bob's junior year of high school, he is listed as a defensive starter. *Courtesy Bob Pruett.*

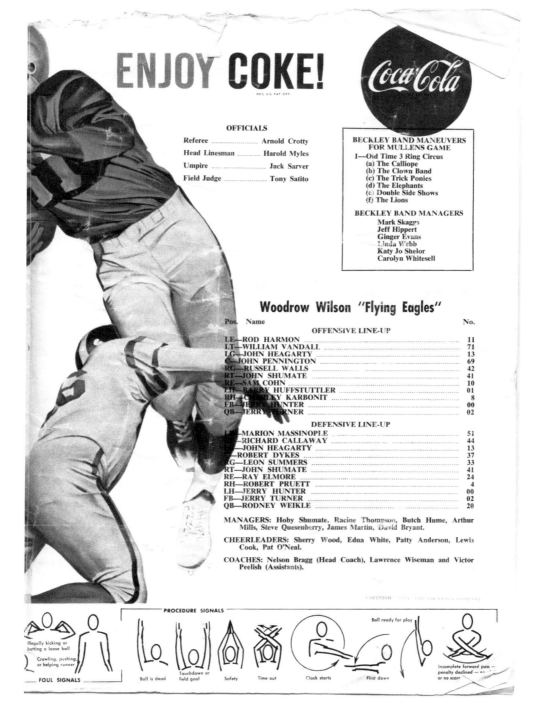

ENJOY COKE!

*Coca-Cola*

OFFICIALS

Referee ..................... Arnold Crotty

Head Linesman ........... Harold Myles

Umpire ..................... Jack Sarver

Field Judge .................. Tony Satito

BECKLEY BAND MANEUVERS
FOR MULLENS GAME
1—Old Time 3 Ring Circus
(a) The Calliope
(b) The Clown Band
(c) The Trick Ponies
(d) The Elephants
(e) Double Side Shows
(f) The Lions

BECKLEY BAND MANAGERS
Mark Skaggs
Jeff Hippert
Ginger Evans
Linda Webb
Katy Jo Shelor
Carolyn Whitesell

## Woodrow Wilson "Flying Eagles"

| Pos. Name | No. |
|---|---|
| **OFFENSIVE LINE-UP** | |
| LE—ROD HARMON | 11 |
| LT—WILLIAM VANDALL | 71 |
| LG—JOHN HEAGARTY | 13 |
| C—JOHN PENNINGTON | 69 |
| RG—RUSSELL WALLS | 42 |
| RT—JOHN SHUMATE | 41 |
| RE—SAM COHN | 10 |
| LH—BARRY HUFFSTUTLER | 01 |
| RH—CHARLEY KARBONIT | 8 |
| FB—JERRY HUNTER | 00 |
| QB—JERRY TURNER | 02 |
| **DEFENSIVE LINE-UP** | |
| LE—MARION MASSINOPLE | 51 |
| —RICHARD CALLAWAY | 44 |
| —JOHN HEAGARTY | 13 |
| —ROBERT DYKES | 37 |
| RG—LEON SUMMERS | 33 |
| RT—JOHN SHUMATE | 41 |
| RE—RAY ELMORE | 24 |
| RH—ROBERT PRUETT | 4 |
| LH—JERRY HUNTER | 00 |
| FB—JERRY TURNER | 02 |
| QB—RODNEY WEIKLE | 20 |

MANAGERS: Hoby Shumate, Racine Thompson, Butch Hume, Arthur
Mills, Steve Quesenberry, James Martin, David Bryant.

CHEERLEADERS: Sherry Wood, Edna White, Patty Anderson, Lewis
Cook, Pat O'Neal.

COACHES: Nelson Bragg (Head Coach), Lawrence Wiseman and Victor
Peelish (Assistants).

PROCEDURE SIGNALS

Ball ready for play

Illegally kicking or
batting a loose ball

Crawling, pushing,
or helping runner

FOUL SIGNALS

Ball is dead

Touchdown or
field goal

Safety

Time out

Clock starts

First down

Incomplete forward pass —
penalty declined — no score

| RE—RAY ELMORE | 24 |
|---|---|
| RH—ROBERT PRUETT | 4 |
| LH—JERRY HUNTER | 00 |

MARSHALL COLLEGE
SCHOLARSHIP COMMITMENT

(In Duplicate)

THIS AGREEMENT or Commitment, made this _20th_ day of _Dec._,
19_6Q_ between the undersigned applicant athlete, the undersigned Athletic Director, and
the undersigned Head Coach.

The applicant wishes to attend Marshall College and participate in
_FootBall_ and the Athletic Director and Head Coach desire to
give the applicant a scholarship for four years, consisting of a maximum of tuition,
fees, books, board and room.

The applicant agrees to meet the admission requirements to Marshall
College, and the Athletic Director and Head Coach agree to recommend the applicant
to the Scholarship Committee of Marshall for the above scholarship for four years;
and even though injured in a collegiate sport, the scholarship shall continue for
four years, subject, of course, to the applicant's eligibility and good conduct.

APPROVED:

_Mrs Roy Pruett_
Parent ( )    Guardian ( )

_Charles C. Snyder_
Head Coach

_Neal B. Wilson_
Athletic Director

_Robert Pruett_
Applicant Athlete

_217 allen ave._
Street Address

_Beckley, W. Va._
City and State

_Woodrow Wilson_
High School Attended

**JOHN HANCOCK —** Bob's signature sealed his future football career at Marshall
University. *Courtesy Bob Pruett.*

"I'm a home body and I love the state of West Virginia," Pruett said. "Marshall was where I wanted to go to school."

Pruett entered Marshall in the fall of 1961. Elsie and Pruett married during the Christmas holidays of Pruett's freshman year at Marshall.

"He was scared to death that he would lose his scholarship, so we were going to keep it a secret," Elsie said. "And that lasted about two days."

At the time the climate at many schools did not condone having married athletes.

The couple's secret became public knowledge thanks to Elsie's mother, who made the mistake of putting a notice in the church bulletin.

"Can you believe that?" Elsie said. "My mother, who never tells anybody anything, put it in the church bulletin. And, of course, students were home for the weekend and, well, they guessed we were married anyway. And, so, one of the players was home that weekend and read the church bulletin and said, 'Are you all married?' and I said, 'No.' And, he was like, 'Yeah, you are,' and it was like, 'No, we're not,' and he said, 'Well, it's in the church bulletin.' And I couldn't believe it, but it was. My mother didn't think anything about it."

Once the news was out, Bob told the Marshall coach, Charlie Snyder, who didn't have the expected adverse reaction.

"There were more football players married then it seemed like," Elsie said. "Nowadays they don't think anything about a football player being married. More of the players are married and you hardly know it. In fact it's probably better, they're more settled down I think."

Elsie and Bob found a lot of strength in their faith. Once they were married, Bob changed his denomination from Methodist to Baptist.

"Of course, I grew up in the church," Pruett said. "But I was a Methodist and Elsie was a Baptist. After I got married and Elsie got to know me a lot better, she was firmly convinced that sprinkling wasn't enough for me—I needed to be dunked. So I needed to be dunked twice. So we went over to the Baptists, you know; Elsie said church let out earlier, that was the reason."

Being married in college set the Pruetts apart from most of the Marshall student body. Compared to today's standard of living, the Pruetts were living in hard times, but they didn't know any better.

"Well, it didn't take that much money," Elsie said. "We didn't know any different. We didn't feel like we were getting by on next to nothing. We just didn't go out much."

Pruett got fifty dollars a month as a stipend for living outside the dorm. During the summers he worked for a company that traveled in a railroad car spraying for weeds along the tracks. Pruett stayed on the road for most of the summer sending his salary home while the company paid him an allowance that he lived on while he was away from home.

"That was nice because most of his meals and everything were taken care of," Elsie said. "And a lot of times he would sleep on the train, so they didn't have any hotel."

The downside of the equation came in not getting to see Elsie much over the summer. But when the second summer rolled around he would not stay away from his bride—and their young son; Rod was born during Pruett's sophomore season. "He'd be ready to leave for the weekend and they'd say, 'Well, you can go home next weekend,'" Elsie said. "He was used to coming home. And finally he said, 'I've had it, I'm going home.'"

Pruett later worked at an Owens-Illinois glass plant where they made different types of glass products. Instead of staying in shape at the local gym—which is the norm for today's college athletes—Pruett kept in shape loading boxcars from the Owens-Illinois warehouse. At night he worked at a local supermarket stocking shelves.

Asked about when he slept, Pruett smiled: "You know, there wasn't a whole lot of time for sleeping. You had to sleep quick."

The couple lived off the money he earned in the summer and from the part-time work he did during the year. All the while he continued to attend school, play three sports—football, wrestling and track—and work when he could.

"He was pretty busy," Elsie said. "He's always been busy. A lot of people didn't know how he did it but it just seemed like he did it all."

According to the prevailing NCAA regulations, freshmen were not eligible during Pruett's freshman year, but Pruett managed to compete in track.

"There were times when I ran track under an assumed name," Pruett said. "We went down to Morehead and they put some of us under different names. They had a grass track. That was the first time I ever ran on a grass track. I don't remember how it turned out."

Playing three sports might have seemed frivolous for a married man trying to support a family. But Pruett's main job continued to be his football scholarship, which meant he was Marshall University property.

"Really, the reason I played the other sports in college was when you

**IN ACTION —** Bob (88) was always near the ball, whether playing offense or defense. *Courtesy Bob Pruett.*

weren't in football, you were involved in an off-season program," Pruett said. "And I felt like I would much rather be competing and playing. If I wrestled and ran track I felt like I was strengthening myself and getting better, but I was also competing. And I liked competing. I felt like I was utilizing my time better doing that and having more fun than I would be just spending time in the weight room or running drills for football."

Elsie became a homemaker, taking care of her husband and their new-born son, Rod. She had never even held a baby before when they had Rod. All of it was new and life was moving fast. Elsie's mother became a cornerstone of support for the couple.

"Mother would come down some but she taught school in Crab Orchard at Crab Orchard Elementary School," Elsie said. "And my stepfather was a principal. My dad died when I was three, so Mother went back to school and got her Master's and she would work during the winter and go to school in the summer. And it was just awesome what she did for us, you know. Her life was ours. She was a role model. She was unselfish and went to church and that was about her whole life."

Newlyweds with a young child, playing college sports, trying to earn money and graduate from Marshall—talk about stress. Looking back Elsie smiles with wonder, "How did we ever get through all that?"

"But we didn't worry about anything," Elsie said. "We didn't worry about money. We didn't worry about where things would come from because they just came. It was good; now it would scare me to death."

Pruett added: "Luckily, I didn't realize how tough it was until I got out and started looking back. When you look back you realize, gosh, how in the world did we do it? Because it was tough. In football, I was the only guy my senior year that played both ways—I played offense and defense. My junior year, some other players did it. Then we wrestled, then we ran track and then we worked and graduated in four years. Looking back on it, I must have been task-driven. We just did what we had to do."

Though young in years, Elsie had the wisdom to understand her husband's passion for sports.

"Bob enjoyed football, he enjoyed track, he enjoyed wrestling," Elsie said. "It was nice to see my husband doing something he enjoyed. He was not at home a lot. And I guess I really didn't think about it. So this was just the way it was. I didn't know any different. When we went out we went to a ball game, which was free. We went down to watch practice, which was free. Going out

RALLY AROUND MARSHALL

WELL DONE....SENIORS!

**1964 MARSHALL UNIVERSITY FOOTBALL SENIORS**

FIRST ROW (Left to Right): Jim Brown, Larry Dexio, John Williams, Bill Winter, Co-Captain; Larry Coyer, Bob Pruett, Jim Cure, Co-Captain.
SECOND ROW (Left to Right): John Bentley, Jim Lewis, Jack Mahone, Joe Willis, Don Van Meter, David Boston, Bob Venters.
THIRD ROW (Left to Right): Barry Zorn, Jim Perry, Howard Cunningham, Paul Turman, Don Dixon, Doug Long, Dennis Gerlach.

PROGRAM SPONSORED BY THE BIG GREEN CLUB, INC., AND THE MARSHALL UNIVERSITY ATHLETIC DEPARTMENT

# Marshall vs. Kent State

2:00 P. M.      Fairfield Stadium      25 Cents

Chapman Printing Company

SATURDAY, NOVEMBER 14, 1964

**SENIOR SEASON** — Bob (88) poses with the Thundering Herd senior class on a gameday program. *Courtesy Bob Pruett.*

Staff Photo by Howard Cazad

**MARSHALL'S MILE RELAY TEAM, WHICH FACES TOLEDO SATURDAY, HOLDS BATON**
*Willie Tucker, Bob Pruett, Arthur Miller And Jack Mahone*

**Big Green Netters To Play Miami** *Friday april 17, 1964*

*March 1964* Advertiser Sports Photo by Eplion

**SNYDER GIVES 'THE WORD'**—Head Coach Charlie Snyder discusses some technical points with three of his returning seniors Monday when Marshall opened its spring drills. Jim Perry, Bob Pruett, Jim Cure listen.

## Toledo Takes Pre-Christmas Bout

BOB PRUETT (white uniform) fights for the initiative in his bout during the MU-Toledo match Dec. 21. He later lost by a decision. Ed Prelaz, athletic trainer and head wrestling coach said that this was the closest the Big Green matmen have come to beating the MAC champs in the history of wrestling at Marshall. The final score was Toledo 16, Marshall 11.

**THREE-SPORTS LETTERMAN** — Besides football, Bob (88) also lettered in track and wrestling at Marshall for three straight years. *Courtesy Bob Pruett.*

# *3.0 Scholastic Mark*

"Whitey" Wilson, where he got that nickname I don't know, but is the athletic director of the Big Green, was telling me all about Beckley's Pruett.

"That boy is going to set a record of winning nine varsity letters at Marshall," Wilson was pointing out. "He not only plays football, but he is on the wrestling squad in the winter and goes out for track in the spring."

But what Wilson bragged about the most—even more than the nine letters he will acquire by next June—is his 3.0 standing in the scholastic world at Marshall.

"And furthermore," went on Wilson, "Pruett is married."

It is an amazing record for the ex-Flying Eagle, who always proved to the fans here in his schoolboy days that he loved to play that football. Put him at fullback and Beckley never had a harder-charging line-crashing back. Stick him on end, defensively, and Beckley never had a guy that loved to block and tackle so much.

Pruett's desire was spelled with a capital D as far as he was concerned. He always played it that way. Evidently he still does.

Sometimes he didn't give out everything in practice, but in a game, Pruett was unbeat-

**BOB PRUETT**
(As A Schoolboy)

able. He has carried this into his sports at Marshall.

"We've had some fellows that may have won five or six letters," Wilson said. "But to play three sports a season for three years — never, at least not in my time here at Marshall."

Bob is listed at 6 feet, 193 pounds on Marshall's football roster. He wears No. 88. He was honorable mention in the Mid-American conference's all-star football team last fall.

**STUDENT-ATHLETE** — In addition to lettering in three sports and being a married college student, Bob maintained a 3.0 grade point average while at Marshall. *Courtesy Bob Pruett.*

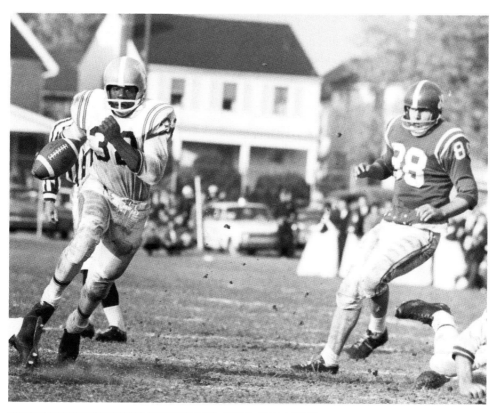

**REDSKINS AND BIG GREEN SCRAMBLE FOR LOOSE FOOTBALL**
*Miami's Myron Williams (Left), Scott Tyler (22), Marshall's Robert Pruett (88)*

**MAC FOES** — Bob got a taste for the Bowling Green (top) and Miami (Ohio) programs while a player at Marshall. *Courtesy Bob Pruett.*

to eat was the McDonald's in Huntington, think about that—going out to eat was McDonald's. McDonald's was new at that time. Oh, McDonald's was just coming in and those French fries. We thought that was just the thing. And the milkshakes, you know, gotta get a milkshake and fries."

Pruett moved from running back to wide receiver during his sophomore season and went on to catch twenty-four passes for 442 yards and four touchdowns. If he had a legacy as a player it came in Huntington on October 5, 1963, at Fairfield Stadium with the Thundering Herd trailing Toledo 18-13 with less than a minute showing on the clock. Marshall needed to cover forty-eight yards to go ahead of the Rockets. Pruett was sent into the game with the play.

"Well, there are very few things you remember, but I remember that play because they sent me in with it," Pruett said. "Howie Miller was the quarterback and we had another receiver named Jimmy Cure, who was the guy that they went to a lot of times.

So here I am, they send me in with the play, and I tell them the play, it was a '94 sprint out, bend in deep'—a four vertical route where you send everyone deep. And I told them it was 94 sprint out, bend in deep."

Pruett paused to chuckle at his recollection.

"I told Howie, 'Throw it to me,' like that's what the coach had told me, so Howie did," Pruett said.

Pruett scampered down the sideline, gave a little juke to the cornerback covering him, and looked back for the football. Miller lofted a pass toward Pruett, who had gone past the defender. At the last instant the cornerback stretched out to try and knock away the pass.

"All he could do was tip it," Pruett said. "I was behind him and I caught it."

After plucking the ball out of the air, Pruett sprinted to the end zone to tie the score at 18. Larry Coyer kicked the extra point, but Marshall was offside, so he had to kick it again. When the ball went through the uprights, Marshall had a 19-18 win and Pruett's most lasting memory as a player had been plated.

"I remember how tired I was suddenly," Pruett said. "I was playing both ways—I played outside linebacker, too, so I was out there for two extra points and then I had to run up the field on kickoffs twice because we were offside the first time, I mean I was about to die. I had just run seventy-something yards. Man, I was spent."

In Pruett's senior season he accounted for both touchdowns in a 14-12 win over Buffalo at Fairfield Stadium; that would be the last winning season at Fairfield Stadium until 1984.

# MU Victory Stuns Lauterbur

## Toledo TD Questioned; Snyder Elated By Play

**By JERRY REED**
**Sports Editor**

"I just can't believe it," Toledo Coach Frank Lauterbur said after the Big Green pulled the game out of the fire in the last minute of play and upset the Rockets 19-18 for the first MU win in the Mid-American Conference this season and the first since 1961.

The atom bomb could not have had as much devastating power to the Toledo squad as did the aerial bomb hurled by sophomore quarterback Howard Miller into the waiting arms of Bob Pruett for the winning touchdown with only :46 remaining on the clock. The pass covered 53 yards and came on the third down and 15 yards-to-go situation.

**The Big Green drove deep into Toledo territory on several occasions, but was halted by the stalwart Rocket defensive squad;**

**TEAMING UP** to provide the winning combination in the 19-18 victory over the Toledo Rockets Saturday were Howie Lee Miller (left), sophomore signal caller, and end Bob Pruett. Miller connected with Pruett on a 53-yard touchdown pass with only 49 seconds remaining in the game.

**BACKBREAKER** — Bob teamed up with quarterback Howie Miller to defeat Toledo with a 53-yard pass play in 1964. *Courtesy Bob Pruett.*

Asked if she enjoyed watching her husband play sports at Marshall, Elsie answered, "Yes and no."

"I guess I was nervous," Elsie said. "I wanted him to do well. It always bothered me, you know, there's tension, but I was always so proud of him."

Pruett graduated from Marshall in 1965 with a B.A. in social studies and physical education. He lettered in three sports for three years while at Marshall, the first athlete in school history to do so. And he graduated in four years, because he didn't have the luxury of lingering.

"We had to graduate because I didn't have any money," he said. "It was all a money deal."

Elsie, who started at Marshall several years before Bob but became a mother at an early age, went back to finish her degree at Marshall, and did so in 1980, earning a B.S. in elementary education.

The Dallas Cowboys signed Pruett to a professional contract after college, but the NFL wasn't what it is today, so he went another direction. The Cowboys offered him a contract of $500, but in order to get paid he had to make the team.

"And at that time we were just finishing college and it was probably bothering him more than it was me because I knew we could always—we got along," Elsie said. "But if you went to camp, you didn't get anything until you made the team. And at that time that was great, you know, but he also had two offers to coach football."

Pruett elaborated further on his decision.

"Well, we had a family," Pruett said. "I felt like we had to go where the money was. In the NFL there were not a lot of guarantees. So we had to earn a living and I'd been living off of nothing. So I needed to go on with my life. Teaching and coaching looked like a better opportunity than pro football at that time, I mean, since pro football was not a guarantee."

Pruett never went to Dallas.

While he understood the economics of his situation after graduating from college—he needed to make some money to support his family—he also recognized a thirst within him. He wanted to coach. And his long-term goal was to be the head football coach at Marshall University.

Pruett had two offers to coach high school football, one in West Virginia and one in Northern Virginia.

"My sister and brother-in-law lived in Northern Virginia, which made that job more attractive," Elsie said. "So, we went up and he got a job at Falls

# NATIONAL FOOTBALL LEAGUE
## STANDARD PLAYERS CONTRACT

### BETWEEN

DALLAS COWBOYS FOOTBALL CLUB, INC., a Texas corporation
which operates DALLAS COWBOYS FOOTBALL CLUB, and which is a member of the National Football
League, and which is hereinafter called the "Club," and ROBERT LEWIS PRUETT of
MARSHALL UNIVERSITY hereinafter called the "Player."
In consideration of the respective promises herein the parties hereto agree as follows:

1. The term of this contract shall be from the date of execution hereof until the first day of May following the
close of the football season commencing in ............ -- 1965 -- .................., subject however, to rights
of prior termination as specified herein.

2. The Player agrees that during the term of this contract he will play football and will engage in activities
related to football only for the Club and as directed by the Club according to the Constitution, By-Laws, Rules and
Regulations of the National Football League, hereinafter called the "League," and of the Club, and the Club, subject
to the provisions hereof, agrees during such period to employ the Player as a skilled football player. The Player
agrees during the term of this contract to report promptly for the Club's training seasons, to render his full time
services during the training seasons and at the Club's direction to participate in all practice sessions and in all
League and other football games scheduled by the Club.

3. For the Player's services as a skilled football player during the term of this contract, and for his agreement
not to play football or engage in activities related to football for any other person, firm, corporation or institution
during the term of this contract, and for the option hereinafter set forth giving the Club the right to renew this
contract, and for the other undertakings of the Player herein, the Club promises to pay the Player each football
season during the term of this contract, subject to the provisions of 17 hereof, the sum of $ 19,000.00 .........., to
be payable as follows:

   75% of said salary in equal semi-monthly installments commencing with the first regularly scheduled

| | | This player remains property of: |
|---|---|---|
| Age: 22 | High School _____ | |
| Ht.: 6' | Semi-Pro _____ | |
| Wt.: 200 | College Marshall | None |
| Pos.: QB | College — UNIV | Name of Major League Club and may be recalled. |
| | Pro Ball _____ | ☐ Yes (CHECK) No ☐ |

## ATLANTIC COAST FOOTBALL LEAGUE
### STANDARD PLAYERS CONTRACT

### BETWEEN

_____ K.D. Pro Football, Inc. _____ which operates
_____ Virginia Sailors _____ and which is a member of the Atlantic Coast Football
League, and which is hereinafter called the "Club," and ...... Robert Pruett ................. of
........ Falls Church, Virginia ...... hereinafter called the "Player."

In consideration of the respective promises herein the parties hereto agree as follows:

1. The term of this contract shall be from the date of execution hereof until the first day of May following the close
of the football season commencing in ............ 1966 ..................,subject however, to rights of prior
termination as specified herein.

2. The Player agrees that during the term of this contract he will play football and will engage in activities related
to football only for the Club and as directed by the Club according to the Constitution, By-Laws, Rules and Regulations of
the Atlantic Coast Football League, hereinafter called the "League," and of the Club, and the Club, subject to the provisions
hereof, agrees during such period to employ the Player as a skilled football player. The Player agrees during the term of
this contract to report promptly for the Club's training seasons and at the Club's direction to participate in all practice
sessions and in all League and other football games scheduled by the Club.

3. For the Player's services as a skilled football player during the term of this contract, and for his agreement not
to play football or engage in activities related to football for any other person, firm, corporation or institution during the
term of this contract, and for the option hereinafter set forth giving the Club the right to renew this contract, and for the
other undertakings of the Player herein, the Club promises to pay the Player each football season during the term of this
contract the sum of $ 100.00 per league game.

**PROFESSIONAL CONTRACTS** — Out of concern for his young family, Bob turned down a contract (top) with the Dallas Cowboys to begin a career in coaching. He continued to play football, signing with the semi-pro Virginia Sailors (later Roanoke Buckskins) of the Atlantic Coast Football League. *Courtesy Bob Pruett.*

Church High School. He stepped right into that."

Pruett's coaching career began as the assistant football coach, head golf coach and head wrestling coach at Falls Church High School in Falls Church, Virginia, in 1965.

"Bob and the football coach, Chuck Sell, were so close," Elsie said. "I think they just bonded. During the games it was actually funny, because it seemed like nobody ever got between the two of them."

At the same time Pruett played tight end, outside linebacker and strong safety for the semi-pro Virginia Sailors, who were later known as the Roanoke Buckskins, in the Continental Football League; the league later changed names to the Atlantic Coast League. The Buckskins operated somewhat as a minor-league team for the Washington Redskins.

"We practiced at a field up in D.C.," Pruett said. "We played against guys like King Corcoran."

Corcoran achieved some acclaim as the flamboyant quarterback of the Pottstown (Pennsylvania) Eagles, a team in the Continental League featured in a memorable NFL Films feature.

"We ended up being the farm team of the Washington Redskins and they'd send coaches down there to drill us and all this other stuff," Pruett said. "Since we had a lot of people who worked, we practiced in the evening, under the lights, like from 7:30 to 9:30 at night. There were a lot of good players in that league. We had players who were on the Redskins' taxi squad playing for us."

Pruett said "playing there was a good experience" and compared the league to the upstart World Football League that came along in the 1970s to offer a brief challenge to the NFL.

"He played football during the season and at the same time he coached," Elsie said. "Sometimes he worked, he coached, he taught, he went and played football—practiced in Washington. And then during Christmas he worked at a toy store after that."

Pruett chuckles when he spins yarns about his experiences on the bottom rung of the professional football ladder, where the conditions were not exactly the Ritz-Carlton.

"One time we went on a bus trip in the cold and the heater went out," Pruett said. "The guys got so cold they were stuffing newspapers under their shirts to get warm because there wasn't insulation on the bus. I can't remember whether the air-conditioner kicked on and wouldn't go off or whether we lost our heat. But everyone was shivering and shaking."

Once they took a road trip to New England to play the Lowell Giants. When they arrived for the Saturday night game a bad thunderstorm made it necessary to postpone the game until the following morning.

"So the boys, they went out that night," said Pruett, who did not go out but heard the story. "And they were drinking and raising a ruckus. Pretty soon they got in a big fight because the whole group was in there messing with the local women, I guess. And one of our players, a receiver who later played for the Jets, ended up deputizing himself. Here he was, the one who started it, deciding he'd help control it. I mean it was just funny stuff."

Another time they were staying at a Holiday Inn that had Indian blankets on the beds. The players began to wrap themselves in blankets while they imbibed and before long they were acting like Indians in a John Wayne movie.

"They ended up in the restaurant, where they tied up two Chinese cooks and told them they were going to scalp them," Pruett said. "Then they cooked up all the food in the kitchen. There was always wild stuff like that going on."

And the labor was far from organized, which Pruett discovered when they went to play a game in Delaware.

"Their players were striking," said Pruett, allowing himself a chuckle. "We were the league champions most years, so we were supposed to win that game pretty handily. And when we went out there to warm up players started showing up for them. Three would come out, then two more. By kickoff they had about thirty players. We were in for the darnedest game that night. They played hard and we barely won."

Pruett laughed about the characters in the league, but they all had a common denominator: all of them were passionate about football. While they might have made a little extra money, the real reason they played was they hadn't gotten playing the game out of their system.

Players worked full-time jobs and practiced twice a week at night in advance of playing a game on the weekend.

"It was a lot of fun," Pruett said. "I mean a *lot* of fun. I met a ton of good guys."

Pruett finally knew he'd had enough after a 1969 game against Richmond. Playing on the punt team he tackled the player running with the ball and caused a fumble. Pruett and the player who fumbled dove for the ball and Pruett got speared in the back, which triggered internal bleeding and prompted surgery.

"I almost died," Pruett said.

## 1969 ROANOKE BUCKSKINS

| No. | Name | Position | Hgt. | Wt. | School |
|---|---|---|---|---|---|
| 67 | Emizie Abbott | T | 6'2 | 255 | Norfolk State |
| 72 | John Cash | T | 6'3 | 250 | Allen Univ. |
| 75 | Marv Crawford | G | 6'3 | 249 | Morgan State |
| 80 | Dick Duenkel | E | 6'0 | 235 | Geo. Wash |
| 64 | John Gawler | G | 6'1 | 245 | Univ. of Ky. |
| 83 | C. Gibson | E | 6'1 | 220 | Livingston |
| 73 | J. Grey | T | 6'5 | 270 | Benedict |
| 27 | Jessie Hines | DB | 6'1 | 200 | Redskins |
| 76 | A. Lederle | T | 6'3 | 275 | Georgia |
| 46 | F. Libertore | HB | 5'11 | 195 | Clemson |
| 5 | T. Manuel | QB | 5'9 | 165 | Jamestown |
| 34 | Whitey Marciniak | FB | 6'1 | 220 | Univ. of Maryland |
| 40 | H. McLeod | E | 6'1 | 190 | Redskins |
| 84 | Phil Norton | E | 6'3 | 200 | |
| 55 | O. Overcash | C | 6'2 | 255 | North Carolina |
| 57 | F. Passerelli | LB | 6'1 | 235 | Wake Forrest |
| 43 | B. Pruett | E | 6'1 | 215 | Marshall Univ. |
| 39 | Clay Singleton | DB-S | 5'11 | 195 | Delaware St. |
| 21 | Terry Stoneman | DB | 6' | 200 | Redskins |
| 26 | R. Taylor | HB | 6'0 | 205 | Maryland St. |
| 4 | A. Tyler | QB | 6'3 | 210 | Livingston |
| 23 | T. Windsor | S | 6'0 | 195 | Univ. of Ky. |
| 62 | J. Costello | LB | 6'2 | 225 | VPI |
| 71 | W. Ward | DE | 6'3 | 257 | Morgan State |
| 77 | J. William | DE | 6'4 | 260 | Redskins |
| 22 | B. Johnson | DHB | 5'10 | 175 | Fla. St. |
| 23 | B. Mitchell | DB | 6' | 187 | Redskins |
| 3 | Ray Harris | K | 5'10 | 175 | Miami |
| 54 | O. Dunlop | LB | 6'2 | 225 | Michigan |
| 74 | C. Brownlee | OFT | 6'4 | 270 | Redskins |
| 44 | M. Shook | LCB | 6' | 180 | Washington |
| 65 | F. Washington | OT | 6'3 | 265 | Washington |
| 61 | D. Lemay | LB | 6'4 | 244 | Washington |
| 56 | B. Nelson | C | 6'2 | 259 | Lenoir Rhyne |
| 86 | S. Henry | F | 6'1 | 175 | |

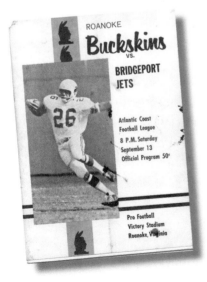

**BUCKSKINS ROSTER** — In the days before NFL Europe, Bob's semi-pro teammates included players from the Washington Redskins. *Courtesy Bob Pruett.*

Aside from football, Pruett had other opportunities. He could have had a State Farm Insurance agency. Another opportunity came from a friend who wanted Pruett to join him in the Secret Service.

"Those opportunities came early in my coaching career," Pruett said. "But, really, I felt like I was called to be a ball coach—nothing more, nothing less. That's what I wanted to do and it's all I ever really wanted to do, so coaching has been my passion. And my true passion was to come back to Marshall and be the head football coach there because the people who I admire most were my coaches: Jerome Vanmeter, who is a legendary high school coach and went to Woodrow Wilson High School in Beckley; and Charlie Snyder, my college coach at Marshall, who was a Marshall graduate."

Pruett spread himself pretty thin with his time, while the couple had three boys—and Pruett continued to have a lot of little boy in him.

Elsie described how excited their boys were when Pruett would come home, often disturbing the tranquility in the house.

"Bob was always wild when he would come in and the kids would be running and screaming and he'd scream and I'd go out the back door and walk around the yard, I mean, especially if the boys had been really bad, you know, I'd think, 'No, I can't take this,'" Elsie said. "So I would just walk around the yard a little bit and then come back in afterward, counting to ten about four hundred times. I'd just gotten them settled down and suddenly they're jumping all over the place."

But Elsie couldn't stay mad at her husband long, even when he added to the madness by bringing home a dog, Midas, a Beagle and Miniature Collie mix.

"He brought that dog home that I didn't want," Elsie said. "We had a fence around our yard, and the deal was Midas was supposed to stay outside most of the time. And, of course, he spent zero time outside. That's Bob. But he always kept things interesting. And it was so nice having little boys, because you can do just about anything and they don't whine and cry."

A family living on a coaching and teaching salary didn't have a lot of resources. But for Elsie and Bob, these were good times.

"It was fun," Elsie said. "I remember having thirty dollars and just figuring out, you know, the groceries and what we'd do. I'd always subtract all the bills at the beginning of the month and we always met our bills. We always had enough."

Pruett coached at Falls Church from 1965 to 1967 then moved to Hayfield

Paul Weber
George Washington Univ

Athletic Director

The
# 1966
JAGUARS FOOTBALL ∞∞ Coaching Staff

Bob Pruett
Asst

Ron Matalavage
Ass't

Dale Larsen
Ass't

Randy Scott
Asst

Chuck Sell
Head Coach

**COACH PRUETT** — 1966 saw Bob as assistant football coach, head wrestling coach, and head golf coach for the Falls Church High School "Jaguars" of Falls Church, Virginia. *Courtesy Bob Pruett.*

High School in Alexandria, Virginia, where he was assistant football coach and head wrestling coach.

Pruett remained at Hayfield from 1967 through 1969 before getting his first head coaching football position at Groveton High School in Alexandria.

"In high school Bob struggled to get that head job," Elsie said. "He was an assistant and they kept saying, 'You're too young,' and he'd say, 'Well, how do you know?' And I remember one job he wanted and they said, 'You're just too young. You're going to be a good head coach someday.' And he was so frustrated because he was head wrestling coach from the beginning.

"And once he got that head high school coaching job they were after him. Every job, they wanted him to come there, and I thought, 'Now isn't this strange?' You know, as hard as he wanted it now, you know, everybody wants him."

Pruett downplayed his getting the job in the folksy way that has endeared him to so many:

"That was my first head coaching job and I got the job because nobody else wanted it, really, they'd lost thirty-one straight games."

Pruett had his work cut out for him.

## *Chapter three*

Bob Pruett took over at Groveton High School prior to the 1970 season. He was excited about the job even though they had a team that he said "couldn't whip butter."

And while Pruett anxiously went about his duties to change the fortunes at Groveton, his alma mater was trying to deal with some setbacks in order to change its fortunes.

On the field Marshall went 0-10 in 1967, which brought an end to the nine-year run of Coach Charlie Snyder. Perry Moss replaced Snyder and posted a 0-9-1 mark, despite attempts by Marshall boosters to take a shortcut to finding success.

Prior to the 1968 season, arrangements were made for approximately 140 players to be shipped in from all different parts of the country to try out for thirty-five scholarships. The

**1973-1978 —** Bob, shown during his head coaching stint at Garfield High School, Woodbridge, Virginia. *Courtesy Bob Pruett.*

3

TRAGEDY AND

OVING BEYOND

move was a recipe for disaster and resulted in 144 alleged NCAA violations.

The Mid-American Conference dealt with the wrongdoings by handing Marshall an indefinite expulsion. Moss went down with the ship, losing his job after one season.

Rick Tolley was promoted from offensive line coach to head coach three weeks before the 1969 season. Under Tolley's leadership, the Thundering Herd's winless streak of twenty-one games moved to twenty-seven before a 21-16 homecoming win over Bowling Green ended the frustration.

While the NCAA dealt Marshall a one-year probation, and they remained suspended by the MAC, there was reason for optimism heading into Tolley's second season.

Fairfield Stadium had been expanded to a capacity of 15,000, and the playing surface was replaced with Astroturf, which would eliminate the sloppy playing conditions created whenever bad weather hovered over Huntington.

Marshall opened what was thought to be a new era of football with a 17-7 win over Morehead State to start the 1970 season. After losing to Toledo 52-3, Marshall rebounded with a 31-14 win at Xavier. But the team would win just one more game before traveling to East Carolina November 14, 1970.

Marshall flew a Southern Airways charter to the game against East Carolina in Greenville, North Carolina. On the flight were many Marshall boosters including a host of community leaders in the Huntington area.

East Carolina defeated Marshall 17-14. After the game, Tolley told reporters: "We had a real nice flight down, and some of them are still flying."

At 3-6, the Thundering Herd had one game remaining on the schedule.

The flight back to Huntington was no doubt full of chatter about "what might have been…if only this, if only that." The air outside the plane turned gloomy as a driving rainstorm whipped up and caused turbulence for the passengers and crew.

The storm might have been an omen. Tragedy was impending.

While attempting to land at the Tri-State Airport in Huntington on a foggy Saturday night—an airport where none of the charter's crew members had ever landed—the plane skimmed along some treetops then crashed into the hillside just below its destination at 7:42. The weather and instrument problems contributed to the disaster. No one aboard survived the crash. All seventy-five passengers died on that terrible night: thirty-seven players, eight coaches, five crew members and twenty-five Marshall supporters—including a state legislator, four physicians and a city councilman. (See p. 59)

Pruett heard about the crash shortly after it happened when one of his brothers called him.

"There are events in your life that you'll never, ever forget where you were and what you were doing at the time when it happened and for me that was one of those events," Pruett said. "I can tell you exactly what I was doing when that plane crashed. I was sitting in the kitchen in Fredericksburg, Virginia, and I had just got through eating dinner.

"I remember it very, very well, just like it was yesterday when I got the call. And I picked up the phone and called an athletic director at Edison High School named Bob Carson because his brother worked at Marshall at that time. And I called to see if he had been on the plane. I was worried about him being on the plane. I knew he really liked athletics and I was afraid that he had made the trip."

Frantically, Pruett began to try and gather as much information as he could. Keep in mind this was during an era where information about news and world events wasn't as readily accessible as it is today.

"When things like that happen, you go into a daze," Pruett said. "Because the athletic director at Marshall at that time was Charlie Kautz and he had been my position coach when I played here. So, you know, I was really close to him. And then I knew some of the coaches that were on the plane. I'll tell you what, the bottom of my heart fell out that day."

A memorial at the Cabell County Veteran's Memorial Field House was held the next day and was attended by over 7,000 people. Many families, a school and an entire community had been devastated, leaving many to wonder just Marshall and Huntington would deal with the future.

Once Marshall decided to continue the football program, they had to figure out ways to build the team back up to where it could compete. Among the fundraisers—and ways to help the team prepare—was a game in the spring of 1971 between the Marshall team and an alumni team. Of course Pruett couldn't resist the lure of playing.

"As dumb as I am, I came back and played in that alumni game that next spring," Pruett said. "I saw all my buddies at that game. I had no business playing—the game had passed me by—but we came back and really had a lot of fun seeing the guys and learning what everybody was doing. I'll never forget some of the players that were in that game for them. They just didn't have very good players. You know, they just had some walk-on guys they were trying out that spring. We wanted to come back and give back and be part of it and it was a fun day and an evening. It was a way for the team to have someone to play and to also raise a little money."

The game turned out to be Pruett's last as a player.

"I really shouldn't have been playing," he said. "I had already gotten hurt and had had the surgery. And I'd recovered, but I remember Marshall was playing with a bunch of walk-on kids. I was playing outside linebacker and hit some kid. And he kept trying real hard and I busted him pretty good. Right then I thought, 'I don't need to be doing this' and I just walked off the field. After that I didn't play any more."

At that point Pruett didn't know, nor did anyone else, whether the school would be able to have a competitive football program ever again.

"The one thing that I am, I'm a real sentimental person and I'm a fan," Pruett said. "I was rooting hard for the Herd to come back. I mean I really wanted them to get back on track."

Pruett had to root for his alma mater and its rebuilding effort from afar since he had to devote most of his efforts toward improving Groveton High.

Several of the players from the previous year's Marshall team had not made the trip to East Carolina. They would be the nucleus of the team new coach Jack Lengyel pieced together. An entire nation pulled for a school that few knew of prior to the plane crash. Even the President of the United States, Richard Nixon, sent a letter to the team telling them everybody in the country would be pulling for them, but they had already won a victory by even putting a varsity squad on the field in 1971.

Because of their unique situation, the NCAA gave Marshall permission to play freshmen in 1971.

The "Young Thundering Herd," as Lengyel labeled the team, did win two games during the 1971 season, the first a miraculous and emotional 15-13 victory over Xavier in the second game of the year. Today, many consider the win over Xavier the greatest in the school's history.

After the dramatic win against Xavier, celebrated widely with cheers and tears for those lost in the tragedy, Marshall settled into a program that would have considered mediocre a step up. In the 1970s, the Herd compiled twenty-two wins in the decade, including a twelve-game losing streak and two losing streaks of ten each. During that stretch some lobbied to disband the football program. The saving grace for the program, however, came in the sentiment that sacking the program would have shown a grave lack of respect for those who had perished in the plane crash.

An interesting footnote about the time when Pruett coached at Groveton was the fact he had the opportunity to coach against T.C. Williams High School in Alexandria in 1971. This is of some significance because of the story that unfolded for T.C. Williams.

The United States Supreme Court issued a ruling in April of 1971 to end all state-imposed segregation in public schools. These were already turbulent times in the United States anyway. The Vietnam War raged, protests were everywhere and the social consciousness of the country was at perhaps an all-time high.

T.C. Williams was a high school greatly impacted by the Supreme Court ruling. And the high school had a memorable season under the helm of Herman Boone, an African-American, who became head coach instead of Bill Yoast, who had held the job.

That team's march to become state champions was chronicled in the Disney movie, "Remember the Titans," starring Denzel Washington as Coach Boone. Among the team's T.C. Williams beat en route to their undefeated season was Groveton. The game was depicted in the movie and the filmmakers exercised a creative license regarding that gridiron clash.

"They took a great deal of theatrical liberties in describing what went on there because when I went to Groveton, they had lost thirty-one straight football games and they said we were undefeated at that time," Pruett said. "I didn't like the way they portrayed me in the movie because, you know, they said I wouldn't trade films with Coach Boone and I had made a disparaging remark toward the coach. Actually, Herman Boone and I are close friends, good friends. Matter of fact, we've talked since the movie. I mean, we were good friends and we used to sit down and talk football together with each other. Other than that, you know, I had talked about T.C. Williams, which is the name of the high school, for a long time because they really, truly were a powerful high school when they consolidated that school.

Typical of Pruett, he enjoyed the movie other than the depiction of the Groveton season.

Pruett commented that the star defensive player, Gary Berteire—who got into a car accident that left him paralyzed—indeed was a great player and not some made up character.

"He wasn't just a good player," Pruett said. "He was a great player."

Pruett said the T.C. Williams High School team "really was that good."

"And Coach Boone did a great good job of coaching them," Pruett said.

"I mean, they were very well coached and they were a fearsome team."

But Pruett added: "I mean, to be honest with you, I don't particularly remember all the racial issues that were in the movie. I'm not saying that they weren't there, because I wasn't over there experiencing them. Basically, I wasn't part of that. And I certainly didn't make racial remarks like they had in the movie. But that could have happened over in Alexandria, I don't know."

Groveton did not have a good football team while Pruett coached there.

"Bad wasn't even a descriptive enough word," Pruett said. "But it's probably one of the things in my life that I'll always remember."

Pruett remained at Groveton High from 1970 through 1972 before moving to Garfield High School in Woodbridge, Virginia, where he was the head football coach, assistant principal, and head golf coach from 1973 to 1978. During that tenure Pruett took Garfield to the state finals in football in 1977.

All the while he thought about taking his coaching to a higher level.

"I never thought about Bob coaching in college," Elsie said. "I didn't know what he wanted, he was always ready to do more. At Groveton he kept saying, 'I don't think I want to be a head football coach. I want to be a principal.' So they let him be assistant principal and the football coach. Well, he did that for a short time and decided that's not what he wanted to do."

Pruett wasn't unhappy as a high school coach. He just burned to be more. And that feeling of wanting to do more resonated within him when Sonny Randle became the Marshall coach prior to the 1979 season. He called Randle before the new coach had filled out his staff and they arranged a meeting.

"I actually took a $10,000 pay cut to come back to try to pursue our dream," Pruett said. "And I think my wife and kids made a big sacrifice. Well, especially when I come back to make $17,000 at the time, which was a $10,000 pay cut to chase our dream—to chase my dream."

Randle remembered Pruett really wanting the job.

"He wanted to get into college coaching," Randle said. "and he wanted to return to his alma mater. I think that he was eaten up with football. But he was real loosey-goosey. A carefree, fun-loving guy who everybody loved."

Randle hired Pruett to coach the defensive backfield.

"I didn't know Coach Pruett before I took the job out there and got a call from him and we were able to meet," Randle said. "He was a very enthusiastic guy, had a lot of football knowledge. I knew he would work his fanny off. And at the time he wanted Marshall to be as good as anybody could want them to be.

From the Gar-Field Boosters Club To:

# BOB PRUETT
# HEAD FOOTBALL COACH
# 1973 - 1978

In appreciation for your accomplishments as the leader of young men and the number one AAA football program in the commonwealth of Virginia.

You are number 1 in the hearts of your players and the Gar-Field boosters.

BOB PRUETT

| Year | Won | Loss | Tied |
|---|---|---|---|
| 1973 | 5 | 5 | 0 |
| 1974 | 9 | 1 | 0 |
| 1975 | 8 | 2 | 0 |
| 1976 | 9 | 3 | 0 |
| 1977 | 9 | 4 | 1 |
| 1978 | 7 | 2 | 1 |
| Total: | 47 | 17 | 2 |

Commonwealth District Championship
1975 - 1976 - 1977

Northwest Regional Championship
1976 - (Runner-up) 1977

Virginia State AAA Championship
1977 - (Runner-up)

East West Prep All-Star Coach
1977

*Special Thanks To:*

Ken's Speedprint
Dale City Exxon
Nick's Pontiac-Oldsmobile
Hardaway Construction Co.
Victory Sports
Holiday Inn of Dumfries
Piedmont Federal Savings &
Loan Association

Triangle Dental Laboratory
Komar's Florist
Hoymeir & Bachman Realty
Globe & Laurel Restaurant
Villa Napoli Restaurant
Shakey's Pizza of Woodbridge
Woodbridge Printing Co.

"The main thing was, here was a guy who had been a very successful high school coach, who was a Marshall graduate. I mean what better credentials could a guy have in selling the university? And here was someone who had been very successful in the coaching world. It was an easy hire, a no-brainer. He was an absolute natural."

"THERE WASN'T MUCH DISCUSSION," ELSIE SAID. "It was like he knew that's what he wanted to do and he took that big pay cut to do it. And that was a really hard time in our lives, probably one of the hardest times that we've faced, because he was gone for about nine months and I saw him twice."

Elsie remained in Fredericksburg because the couple's children were still in school and they didn't want to move them during the school year. The Pruett family, which now consisted of three boys, had always had their dad at night. He had never been away longer than a week in the summer and they went with him to camps and other destinations. He might be late coming in but he was home sometime during the night. So this was a trying period for their family. Elsie focused on getting the kids through school and selling the house while it snowed and snowed during a harsh winter. And the house didn't come close to selling that winter in part because the weather prevented them from even putting a "For Sale" sign in the yard.

"Then the house finally sold," Elsie said. "And we didn't even know to negotiate to move, so we moved ourselves. We packed up and moved the kids and they were established, so I was worried about that, too."

When Elsie and the kids arrived in Huntington it didn't get much better.

"It was funny because we had almost a new house in Fredericksburg—it was nine months old when we moved in it—and then we came to Huntington and the prices were sky high," Elsie said. "And we went down in housing quite a bit."

Still, Huntington felt like home. Pruett's father had died by then, but his mother still lived in Beckley and it felt good to be close to her. Pruett had made sacrifices and in the process had asked his family to make sacrifices as well, but the move felt right. Elsie saw new life in her husband.

"Seemed like he really loved it, everything was exciting and new," Elsie said. "Yeah, he needed that. About every six years he wanted something different. Didn't matter where we were, he would always talk about moving and

**MARSHALL ASSISTANT COACH** — Bob, shown here in a friendly round of tug-of-war, was hired in 1979 by Sonny Randle to coach Marshall's defensive backfield. *Courtesy Bob Pruett.*

I'd be like, 'Oh, no, we're just settled.' I tend to nest, so I would always tell Bob, 'I nest and then you tear up my nest, move me somewhere else.' But he likes the newness and the challenge, something different."

After coaching the defensive backs his first two seasons at Marshall, Pruett became the defensive coordinator. He spent two seasons in that role before Al Groh came calling. Groh, one of Pruett's close friends, got the head job at Wake Forest in 1981 and in 1983 offered Pruett a job coaching the defensive backs. Pruett evaluated his situation and decided a move would be best.

"After four years at Marshall, I realized if I ever wanted to get back to Marshall as the head coach, I needed to leave to come back," said Pruett, noting that his leaving his alma mater was no slam on the coaching staff. "We had some good coaches—Jim Cavanaugh, Jim Grobe, Bill Stewart—we just didn't have very many good players at the time." But this was at the beginning of the building process for Marshall.

Wake Forest felt like a good fit to the Pruett family; they liked the school and the city of Winston-Salem.

Pruett coached the defensive backs his first two seasons at Wake Forest, and the Deacons went 4-7 and 6-5; in 1985, Pruett became the defensive coordinator and the team went 4-7 and followed in 1986 with a 5-6 record. After the 1986 season, Groh and Wake Forest had a contract squabble.

"Al got fired or resigned, or whatever, it was over his contract, he wouldn't sign his contract," Pruett said. "It was the darnedest thing how it happened.

"Al was really doing well for Wake Forest. We'd had a losing season, but remember, this was Wake Forest—I mean, we'd had a good season. Al hadn't told us anything, but he was arguing over some clause in his contract and he and the athletic director were going round and round. Al had gone a whole year and not signed the contract. Anyway, we were all out on the road recruiting when push finally came to shove and the athletic director told him he had to return to Winston Salem and sign his contract."

Pruett was in Florida recruiting and had taken Elsie with him. While he visited prospective recruits, she stayed at the beach. When they made their return trip to Wake Forest from West Palm Beach they were accompanied by a recruit, who would be making his campus visit. They flew into Tampa on the way back to Winston-Salem.

"When we got off the plane, there was an announcement that said, 'Passenger Bob Pruett, Piedmont Airlines, please come to the white phone for a phone call,'" Pruett said. "You think the worst when you get paged like that.

I had no idea why anybody wanted to talk to me on the phone at the Tampa Airport. So I picked up the phone and I had a message to call my secretary. I called her and she told me Al was resigning at 1:30 that day."

Pruett is a man who knows how to roll with the punches, but in this case he was stunned. He was under instructions to send his recruit home, which he disregarded.

"I figured the way my luck was going the plane was going to crash anyway," Pruett said.

Once the plane took off from Tampa, he leaned over to Elsie and told her: "We're without a job."

When Pruett returned to Wake Forest he wasn't given any news on the status of his job.

"So I just went in to work and kept working," he said. "I kept on working and recruiting and everything. I didn't know who was going to be hired and, of course, I was looking for a job since I didn't know if the new coach was going to want me. Most times they want to hire their own staff."

Bill Dooley, Virginia Tech's coach, was hired to take over Wake Forest. Meanwhile, Pruett interviewed for the head job at Salem College, an NAIA school in West Virginia.

"I was on the road when Salem called me," Pruett said. "I didn't have any of the right clothes for an interview, so I had to stop and buy a sport coat, a shirt and a tie. And while I was at the interview, I got a call where I was told they'd hired Coach Dooley and he wanted the whole staff back there. So I had to drive through a heavy snowstorm to get back to Winston-Salem for the interview. And, really, that was one of the two prospects I had for a job. The other one was a State Farm Insurance agency that wanted to talk to me about becoming an agent for them. Which I had the opportunity to do before, but I didn't want to do it. Financially, we would have been a lot better off, but I wanted to be a ball coach."

Pruett had to take a step backward at this juncture, moving back to secondary coach after Dooley hired Gary Darnell to be the defensive coordinator. Such a move can be hard for a coach to swallow, but in this case the move was softened because of Pruett's friendship with Darnell.

"And so, it would have been a lot tougher if I hadn't had a good relationship with him," Pruett said.

The Deacons went 7-4 in Dooley's first season in 1987 and Darnell left Wake Forest to go to the University of Florida to take the defensive coordinator position. Pruett became defensive coordinator again in 1988 and the Deacons went 6-4-1 before Pruett was moved back to defensive backs coach in 1989.

"When I became the coordinator under Dooley, he had some coaches on his staff who had been with him at Virginia Tech and they resented me being the coordinator," Pruett said. "I didn't solicit the coordinator's job, he just offered it to me. As a matter of fact, at that time Gary Darnell was trying to get me to come to University of Florida with him to become a position coach. And Coach Dooley offered me the coordinator job and I took it for a year, but the chemistry wasn't right there. So I just stayed on as the secondary coach the next year and then left."

Pruett believed the experience he got at Wake Forest would help qualify him for the Marshall job, which became open after the 1989 season.

Marshall athletic director Lee Moon interviewed Pruett for the job.

While they sat in a motel room, Moon spoke frankly with Pruett, laying out some important criteria for advancement.

"Lee told me, 'You know, Bob, I think you're a good football coach, but we're Marshall,'" Pruett recalled. "Coach [George] Chaump had done a good job and had taken them to the National Championship game, and they had been the runner-up. Lee said, 'We're a team that has come along to the point where we feel like we need someone from a school that's playing in bowl games and on television to help the image of our football program.'"

Moon went on to tell Pruett he thought he was going to be a great head coach one day, but that he needed to broaden his horizons and gain more experience. Jim Donnan, who had been the offensive coordinator at the University of Oklahoma, had more impressive credentials than Pruett.

"He fit all of their criteria, so he got the job, and rightfully so," Pruett said. "I wasn't bitter that he got the job. But it was disappointing. It also brought me a realization at the time: Wake Forest and Marshall had been my only two college coaching experiences."

He took Moon's words to heart and recognized that he was at a professional crossroads. Taking the easy route would have meant staying at Wake Forest. But if he truly wanted to reach his ultimate goal of becoming the head football coach at Marshall, he knew what he had to do and it required a new approach. Making his decision easier was the situation at Wake Forest where he was no longer happy.

"The chemistry wasn't there and I wasn't having a lot of fun," Pruett said.

"I think that made it easier for me to leave. But I will say that we really enjoyed our time at Wake Forest. We thought it was a great place. We loved the city and I still have two grandsons and my son and daughter-in-law who all live in Winston-Salem. We enjoyed every second that we were there. I think it's a great town, a great place to live. Everything about Wake Forest was really, really good, a really great experience, except for three hours on Saturday. And I'm not trying to be negative, that's just the fact. The academic requirements are such that it's hard to get the athletes. I think they've had great coaching over the years and it's doesn't have anything to do with coaching. I think Jimmy Grobe, who is there right now, is a great football coach. But, eventually, Wake Forest will get to you, just as a lot of schools do. It's a tough place to win. And even though I thought we did pretty well, we were playing so many homecomings that we were taking our own float. I mean we went down to Mississippi State and it wasn't homecoming, we had to tell them our float was the team bus, you know."

Pruett chuckled at the memory.

"But Wake Forest is a great place to coach and work and I think you have to be a very special person to be able to survive at a school like that and you have to understand how you build a program there," Pruett said. "Because you're going to have some years where it's not quite as good as you would like because what you have to do at the Wake Forests of the world is during the years when you're good, you have to make sure you play enough of your young kids so you can continue to compete. What happens is you're not quite as big and you're not quite as fast as the people you're playing so you sort of play young kids and beat them into knowing what to do and how to be tough. And after that they graduate, you see what I'm saying, so you start all over again. It's a vicious circle."

Pruett had a relationship with Ole Miss coach Billy Brewer after Brewer's son, Gunter, played at Wake Forest. So when a coaching vacancy opened up on Brewer's staff, Pruett went for it, becoming the defensive backs coach for Ole Miss beginning in 1990. The Pruett family was headed for Oxford, Mississippi, where he would experience Southeastern Conference Football.

The news didn't sit well at home when Pruett told Elsie he wanted to move on to a new destination to get the experience he needed.

"I told Bob I thought it was ridiculous, that he could stay at Wake Forest and gain the experience he needed," Elsie said. "And that if he could survive, that would show more, him staying at one place. That the coaches who hopped around were not doing well in my opinion."

But once again, chasing Pruett's dream, the family moved.

During Pruett's first season in 1990, Ole Miss lost out to Tennessee for the SEC championship, but went 9-2 to earn a spot in the Gator Bowl, where they played Michigan.

"Going to my first bowl game was a big moment for me," Pruett said. "Going to bowl games is what coaches want to do. You always want to coach against the best teams and the best players."

After Pruett's second year at Ole Miss he attended a coaching convention in New Orleans, which led to his being asked to become the defensive coordinator at Tulane. Buddy Teevens, who had been impressed with Pruett after visiting him to study his defensive schemes at Wake Forest, was Tulane's new head coach.

"I really wasn't looking for a job," Pruett said. "And that offer just sort of came out of the blue. I thought about it and decided it would be a good move."

Part of what made Pruett attractive for the job was his penchant for being able to come up with successful schemes for teams that traditionally had less talent than the teams on their schedule.

"I think that the thing that helped me was that I'm a football junkie," Pruett said. "I was constantly calling and begging and talking football with people so we could have the schemes to be successful, because we certainly weren't able to always have the fastest people. But one of the things that I've always said was that the best players don't always make the best team, but the best team always wins. And I've always used that philosophy."

Pruett explained that devising such schemes begins with knowing the opponent.

"We wanted to really, really understand our opponents," Pruett said. "We would do extensive studies on their schemes so we completely understood what they were doing. That way we knew what they were attacking and how to attack what they were doing."

Ultimately, the frustration of coaching at places like Wake Forest and Tulane is the knowledge one can only do so much to "coach 'em up."

"I mean, at a Tulane or a Wake, you can coach them up all you want, but it still comes down to talent after that," Pruett said. "You know, in the coaching profession you can only do so much with smoke and mirrors. And it was frustrating. I mentioned earlier that that was the great thing about Wake Forest, every day of the week it was a wonderful coaching job except for the three hours on Saturday. And what I meant was you worked your buns off and the reward at the end of the day just wasn't there. Because we'd go and play some-body really close and then at the end of the day, we'd come up short. The reward at places like that comes when you go and beat somebody and you know they had better people than you did. But those days were a lot fewer than the days where you'd play a close ball game and end up getting beat."

Having noted the frustrations about coaching at places that had trouble winning, Pruett said he wouldn't give back those experiences for anything.

"I think those lessons and those methods and going through that is what really helped me become a stronger football coach," Pruett said.

By the time Pruett moved to Tulane, Elsie had climbed aboard to em-brace the strategy her husband had employed for moving up the coaching ladder.

"We loved Ole Miss and wanted to stay there, but then we went to Tulane and Florida," said Elsie, who said she finally understood why moving was the right strategy. "I could see then why it was important to move around because as assistant coach you only know the other assistant coaches and your players and maybe your neighbors. The more athletic directors and college presidents you met, the better your chances were to advance."

Pruett spent two years at Tulane with Teevens.

"Tulane was a great experience," Pruett said. "We played great defense at Tulane. And we weren't a very good football team."

Teevens' goal was to build the Tulane program to where they could com-pete against a high-caliber schedule.

"At Tulane, I got to be a coordinator against some really good teams be-cause they basically played an SEC schedule," Pruett said. "I think playing those kinds of teams made for a growing and a learning experience."

But there were the bumps and bruises suffered from having inferior tal-ent.

"I'll never forget, we went down to play Florida State and it was the last game of the year," Pruett said. "And I can't remember why, but some of the seniors didn't make the trip for whatever reason and we were beaten miser-ably. They were honoring Burt Reynolds and Walter Payton and giving leather Florida State jackets to them and they beat us something like 70-7. That was my first experience at Florida State.

"Funny thing was, that same year, we played Alabama, who won the national championship, and we played them at their place and the score was like 16-7. In other words, we had some great games and great experiences."

Tulane served as a stepping-stone to the most prestigious job Pruett had as an assistant when he became the defensive coordinator at the University of Florida.

Pruett knew Florida Coach Steve Spurrier from coaching against him when he was the coach at Duke while Pruett was at Wake Forest.

"We had been successful, he liked our schemes," Pruett said.

So when Pruett was in Florida recruiting for Tulane and read how upset Spurrier was about his defense, Pruett picked up the telephone and called Spurrier on a whim.

"Coach Spurrier happened to answer the phone," Pruett said. "And I just told him I'd been reading in the paper and saw that he was unhappy and was thinking about hiring a secondary coach. I told him if he was interested in considering me, I would be interested. Then I didn't really hear any more from him until he was calling around getting recommendations from people and they called and told me he'd called. And then I got a call and they wanted me to interview.

"I'll never forget when Coach Spurrier offered me the job at Florida," Pruett said. "Of course, that was one of those dream jobs, too, to be the defensive coordinator at the University of Florida in the Southeastern Conference. I was in the Holiday Inn there in Gainesville and I had interviewed. We were waiting to go out to dinner and I had just showered and they called and offered me the job. And I stood in the middle of the bed and did a dance, I was so happy.

A lackluster response from the media followed when the news of Pruett's hiring broke.

"I was hired and they had this press conference on Monday and the Jacksonville newspaper said, 'Bobby Who?'" Pruett recalled. "And I think about five or six days later, we had to start spring practice. So I had to put in the whole defensive scheme in five or six days."

Pruett's devising a defensive scheme came in advance of his first coaches meeting where he gained a little insight into Spurrier's quirkiness. Pruett smiled recalling the meeting at which Spurrier told his coaches, "Okay, boys, this is how we're going to do it." Spurrier then changed nearly every coach's responsibilities.

"None of them knew any of this was coming, including me," Pruett said.

"Since I was the new guy they all looked right at me like I was the culprit."

According to Pruett, the staff had quality coaches throughout, but suddenly they were all coaching new positions. On top of that, Pruett had to teach the defense a new scheme.

"We had to get our drills together in four or five days to get ready for spring ball against one of the most potent offenses in college football," Pruett said. "And after about three or four days, Coach Spurrier came and made everybody go play golf. He said we were working too hard. So, it certainly was different. It was fun. It was exciting. It was demanding, but we had to adjust and I had to get the coaches all pulling together on defense and believing in me and doing those things. And they did. In other words, it was an adventure to say the least. But it was a learning experience."

In hindsight, Pruett believed the coaching changes came because Spurrier was looking for a drastic change and the resulting shock effect.

"And that was his method of doing things," Pruett said. "He certainly got everybody's attention, including mine. When somebody asks me about him what I say about working for Coach Spurrier is that he was a very demanding guy from the standpoint he wanted you to scratch where it itched. And if you couldn't scratch, he wanted to help you a little bit and then, if you still couldn't scratch that itch, he'd get him another scratcher."

Pruett spent the summer before his first season with the Gators trying to scratch what itched Spurrier.

When Spurrier hired Pruett to join him at Florida, he talked about Georgia and Tennessee as being the two teams that scored the most points on him. Wanting to please his new boss—and following old habits—Pruett went to Penn State to pick the brains of their coaches. Penn State had played Tennessee in a bowl game and had done well. Pruett figured he didn't have to reinvent the wheel to learn how to stop the Vols. He also talked to some coaches who had coached at Tennessee in attempt to learn their new offensive scheme. He followed suit in uncovering information about Georgia.

Pruett logged away what he learned over the summer about both teams and put everything in a book. In addition, when Pruett talked to other coaches via the coaching grapevine, he solicited their opinions on how to defense different schemes.

"During that year we went to Tennessee and shut them out 31-0," Pruett said. "I think that was the first time they'd been shut out in a long time at Knoxville. Later that year we beat Georgia and we intercepted three balls and scored touchdowns on defense. So the work in the off-season really paid off in just understanding what our opponents were doing."

Pruett was a defensive coach in the land where offense ruled. Cohabitating in that situation has felled even the best defensive coordinators. Pruett understood what he was getting into when he went to Florida.

"One of the things you knew with Coach Spurrier, he wanted the ball," Pruett said. "He wanted to call plays. And I'll never forget: We were playing Ole Miss and we jumped up on them 21-0. We lost a couple of defensive backs in the ball game and they had a couple of good receivers and a quarterback that could throw the ball. And what they did was spread us out, which limited us in what we could do.

"I knew we were good enough to win the game and they couldn't beat us. We just couldn't give them cheap scores. So we got fairly conservative on defense and played a two-deep coverage."

By employing the two-deep coverage, Florida could not smother the run.

"Our guys weren't really excited about playing Ole Miss because they were a lot better than Ole Miss anyhow," Pruett said. "Anyway, Ole Miss ended up getting some first downs running the ball and ended up holding the ball on us a little bit. We won the ball game 36-10. Beat them pretty good, but we didn't have the ball a lot on offense. In other words, they took the air out of the ball. They were just going to run it and run the clock and make sure they didn't get beat bad."

Spurrier was cranky afterwards because his offense didn't get their hands on the football enough. During the game Spurrier told Pruett, "Bobby, get them off the field and let them score. I want to call some ball plays."

Pruett's first year didn't exactly have a happy ending. Florida went to Tallahassee and built a 31-3 lead only to watch FSU come back and tie them 31-31.

Pruett caught a lot of blame for changing the Gators' defense in the fourth quarter of the game played at FSU's Doak Campbell that came to be known as "The Choke at Doak."

"That one was pretty tough to deal with," Pruett said. "You know, to be honest with you, we were lucky we didn't lose the game. Because the way the momentum had changed, if they had gone for two they probably would have won the football game.

"Because what happened is the momentum turned against us and their crowd got back into the game. I remember looking at the game on film and at the end of the third quarter, FSU had less than 200 yards of offense—they had almost 300 yards of offense in the fourth quarter."

The defense always takes the heat whenever a turnaround the magnitude of the "Choke at Doak" occurs. But the Gators' offense didn't do much to help the defensive effort.

"We were up 31-3 in the fourth quarter and they scored," Pruett said. "And all we've got to do is run the football and it's over, because they don't have enough time. And we throw that thing around and turn it over on first and second down. But you just have to understand that's Coach Spurrier's style. So, if that's his style, you had to coach to that style."

When Pruett went to work the Monday following the FSU game he saw a reminder about what had happened in Tallahassee.

"Right by the practice field there was a little fraternity house where they had a big piece of plywood out on the lawn propped up and it said 'Pruett sucks,'" said Pruett with a little grin.

Later he visited the house and kidded with the residents about the sign.

"I made light of it and went on," Pruett said. "Because, ultimately, we should have won the football game. And we didn't. You can sit around and make excuses or reasons for losing or not being successful, but the bottom line was that no matter what the reason was, we were good enough for three quarters to shut Florida State down and we should have been able to do it for the rest of the ball game. We didn't get it done. But they had a good football team too."

Florida handed undefeated Alabama its first loss, 24-23 in the SEC Championship game the following week, and Pruett saw a different sign at the house across from the practice field.

"We played well against Alabama, so they changed the sign to where it read, 'Much better, Coach,'" Pruett said.

Being under a microscope was something new to Pruett and something he experienced immediately in the Gators' opening game of the 1994 season against New Mexico State.

"The first game I coached at Florida I was all happy because I had always wanted to have really good people and be able to do about whatever we wanted to do on defense and stuff like that," Pruett said. "And I think about the first or second play of the game we call a blitz and a defensive back falls down and they score a long touchdown. We were playing a team that we should beat. So, I mean, that's about the first or second play of the game. That's my first experience as a defensive coordinator. So that wasn't a real good one."

Florida ended up playing FSU in the Sugar Bowl following the 1994 season, making for a rematch of the tie game in Tallahassee.

"I was kind of snakebit against FSU that first year," Pruett said. "The night before the game we were going to have a meal in the Superdome and one of our linebackers and a defensive end get in a fight over a card game. And they start pushing and shoving each other and one of the kids is drinking a bottle of Gatorade and it breaks and hits him on the side of the head and cuts him pretty good. One of the guys was one of our top defensive player and the other was a pass-rushing defensive end."

FSU won the game in overtime 23-17.

"That incident was a big, huge disruption for our defensive team," Pruett said. "But all of those things were huge learning experiences for me."

Pruett made a note to himself that his off-season project would be to study FSU the way he had Tennessee and Georgia.

"We just really wanted to understand what they were doing," Pruett said. "So the next summer we tried to learn more about them and it really helped us understand them. We went to Virginia Tech because their offensive coordinator had been at South Carolina. The head coach at South Carolina was Brad Scott, who had run the offense at FSU. In other words, I'd go everywhere and just try to keep piecing together as much information as I could about an opponent. I figured you couldn't get all the information you wanted at one place, but if you kept digging by going ten different places, you'd accumulate enough to where you had information that could really be a great benefit. My thought process was, and always has been, if you knew enough about your opponent at strategic times—what they were thinking or how their scheme worked, stuff like that—you'd have a better chance of winning the game."

The following year Florida defeated FSU 35-24 to highlight an undefeated season that led them to the Fiesta Bowl and their meeting against Nebraska where they were humiliated.

Despite having to face the heat, coaching at Florida proved to be a wonderful experience for Pruett.

"We played for and won the SEC championship both years I was there," Pruett said. "Everybody wants to play for championships. I got to work with great players and great coaches, which was quite an experience. And the fans, their fans, basically I thought were great fans.

"The things I experienced and learned at Florida were invaluable. Because I learned some tough lessons and when I say 'the tough lessons,' well, you learn how to work through things and around things to manage things. Having been at Marshall, Wake Forest, Ole Miss and Tulane, you were sort of at the have-nots. Ole Miss wasn't quite that bad, but, in comparison to everybody else in the SEC, they were. Then I went to Florida, which is the privileged. So I learned how to be a champion and how hard you had to work to try to get there. And I got the experience of how a champion acts and how they are expected to win and what the Florida fans' expectations and demands were."

Once Pruett landed the job at Marshall, he cobbled together the lessons learned while coaching the have-nots with those he learned during his two years at Florida to form what he considered to be the best plan to make Marshall a champion.

---

### In memoriam of those who perished in the Marshall plane crash

| | | |
|---|---|---|
| Capt. Frank Abbott | Art Harris | Phyllis Preston |
| James Adams | Art Harris, Jr. | Courtney Proctor |
| Mark Andrews | Bob Harris | Dr. H. D. Proctor |
| Charles Arnold | E. O. Heath | Helen Ralsten |
| Rachel Arnold | Elaine Heath | Murrill Ralsten |
| Mike Blake | Bob Hill | Scotty Reese |
| Dennis Blevins | Joe Hood | Jack Repasy |
| Willie Bluford | Tom Howard | Larry Sanders |
| Donald Booth | Cynthia Jarrell | Al Saylor |
| Deke Brackett | James Jarrell | Jim Schroer |
| Larry Brown | Ken Jones | Art Shannon |
| Tom Brown | Charles Kautz | Ted Shoebridge |
| Al Carelli, Jr. | Marcelo Lajterman | Allen Skeens |
| Dr. Joseph Chambers | Richard Lech | Jerry Smith |
| Margaret Chambers | Frank Loria | Jerry Stainback |
| Roger Childers | Gene Morehouse | Donald Tackett |
| Stuart Cottrell | Jim Moss | Rick Tolley |
| Rick Dardinger | Barry Nash | Bob Van Horn |
| David DeBord | Jeff Nathan | Roger Vanover |
| Danny Deese | Pat Norrell | Patricia Vaught |
| Gary George | Dr. Brian O'Connor | Parker Ward |
| Kevin Gilmore | James Patterson | Norman Whisman |
| Dave Griffith | Charlene Poat | Fred Wilson |
| Dr. Ray Hagley | Michael Prestera | John Young |
| Shirley Ann Hagley | Dr. Glenn Preston | Tom Zborill |

## Chapter four

Bob Pruett had spent most of his adult life coveting the Marshall head coaching position—a job he didn't know if he would ever land—then suddenly he had it. What happens when your dreams come true? Anxiety easily can follow attaining a long-time goal. One can entertain thoughts of failure, or an emptiness can accompany the glow, because what's left to accomplish?

Pruett didn't need therapy. He needed to come down out of the clouds.

"No, getting the job was just so exhilarating," Pruett said. "I was so excited about the opportunity, it was like a huge shot of adrenalin, I mean, here's a real challenge. I'm following Jim Donnan, who had done a fabulous job and won a national championship and played for three or four and was

**HE HAS ARRIVED** — With a serious look on his face, Bob settled into his dream job of coaching his alma mater. *Courtesy Marshall University; photograph by Rick Haye.*

*4*

# FULFILLIN

A DREAM

runner-up three or four times. He had enjoyed great success, too. Maybe I should have been scared, but there wasn't anything scary or overwhelming about getting the job. There wasn't anything other than, let's get into this thing and let's just see where it takes us. This is a new adventure. This is exciting and this is a huge challenge for us. Let's just jump into this thing and give it all we've got and see what happens."

Pruett returned to Marshall after being at Florida, a program that had been the runner-up to the national champions. The Gators had NFL type players up and down their numbers to play the types of schemes Pruett wanted to employ. Most coaches can only dream about having those types of players to coach.

Now Pruett would be at Marshall, where the talent level wasn't the same.

Team meetings gave Pruett his first up-close look at the team he inherited at Marshall. Immediately he noticed a size differential.

"The biggest difference from Florida—because we really had a good football team at Marshall, and I knew that—was at a bigger school like Florida, they've got so many more players," Pruett said. "In other words, Florida had a lot of good players. There were first team players, second team players and third team players. And you could just keep going and going. No doubt, we had a lot of great players at Florida. But I really didn't consider that an issue. Having been at Marshall in the past as a player and a coach, I noticed how much better the players were than when I'd been there before. So I don't remember the talent level really being an issue, because as a coach I've always believed you just have to coach up the players you have to try and make them better. Just go out and play and see what happens."

Donnan had done a wonderful job during his years at Marshall, putting the team on the fast track toward where it wanted to go in 1997: Division I-A. Donnan's first season was 1990 and under his guidance Marshall became a I-AA bully, winning the national title in 1992, becoming runners-up twice and making it to the final four one other time. And when Donnan left Marshall to assume the Georgia job, he didn't leave the cupboard bare.

"Well, you know, we had some good players at Marshall," Pruett said. "Coach Donnan had recruited some good players. Matter of fact, a couple of them went with him to Georgia, Olandis Gary, and Jermaine Wiggins. Both of them ended up playing in the NFL. Olandis Gary became a 1,000-yard rusher for Denver."

Pruett spoke frankly with his team during that first team meeting. He respected the track record of what the group had accomplished, but he wanted more.

"They were accustomed to playing for championships and had been in I-AA National Championship games," Pruett said. "But we wanted to win them. We wanted to compete for championships. I told them we wanted them to compete as hard in the classroom as they did on the football field and that my door would always be open to them to talk. If they had a problem, I expected them to come and present that problem to me if they didn't like what was going on. Because if I didn't like what was going on, I would find them. And I'd give them my cell phone number, my office and home number, whatever. And I said this is the way it's going to be and I would be expecting them to go to class. We expected them to be good citizens and we expected them to be great football players."

Since Pruett had left Marshall, Pruett noticed changes at the university he loved. Marshall had updated their program with a new stadium—Marshall Stadium—and they had updated facilities. Marshall played in the Southern Conference.

"Facility-wise we were by far better than anybody else in our conference," Pruett said. "And then the energy level in Huntington and the surrounding area, well, the interest level had just gotten so much better than it had been during the period from 1968 to 1982 when Marshall was the losingest football program in America. Obviously, the setback of losing the team in the crash had been the major factor in that."

Upon taking the job, Pruett had a conversation with Marshall President Wade Gilley, who wanted to size up just how high Pruett wanted to set the bar.

"Where do you think you can take this program?" Gilley asked.

"Well, as quickly as possible, I'd like to get it to the Southern Miss, East Carolina level," Pruett told him.

In the mid 1990s, Southern Miss and East Carolina were Top 25 teams.

"East Carolina had gotten even higher than that," Pruett said. "But, you know, they were Top 25 at both programs. And that's where I felt like we wanted to try to get to as quickly as we could."

More immediate was the task at hand, which was to try and improve on the success the Herd had enjoyed the previous season. This was no small order.

Chad Pennington began the 1995 season as the Herd's third-string quarterback, which is the place you expect a true freshman to be in his first season on campus.

All of that changed in a game against Georgia Southern September 16, 1995, when the starter, Larry Harris, went down with an injury and then Mark Zban, the backup quarterback, also got injured. Pennington entered the game and looked as cool as the other side of the pillow while completing fourteen of twenty-three passes for 164 yards and a touchdown.

Pennington started the next week against the University of Tennessee-Chattanooga.

Despite throwing six interceptions, Pennington led the Herd to a 35-32 victory. He also threw three touchdowns and had 284 yards passing.

In addition to showing promising ability, Pennington demonstrated great leadership qualities. The Herd got on a roll with Pennington, going 10-1 with their freshman signal caller at the helm; their only loss with Pennington at quarterback came at home when Appalachian State beat the Herd 10-3. Marshall finished with a 12-2 record to earn a spot in the Division I-AA playoffs.

Marshall's offense also had senior running back Chris Parker, who finished his career with more than 4,500 rushing yards. Complementing the offense was a smothering defense that allowed only 246.4 yards and 15.7 points per game.

In the playoffs they defeated Jackson State and Northern Iowa before upsetting No. 1-ranked and undefeated McNeese State 25-13 at McNeese State to reach the title game for the fourth time in five years.

Marshall led Montana 20-19 late in the fourth quarter of the contest played in Huntington before the Grizzlies drove down the field and got a go-ahead field goal. Pennington drove his team to the Montana forty-six to give the Herd one last shot. But kicker Tim Openlander's attempt at making a 63-yard field goal didn't reach the goal post and Montana had a 22-20 win.

Pennington's numbers were just short of astounding considering he was a true freshman. For the season, he completed 61.9 percent of his passes for 2,445 yards and fifteen touchdowns. He had five games with more than 200 yards passing and was named Southern Conference Freshman of the Year. In addition to having a great quarterback, Pruett would have most of the cast from the previous season on his first Marshall team.

"Oh, yeah, yeah, I could see we had good ballplayers," Pruett said. "We had a good team, but we needed to get some depth."

**FRESHMAN QB —** One of the players Bob inherited from Jim Donnan's tenure was a skinny kid from Knoxville, Tennessee—Chad Pennington. *Courtesy Marshall University; photograph by Brian Tirpak.*

Pruett didn't try to copy Donnan upon taking over. However, it would have been foolish not to recognize the great success Donnan had enjoyed. So he did not change everything, adding his own approach where he saw fit.

Pruett retained four coaches from Donnan's staff: Tim Billings, Mark Gale, Tony Petersen, and Brian Dowler.

"That really helped in the transition," Pruett said. "They were all good coaches and I kept them. And we just went to work. I didn't feel threatened or challenged by the past success because you're going to be judged on your merits. But the thing I tried to do was praise what the people before me had done because they deserved it and they earned it. I wanted to say all positive things about those guys and alter the things I needed to alter to fit me.

"Having been a coach and having worked under good people, I realized that I couldn't be Bear Bryant or Steve Spurrier; I had to be Bobby Pruett. But I could certainly learn from those people and the things within their systems or their personalities that fit within mine. I learned from them and tried to incorporate those things that I learned from each one of the guys I'd coached for. I learned from those guys and tried to take the positive things. I also tried to learn from the things they did that didn't work."

Having attained his dream job, Pruett could see how the journey he had taken—traveling from school to school—carved out a perspective he might not have attained had he not become such a well-traveled coach. Maturity accompanied him to his new job as the Marshall coach at age fifty-two, and he could see how all of his experiences had meshed together to give him a different way of looking at things.

"I think being a head high school coach at a large high school and an administrator there really shaped my perspective," Pruett said. "Then the experience at Florida of handling the media, because the defensive coordinator at Florida with Spurrier was such a high profile spot, those things and my age when I got the job."

Pruett's down-home, folksy personality also won people over.

"I didn't feel like that I had anything to prove from the standpoint of the way I tried to do things," Pruett said. "I realized that ultimately, what happened while I was there would be determined by what we did. We would make that happen. And I didn't need to get all the credit. In other words, if it's good, there's going to be enough ice cream for everybody; and if it's bad, all of it will melt on my plate. Luckily, we had enough for everybody and that's the way I wanted this to be, a community program. I wanted it to be something that everybody could enjoy and everybody could be part of. Sometimes I think coaches, even businessmen, are afraid that somebody will overtake them. But basically, either we all succeed or it doesn't matter anyway."

In that vein, Pruett remembered what he had liked about working for certain coaches.

"During my coaching career I always wanted whoever I worked for not to take away my creativity," Pruett said. "And what I wanted to do was hire good people around me. I felt like I had enough confidence in what I was trying to accomplish that by evaluating people, I could hire good coaches. And that was probably one of the things we were able to do, hire really good coaches, set the program, set the direction, and let them run with it. Handle their responsibilities. Each of the coaches was the head coach of his position. The coordinator was the head coach of the offense, defense or the special teams, and then I was sort of the next guy. And by doing these things and letting these guys stay under the umbrella that we had set for them and by making it clear what the umbrella was, that enabled me to develop the things in the program that needed to be developed, fundraising, program raising: doing all the things we needed to do. I could still run the football and still do the promotional things that had to be done to take a program like Marshall from Division I-AA to Division I-A to a Top 25 program and change the perception in the country."

Pruett worked hard to make the Thundering Herd the community's team.

"It never was my team," Pruett said. "It was *our* team. It was our community team, everybody out there. You always want to sell the community and the family concept. And we were able to increase the average attendance from 17,000 a game up to around 28,000. That was just part of the system of what we wanted to try and do. It was such a thrill for me to get to come home and to be back in the state."

He made it a point to get out and talk up Marshall football.

Pruett spent a lot of time and energy his first season at Marshall speaking at over 200 engagements. In return for those speaking engagements he usually got an "atta-boy."

"But that atta-boy is what it's all about," Pruett said. "Image is everything. College football is a business. We're just in the people business and athlete business and passing a little ball around. But any type of business, or product, you have, you want to get it a brand name, IBM, AT&T, whatever. These are all brands that are recognized. And what we wanted to do at Marshall was establish the brand. So, I didn't change the helmet. I didn't change the jersey. I didn't change the pants. When we ran out onto the field on TV and people saw the white hat with the 'M' on it, I wanted people to know what team it was. That it was Marshall University."

Pruett took one look at the hand he'd been dealt at the start of spring practice and had a good feeling about his team. This was a team a coach could look at and expect it to run the table.

"Oh, it was a good team," Pruett said. "Everybody knew that. I mean, they were the runner-up in the National Championship game and most of the players were back. So expectations were high."

Tweaking the offense and defense would be part of Pruett's agenda that spring.

"Well, we implemented our offense and our defense," Pruett said. "I mean, that part of it was all new. We went strictly to a one-back offense and threw the ball around. Like what Steve was doing at Florida."

Much of the success for that kind of offense is contingent on finding the best match-ups to exploit, which Pruett had studied Spurrier doing masterfully at Florida.

"We wanted to be wide open, 'Fun 'N Gun' like Florida, but we were a bit more intent on running the ball than Coach Spurrier was," Pruett said. "On defense, being a defensive guy, we wanted to be able to create turnovers and that type of thing."

The new offense went over well, generating an air of excitement among the players.

"When he came in, Coach Pruett brought in that Florida Gator style of offense," said Doug Chapman, a red-shirt freshman running back at the time. "As a running back it can either be a positive or a negative. It's one of those offenses where, if the passing game is going, you might get the ball six times in the game. At the same time you've got to look at it from a more optimistic side. If the passing game is going, that's spreading out that defense more and getting that extra guy in the box. Then when it's time for you to run it, instead of getting a three-yard gain, you get a twenty-yard gain or you take it all the way.

"It's all about what you make it. We had a great offensive line and I had the ability to catch the ball out of the backfield. They moved me around a lot. So it was a fun offense to play in, that West Coast, wide-open offense. I enjoyed every moment of it."

On defense Pruett said he wanted to be able to have something where they could "crowd a lot of people around the line of scrimmage" if Marshall was playing a heavy run team.

"But, because of the success that we were having at the University of Florida, I knew that if we got to throwing the ball around like Coach Spurrier was doing—even old dummy me could figure this out—it wouldn't be long before somebody else was going to figure out pretty well how to try and stop us," Pruett said. "So we needed to have something in our package that could help us versus the passing game. So we had a little combination of both the pass and the run."

Establishing his personality while also establishing a measure of discipline for Pruett's players shed light on another aspect of his job his first spring.

"We had players get into scuffles in bars and we had to get that under control, you know, fighting," Pruett said. "We were running them and doing some things and I had a team meeting after about the third fight and told them that we had to quit it. And I said, 'Thing of it is, ain't none of it your fault.' I said, 'Look back there at so-and-so.' Everybody in the room turned and looked at him. The whole side of his face was bruised from fighting. Then I said, 'Look at so and so.' Everybody looked at him. His face is black and blue. And I said, 'He's saying he won?' Well, they all laughed."

Pruett said one of the players, who he referred to as Poochie, stood up in front of the team and said the fight hadn't been his fault.

"I was just standing there and this guy hits me," the player said.

Pruett thought to himself, "My player is six-foot-five, 305 pounds and this guy, who weighed about 195 pounds, decides to pick on my player and hit him?"

"Now this don't make sense," Pruett said. "So I said, 'Poochie, you're in a fight. I get a call and you're telling me a bunch of guys jumped you outside of Sam's Iguana?' I said I could understand that. But, I said, 'The complaint I got is that you knocked down the door of a fraternity house and beat some guy up.'"

"Well, I just came back and got my buddies and then I went back and the guys jumped me, is all," Poochie said.

"Guys, this ain't going to work," Pruett told his team. "We're going to have to send somebody home. We can't have this."

Pruett said the discipline came down to getting his team under control by making them understand how they had to act and that there were rules that had to be followed. He finished by telling them: "I'm on your side, but just like your dad and mom are on your side, if you get out of bounds, you've got to get back in bounds."

Spring practice told Pruett he had a good group of talented players, and he could see he would have no problems at quarterback.

"We knew we had two really good quarterbacks," Pruett said. "We had Chad Pennington and Mark Zban, who had transferred from Ohio State. He was from Huntington. He was an outstanding quarterback. We had two really good players at the position, so who was going to start there really wasn't an issue."

Pruett loved Pennington, but had some concerns.

"Going through spring practice, the only thing that we felt like with Chad was, 'Gosh, here is a fabulous quarterback, but he's a hundred and seventy-five pounds' and even though he was a very accurate thrower, he didn't quite have the strength yet that he needed," Pruett said. "He just needed to get in the weight room and get bigger and stronger.'"

Pruett also recognized that his team lacked depth.

"We needed to add some depth and we addressed that after spring practice," Pruett said.

Depth, and talent, would come.

On February 13, 1977, Randy Moss was born in Rand, West Virginia, an area located just outside Charleston. Mining provided the most jobs for the locals, so entertaining thoughts of leaving Rand required an imagination. Most of Rand's population was born in Rand and remained in Rand.

Moss was raised by his mother, Maxine, a single parent, who worked hard to keep a job as a nurse's aide while doing the best she could to raise Randy; a situation that left Randy alone much of the time. She impressed upon her son the importance of attending church and she did not tolerate alcohol or bad language.

Maxine's workload left her tired and run down, which became a motivating tool in Moss's life. If he ever became successful, he would see to it that he could take care of his mother where she could kick back and not have to work so hard.

Once he began to participate in athletics, Moss began to understand sports could be his ticket toward realizing a successful future. Clearly he had special athletic gifts that left jaws dropping in his small community, whether he was playing football, basketball or running track. Envisioning Moss playing in the NFL or NBA didn't require much of an imagination, even in Rand.

By the time Moss was a senior at Dupont High in nearby Belle, West Virginia, every coach in the country knew who Randy Moss was. Already he'd led Dupont to state football titles as a sophomore and junior in 1992 and 1993. He had unique gifts: speed, hands, agility, quickness, and jumping ability. In his senior season he was named the State of West Virginia's Player of the Year in football and basketball. Notre Dame coach Lou Holtz called him the best high school talent he had ever seen. To call Moss a blue-chip prospect would have been like calling Secretariat a plow horse.

"On the football field he didn't seem human," said Tim Stephens, a sports reporter for *The Huntington Herald-Dispatch.* "I saw him a little bit in high school. I saw him against a really good football team, Ironton, Ohio. They're a real super power in Ohio. In fact they beat Moss' team, Dupont, which was West Virginia state champion.

"Randy performed against them. He was just a heckuva a player. You could tell on the basketball court what an athlete he was, but he was more than an athlete, he was a football player, too. He wasn't just a package of skills in a six-foot-five, 210-pound body. He was the real deal, he was more than just an athlete—he was a total package football player."

Notre Dame, Florida, and Tennessee appeared to have the best shot at landing the incredible talent. Notre Dame won the sweepstakes, but there would be baggage.

Moss was involved in a fight at Dupont High in March of 1995, and since he was eighteen, he was charged as an adult and sentenced to thirty days in jail. Dupont expelled him from high school and Notre Dame rescinded his scholarship. But everybody who had spent time with Moss recognized re-deeming qualities in him, which is why Holtz called FSU coach Bobby Bowden and encouraged him to give Moss a shot. Bowden had dealt with many play-ers with problems in the past, and agreed to bring in Moss on the condition he sit out his first season.

Moss did not suit up for the Seminoles as a freshman in the fall of 1995, but Florida State looked like a good fit for him. He didn't get in any trouble and made his grades. And he did open a few eyes when he took the field to participate in the team's 1996 spring football drills. FSU traditionally produced a host of NFL talent every season, but even among such a group that included the likes of Tra Thomas, Peter Boulware and Warrick Dunn, Moss stood out.

Moss broke Deion Sanders' FSU record in the forty with a burst of 4.32, earning a phone call from the FSU legend. Add to the speed a 38 inch vertical leap and Moss looked like a pass catching machine to the Seminoles, who could not believe how well he caught the football and how effortless he looked doing it.

Unfortunately for Moss—and FSU—Moss tested positive for marijuana before serving his time in jail for the assault conviction. Testing positive for marijuana violated the terms of his probation, so his probation was revoked and another ninety days were added to his sentence. Bowden took action by terminating Moss' scholarship.

Moss did considerable soul searching while spending time in jail and would say that he was humbled by the episode. And his college options had thinned considerably through his actions. But fortunately for Moss, a third chance sat on the horizon in Huntington, West Virginia. Obviously, Moss was aware that Marshall would be a Division I-AA school for its final season in the fall of 1996 before moving up to Division I-A. Moss contacted Pruett and asked Marshall's new head coach if he would be interested in having him come to Huntington. Any coach would love to have a Randy Moss running pass routes, but at what cost?

Pruett told Moss he would welcome him if he could stay out of trouble.

"I recruited Randy at Florida," Pruett said. "Randy made only three official visits out of high school: Notre Dame, Tennessee and Florida. He didn't make an official visit to Florida State; it's just where he went when Notre Dame turned him down.

"We were trying to get him to come to Florida, but one of the issues was Randy was a qualifier out of high school. He was a pretty good student, but, I think if your ACT score is—he met the requirement—but it had to be a certain level at Florida and Florida State or you had to go to summer school. Florida State had some kind of program that paid for the summer school and Florida didn't. That was one of the factors for him choosing Florida State. Plus, I think he liked Florida State. So he went there and then, when it didn't work out there, I had a relationship with him from when he was in high school. And, if he was going to transfer, he needed to go down a level [to Division I-AA or lower] or he would have had to sit out another year. Randy really wanted to play two years of college football and go to the NFL. So he came to Marshall."

Pruett downplayed his part in facilitating Moss' arrival, but it wasn't an easy endeavor. Pruett was a new head coach expected to keep the flame burning at a program that had reached some lofty heights under its previous coach, Jim Donnan. Now here he was, the new coach, sticking his neck out for a controversial player many considered a hoodlum. To some this signaled Marshall had lowered its standards in the name of creating a better football team. Pruett, like every college coach in America, understood what Moss could do for the program as an athlete, but he also felt like he was doing the right thing by giving Moss another chance.

"I had recruited Randy when he was in high school and met his mom— and what a tremendous lady—and met Randy and he had come to Florida on an official visit," Pruett said. "And, honestly, I can say that Randy was a joy for me. In other words, I think he's one of the best things that ever happened to Marshall University and the State of West Virginia. And I felt like as long as you were up front with Randy and honest with him and dealt with him in a fair manner that he would work extremely hard for us, and he wasn't any different than a bunch of other guys that we'd coached at a lot of other universities.

"In other words, when anyone is growing up from seventeen years old to twenty-nine, I hate to think some of the things I did would have been as scrutinized as everything that Randy did was just because he was a fabulous athlete. He was *Parade Magazine*'s player of the year. He was Mr. Basketball in the State of West Virginia. He won the state 100 meters. I mean he was fantastic. He could have run in the Olympics. So everything was scrutinized. Everybody knew who he was and Randy, you know, maybe some things had happened in his life that I'm sure that he wished had not happened or that he would have done differently, but he got in a fight. That's the way I looked at it and he admitted to smoking pot. But him coming to Marshall had the support of the president of the university and I think that him being an in-state guy helped the situation, too."

Pruett was at an alumni golf outing in Logan, West Virginia, when he got the news Moss would be attending Marshall.

"And you talk about somebody that was excited—I was elated," Pruett said. "We'd gone through spring practice with the players we had and then Randy Moss was coming. I knew what we were getting and that the fortunes of Marshall football were turning because not only were we getting a great player, we were getting a guy I considered the best player in the country. Certainly the best athlete, who I thought was the best player, and easily the biggest impact player in the country. And I had the quarterbacks who could get him the ball. Jiminy Christmas. It was just such a huge event for Marshall football and our program when he came."

The "rubber chicken" circuit is one of the toughest things a coach has to do during the off-season, but clearly, the rubber chicken tasted better the day Moss said he would be attending Marshall.

"Oh, everything tasted better that day, can't you see?" Pruett said. "And I was excited for Randy because I had gotten to know him. And I really, really liked him. As much as he would be helping us, I knew Marshall University would be a good fit for him, too."

In addition to Moss' arrival prior to fall practice, Pruett welcomed a familiar face from the University of Florida, Eric Kresser.

Kresser starred at Palm Beach (Florida) Gardens High School, where he passed for for 5,364 yards and forty-four touchdowns, earning all-state honors in Division 5-A and even received All-American honors from High School Recruiting Service and Blue Chip Report. Having a big arm and big aspirations, Kresser sorted through his many suitors before finally deciding to attend Florida, where Florida coach Steve Spurrier employed his wide-open style of football and the Gators were perennial National Championship contenders.

Kresser looked the part of the made-to-order quarterback any college coach would love to have sign on the dotted line. He stood six-foot-two, 209 pounds and his arm leaving high school possessed the strength of an NFL quarterback's.

Unfortunately for Kresser, being the most physically talented never insured a quarterback a starting spot in a Spurrier offense. Danny Wuerffel, who would go on to lead the Gators to a National Championship in addition to winning the Heisman Trophy, caught Spurrier's eye first. And when Wuerffel played well, Kresser was relegated to a permanent position on the bench.

Still, Kresser went into spring practice with the Gators in 1996 ready to compete for the job. In Kresser's mind he had won the competition with Wuerffel and the other Gator quarterbacks, but he did not win the starting job. Thus, Kresser was left with the prospect of sitting the bench his senior season—unless Wuerffel got hurt—or making a drastic change.

Given the fact Kresser's goal was to play quarterback in the NFL, the drastic change idea won out. After all, a quarterback had a lot better chance to gain recognition from NFL scouts if he played his senior season. But in order to transfer somewhere else and not have to sit out the 1996 season, Kresser, like Moss, needed to transfer to a lower level of college football.

Kresser already had a working knowledge of the Huntington area. He had been born in nearby Cincinnati and had relatives in Charleston, West Virginia. In addition, he had a familiarity with the new coach at Marshall who had been the defensive coordinator at Florida.

"Obviously Eric was unhappy at Florida because you had Wuerffel and he had kind of won the thing over," Pruett said. "Eric had a strong arm. He could have been a starting quarterback anywhere else in the SEC. At Florida, though, he was just behind Danny Wuerffel. The thing about Spurrier is this: the most talented guy physically is not always going to be Spurrier's choice at quarterback. Wuerffel was the guy who had the most success, so Coach Spurrier wasn't going to change that. But he didn't want to see Eric go. He knew he had some talent. I think he even told Kresser he'd let him start two or three games [in 1996] if he'd stay. Kresser started a game or two my last year at Florida. He's a very talented player.

"But I had no idea that he was going to transfer or even wanted to transfer. But Eric and his dad had decided to transfer and that's when they contacted us. We didn't contact him. And they were contacting a couple of other universities. We went through spring practice and didn't know he was going to transfer."

Pruett and company didn't promise Kresser he would be the starter.

"We just promised him an opportunity, because I saw where it would give us an opportunity if we did that," Pruett said.

Kresser could see himself playing in the NFL if given the chance. Going to Marshall and winning the starting quarterback job would afford him the opportunity to showcase his talents for NFL scouts. There were no guarantees, but Kresser recognized the job could be his, so he made the decision to transfer to Marshall.

Ironically, Kresser had made a weekend visit to Marshall several months earlier, prior to making his decision and was hosted by Pennington, the guy Kresser ultimately would bench by his electing to change addresses.

Kresser's transferring enabled Pruett to make one of the biggest decisions of his coaching career prior to his first fall practice: opening up the quarterback position for competition.

# Chapter five

Building a program can mean difficult decisions for a coach. Bobby Pruett faced a whopper of a problem heading into fall practice prior to his first season as the Marshall coach, albeit, a pleasant problem. The kind of problem most coaches would love to have. Still, Pruett recognized the situation and the possibilities it had to explode in his face if not handled properly.

Eric Kresser would compete for the starting quarterback job with Chad Pennington—the resident Marshall golden boy and champion of resurrecting the Thundering Herd's previous season—and such a prospect was unsettling to some.

"We let them compete," said Pruett, who acknowledged he was already leaning in one direction for the route he would take. "If Eric won the job, I saw where it would give us an opportunity for the program. Chad was a skinny kid that

**KRESSER ARRIVES** — Eric Kresser (15) followed Bob from the University of Florida to Marshall, as Danny Weurffel was firmly entrenched as the Gators' starting QB. *Courtesy Marshall University and marshall.edu.*

5

# REDSHIRTING

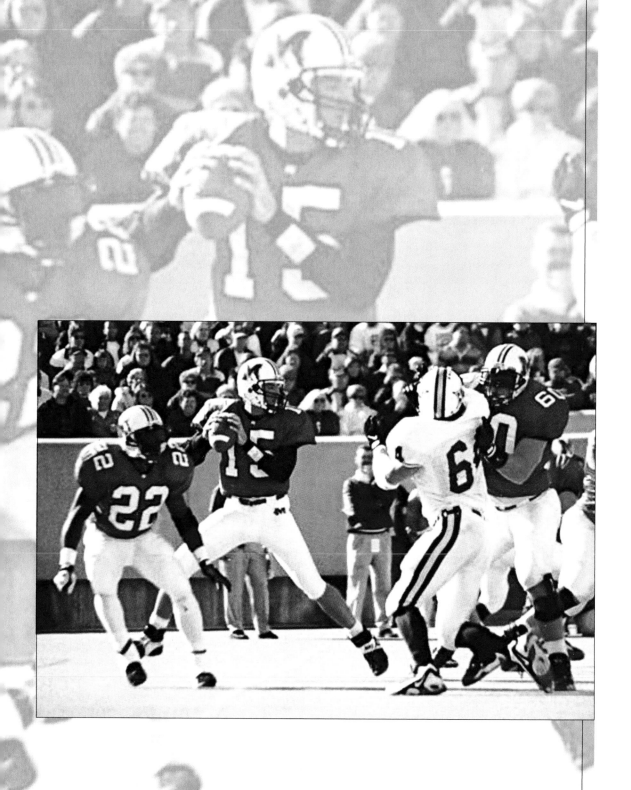

# PENNINGTON

needed to get bigger and stronger."

Pennington, who had had the glorious freshman season, also had Marshall roots. His mother, Denise, attended Marshall for four years to earn a degree and his father, Elwood, had played football at Bluefield State before attending Marshall his final two years of college.

The Penningtons settled down in Knoxville, Tennessee, where both became teachers. Denise taught ninth-grade English and Elwood, physical education; he also coached high-school football.

If there was one thing Chad caught on to at an early age it was how to be engaging. He developed an outgoing personality and had a magnetism that drew people to him. In short, he was a dream kid, eaten up by football. Knoxville was University of Tennessee country and Chad grew up dreaming of being the quarterback for the Volunteers.

Football was a dream, but his intellect looked like it would provide a living for him in his future. He had a lot of interests and a photographic memory. Chad's intelligence, coupled with the fact his father was a football coach, added up to a quarterback who knew what was happening on a football field. Elwood and Denise decided to send Chad to Webb School of Knoxville, a private high school. That decision came primarily because Elwood coached at Halls High School and Chad's parents didn't want to create the situation where the father and son had to worry about what went on at football practice every day once they sat down to eat dinner.

Chad didn't exactly have a stellar high school football career, in large part because of the wing-T offense his school used. Chad had average speed and the wing-T is a run-oriented offense, so the two elements weren't the best combination. In addition, his body had yet to fully develop. But like a puppy, if one looked hard enough, they might have seen the potential for him to fill out—he wore size 13 shoes by age thirteen.

Chad had potential, which was noticed at a football camp at Marshall University prior to his senior season at Webb.

"I had watched [Marshall] on television in '92 and they won the I-AA championship with Coach Donnan," Chad said. "But other than that, I didn't know much about them."

Elwood had a friend, Jack Daniels, who was the coach at Soddy Daisy High School in Soddy Daisy, Tennessee, and Jack had two players that went to Marshall from the school, Tim Martin and Jermaine Swafford.

"And it just so happened that Tim was in town one weekend the summer before my senior year and we had thrown a little bit," Chad said. "And so Coach Daniels told me I ought to go up to camp at Marshall. He said it was a smaller camp and that I could go up there and just have a good time and learn some things. You know, nothing other than that was planned. I wasn't trying to go up there and get a look or anything. I just thought it would be a good chance to go up there and go to a smaller camp and get some individual attention. So, I went to camp. And it was funny, before I left for camp I told my dad, 'Wouldn't it be funny if I had a good camp and they offered me a scholarship? Wouldn't that be amazing?' And we both just kind of laughed and giggled at the thought, thinking nothing was going to happen at the time."

Only Division I-AA schools Tennessee-Chattanooga and Middle Tennessee State were interested in Pennington at the time. But Pennington showed well at the summer camp.

"I had a really good camp," Pennington said. "Coach Donnan liked what he saw. After the camp they started recruiting me and eventually they offered me a scholarship."

All Tennessee offered Pennington was a chance to walk-on, so he elected to attend Marshall, which led to the incredible freshman year Pennington enjoyed.

And now Pruett was going to try and take away Pennington's job? Could clubbing baby seals be far behind?

Pennington knew Pruett might red shirt him during the 1996 season.

"When Eric Kresser transferred to Marshall I knew that the possibility existed that they would red-shirt me," Pennington said. "Coach Pruett had talked to me about having a year to develop because he was really concerned I couldn't throw the corner route that well. He was concerned about me being able to get stronger and developing more arm strength and getting bigger. And he told me how he wanted me to be the quarterback to lead Marshall football into Division I-A. We talked about how it was a big challenge for our school to move up to I-A and he wanted me to be there for that and be the leader for three years and to use this time during the '96 season to get better physically and mentally and really use it to my advantage."

Pennington had always trusted in his coaches and in their wisdom. And with his father being a coach, Pennington had always been around great coaches who had wisdom and could foresee things into the future that were best for him as a person and as an athlete.

"So I just put my trust in him and tried to make it work," Pennington said. "And it did work."

Pruett did tell Pennington he would let him compete for the starting job during two-a-days at fall practice.

"So, obviously, I did not want to read between the lines," Pennington said, "and I just tried to prepare myself as hard as I could and tried to compete during two-a-days and give it a shot. But, in the end in the back of my mind with my dad being a coach, I understood where Coach Pruett was coming from and I knew it was a win-win situation for me because I'd have three years of Division I-A and be stronger and bigger and better because of it. But, you know, Coach Pruett was not a fan favorite of my mother for a while—or my grandmother. But they're over it now."

Pruett called the competition "pretty equal."

"It was pretty equal, but, with it being equal, I really wanted to red-shirt Chad, because—for him—he needed to red-shirt," Pruett said. "Chad competed and we really didn't make the final decisions until the last scrimmage in the fall. And we brought Chad in and I sat him down and explained to him what I wanted to do."

Pruett shot straight with Pennington.

"I think Coach Pruett has always been a coach that is easy to approach as a player," Pennington said. "To me, I always felt like I could walk in his office at any time and talk to him about a situation, even when I didn't know him that well. And I know, on the field, he always made us feel comfortable and relaxed and gave us that sense of confidence we needed. No matter what the challenge was if we just believed in ourselves and did what we were coached to do, we would win football games. And so it was that same aura, that same attitude that he used with me as far as making me feel comfortable about the situation, even though it was a tough situation, and trying to get me to foresee into the future about how good things could really be if I would just continue to work hard and use the year to my advantage."

Pruett always tried to be honest with his players, even though decisions like the one regarding Pennington were tough.

"With Chad and all the players, I was like, 'This is what I'm thinking,' you know?" Pruett said. "And 'just tell me what you're thinking' and just treat them as adults and not BS them. And I think that's one of the strengths that we had in our program is that when I told them something, they knew that that's the way it was, especially at that time; and, if it changed, I would tell them. In other words, I was very honest and open with them and told them this is the way it is. This is what we've got to do and what we're going to do. I think that Chad's grandmother, who is a great lady who I love to death, I think she'd like to hit me with an umbrella. It's just like I'm a grandparent, too. And I think Chad's mom, who is a great lady—Denise, and we really love her to death and have great respect for—well, she didn't care too much for the decision either. I think Chad and Chad's daddy handled it well. It wasn't something that was the most popular thing with everybody. Chad's dad, being a high school football coach, and Chad, they bought into it, but it just took a unique kid to do that. There was a lot of trust. Here's a guy that comes in and they didn't know me from a jar of Vicks. Or even the community or whatever didn't know me from a jar of Vicks and this is my first season and I'm taking the golden boy and trying to do what I think is the best for the program and the best for him."

Pennington might have understood the rationale behind the decision, but that didn't make things any easier for him.

"Well, it's not easy when you've just started and helped lead your team to the National Championship game and you're a field goal away from winning the I-AA National Championship," Pennington said. "And then you have to come in the next year and red-shirt and sit back and watch a guy who's just coming in there to play one year and who has not been through the program. It was tough. It was definitely tough."

Kresser won the job on the basis of talent, his knowledge of the Florida offense—which Pruett had implemented during spring practice—and the fact Pruett wanted Pennington to build himself up physically.

"Red-shirting Chad was good for Marshall and good for Chad," Pruett said. "But the way that Chad handled the red-shirting and the way his parents handled it—his dad's a coach, which helped—and his mother, made all the difference. With all the success he had the previous year it was a tough thing for them to buy into this plan. If Chad and his parents hadn't handled it the way they did with such great class and worked within the program and worked with me and done this, he could have transferred to Georgia along with those other two guys. Or just left the program and been mad. Instead he handled it with great class and understanding in relation to everything about the situation. If he hadn't it could have been devastating. Chad was fantastic. It was a tough deal, a really tough deal. It was a win-win deal for Marshall University, but it was a tough deal for Chad and his parents."

Marshall players weren't so sure about the decision to start Kresser, either.

"I'm not going to lie, with Randy [Moss], there wasn't a big transition because we needed a wide receiver," Doug Chapman said. "But I know me, and some of the others were a little adverse toward Eric when he first got there. Chad's our brother, that's the guy we came in with and this guy's coming out of nowhere and Chad's red-shirting. So all of us were like, if you're starting, you'd better be damn good.

"But Eric came in there. Eric and Chad were two different quarterbacks. But at the same time they both got the job done. Eric came in and picked right up. He knew the offense already from Florida. We had to learn it. He helped me. He helped our offensive line. He helped our receivers. He was one year removed from a national title game. When you look at a guy who has been in a situation like that, if he's going to give you some advice, you've got to take it a little more than you would from somebody else, because he's been there playing and competing in one of the best conferences in college football. He brought that to the table and I think that helped everybody pick their game up and grow a little bit more as a football player. But, like I said, I'm not going to lie, we were a little pessimistic about Eric at first, new guy coming in. But he fit in perfectly and it worked out well."

Chapman and company weren't the only ones second-guessing the decision to use Kresser over Pennington; even Pruett's quarterback coach, Larry Kueck, who is still at Marshall, wanted to play Pennington over Kresser.

"Larry really wanted to play Chad and for a lot of reasons, because of his knowledge and his understanding of the offense, stuff like that, and the way he was keyed in to the game and his learning," Pruett said. "And so Chad is probably the one that made that thing work, because, if he hadn't have done what he did and been acceptable with all that stuff, it wouldn't have worked. If Eric would get hurt, we would use Mark Zban. But I saw great, great potential in Chad Pennington and these other two guys were seniors. If Chad had a year to red-shirt, he'd get bigger and stronger and learn the offense. There'd be unlimited potential for Chad."

Pruett recognized if he were to be successful a lot of that would be dependent upon his trying to mesh the newcomers with the quality players that had been on the 1995 team that had been a whisper away from a championship.

"You've got the guys who are the stars and then all of the sudden you bring a Randy Moss in and then the star receiver who is already there is like, 'Well, am I going to get my share of the balls thrown to me?'" Pruett said. "I mean, nobody said that, but you've got to understand you had another quarterback in here."

Potentially leading to insecurities and any number of confusing thoughts.

Pruett understood that whenever a coach was handling young people he had to be up front and straightforward with them in addition to being honest and letting them have a chance to compete. And he had to show them he wouldn't play favorites.

Moss' talents spoke louder than anything anybody could say; he opened the eyes of his new teammates immediately.

"I'd never seen anything remotely close to him," said Giradie Mercer, a freshman defensive lineman in 1996. "I had been hearing about this guy forever, that this was the guy to have, and he ends up playing at the same university that I do, so you want to go out and see him, like, 'Hey, what's this guy all about?'

"I vividly remember the first day of practice. Everybody is talking about how fast Randy is. So he comes out the first day of camp and runs a forty. I'm sitting there watching with a few other guys and we watch him run. Then I'm saying, 'I don't know that looks like about a 4.6, a 4.5 at best. But by the time we get a chance to hear what the forty numbers are, one coach had 4.29 and another had 4.31. I'm like, 'What!' I heard this statement made before about Walter Payton; the statement was, The great ones make it look easy. And sure enough, this guy Randy Moss is running a phenomenal forty time and the guy's not even breaking a sweat. He is without a doubt the first player I have ever seen up close in person to have what I have defined as 'give up speed.' And if you're wondering what give up speed is; that's when someone is so fast, you just give up instead of trying to catch him. You see this guy start pulling away and you're like, I'm not going to burn up all my energy trying to chase this guy."

Mercer attended high school in Washington, D.C., then went to Hargrave Military Academy in Chatman, Virginia, before attending Marshall in Pruett's first season. Mercer, who described himself as 235 pounds of "twisted steel and sex appeal" at that time said the physical demands of Pruett's practices weren't bad.

"I remember the focus of the camp as being 'We have the players to get into the National Championship; let's go out here and get it done,'" Mercer said. "Obviously that year we brought in Randy Moss and Eric Kresser and it was a new style. It was a big change of philosophy, not only for the young

**THE GAME-BREAKER —** Wearing Bob's number 88, Randy Moss took little time to establish himself as *the* receiver in college football. *Courtesy Marshall University; photograph by Rick Haye.*

guys coming in, but for the guys who had been there and who had been so successful under Coach Donnan. He came in here with a different philosophy in terms of the offense. I think it really brought a lot of excitement to our campus. Throwing the ball all around the field. The fans were all excited, the players were excited. He really brought a different kind of air to Marshall University. With Randy Moss and Eric Kresser and what was already there, it was like, 'We know we're going to go undefeated. We're going to win the national championship.'"

*Chapter six*

Marshall entered the 1996 season as an overwhelming favorite to win the Division I-AA championship. The Thundering Herd, which had finished as the runner-up the year before, had a new product managed by their new coach Bobby Pruett that featured impact players Eric Kresser and Randy Moss. A great sense of anticipation awaited the premier of the new product when it rolled out of the showroom in its first game of the season against Howard University.

Moss drew the most curiosity. College football fans had been waiting for his arrival ever since Notre Dame signed him then denied his admission. Kresser also drew his share of interest. If it hadn't been for Danny Wuerffel, Kresser would have been running the show at Florida, where Gators head coach Steve Spurrier complimented Kresser by saying he could

**AROUND THE WATER COOLER** — Before the season even got underway, Randy Moss was a hot topic of conversation in both the Huntington area and across the country. *Courtesy Marshall University.*

6

A HIGH TA

ENT START

have been the starter at seventy-five percent of the Division I-A schools.

An editorial in the *The Huntington Herald-Dispatch* stated that allowing Moss into Marshall mocked the idea that school athletics were part of character building.

"Public opinion was mixed," sportswriter Tim Stephens said. "Most people were excited that he was obviously a great talent and he was a West Virginia kid. There were some people worried, obviously, about Marshall's reputation as a second-chance school. Bringing in someone who had been kicked out of Notre Dame then kicked out of Florida State eventually. … I think most fans were excited about having that caliber of football player on the field. I think there were more people glad to have Randy here than upset about him coming into the program."

Perhaps even more so than Moss, Kresser was underneath the microscope of Marshall fans since he was taking Chad Pennington's place.

"Chad didn't have the following he had by his senior year, when he was everyone's golden boy," Stephens said. "The fans were excited about getting a quarterback from Florida, but there was still some apprehension. The previous year Pennington had gotten them to the I-AA National Championship game. He was a very intelligent and capable quarterback, and now he's being supplanted by somebody Bobby's bringing in for one year."

Adding steam to the anti-Kresser sentiment was the fact Kresser didn't hide his reasons for coming to Marshall: he wanted to showcase himself for NFL scouts. One rumor even said he planned to transfer back to Florida after football season to complete his degree.

And there was Pruett and all the changes he brought with him.

Pruett had changed from Donnan's two-back, pro-set offense to the one-back "Fun 'N Gun" and he'd brought in Moss and Kresser. A lot of people wondered why the new coach was tinkering with the formula that had allowed the team to win sixty-four games in the 1990s, which tied them for the most wins of any team in the decade.

"Donnan had been really successful," Stephens said. "They were unsure more than anything with Bobby. Here's a guy who comes in and plays up being just a dumb ol' boy from East Beckley—though he's very sharp on and off the field—but he plays that up and comes off as the good ol' country boy. And a lot of fans were really unsure of what they were getting. They were afraid that they'd hired somebody who was in over his head.

"When Bobby was hired they were afraid that everything that had been built from the crash on up through all those coaches was going to go out the window. But Bobby Pruett quickly put those fears aside."

Pruett didn't think about the negatives; he simply reveled in the fact he would begin his run at his dream job on September 7, 1996.

Pruett's first game day prior to the first game would establish his routine for future game days. Being a creature of habit and a superstitious guy, what he started on that first game day would become his game-day routine.

He rose early and "piddled around in the yard," then went to the football offices to meet with his coaches. Afterward he and the other coaches met with recruits visiting the campus. Since most of the games were at 7 p.m., the team would have chapel in the early afternoon before eating lunch together in the Student Union Building. Pruett understood the importance of giving his team the right fuel prior to games.

"We changed their menu," Pruett said. "I don't know what their menu was before, but we changed the menu to give them a variety of things that would give them energy. But we didn't have big hunks of meat. It was more like the menu we had at the University of Florida."

After the meal, the coaching staff didn't do anything with the team until they arrived two hours before the game. Pruett enjoyed walking from the different venues for the coaches meeting, chapel and lunch. Once he had finished lunch, he made his way across campus toward the stadium, cutting through the parking lots where he'd kibitz with tailgating Marshall fans.

"Seeing people like that, just creates a little bit of a buzz," Pruett said.

The buzz felt a little more electric prior to the Howard game. Many family members and friends were on hand to share the special moment with Pruett. Normally, Pruett did not get too nervous prior to games.

"The coaches will tell you I'm pretty calm up until twenty minutes or so, right before kickoff," Pruett said. "That's when I really get nervous before a game. Sometimes you're able to get through it because you go through your routine, but I'd really get nervous before the game. That's just me. Once the kickoff starts, I'm fine. But I was pretty nervous before the Howard game."

Many years and memories washed across Pruett's consciousness leaving the locker room. When the Marshall fight song played as the team ran out of the tunnel, Pruett felt chills all over his body and he began to think about all of the work he'd put in over the years in advance of landing the Marshall job. And there were the memories. If Pruett squinted his eyes he could almost see the tipped ball in the Toledo game just before he snatched it from the air and raced into the endzone for the winning touchdown, slugging it out on the lower rung of professional football, the countless high school football games and all the moves from place to place pursuing a dream he might never realize. It seemed like it was only yesterday when Sonny Randle offered him the chance to return as an assistant to the university he loved so. And there was the memory of the unfortunate members of the 1970 team and those from the community who had perished in the plane crash. The school and the community had rallied around a disaster and had literally risen from the ashes.

"I'm a romantic, I guess," Pruett said, "a sentimental-type guy. I mean Marshall had been so good to me and I had all the great feelings that I have about Huntington and the state of West Virginia. What a lot of people didn't understand was that I spent thirty-one years trying to get back to West Virginia. Which is funny since a lot of people think they need to get away from it. Because I just enjoy the people there, I really do. They're my kind of folk. You know, they're good people, they're loving people. They're kind people. And I wanted to make a difference. We wanted to make a difference in southern West Virginia to give us something to be proud of. There have been a lot of great accomplishments in West Virginia and we shouldn't be ashamed of our state. And to be able to come back home to be the head football coach and run out there, well, it was a big moment."

Finally, the kickoff for the first Marshall game of the Bobby Pruett era came in front of a crowd of 26,054 at Marshall Stadium.

After all the anticipation about seeing Moss and Kresser in Marshall uniforms, they had to wait approximately ten minutes into the game before Kresser delivered a tight spiral to Moss on a post pattern. Moss—wearing the same No. 84 worn by Pruett during his playing days—gathered in the pass and ran into the end zone to give the Herd a 10-3 lead.

Marshall Stadium erupted in raucous cheers of acceptance for the new quarterback-receiver tandem.

"There was a lot of jealousy flowing around the football team and on campus," Moss told *The Sporting News* afterward. "With us coming in from Division I schools to a Division I-AA school, they kept hearing that this guy is gonna start and that guy is gonna start, and it didn't seem fair to the ones who were already here. I told them from the get go that it doesn't matter if I start. I just want to play. But it all died down once we got out here and they saw us play ball."

Kresser remembered well the pressure to perform he and Moss felt.

"I remember hearing someone say at the beginning, "These guys better go 15-0," Kresser said. "I think the thing that made the move easier for me was the fact there was a new head coach, a head coach who had seen me playing quarterback during major college football games. So I felt like Coach Pruett was really going to give me a chance to play."

By the time the game was over, Moss had three catches for 134 yards and one touchdown. In addition, he had 142 yards on five kickoff returns and he threw a block on a sixty-five yard touchdown run that put the game away.

Kresser completed nine of the nineteen passes he threw for 118 yards and the touchdown to Moss before tweaking his ankle in the third quarter.

"Randy Moss and Eric Kresser turned out to be a great thing for the team," said Randle, the former Marshall coach and color commentator for Marshall's TV network. "But it really helped that they got off to a good start. Everybody was expecting Marshall to win a national championship. If they would have lost [with Moss and Kresser] it could have gotten ugly."

In addition to the work done by Moss and Kresser, Marshall gained 236 yards rushing with Erik Thomas doing most of the work by accumulating 173 yards on eighteen carries. And the defense allowed just one touchdown in the second half in the Herd's 55-27 victory.

Pruett felt relief after the game, but he wasn't particularly pleased with the game his team had played.

"We rose to the occasion in the second half," Pruett told *The Huntington Herald-Dispatch*. "The second half was better than the first. Am I pleased? No. We can be much better than that. We are much better than that."

Still in the establishing a routine phase of his coaching days at Marshall, Pruett finished his press conference after the game then headed to Gino's Pub, known as "The Pub," where he talked to fans to recap the game and to tape his TV show. Then he returned to the stadium with the coaches, their wives and other friends of the program to a catered box the athletic director had. After visiting with everybody, Pruett and Elsie headed home around 2 a.m. and Pruett didn't sleep a wink.

"I was all geared up and kept replaying the game, that's the way it would be after every game," Pruett said. "But after that first one, it's like, I'd been at Florida, and I'd been at Wake, Ole Miss, so the last three, four, five years, I was really playing at a high level of football. And I didn't know how good Howard was. And I didn't know how good we were. Being the defensive guy I was, every play where they made over three or four yards, I was thinking,

'How can we get better?' So I'm analyzing every little thing I'm doing wanting us to get better.

"Then I'd go through a gamut of emotions. 'Are we as good as we think we are? Are we bad? What've we got to do? It's just a whole bunch of things that you go through and you experience. You cease being the head coach of the defense. Now you've got so many different things you deal with than when you handle the offense or the defense and you're in your own little world and you can be critical, like, 'If the offense had done this or that.' But when you're the head coach, you're worrying about everything all the way down to if we had enough people there to pay the bills. I mean, just all these different things. Is anybody going to go out and get in a fight after the game? And then it's Sunday and you start all over."

In the background, Pruett continued to show a genuine concern for people outside of the football arena. Typifying this concern for others was the story of Matt Haymaker, who had lost an eye from a gun that malfunctioned. The accident occurred during the 1996 season and almost cost the youngster his life.

Pruett found out about what happened and took Matt under his wing.

"He'd heard about Matt being in the hospital and he started calling him," said Tim Haymaker, Matt's father. "He was in this dark room in the hospital and had a morphine pump going. Bobby would call him two, three times a day. It was just incredible. Giving him a pep talk. Matt's always been a Marshall fan. So Bobby just became his friend."

Once Matt got out of the hospital, Pruett continued to pay attention to the youngster.

"Bobby had him to the football game," Tim Haymaker said. "Gave us sideline passes. The day we were there Matt had a patch over his eye and a big scar on his face. Bobby let us go into the locker room before the game. Then, when we started out onto the field, Bobby realized how sunny it was outside. So Bobby, who is very caring and very interested in every detail, went back to his office and came back with a pair of sunglasses that he said Coach Spurrier had given him and he told Matt he wanted him to have them. He was that concerned about Matt getting the sun in his eyes. He was just genuinely interested in him."

Marshall's second game of the 1996 season saw West Virginia State visit Marshall Stadium on September 14. With the talent differential decidedly in favor of the Thundering Herd, Pruett acted accordingly, substituting liberally in the first half en route to a 35-0 lead. In the second half Pruett had his troops keep the ball on the ground, running the ball on all thirty of their offensive plays before finishing with a 42-7 victory.

Though the West Virginia State game was early in the season, the breather came at the right time since the Herd had to travel to Statesboro, Georgia, the following weekend to play tough Georgia Southern.

Doug Chapman was a red-shirt freshman at the time and remembered the game because starting running back Erik Thomas did not dress due to the flu, making Chapman the starter for the first time in his collegiate career.

"I was a wreck that whole week," Chapman said. "I was nervous. I didn't want to let the guys down. We hadn't lost a game. Coach Pruett called me into his office after the Monday practice and we talked. He told me, 'I want to give you a piece of advice. Never worry about things you can't control.' Then he sat down and explained it. It didn't really make sense until after the game. And I had a great game. That line just stayed in my head. And I'm like, 'I can't control what the left guard is doing. I can't control the crowd. But I can control my game preparation. I can control what shape I'm in. I can control my focus.' And the thing is, as a football player that's a strong piece of advice, because sometimes you play outside of yourself. I was young at the time and I think that was something that helped me as a player make it to the professional ranks because I quit thinking about a million things and just focused on the important things that Doug Chapman had to do. That was just one thing out of a lot of things he helped me with."

Chapman gained 130 yards on twenty-four carries and one touchdown to lead a 29-13 win over Georgia Southern in their Southern Conference opener.

"Coach Pruett had a good feel for his guys," Chapman said. "He knew his guys. And he could sometimes walk in there and call a guy to his office, because maybe a look he saw on his face, and find out something was going on back home. Or he's not doing well in a class. A lot of players don't feel comfortable talking to a coach like that. But Coach Pruett always had an open-door policy. He was known for these sayings that everybody started calling Pruettisms. I can't even remember all of them, but I remember this one. He'd ask a guy if he was lying, and the guy'd be like 'I'm okay coach.' And Coach Pruett would say, 'You're pissing on my back and telling me it's rain.' I think he helped the guys more with off the field issues than on the field. You talk to some of the players, especially the guys who were there when

I was there."

Pruett had recognized Chapman's ability and believed in him.

"Doug was going to be a great back," Pruett said. "We knew he was going to be a great back. He just needed to play. Matter of fact, Donnan was trying to play him at defensive back. But that was a tough game to break in, Georgia Southern at Statesboro. And Doug was just the type of guy that just needed a little bit of love and you wanted to give him a little self-confidence and then he was going to go. I just reassured him that we knew he could do it, that we knew he could be a really good player for us."

While Pruett's talk with Chapman helped ease his running back's mind, Pruett's work in front of a projector looking at film helped the Herd pull off their biggest play of the game. Leading 16-13 with just over eight minutes remaining in the third quarter, the Herd lined up for a field goal at the Georgia Southern twenty yard line. But instead of kicking, holder Mark Zban picked up the ball and ran for a seventeen-yard gain to the Georgia Southern three. Chapman scored on the next play for a 23-13 lead.

"We saw it on film and thought we could do that," Pruett told *The Huntington Herald-Dispatch*. "Any time we see something like that on film, we're going to take advantage of it if we can."

Kresser, who had been hobbled by a sprained ankle, played his first full game as the starting quarterback and flourished; he completed twenty-three of thirty-six passes and scored three touchdowns, including a forty-two-yard touchdown pass to Randy Moss that gave the Herd a 10-0 lead.

The Herd returned to Marshall Stadium September 28 to play Western Kentucky, considered by many to be a sleeper, and the Hilltoppers made it close for the first twenty-eight minutes when they trailed the Herd 10-3. Then Chapman's nineteen-yard touchdown run expanded the lead to 17-3. By the time the game had concluded, the Herd had put twenty-seven unanswered points on the scoreboard for a 37-3 victory to move to 4-0.

Continuing to roll, Marshall scored on its first five possessions against the University of Tennessee-Chattanooga on October 5 en route to a 45-0 win in front of a Marshall Stadium crowd of 22,078. Kresser completed twenty-two of thirty-two passes for 296 yards and two touchdowns; Tim Martin caught nine passes for 139 yards and Moss caught six for 96 yards and a touchdown.

Marshall traveled to Lexington, Virginia, on October 12 to play VMI and staggered the Keydets with five touchdown drives—none of which lasted more than a minute and a half. Kresser to Moss set the tone early when they hooked up on a fifty-nine-yard touchdown to finish off the Herd's first possession. VMI answered with an eleven-play, sixty-one-yard drive for a game-tying touchdown before Martin returned a punt sixty-seven yards for a touchdown and flanker Anthony Dixon scored on a seventeen-yard reverse to build a 21-7 cushion.

Despite a decided speed advantage, the Herd looked lethargic at times against VMI. Pruett expressed his displeasure with his team's play before the start of the second half, but the team seemingly continued to go through the motions as the Keydets outscored them 10-0 in the third quarter and cut the lead to 38-20 with just over seven minutes remaining in the game. But after Marshall recovered an onside kick, Erik Thomas scored on a forty-six-yard touchdown run and the Herd took a 45-20 win to move their record to 6-0 and to 3-0 in the Southern Conference.

Afterward Pruett credited VMI for their performance and expressed displeasure with his team's lack of enthusiasm.

Given his team's level of talent he had to guard against complacency. Western Carolina was next on the schedule and the team's intensity level certainly was a legitimate concern.

The Catamounts traveled to Marshall Stadium and quickly experienced the Herd's high-gear offense up close and personal. Kresser to Moss accounted for the Herd's first two touchdowns on strikes of twenty-five and twenty-six yards. Kresser completed seventeen of twenty-three passes for four touchdowns on a day that saw the Herd put up 629 yards of total offense.

Meanwhile, the Herd's defense limited the Catamounts to three plays and a punt on their first eight possessions of the game. In the end the scoreboard read 56-21, but Marshall clearly could have named the score.

Western Carolina Coach Steve Hodgin called Pruett a "gentleman" after the game, noting that Marshall could have scored 100 points had he wanted his team to do so.

On October 26, Marshall traveled to Boone, North Carolina, for a critical game against Appalachian State. If any game looked like it had a chance for derailing the Thundering Herd's quest for a national championship, this one had all the trappings. Marshall had not won at Boone since 1987 and Appalachian State was ranked 20th in the Division I-AA poll.

A crowd of 23,458 showed up on a rainy day at Kidd-Brewer Stadium to see if the upset would happen. Everything seemed to be falling into place after the first half when the Mountaineers took a 10-7 lead to intermission.

The game marked the first time in the 1996 season when the team trailed at intermission. Pruett laid down a challenge to his team at the half.

"We had better players and a better team," Pruett said. "So we told them they needed to get out there and play like it."

Marshall quickly answered in the second half when Tim Openlander kicked a forty-four yard field goal to finish off the Herd's first drive of the second half. Later in the quarter with the Herd at their own 28, Kresser noticed the Mountaineers' safety didn't move toward a gap in the middle of the field. Exploiting the weakness, Moss shot between the defenders to find a seam in the middle. Kresser delivered a strike to Moss, who hauled in the pass and sprinted to the end zone for a 17-10 lead. Martin's thirty-one-yard touchdown reception early in the fourth quarter put away any thoughts of an upset and the Herd had a 24-10 win.

"I think the Appalachian State game was the point where we thought we could go undefeated," Kresser said. "It was the first time we had to come from behind at half-time to win. It gave us momentum going into the second half of the season. We played some good teams. Most teams had a few standout players who should have played Division I-A."

The victory moved the Herd to 8-0 and 5-0 in the Southern Conference, which tied East Tennessee State for first place.

"We had terrific talent, but the team was still learning how to play together," said Pruett about some of the games being close. "We had a new system and we brought in Kresser, Moss, Jerrald Long, and Andre Goines. In other words, they weren't part of the team. All of them were learning to be a team. You know, the best players don't make the best team. It's just like the New York Yankees. When they're not playing well, it's, 'What's wrong with the Yankees? What's wrong with the Yankees?' That's all you hear, They've got the best pitchers. They've got the best hitters, but they're not the best team. The best players don't always win. The best team wins. So a lot of times you had to learn to be the best team. And that first year, early on, we had to learn to be the best team, pulling together, believing in each other and liking each other."

Not to be forgotten was Pennington, who patiently watched the Kresser to Moss connection and thought about being at the helm the next season. He continued to lift weights and to do what was necessary to strengthen himself while staying remarkably positive during what amounted to a difficult season for him personally. Pruett would credit Pennington time and again for the remarkable way he handled the season, particularly when Pennington knew he could be doing the job had it been his in 1996. Pruett also tried to make sure Pennington felt connected to the team and that the team felt connected to Pennington.

"We red-shirted him but he took all the snaps as the second-team quarterback even though he never played any," Pruett said. "We had Mark Zban, who was an outstanding kid, who could play if Eric got hurt, which he did. What I didn't want was for Chad to be out there running the scout team. I wanted him to be the player everybody knew we were coaching up to play every game the next season and be someone special for three years. I think being the second-team quarterback paid off in the leadership department, too."

And Pruett knew Kresser would help Pennington.

"Coach Pruett always did a good job of making sure that the older quarterbacks helped out the younger quarterbacks," Pennington said. "And when you're the starter at Marshall, one of your duties is to mentor the younger guys and set an example. So, you know, I learned what an NFL arm looked like when I watched Kresser play. He had an outstanding arm and could throw with the best of them and he understood that offense really well from playing it at Florida."

Marshall returned home November 2 to play The Citadel and trailed the Bulldogs twice in the first half by scores of 7-0 and 10-7. The Herd overcame both deficits to build a 28-19 lead late in the third quarter when Larry McCloud intercepted a pass and the junior linebacker returned it thirty yards for a touchdown.

A notable mistake made by the Bulldogs' defense was trying to use one-on-one coverage against Moss, who caught touchdown passes of thirteen, fourteen, and sixteen yards to break Troy Brown's school record of sixteen touchdown passes that had stood since 1992. Moss also returned a kickoff of eighty-eight yards in the game.

If anything, the two challenges—albeit brief—against Appalachian State and The Citadel were excellent tune-ups for their November 9 meeting with East Tennessee State in Johnson City. A win for the Herd would mean at least a tie for the Southern Conference title heading into their regular season finale against Furman.

The Bucs obviously watched tape of the Herd's game against The Citadel as they double and triple covered Moss for most of the game and were relatively effective in stopping him until he caught a seventy-two yard touchdown from Zban. Moss' touchdown tied Jerry Rice's NCAA record of catching a touchdown pass in ten consecutive games and, unfortunately for the Bucs, it gave Marshall a 34-3 lead.

East Tennessee State actually held the Herd scoreless in the first quarter, earning the distinction of being the first team to do so. And Marshall led just 10-3 at the half, but this was a confident Herd that knew the proper adjustments would be made at the half and they would respond to the challenge.

Marshall scored on its first four possessions of the second half to build a 27-3 lead and put the game out of reach.

On November 16 Furman visited Marshall Stadium to play the 10-0 Thundering Herd, who hoped to claim the distinction as outright Southern Conference champions and finish the season 11-0. But it wouldn't come easy.

The Paladins, a long-time rival of the Herd, ran the option with precision in the first half to put up some big gains and lead them to a 14-14 tie until twenty-three seconds remained in the first half when they kicked a field goal to take a 17-14 lead.

Unfortunately for Furman, they didn't handle their good fortune with the grace Marshall felt they should have.

According to Marshall players, several Furman players and coaches taunted them as they went to their respective locker rooms in addition to punching the "Herd" on the padding around the goal post while they passed by.

"I remember their players punching our goalpost at halftime, like they were kicking out butts," Kresser said. "Why they would do this when the game was only half over I don't know. They were yelling all kinds of things. I didn't pay to much attention to the actual words. All I know is we won that game 42-17. And it gave us some motivational material to use in the next game."

You don't awaken a sleeping giant, which Furman learned the hard way.

Three plays into the third quarter Marshall's senior linebacker Jermaine Swafford intercepted a pass and covered the thirty-three yards between him and the end zone to give the Herd a 21-17 lead. Midway through the third quarter, Kresser connected with Thomas to put the Herd up 28-17. Doug Chapman's two touchdown runs in the fourth quarter finished off the 42-17 rout that had once been a close game.

Immediately following the game Marshall players celebrated on the field, thanking the 22,681 fans in attendance for the game. The Thundering Herd was 11-0 and the Southern Conference champion after completing its first undefeated season since 1919.

# Chapter seven

Bobby Pruett and Marshall's Thundering Herd needed just four wins in the Division I-AA playoffs to go wire-to-wire for the season after starting the year as the overwhelming pick to take the title they had come so close to capturing the previous year.

Delaware would be the Herd's first opponent and the Blue Hens coach, Tubby Raymond, expressed his displeasure about playing the first game of the playoffs at Marshall Stadium—and the fact the Herd would be playing at home for as long as they remained in the playoffs. Raymond had seen the films—Marshall had an incredible collection of talent—and they got to play in Huntington to boot?

Marshall had a suitable stadium for hosting the NCAA Division I-AA playoffs and had contracted with the NCAA to

**SAY HELLO TO MR. MOSS** — The Delaware Blue Hens, for better or worse, got the full Marshall treatment upon arriving at Marshall Stadium on November 30, 1996. *Courtesy Marshall University; photograph by Tom Wildt.*

7

AN UNDEFEA

TED SEASON

do so. Selling tickets to Marshall season-ticket holders in their season-ticket packages was a part of the deal. And those season tickets included admittance to the East Division playoffs of the MAC. Of course the arrangement coincided with a nice run by the Marshall football program, which had been the root of Raymond's displeasure.

Home field or not, Marshall flexed its collective muscle against Delaware November 30, 1996.

Randy Moss led the offense with eight catches for 288 yards and three touchdowns—two came within a sixty-six second span in the second quarter—effectively setting a record for receiving yardage in a single game for Marshall, the Southern Conference, and a playoff record.

Eric Kresser continued to dazzle in the quarterback spot, completing eighteen of twenty-five passes for 449 yards, and Doug Chapman chipped in 128 yards and two touchdowns in nine carries during the contest for 689 yards of total offense. When the final gun sounded Marshall had a 59-14 win.

"That was just a terrific offensive game we had against Delaware," Pruett said. "Easily one of the best performances by our offense that whole year, I was really pleased with that one."

In addition to advancing to the second round, the Herd had made a believer of Raymond, who said afterward that he had been around for a long time and had never seen a better long passing attack than Marshall's.

Raymond also said his team had not played a Division I-AA team, but rather a Division I-A team—a comment that got under Pruett's skin.

"He said that we had transfers," Pruett said. "So the press tells me, 'Coach Raymond was upset because you had transfers,' which he had a bunch on his team, too. So I said, 'I didn't realize that was a rule just for us.'"

Next up for Marshall was a December 7 rematch with Furman, Marshall's long-time rival that had disrespected the Herd during their regular-season meeting.

"That first game came back to bite [Furman] in a real big way in the playoffs," said Tim Stephens, who covered the playoff run. "Bobby used that as motivation."

Marshall players and fans alike wanted nothing better than to make a statement to the Paladins.

Marshall's defense didn't let the Paladins get any closer to their goal line than the Marshall twenty-seven the entire game and they were limited to nine yards rushing on thirty-three carries. The first time the two teams met. Marshall trailed 17-14 at the half. This time the Herd took a 24-0 lead to the half built on two Randy Moss touchdown catches, a Doug Chapman touchdown and a field goal.

And there were no incidents with the Marshall goal post as there had been during the regular season contest—state troopers stood guard to insure that fact.

The second half brought out more of the same flavor from Marshall when the Herd added thirty points to make the final score 54-0.

"It's the only time I saw Bob, I won't say run up the score, but put one on another team," Tim Stephens said. "And it was just the most dominating performance I've seen a Marshall football team have—ever. Furman did nothing. They couldn't throw it. They couldn't run it. Their defense couldn't stop Marshall at all. And Marshall's fans took great delight in that game and I know the players had a lot of fun with beating Furman in that way as well."

Northern Iowa came to Huntington as the Herd's opponent in the semifinal round, marking the third time Marshall and Northern Iowa faced each other in the playoffs. Marshall won both of the first two games.

Marshall made it three in a row in the playoffs and over Northern Iowa in relatively easy fashion on December 14. The Herd took a 10-0 lead to the half and expanded it to 24-0 by the end of the third quarter before finishing with a 31-14 win on an uncomfortably cold afternoon at Marshall Stadium when just 14,414 showed up to watch. Marshall's victory moved them into the finals for the fifth time in six years and set up a rematch between Marshall and top-seeded Montana, which dominated Troy State 70-7 in the other semifinal.

Marshall took the field for the final time as a Division I-AA school on December 21, 1996 as they were prepped to make the jump to Division I-A and the Mid-American Conference beginning in the fall of 1997. What sweeter way to leave the lower level?

Tubby Raymond had already suggested Marshall's talent level was more fitting of a Division I-A school, anyway.

A crowd of 30,052 showed up at Marshall Stadium to see their beloved Herd play unbeaten Montana to try and complete their incredible run through the 1996 season.

Kresser and Moss—the two most prominent newcomers to Marshall for the 1996 season—would most sway the outcome of the championship.

Marshall appeared to be peaking at the right time, but would it be enough against the high-powered Montana offense led by All-America quarterback Brian Ah Yat?

Kresser went deep to Moss on the game's first play forcing Montana cornerback Billy Ivey to do all he could to stop Moss by interfering with the catch. Kresser went to Moss again seven plays later to cap the Herd's first possession with a nineteen-yard touchdown to give Marshall a 7-0 lead.

Ah Yat answered by driving his team to the Herd's twelve. But when he passed to Joe Douglass the ball bounced off his receiver right to Marshall cornerback Larry Moore, who snatched it for the interception. Seven plays later, Chapman darted through the Montana defense for a dazzling sixty-one-yard touchdown to make the score 14-0 Marshall.

"Our offense was a lot like Florida's in that everybody talked about the passing, but the running game was a big part of it," Pruett said. "You had to take the running game when it was there. In the championship game in '96, Doug had a huge, long touchdown run that turned the tide of the game early. I mean, just sort of broke their back, because Montana had a high, potent offense and we went down and scored. When you run the ball down somebody's throat, it's demoralizing. When you throw it over their head, they have a tendency to think, 'Aw, dumb DB.' You know, one guy got beat, not the team. They take it a little more personal when they get run over. And Doug hit that long, sweet play, and it really just broke their back."

Ah Yat then fumbled and John Grace recovered to set up another Kresser to Moss score; this one covered seventy yards and gave the Herd a 20-0 lead early in the second quarter. By halftime the Herd had a 23-6 lead.

Kresser hit Moss for a fifty-four-yard score to start the third quarter and one of twenty-eight yards to start the fourth quarter en route to the 49-29 victory, which gave Marshall its second Division I-AA championship in five years.

"That game, I'll never forget," Pruett said. "I called up to the coaches in the press box and I said, 'The fat lady is singing.' Then I told them I wanted all the coaches to come down on the sideline that we'd just call the rest of the game from the sideline. And I said, 'If we play these kids, they'll know they did get to play in the national championship game and we'll just play a vanilla defense. If they score, it's no big deal.'" In the past the Herd had caught some flack for losing in the title game in 1987, 1991, 1993, and the previous season on Montana's field goal in the closing seconds of the game. Afterward Pruett spoke for his team when he said: "They felt they let an opportunity slip away a year ago. They weren't going to let it happen today."

In addition to accounting for four touchdowns, Moss had nine catches for 220 yards; Kreser completed eighteen of twenty-eight passes for 324 yards.

"I never thought it would feel this good," said Kresser afterward.

Balancing it all out was the running of Erik Thomas and Chapman, who ran for 114 and 104 yards respectively.

Marshall's defense held Montana to six points and 220 yards through the first three quarters—when the outcome was remotely still in question.

"That game was what everyone was waiting for all year," Kresser said. "A rematch with undefeated Montana made it even better. I played in some pretty big games at Florida, and this was better than all of them."

By winning in the fashion they did all season, Marshall fueled speculation they were the best team in Division I-AA history. Backing the argument was the fact they were only the second undefeated team in the division's history and the fact that they won their four playoff games by an average score of 48-14 and finished it off with a rout of Montana, which had won twenty-one consecutive games. In addition, Marshall had played for the title four times in the 1990s and had won twice.

Kresser tied a school record for touchdowns with thirty-five, and ten players were honored with All-America honors and seventeen were named All-Southern Conference. Moss finished with seventy-eight catches for 1,709 yards and twenty-eight touchdowns, tying the Southern Conference career record for touchdown receptions. Moss' twenty-eight touchdowns tied Jerry Rice's mark for most ever in a college football season and his 1,073 yards receiving and nineteen touchdowns in the regular season set NCAA single season records for a freshman. He set NCAA I-AA regular season records for consecutive games with a touchdown reception (with ten) and he also had most yards receiving in a playoff game (with 288). Moss scored more points in one season than anybody else ever had in Southern Conference history with 174. He also tied the Southern Conference record for career touchdown receptions and beat the old Marshall record by two, which Mike Barber had set from 1985 to 1988. In addition, Moss led Division I-AA in kickoff return yardage with 34.0 yards per game. Moss was also named first-team All-American by five different organizations.

Pruett became the first coach in college football history to have a 15-0 record and a national championship in his first year as a head coach. Chevrolet and the All-American Football Foundation named Pruett the National Coach of the Year.

**THE INFAMOUS SOCKS —** Although his athletic skills were more than capable of drawing attention, Randy Moss added a personal touch to his uniform. *Courtesy Marshall University.*

"Well, that year was a storybook year," Pruett said. "We won the National Championship on Elsie and my wedding anniversary, this was a storybook thing, going back to my school, my dream job. Going into that season, if we hadn't won the National Championship we would have caught some heat. But we had good players, a lot of talent on that team. I thought we would be a great team. And we were."

Pruett and Elsie celebrated their anniversary by attending that night's Marshall basketball game. And by Monday, it was time to start getting ready for the 1997 season.

## *Chapter eight*

Heading into the second year of the Bob Pruett Era at Marshall, the team faced challenges in replacing the departed, such as Eric Kresser, defensive tackle Billy Lyon, cornerback Melvin Cunningham, and guard Aaron Ferguson. Replacements were either already at the school or in the process of being recruited.

Pruett had coached at the Division I-A level and knew the kind of fuel he needed to run his football engine. That meant athleticism over size. Linebacker John Grace typified Pruett's ideal.

"John Grace is a good example of the kind of player we wanted," Pruett said. "He was a great player. He came in the year before I got there. But he's an example of what we were trying to do. He was an undersized player, wasn't six-four, but,

**STEPPING UP** — Randy Moss was an integral part of Marshall's move to Division I-A. *Courtesy Marshall University.*

*8*

# PREPPING FOR

THE NEXT LEVEL

you know, he had heart and he was a guy who made plays. That's what we tried to do when we evaluated people."

Pruett believed in players who dominated the league where they played, which he and his coaches used as a gauge when they evaluated players to put on their shopping list to be recruited.

"When we looked at players on film, we wanted ones that would jump out at us," Pruett said. "You have all these different things you look at and all that other stuff, but if he wasn't a dominant force and made a lot of plays, he was a hard sell for me. Yeah. I wanted guys that made plays. You sort of keep a little chart on how many plays they make in a game. If they play a whole game and don't make a tackle, it doesn't really make a whole lot of difference how good they are."

Pruett and company wanted a team built on speed.

"That's exactly what we did," Pruett said. "If you talk to anybody else in our conference, the Mid-American Conference, they'll tell you that. We changed the dynamics and the complexion of the Mid-American Conference because we came in and we were just faster than they were."

Pruett didn't want to go into areas of recruiting where there were a lot of schools like Marshall. While they loved recruits from Ohio, the MAC was saturated with Ohio. Besides the biggies, Ohio State and Michigan, Cincinnati, Louisville, and Kentucky all ventured into Ohio to recruit, which made the recruiting battles less time efficient than other areas.

"We felt like that there were other areas where we could go to and get more speed," Pruett said. "We could be bigger, faster, stronger, you know, that whole deal. And that's what we did. We went to areas where people knew us and understood our program because they'd seen it on TV, areas such as Mississippi and Tennessee, Virginia—especially the D.C. area—and Florida. We wanted to go to the areas that played really good football, where winning meant something to them and get good kids that wanted to win and wanted to play hard. And that's what we did."

Given the MAC's slug-it-out-in-the-trenches type of teams constructed to play in bad weather, some might have thought Pruett was taking a risk by building a team based on speed rather than muscle.

Pruett laughed at the suggestion.

"I'm not real smart," he said. "You know, the way I figured it, if we were faster on dry land, we'd be faster still in mud. But we played on an artificial surface—at least for all of our home games. And most of the schools in the

MAC played on turf. We had to play Bowling Green and Miami on grass. Kent State, Akron, Western Michigan, Eastern Michigan, Toledo and, at that time, Central Michigan, all had artificial turf. So we felt like we could get away with it."

Pruett knew the kind of players he wanted to recruit, raising the question: How does one go about procuring such players? His solution was to hire go-getter assistants who knew how to go into a recruit's home and close the deal. Having those kinds of assistants is vital for any college program because talent is the lifeblood of any program.

Prior to his first season, Pruett brought in Gunter Brewer from East Tennessee State and made him the recruiting coordinator and he hired Larry Kueck to be the quarterbacks coach. Kueck had been the coordinator at Southern Miss and had a world of experience in recruiting—he'd been around, and he ran the offense, too. All told, Pruett retained four assistants from Donnan's tenure and brought in five of his own.

"Recruiting is all about organization and understanding what needs to be done and being able to deal with people," Pruett said. "The one thing I did when our guys first came in was to stress the importance of recruiting. The recruiting part of it is so key. It's vital to the success of your program. It was just imperative for us to have good recruiting classes and we were able to do that because our guys worked extremely hard at it and we had a system of evaluating guys. We did a good job as a staff looking at film and everybody agreeing on it. We didn't make a lot of mistakes. We were very fortunate and I had very, very good coaches who dug into recruiting hard and they were loyal, which are the staples it takes to win."

Another feather in Pruett's cap where recruiting was concerned stemmed from the fact he'd coached in Florida and had recruited a state rich with football talent for two years. High school coaches in Florida knew Pruett.

"And that really helped in recruiting," Pruett said. "It also helped us in Georgia and it helped us everywhere we went because people knew what we were trying to do at Marshall. It was a whole organized thing. We were winning more games than anybody in the country, so we were going to have good players. When you do that you're going to have some good players.

"And then, in the second year, we started pushing Randy Moss for the Heisman Trophy, which was unheard of for a school like Marshall. I mean, here we are, the first year in Division I-A football and we've got a legitimate Heisman candidate, okay?"

PRUETT RECOGNIZED A SEVERE DISADVANTAGE Marshall would be operating under by moving up to Division I-A.

"We were very limited financially, so I had to do a lot of fundraising to get the things that we needed that weren't in the budget," Pruett said. "Like getting fans for the sidelines, or putting our championship banners in the stadium. I had to raise the money to do that. Putting down tile in our facility building to replace the worn out carpet. Buying computers for our coaches. So winning football games is part of the job at Marshall, but the other part of the job is doing the things necessary to keep up with your competition as you climb up the ladder of national prominence. So I had to go find the money, raise the money to buy the computers. And as computers go, you've got to constantly update the computers. That was a big battle. And video equipment, we had to constantly find ways to upgrade our video because we just didn't have the money. When I got there, we had $125,000 in the recruiting office, which was very low. You had to improvise and make do with what you had. When I got to Marshall, we didn't have an academic support system. The lady who was handling the academic support system had left to take another job, and we didn't have anybody else. So we had to redo all that. That was a constant thing because we had to take some chances academically on kids to win. Because to get a good enough athlete, if you're going to do that, you've got to make sure that they have a chance to have the means to be successful academically. Probably the best thing I did in gaining the confidence of the players was showing them I was very deeply concerned about how they did academically and wanted to furnish their support system and the support of the coaches for them to have a chance to graduate with a degree. And our graduation rate was phenomenal."

Dear to Pruett and integral to Marshall's recruiting was the Buck Harless Student-Athlete Program. The program was developed in 1981 with the purpose of aiding Marshall student-athletes in their pursuit of a degree while also staying in tune with the athlete's eligibility.

In addition to being housed in an excellent facility, the Marshall H.E.L.P. program, founded by Dr. Barbara Guyer, had a superb staff of counselors and specialists. Among their capabilities was the wherewithal to recognize and deal with learning disabilities. Pruett saw the program as a tool to help his football team's players achieve academic goals or to recognize learning disabilities that might hinder achieving such goals. Pruett also saw the program as a major recruiting tool.

"I think that what we did was win the parents over," Pruett said. "Now, if you cut open the heads of the majority of college football players—not all of them—but if you cut their heads open, footballs and naked women would run out of them. And that's what they thought about. But mom and dad certainly thought about the academics and the leadership and the guidance and that type of thing is what we wanted to give them. All athletes are high-ego, risk-taker type people. So you have to be able to manage that process. I think that I've always worked on the principle that says you can be programmed for failure. You have to exploit your strengths and manage your weaknesses. Well, the strength of a lot of these guys was they ran fast, they had high energy, and when motivated they were capable of doing a lot of great things. The weakness for a lot of them was that English wasn't as important as a football game. So you had to get past that and get to the English book. We tried very, very hard and talked a lot about how we wanted them to compete as hard in the classroom as they did on the football field. And I think that one of the strengths of our success was that we got them to compete in everything that they did and that helped them off the field, on the field and in the classroom. We tried to get them to take pride in everything they did and the image they projected. I think that's one of the things that pushed them on. Gave them confidence and self-worth in a way that they really didn't know about before."

Yes, Pruett wanted to recruit the best athletes, but he also wanted them to get an education while at Marshall.

Moving up to Division I-A and the MAC meant a different level of competition for the Marshall program. Did Pruett feel like his brand of football—specifically offense, would work against the improved composition of the teams they would be playing?

"What I'd learned at all the other spots I'd coached at was simple: speed kills," Pruett said. "And being a defensive guy and coming from Florida—where I'd seen the type of ball that Coach Spurrier taught and played—convinced me we wanted to throw the ball around. We wanted to do that because that gave us a lot of trouble on defense and we felt like we had a pretty good handle on what was going on. I had a vision in my mind of what we wanted to do and we put that together offensively.

"Defensively, we wanted to attack people and be sound and keep it at a level where our guys could understand what was going on."

In order to get to the level of athleticism he wanted, Pruett said they had to take some chances on several kids who would be academically challenged by the curriculum at Marshall.

"We couldn't get twenty-five guys who could all play at Division I-A level, so we had to take some chances on them academically," Pruett said. "By taking some chances you ran the risk of programming yourself for failure if you didn't simplify things. You had to be able to keep it within a grasp that's not too complicated so we could let these guys play ball.

"You know, I had coached at Wake Forest and Tulane and we had a lot of guys there who had scored 1300s and 1400s on their SATs, guys who could split the atom, know what I mean? But fast feet and fast minds don't always go together sometimes. I found out when we got to Florida, the guys that could really run could make up for mistakes. Now, I also found out that if they went in the wrong direction, they were a long way from where they were supposed to be. So we had to make sure we did a really good job of training these guys. Putting them in a scheme that they understood and where they knew what to do. And by doing that, that gave us the best chance to win."

Going back into the MAC for the 1997 season brought an historical significance to Marshall, which competed in the conference from 1954 to 1968 when the school was suspended indefinitely after the "quick fix" performed by the school's boosters resulting in 144 alleged NCAA violations. Add to that the reality the Herd would open their season—and their step up to Division I-A—against instate rival West Virginia.

"We had not previously played anybody on our schedule or anybody on our schedule that had played them," Pruett said. "In other words, we had no way to gauge how we were going to be and in the community there was a lot of apprehension because it was about a fifty-fifty split whether we should have stayed Division I-AA or gone Division I-A because of the uncertainty of being able to compete in Division I-A football. They really didn't have anything they could rely on about anybody that moved up and had any type of the success. A lot of people thought they were doing the wrong thing because Marshall had never been able to win on the Division I-A level. So the question was kind of out there, 'Do you want to be a small fish in a big pond or a big fish in a small pond?'

"I'll never forget the president, Dr. Gilley, who was very athletic-oriented and supportive of athletics. When I went to Marshall, his vision was, 'We're in the Southern Conference going to the MAC, trying to get to Conference USA.' Now, we have a vision. We just kept that vision. We just kept pushing the envelope. Pushing the envelope to try to get better, to where we're ranked in the Top 25, then the Top 10, always trying to get better. I didn't think about it back then, but I guess there was a lot of pressure. Because, you know, not only are we going into Division I-A football, we're pushing a guy for the Heisman Trophy, we're going into a conference we got kicked out of and we hadn't had a winning season in Division I-football forever. On top of that, we hadn't played anybody that was on our schedule or even played anybody that had played somebody on our schedule."

Going with the understated, Pruett added: "You know, it was an interesting time."

Pruett felt invigorated by it all.

"I mean, to be honest with you, I never really thought about, until right now, all those things that were going on then," Pruett said. "I was so excited to be the head football coach at Marshall. Not being successful didn't enter our minds. We never talked about it. Never dreamed we weren't going to win. We were just trying to figure out how we were going to do it and by how much."

The team, too, felt a buzz about moving up to a higher level of competition.

"I think it was pretty exciting because when I first signed with Marshall I was not aware that they were going to go to Division I-A," Rogers Beckett said. "But when I did find out, it was good. It was exciting because a lot of guys on the team didn't have a chance to go to a Division I-A team, for whatever reason."

No longer did Marshall's schedule contain the likes of VMI, Georgia Southern, Appalachian State and Furman. Replacing them were the likes of Miami of Ohio, Bowling Green, Ohio, and Toledo.

Marshall joined the MAC along with Northern Illinois, which expanded the conference to twelve members and divided into Eastern and Western divisions. Marshall would compete in the East with Akron, Bowling Green, Kent, Miami, and Ohio.

The MAC would experience a change as well, as its champion would be decided by a MAC Championship Game played December 5, 1997, in Huntington, with the winner earning a bid to the Motor City Bowl in Detroit.

Among the benefits of moving to Division I-A for Marshall, and the football program, were increased national exposure and more athletic scholarships. Also accompanying the move were higher academic requirements. Freshmen were required to maintain a 1.6 grade point average in the Southern Conference and it progressed each year accordingly: sophomores 1.7, juniors 1.8 and seniors 1.9. Freshman and sophomores in the MAC needed to maintain a 1.8 and juniors and seniors a 2.0.

Marshall had approximately forty players that did not meet the MAC requirement in 1996, so they had to work hard in the classroom to meet the new standards they would be held to in Division I-A.

Passion goes a long way. And after one year on the job, the Marshall football coach continued to have an unsurpassed passion for his job and everything about it—even the rubber-chicken circuit.

"I can never remember a time when he would not go out and help support, not only athletic fund raising, but anything that would help support Marshall or the Tri-State community or the state of West Virginia," said Lance West, Marshall's athletic director from 1996 through 2002. "He was very, very unselfish. He also involved Elsie, his wife. He did anything he could possibly do to bring her to these events. I think that spoke well about his persona for allowing people to feel good about supporting his alma mater and Marshall. And he always did it with a great sense of humor."

The reaction Pruett got from the gatherings was always positive and for good reason.

"He was great," West said. "As soon as we showed up he'd sign autographs and we were usually the last to leave by taking pictures as we're traveling from city to city or event to event. He was always eager to interact with people and he always spoke about our university. And I thought that was very telling, a football coach really selling everything at the institution."

To Pruett it was all part of the job. And he did love the job.

While Marshall had lost a number of great players from the 1996 championship team, they were returning a quality lot. The returning group had enough respect for what they had accomplished to be picked in the MAC media poll to finish second behind Miami in the Eastern Division.

And there was the great equalizer. Marshall still had Randy Moss, perhaps the best athlete of his generation. Pruett recounted a Moss anecdote shortly after completing his first football season at Marshall.

"I'll never forget after his first year there, he's walking across campus and the track coach asks him, 'Would you come and run the Southern Conference Indoor Track Meet?'" Pruett said. "This is like on a Wednesday. Randy's not doing anything but playing a little basketball, so he says, 'Yeah, I'll do that.' Then on Thursday, they give him a pair of track shoes and he goes out to practice to see if they fit. That's about all he did. Friday, he goes and runs in the meet. He won the 60 and set the conference record and had the fourth fastest indoor time in the 200 meters indoors in the country. And they said he warmed up lying on the track listening to a Walkman. He's a phenomenal athlete. He's just blessed with all this stuff. I mean, he got the nickname, "The Freak," because of the freakish things he could do athletically."

Pruett added that another feature setting Moss apart from others was his competitive fire.

"I mean, I've never been around anybody that competed the way Randy Moss competed," Pruett said. "I mean, he came ready to play every game. And he was a great leader for us. I'm talking about a great leader. He did so many phenomenal things, but I think one of the big things that happened with him is he matured. Randy was a pretty good student, he went to class, had over a C average. He went to class and did his work. I had no complaints about Randy Moss. I was tickled that he was part of our program."

Pruett said Moss "bought into the Marshall program" and actually managed to improve prior to his second season at Marshall. He also was up front with Pruett about his intentions.

"He said he wanted to be there a couple of years and go on to the National Football League," Pruett said. "And when he left, he did go on to the National Football League, and that's where he belonged. He was that good."

Moss' presence helped perpetuate the perception that anybody could coach Marshall. But appearances could be deceiving.

"Bob brought some great talent in there, no question," Sonny Randle said. "You know, good players make good coaches. So Bob was real smart when he had Randy." Randle offered a little chuckle. "But coaching a guy like Randy is not as easy as it looks. Bob was smart to let Randy Moss do his thing. Having him fit, making him fit, believe me that took a certain amount of genius. It really did, because he could have very easily gone over the top. But he always kind of kept him right there. He gave him as much rope as he needed to give him without letting him hang himself. And that takes a lot of coaching ability. It's a lot tougher to coach the great ones than it is to coach the good ones."

Stepping out of the background to the forefront to once again lead the Herd's offense and get the ball to Moss was Chad Pennington.

"My best day was the day of the National Championship Game,"

Pennington said. "Because I knew that after that game I was no longer a red-shirt. So it was a great experience for me to be able to experience a Division I-AA championship game and watch us win. Then I knew it was my time to take over, from that day forward to lead this program where it needed to go."

West Virginia sat on the horizon and every Marshall fan eagerly awaited the contest all summer.

"Well, you could just feel the buzz around the whole state of West Virginia the entire off-season leading up to the 1997 season," Pennington said. "That's all West Virginians talked about was the 'Front Yard Brawl,' as they called it, because the 'Backyard Brawl' is the West Virginia-Pitt game. The buzz around the state was unbelievable. I can remember all the media attention leading up to the game. It's the first thing that I was asked about during spring practice and the first thing that was asked the first day of two-a-days in August. The questions continued all the way up to the game. All conversation was built around that game."

At fall practice Pennington also became aware of the benefit of having red-shirted the previous season.

"During two-a-days I saw how much stronger and better I had gotten from the 1995 season by using the '96 season to get better," Pennington said. "When I saw that transformation in two-a-days, I could really tell the difference and it really gave me a sense of confidence that I could do this, because I'd taken a year off. When you do that, when you don't play for a whole year, you feel like you may lose your senses as far as the game is concerned. But I didn't feel that way. I felt very comfortable and very confident and I was excited about the potential of what we were going to be able to do in '97."

Pennington spoke of the gains he'd made in strengthening his body, noting that in 1995 he weighed in before the season at six-foot-two, 186 pounds. In 1997 he'd advanced to six-foot-three, 208 pounds. Weight and muscle that would help him throw the deep corner route, which had not been one of Pennington's strengths during the 1995 season.

"And it wasn't as much strengthening my arm, because I think arm strength is just a God-given talent, but strengthening everything around my arm, with my core muscles, my abdominal muscles, back muscles, hips, to be able to use my entire body to increase the velocity of the ball. I could really tell the difference."

Pruett immediately noticed the difference in Pennington and could see that the improvements would open the door to certain plays that Pennington

118

could not have done prior to his red-shirt season.

"We knew Chad was special that first year I was there," Pruett said. "He just needed to get bigger and stronger. There was never a question in our mind that he wasn't going to be a great player for us. Chad is a tremendous worker. There's not anything that you could ever ask that kid to do that he wouldn't do to get better. I've never been around a kid that would work so hard to do the things necessary to get good. I mean we talked about what he needed to do and he did it. He got into the weight room and he just did what it took. He worked at football. He worked at everything. By the start of the next season he'd gotten stronger and could make all the throws. He was always a very accurate passer. We just needed him to get a little stronger arm than he had at first. And boy did he, whew!"

Specifically, Pruett needed Pennington to improve on the corner cut.

"We made a living throwing the corner cut," Pruett said. "And we wore people out on the corner cut. We had a special way that we tried to throw that. Chad improved to where he was very proficient at it. Once he could start making stronger throws on that route, it just turned everything around for us."

Pennington couldn't wait to crank up the offense and use the weapon he hadn't had his freshman season—Randy Moss—and lead the team into Division I-A, but he knew the team had some limitations.

"We all knew that we had a really good team," Pennington said. "Most people just looked at us as a I-AA team, but we knew we had a very good shot to compete against anybody. But, as far as our starting eleven on both sides, we had a solid team. We were really good. And so it was pretty exciting. And having Randy Moss out there, you knew that anytime you were in trouble, Randy was going to give you a chance to win and a chance to make plays. The one thing we were lacking in '97, because of the difference in scholarships from I-AA to was depth."

Pennington said even at the beginning of the 1997 season Pruett had already begun sharing his thoughts on the future of Marshall football.

"Even then, Coach Pruett and I always talked about the future and we knew we had a good team in '97," Pennington said. "We knew we could be good in '98, but we knew '99 was going to be a really special season if we stayed healthy. Because the class that I came in with, we had some really good players, young players at the time, who were contributing in '97. We would all be seniors in '99 and we would have a well-built football team. And that was kind of our target, you know. We wanted to win the MAC championship every year over the next three years, from '97 to '99, and just keep building on that. We even talked about an undefeated season when we got to '99 and how that was definitely a possibility because of all the talent we had."

Marshall operated on a shoestring budget, which had Pruett constantly looking for ways to improve while under the gun of financial constraints.

"We were constantly fighting our budget," Pruett said. "In other words, for a Division I-AA school, we were pretty good. But, for a Division I-A school, we had no money."

Prior to the 1997 season, Pruett managed to incorporate having a project stemming from their low budget into a come-together sort of activity for his team. He looked out at his practice field and noticed there was a lot of clay in places where grass should have been.

"So I got our Quarterback Club to buy two truckloads of Bermuda grass sod for me," Pruett said. "And the first truckload came in during two-a-days."

Labor costs were a line item for most budgets, but Pruett had an idea. Why pay for labor when he had a source of free labor in his freshman class? Which is how and why approximately thirty incoming freshmen at Marshall University grudgingly went into the land care business.

"We took our shoulder pads off, kept our bottom clothes on, our t-shirt, and went up and unloaded and laid a truckload of sod on our practice field," Pruett said.

When the two truckloads did not cover all of the spots, they bought another truckload. This time the whole team worked to place the sod.

Pruett couldn't resist prodding his team while they labored.

"Do you all think Coach Nehlen up there at Morgantown is laying sod?" Pruett asked them.

"But those were things that we had to do to get our team ready," Pruett said. "Any time we needed stuff, to be honest with you, we took the philosophy that we were going to find a way to get it done. No matter what it took, we'd find a way to get it done."

**TEAM BUILDING** — With an approach based on speed, teaching techniques, and extensive study, Pruett began molding a Marshall team unlike any previous. *Courtesy Marshall University; photograph by Marilyn Testerman-Haye.*

# Chapter nine

Heading into the 1997 Marshall-West Virginia contest, the last time the two teams had played was in 1923. The Mountaineers beat the Herd that day 81-0 and that was that. West Virginia simply refused to play Marshall thereafter based on the fact they saw no value in playing the Herd.

"(West Virginia) Coach Nehlen fought the game," Pruett said. "He didn't want the game. He didn't like all the hullaba-loo because they had everything to lose and nothing to gain. But we wanted the game and I wanted the game. I wanted the game because I thought it was really good for a number of reasons. It was really good for Marshall's program to have the game and it was good for everybody's budgets. Now, West Virginia argued against that because they felt like they had more to lose. It wouldn't have anything to do with money.

**HOLDING HIS OWN —** Randy Moss demonstrated to WVU players that he was perfectly capable of bringing game. *Courtesy Marshall University; photograph by Rick Haye.*

9

# CHALLENGING

# THE BIG BOYS

The money was there. It was proven. But I wanted it because I felt that one of my sole objectives of my coaching career was to develop football and athletics in the state of West Virginia.

"The game came together kind of quickly," Tim Stephens said. "They'd been wanting to schedule it for years. People were fired up about it. Marshall's first game in Division I-A and against West Virginia, who everyone thought would never, ever play them. There was a buzz all over the state.

"I remember Coach Pruett and Coach Nehlen going around the state promoting the game. It was very cordial, obviously, but they did a great job of stirring up the state for that game—not that it needed a whole lot of stirring. But I remember Coach Nehlen being at a function in Charleston and he was talking about a student going to WVU, and he said, 'Yeah, she's going to WVU,' and Bobby jumped up and said, 'Oh, she couldn't get into Marshall?' And Nehlen kind of smirked at him, like 'That's pretty good.'"

Pruett enjoyed his role of giving West Virginia the needle.

Given the fact some questioned Marshall's sanity for moving to Division I-A, it was reasonable to assume some doubts would be created in the minds of Marshall players regarding whether they belonged or not. But Pruett and his staff refused to allow doubt to creep into the equation.

"Having been born and raised in West Virginia and having gone to Marshall, I felt like Marshall had been slighted for some time," Pruett said. "I had great respect for Coach Nehlen and the West Virginia program and I still do. I mean they were and still are a dynamic program. But we had to do what was best for *our* program. Do what we needed to do to build it and gain respect for it. The one thing that I learned from being a high school coach and from being in coaching so long was that you needed your players to have confidence and they needed to believe in your system. They needed to believe they could win and do all those types of things, so we never, ever talked about losing. Losing wasn't an option. We talked about how good we were going to be."

Pruett said they simply ignored any comments contrary to what he told his team about their ability to win.

"Our deal going into Division I-A was going to be 'damn the torpedoes,'" Pruett said. "We wanted our guys to think that we're pretty good and that we weren't going to be second best to anybody. Didn't matter who we were playing, WVU or Ohio State or whoever; we wanted our guys to feel like, 'Put the ball down and let's play ball.' And that's one of the things that we even put on

**ON TARGET** — Billy Malashevich, with Mark Zban holding, during the WVU game.
*Courtesy Marshall University; photograph by Rick Haye.*

our playbook cover. 'Put the ball down.' You know, we'll play in the parking lot. Just play. We're not saying we're better than anybody. But we'll play. And if you look at our scheduling, you'll see I continually tried to schedule up. We scheduled Florida. We scheduled Georgia, Ohio State, Tennessee, Kansas State, Virginia Tech, and we constantly begged to play West Virginia. During that second year, we had a chance to schedule Clemson. The athletic director came in and said, 'Do you want to play Clemson? They want to play a game.' This is Clemson, a team that had won a National Championship and all that. I'm like, 'We'll take that game, I think we can win it. We're going to have a really good team. That's going to be Chad's senior year.'"

On the Marshall campus a massive pep rally took place on the eve of the West Virginia game.

"That pep rally before the game, that was the equivalent of Marshall playing the National Championship game in the first game of the season," Giradie Mercer said. "So the tough thing about that is you have an opportunity to play a good team, because that was probably one of West Virginia's last great teams. They had a lot of good players. We went into that ballgame with the mindset we were going to upset those guys."

Pruett wanted to make sure his players didn't take the press clippings about West Virginia's parade of stars too seriously.

"Well, we thought we had a pretty good football team and we just tried to tell our guys we could go up there and play with them," Pruett said. "They had a whole bunch of guys that were good players. I mean they had some great players."

West Virginia was loaded with talent. Nevertheless, Pruett was confident of his team's chances and was outspoken about his belief that if they beat their in-state rivals they had a chance to win all of their games.

"I'll never forget Elsie and I walked out on the field two hours before the game up at WVU and some of their student fans were up there and they yelled, 'Pruett sucks,'" Pruett said. "And I turned around to Elsie. I said, 'Elsie, what've you been doing? They're yelling at you up there.' People got a kick out of it. But I was usually pretty loose before the games. I mean, the players will tell you I was always loose before the game. And it was a great experience. That's maybe the biggest thrill that I've had."

The thrill of being on the field in Morgantown quickly took a turn for the worse during pre-game warm-ups when Doug Chapman ran into one of the team's managers and got a bad enough charley horse in his leg that he could not play.

"Doug was a hard, slashing-type runner and the more you gave him the ball, the better he ran," Pruett said. "Not having him for that game is one of the things that really, really hurt us. Llow Turner had a big ball game for us, but Doug was our guy."

Even though they struggled at the beginning, Marshall eventually flexed their muscle and showed they belonged against the Mountaineers, running up 381 yards of total offense against a West Virginia defense that led the nation in total defense a year earlier limiting opponents to 217.5 yards per game.

But the game began ugly when Marshall looked to be in awe of finding themselves on the same field as West Virginia.

"You know, you go up there to play in that atmosphere and then we don't make a first down the first time we have the ball and we have to punt," Pruett said. "They didn't even rush the punter, but we made a mistake and they blocked the punt. Next thing I know, we're down 21-0."

Rogers Beckett saw a tangible difference in the competition against a Division I-A school.

"The thing I remember most about that game was the speed and tempo of the game," Beckett said. "The players were physically stronger. Division I-AA had good players, but that was definitely a step up. What I really got from that whole year was that I had to get stronger in order to continue where I could perform and be somewhat good at it. I think everyone on the team felt that way."

Tim Stephens covered the West Virginia game.

"West Virginia jumped out to a big lead," Stephens said. "They blocked a punt and scored early, and they're up 28-3, and I'm thinking, 'Holy cow, welcome to I-A. Maybe this team is ready for the MAC, but maybe not quite ready for this level.' West Virginia seemed so fast that day."

"Our guys were upset at halftime," Pruett said. "They knew they could play better than they were playing. And we came back."

Marshall overcame the 28-3 deficit to take a 31-28 lead with just over twelve minutes to go in the game after Randy Moss hauled in a pair of touchdown passes.

"When Marshall comes back they've got a 31-28 lead in that game and Moutaineer Field is dead silent except for a little patch of green," Stephens said. "You could see a look on the WVU fans' faces, 'Oh my God, we can't lose this game.'"

**UNDER CENTER** — Chad Pennington led a second-half comeback that gave Mountaineer fans pause. *Courtesy Marshall University.*

Two late interceptions hurt the Herd's cause and they came up 42-31 losers.

"We ran out of gas in that game," Pruett said. "West Virginia had better depth than we did and it turned out to be a big factor in the game and we ended up losing to a very good West Virginia team."

Mercer remembered a game that had a wave of emotions.

"I think at halftime they thought they had won the game, and obviously, it ended up going back and forth," Mercer said. "That was the biggest game of anyone's career at Marshall. There wasn't an empty seat in the house. And it was just really one of those good things for the State of West Virginia."

Though their team had not won, Marshall fans seemed satisfied with the result. They had not gotten blown out 81-0, they had scared the Mountaineers, and they had shown they belonged in Division I-A. Inside the media room prior to the post-game press conference the media scurried about talking up the way the Herd had almost come away with the upset. Like the fans, the media saw Marshall winning on that Saturday afternoon even though they had lost.

"WVU came back and won," Stephens said. "But Marshall showed that day that 'Yeah, we belong in I-A and we can play some good teams in I-A and compete very well.'"

Such a mindset might have worked for the fans and even the media, but Pruett did not buy into the same logic. First, he was proud of his team for the way they played.

"We've been Division I-A for three weeks," he said after the game. "I'm proud of our guys."

And Pruett felt the game had a higher calling than West Virginia or Marshall being the winner.

"Without question, no matter what the results of the ballgame, everybody's a winner," said Pruett, noting what a plus the game was for the State of West Virginia.

"The strong point of that game was that we really showed to ourselves that we could compete on this level against a quality football team that was very well coached and had a lot of good players on it," Pruett said.

While Pruett had the perspective to see the positives stemming from the game with West Virginia, he conveyed a different message to his players in the locker room and to the fans of Marshall afterward.

In Pruett's eyes, Marshall had played sixteen games since he had become the coach and they had just taken their first loss. To his way of thinking a loss was a loss and there were no moral victories.

"We don't look at this as a moral victory," Pruett told reporters. "It's a loss. We came here to win this football game. That was our goal."

Pruett was not content and he certainly did not want his players to be content. Going out and playing a good game might be good for some teams, but it wasn't good enough for Marshall—at least not on his watch. He'd been there and done that at other programs such as Wake Forest and Tulane, where playing a team tough was enough to make everybody happy. Pruett wanted more for himself. He wanted more for his players. And foremost, he wanted more for Marshall University.

Pruett did revel in the fact that Marshall and West Virginia had played each other, a game he had wanted to see scheduled his entire life. But the moment had been fleeting.

"They had scheduled the game with West Virginia prior to me getting the job," Pruett said. "They had originally scheduled four games with West Virginia, all four of them were going to be played at West Virginia. And then they were squabbling about having at least one of the games at Marshall and WVU wouldn't do that. So as a compromise they played the one game in 1997 and then they were supposed to negotiate the future games. Well, it was reported that when we went ahead of them in the fourth quarter, the president at WVU made the statement to some of our fans along the lines of 'If I get out of this it won't happen again.' They wouldn't play us again. They just figured it was too big a risk."

Pruett was disappointed the series was discontinued after just one game.

"I thought it was a huge mistake," Pruett said. And they kept making excuses for why they shouldn't play the game. To me, I thought the next logical step would have been to create a huge rivalry within the state. I felt like the rivalry between West Virginia and Marshall would grow just like any rivalry. And I thought that we needed that for the fans, for the programs, for all those things because of the changing dynamics, the changing of conferences, changing of people, and all that stuff."

Pruett needed to put the West Virginia game in the rear view mirror and prepare his team for its next game against Army at Michie Stadium in West Point, New York.

The Cadets were coming off one of their best seasons in years and had made an appearance in the Independence Bowl. The game would be the 1,000[th] football game in Army's storied history.

"We had opportunities to win the West Virginia game, and, you know, that's football," Pruett said. "So what we wanted to do was build on the experience. We tried to use what happened in the ball game to make us better and that's the way we dealt with it. We came back and, just like any other time, we didn't want to tear our guys down. In other words, I tried to be a positive coach. I know there were times when I got after them, but we wanted to build on the West Virginia game. They were disappointed because it was certainly a big game for us, and our program, because it was West Virginia and it was our first loss. I mean, we were disappointed, but that's one thing about football. We didn't have a long time to feel sorry for ourselves, because we had to go to Army the next week. And no matter how you sliced it or diced it, that was going to be a tough, tough chore for us. They were a pretty good team at that time. They were beating Conference USA schools."

Marshall had Army's respect going into the game. Their coach, Bob Sutton, called the Herd a "pretty doggone good football team," noting they were used to winning and they did have Randy Moss, adding what amounted to an understatement when he said, "When he catches it, it's exciting."

Pruett's offense was predicated much of the time on how the defense treated Moss.

"Basically, we'd put Randy out there at wide receiver and the premise of our offense was if there's one guy out there on him, we throw him the ball," Pruett said. "If there's two out there, we threw him the ball most of the time, and if there were three guys covering him, well, we threw him the ball about half the time. You know, he was just so dominating. Remember, Randy was one of the best college football players to ever play the game, maybe even *the* best."

However, Marshall's offense amounted to more than Moss. They had quality backs in Turner and Chapman, whose work opened up the passing lanes for Moss and other receivers. And they had Pennington, a quarterback with intelligence and physical skills, getting them the ball.

Army appeared up to the task against the Herd, driving the ball up the field seventy-yards on their first possession before fumbling the football at the Marshall six-yard line.

On the third play after recovering the fumble, Moss caught a screen, hurdled one defender, stiff-armed another and didn't stop running until ninety yards later when he was standing in the end zone. A Carolina Panthers scout

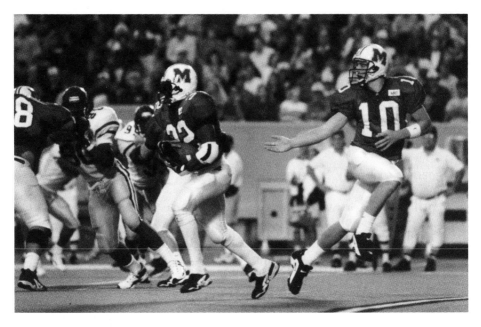

**RELIABLE TANDEM** — Pennington hands off to Doug Chapman, his Marshall roommate. *Courtesy Marshall University; photograph by Marilyn Testerman-Haye.*

sitting next to Stephens seemed awestruck. "He just sat there with his mouth agape," Stephens recalled.

Army successfully moved the ball on their next possession, putting together a fifteen play drive that covered fifty-seven yards before Army quarterback Johnny Goff threw into the end zone only to have Marshall's Larry Moore pick off the pass. Six plays later Pennington hit LaVorn Colclough for a thirty-six yard touchdown.

Moss clearly was the big difference in the Army game, catching five passes for 186 yards and two touchdowns. The second one was a back-breaker coming on the first play of the second half. Moss hauled in the pass, tore away from a defensive back, then ran seventy-nine yards for the touchdown.

Marshall's defense had done its job as well—setting up three touchdowns with turnovers—despite what the numbers said. They had bent, but never broken, allowing 527 yards of total offense and losing the time of possession battle as the Army offense held the football for close to forty-two minutes of the sixty-minute contest. But when the final gun sounded, Marshall was back in the win column at the Division I-A level with a 35-25 victory.

The defense came through against Army, but Marshall would be suspect against the run throughout the 1997 season. At one point Pruett criticized the defense in a newspaper article, which upset Giradie Mercer.

"I got so mad at him that I actually thought about transferring," Mercer said. "I got so mad I kept the article. Coach Pruett made a comment in the paper that we were not very good at stopping the run at all. We had some younger players on defense—including me—Ricky Hall was a junior, who just got his first chance to start that year. And we had some new linebackers, two new outside linebackers, John Grace and Andre O'Neal. So our first seven weren't as experienced as they had been in the past. But with that being said, he directed a lot of criticism at the run defense. He said that instead of having guys who are six-five, 290 like he had at Florida, he now was at a point where he had guys who were six-one and 265. He said with guys that big we would never be great on defense and we'd just try to hold the other team and do what we could to try and get the ball back to our offense. A lot of guys took offense to it. But really the bigger problem was we just didn't have many guys with a lot of experience and anytime you lose as many guys as we did after that '96 team you're going to have some growing pains. Obviously, as the year went on we got a little better."

Already on most college football experts' short list of best players in the country, Moss was ready for the NFL. He did not say he would be leaving after the season, but most knew his leaving was a foregone conclusion. Pruett knew it, too, and talked openly with Moss about what the NFL was all about.

Pruett told Moss there was nothing on the playing field he would have to get used to when he got to the NFL—Pruett knew Moss would excel once in the NFL—but he conditioned Moss to the idea of learning how to take care himself off the field, like having a lot of money and knowing how to manage it and the relationships often accompanied by suddenly having wealth.

Counseling Moss and others on life outside of football endeared Pruett to his players. This was the good stuff, the fiber that made lasting relationships and what made Pruett special.

After the Army game, Marshall followed by defeating Kent State 42-17, bringing Western Illinois to Huntington for a date with the Herd at Marshall Stadium and the first play from scrimmage brought about the kind of action that endeared Pruett to the Marshall faithful.

Moss and Colclough were lined on one side of the field in a pass formation. Pennington took the snap and faked a play-action pass to Moss' side

**ANOTHER WEAPON** — In addition to Moss, Marshall had an outstanding posses-sion receiver in Nate Poole, shown here against Ball State. *Courtesy Marshall University; photograph by Brett Hall.*

then went the other direction with a screen pass to Turner, who caught the ball and ran eighty-four yards for a score.

A lot of coaches would have taken the credit for the call themselves, but not Pruett, who said Pennington had wanted to do it based on the feeling the Western Illinois linebackers would go Moss' way. When the play didn't go to Moss, Turner went undetected out of the backfield.

The Herd went on to defeat the Leathernecks 48-7. Wins over Ball State, 42-16, and Akron, 52-17, started to make the jump to Division I-A appear as routine as walking outside to retrieve the morning paper. Against Ball State, Moss and Pennington connected for five touchdowns to set a school record.

Pruett, though normally locked in on the action on the field, maintained his sense of humor. He always liked to look around at what was going on in the stands from time to time and often was rewarded with a good laugh. The Ball State game brought one of those moments.

"There was this one guy walking around wearing one of those big, tall hats," Pruett said. "The ones you see at the carnivals, like one of those 'Cat in the Hat' hats. And he had a sign on the hat that said, 'Randy Moss.' He also had a big, rolled-up sheet of paper that said 'reefer' on it, like he's smoking pot. The fans in the MAC, they were always on our people, but they're pretty creative and they could be funny."

The Herd got a wake up call October 18, 1997, at Miami of Ohio.

Facing a tough MAC opponent and playing poorly, Marshall got humiliated 45-21. Though the defeat gave the Herd only its second loss in two seasons, it was devastating because of its ramifications. A major goal for Pruett and his team entering the 1997 season was to gain entry into the MAC Championship Game. Losing to Miami, traditionally a MAC heavyweight, cast a pall over any hopes the team had of attaining one of its top goals for the season. Miami would have to lose twice in order for Marshall to have any chance of winning the MAC's East Division title.

Pruett understood the damage inflicted on his team by the loss at Miami. He assessed the situation, then told his team they controlled only what they did.

"We needed to take care of our own business," Pruett said. "We needed some help to win the championship. Miami needed to lose twice. But that was something we had no control over. I told the team we just needed to keep winning and we'd see what happened."

In other words, no reason for his players to worry about things they couldn't control.

The team responded and played with a passion equal to their coach's. After the Miami loss, Marshall defeated Eastern Michigan 48-25, Central Michigan 45-17, Bowling Green 28-0, and Ohio 27-0. Marshall had done what they needed to do and Miami had not, losing twice to allow Marshall to win the Eastern Division and earn a spot in the MAC Championship.

In the Ohio victory, Moss caught his twenty-second touchdown pass of the season with two minutes remaining, which tied the NCAA single-season record. The touchdown demonstrated his catching ability, the resulting celebration toss showed he could pass, too, as he cocked and fired the ball over the end zone stands.

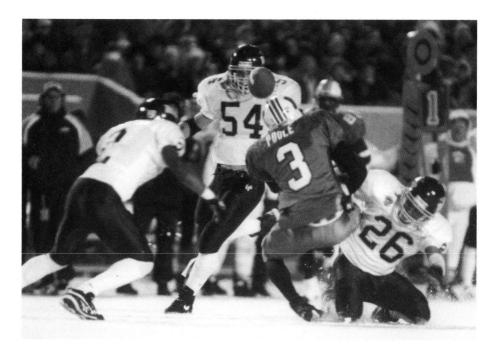

**THE SNOW BOWL** — Nate Poole gets separated from the ball against Toledo. *Courtesy Marshall University; photograph by Brett Haye.*

Had any of the joyous Marshall fans had an opportunity to throw the ball they might have thrown it even farther, for their team—which had been kicked out of the MAC twenty-eight years earlier—was back and was far better than before. A victory over Toledo in the conference title game would put the 9-2 Herd in a bowl game for the first time since the 1948 Tangerine Bowl.

On December 5, 1997, Toledo visited Marshall Stadium to play the Herd for the 1997 MAC Championship; the winner would go to the Motor City Bowl in Pontiac, Michigan.

Light snow in Huntington was the forecast for the game that was played on a Friday night to accommodate an ESPN 2 audience. But by kickoff enough snow had fallen to cover the field with a layer approximately an inch thick.

The game instantly came to be known as "The Snow Bowl" and saw Toledo slog their way to a 7-3 lead at the half.

"Toledo had a defensive back who ended up playing in the NFL, he was pretty good, so they had him playing one-on-one against Randy," Pruett said. "So I told my offensive coordinator, 'You need to throw the ball to Randy

**NATIONAL TELEVISION —** ESPN2 carried the MAC Championship, where viewers across the country were given a taste of the Division I-A upstarts. *Courtesy Marshall University.*

during the second half.' He said, 'I'll throw it to him every damn time.' And I said, 'Man, you're beginning to understand.'"

Pennington found Moss twice for touchdowns in the third quarter and Billy Malashevich kicked his second field goal to give the Herd a 20-7 lead. Pennington to Moss accounted for another score in the fourth and Doug Chapman added a late touchdown to give the Herd a 34-7 lead. Final score: Marshall 34, Toledo 14.

Pennington led the nation in touchdown passes with thirty-nine, establishing a record for a sophomore. He also set a single-season MAC mark with 3,480 passing yards.

After losing its first game of the season, the Herd went 10-1, becoming the first team in history to win ten games in its first season in Division 1-A. Best of all, Bob Pruett and his Marshall University Thundering Herd were champions of the Mid-American Conference and headed for Pontiac.

"I think the West Virginia game was certainly a highlight of that first year in Division I-A for us," Pruett said. "That was a big event in the state and for us and for everybody involved. I think we really shocked the rest of the MAC by how good we were. Going into the 1997 season they really had no idea we were that good. So they were stunned. And then we handled Toledo pretty easily in the championship game."

Toledo coach Gary Pinkel would later say that Marshall's style changed the dynamics of the conference as all of the conference's teams began to change their offense.

"They started running our offense, they started changing their recruiting, they were following us around recruiting," Pruett said. "I mean it was really pretty funny."

Pruett, like most Marshall fans, also particularly enjoyed watching Moss play.

"He was just awesome to watch," Pruett said. "Besides that, his leadership skills were unbelievable. And the things that he was able to do for us. Watching the plays he made for us, whew! Randy was just special. Every game you'd go out there and you had no idea what you might see. He was a Wide World of Sports highlight waiting to happen every time he went on the field. But one thing I always knew: we were going to get great effort from Randy. He did that for us. Randy is such a competitor and, where he is really misunderstood is he really wants to win. He's got a great burning desire to win. And when he doesn't win, he really gets disappointed and he wears his emotions on his sleeve. He is so confident in his skills he has a tendency to blame himself. He thinks he could have done more. Randy is just a lot different person and player than people think he is."

In a season of firsts, Moss brought another major first to the Huntington campus: Marshall University's first Heisman Trophy candidate.

Moss finished the regular season with 2,178 all-purpose yards, good for first in the MAC and third in the NCAA, and twenty-five touchdowns, which almost doubled the previous conference record of thirteen set the previous year by Kent's Eugene Baker.

On December 13, 1997, Moss joined Tennessee quarterback Peyton Manning, Michigan defensive back Charles Woodson, and Washington State quarterback Ryan Leaf in New York at the Downtown Athletic Club as an one of the invitees to the Heisman Trophy presentation.

"It was just a phenomenal event for our school and for everybody involved,"

**DELEGATION** — Marshall was represented at the 1997 Heisman ceremony by (l-r) Mary West, Bob Pruett, MAC Commissioner Jerry Ippoliti, Elsie Pruett, and Marshall Athletic Director Lance West. *Courtesy the University of Tennessee.*

**SHARP-DRESSED MAN** — Randy Moss raised a few eyebrows by sporting cornrows and sunglasses at the Heisman award ceremony. *Courtesy the University of Tennessee.*

said Pruett, who was part of Moss' entourage to New York. "I mean, here we are, Marshall University. We had just got into Division I-A football and we're in New York."

Pruett has a trophy case at his house in Huntington with many commemorative items and photographs from that first trip to the Downtown Athletic Club.

Despite Moss' lofty credentials and his incredible athleticism, Woodson won the award, even though he later admitted Moss had had a much better season than he did.

"One thing about Randy Moss, when he got up there, he was the leader up there among the other candidates," Pruett said. "They were following him around. He didn't win it, but they were following him around."

Moss did win the Biletnikoff Award as the nation's top receiver.

HUNTINGTON FELT ELECTRIC IN ANTICIPATION of Marshall's December 26, 1997, match-up with 7-4 Ole Miss of the powerful Southeastern Conference in the first-ever Motor City Bowl in Pontiac's Silverdome.

Mississippi, which finished in a tie for third in the West division of the SEC, had a running game bolstered by John Avery, who had 4.3 speed in the forty-yard dash and he rushed for 100 yards six times despite missing the first three games of the season with a dislocated elbow. The Rebels also had a quality passing game led by Stewart Patridge, who set single-season school records for passing yards, completions, and total offense, and tied the mark for completion percentage.

Marshall looked overmatched when the game began. Patridge completed a fifty-four yard pass to Grant Heard, leading to Avery diving into the endzone from the one for a 7-0 Rebel lead after only twenty-four seconds had ticked off the scoreboard.

Mississippi quickly discovered two could play explosive football.

"Two plays after getting the kickoff they scored," Pruett said. "So in their minds they're going to run over us, see."

Marshall started at their own twenty after receiving the kickoff. On the first play, Pennington stepped to the line to read the defense and immediately picked up on the fact Ole Miss had walked a corner up to play bump-and-run with Moss. After not believing what he was seeing, Pennington called Moss' number.

**MOTOR CITY BOWL —** For the first time in nearly six decades, Marshall made it to a postseason bowl game, versus Ole Miss. *Courtesy Marshall University.*

"They thought they could play bump and run with Randy," Pruett said. "The cornerback was the SEC sprint indoor sprint champion, and Randy ran by him like he wasn't even there. I mean that call was a no-brainer. Anytime anybody tried bump-and-run against him we went downfield. That was who we were. That was part of our system."

The eighty-yard touchdown tied the score at 7. Two touchdowns had been scored on three snaps and the game was only forty-one seconds old. Yes, the track meet was on in the inaugural Motor City Bowl.

Pennington completed twenty-three of forty-five passes for 337 yards and three touchdowns; Chapman ran nineteen times for 153 yards and a touchdown.

But the heat and Patridge's passing took their toll on Marshall.

The Silverdome turned into an oven once people were inside and the game began. Marshall was not prepared for the toll that heat would take on the team.

"That game proved to be a learning experience for the players," said Giradie

**HOTHOUSE —** Concerns at depth, combined with playing inside, wore Marshall down by the fourth quarter. *Courtesy Marshall University; photograph by Rick Haye.*

Mercer. "But not only was it a learning experience for the players, it was a learning experience for the coaches as well. What we did in that bowl game, we got into a situation where we were probably finished as a team—I know defensively—at the end of the first half. I remember me, personally, suffering with cramps along with a few other members of the defense. It was hot, but I think the best thing that probably came out of that game was the coaches decided we were going to start rotating to keep everyone fresh. Out of that game came the development of depth at Marshall.

"One of the things we did that up until that point we hadn't done a lot of was rotating," Mercer continued. "In Division I-AA you could kind of get up on people and just kind of play who you wanted. But [in Division I-A] we were going to be playing teams where we'd be in the game right to the end. Which was something different for Marshall. We got into I-A where we were playing these long drawn out games like a heavyweight fight. Like Mike Tyson always being able to knock people out early on, but when you take him the distance, he's not used to handling it. Doesn't know how to act. Doesn't know how to put himself in position to win the fight. That was one of the things that came out of that Ole Miss game. And after that year we always went into the bowl game with the mindset that we were going to play a lot of guys, make sure everyone knows his assignment. And, that everyone is in the mindset and frame of mind to play the game."

Pruett's team was dehydrated and drained. He even told the offense they needed to hold the ball a little bit to try and run out the clock so they could rest their legs.

"We hadn't played many snaps and we weren't a team that was in bad shape," Pruett said. "It's just that teams die in heat when they're not used to it."

A dead-tired Marshall defense was no match for the passing of Patridge, who led the Rebels to two third-quarter touchdowns and a 21-17 lead. Before it was over, the lead changed five times in the second half.

Pruett said the depth problem stemmed from the lack of seasoned talent. Making the transition from Division I-AA to Division I-A meant Marshall could expand their number of scholarships from sixty-five to eighty-five. But since those additional athletes were mostly incoming freshmen, Marshall didn't really have the depth of a long-time Division I-A school like Mississippi.

"We had depth for the Mid-American Conference, but, when you get into the SEC and the top echelons of bowl teams, what happens to you is you run up against a team that has greater depth and you're in trouble," Pruett said.

Depth and Deuce McAllister, a talented running back the likes of which Marshall had not seen all season.

"He came in and broke our backs running the football in the second half," Pruett said. "We were able to contain Avery, but McAllister hurt, and what happened, they also had a good quarterback and good receivers. So we had to put enough people in the core, in the box, to stop the run. We needed to be able to play a one-deep, a free safety, man free, which was our best coverage to stop them from throwing the football.

"We didn't have depth at the corners and our starting corners got dehydrated. With all the guys in the box and inexperienced guys at the corners, they'd throw the ball over their heads. So we ended up having to play a two-deep coverage that doubled the wide-outs to help the cornerbacks. When we did that, we took a guy out of the box and they were at the line of scrimmage checking on us."

And Mississippi exploited the weakness.

"We were getting bled by them running the football, taking a slow death instead of a quick death," Pruett said. "And we were just dehydrated and that's the depth thing. That's what hurt us depth-wise."

Chapman's nine-yard touchdown run capped a nine-play, eighty-eight-yard drive to give the Herd a 31-27 lead with 2:57 remaining. But Ole Miss marched the ball right back up the field until McAllister's one-yard touchdown run with thirty-one seconds left on the clock gave the Rebels a 34-31 lead. But Marshall had more left.

Pennington found Moss for a forty-yard completion, which would have put them in field goal range, but Moss had the ball stripped away and Ole Miss recovered—game over.

Several Marshall's players believed the Ole Miss player had not been in possession of the ball and got emotional to the point of removing their helmets and barking at the officials about the call. In the face of disappointment, Pruett showed class when he addressed the fumble call: "It's a judgment call, and we would have loved for it to go our way. But the referees didn't beat us. Ole Miss beat us."

While many of the Marshall faithful felt like the Herd should have won the game, most were generally happy with their team's showing—somewhat like they were following their opening game loss against West Virginia. Once again, Pruett felt inclined to step in to continue conditioning the fans, the alumni and most of all his football team with his post-game remarks.

"We don't like the idea of losing," said Pruett afterward. "Now we have an idea of how far we have to go to compete with teams like Ole Miss and West Virginia."

Pruett added the dialogue, which included the statement that would define his years at Marshall.

"After that game we're in the press conference and a reporter says, 'Coach, aren't you really proud of your football team tonight after you all played an SEC school the way you did?' And I said, 'I am very proud of our effort tonight, but at Marshall we play for championships and we played for one tonight and didn't win.' I said, 'This is the first one that we played for that we didn't win,' because we'd won the divisional championship and the Mid-American Conference and we'd won the national I-AA championship. So that was the first championship that we'd played for and lost.

"It was all a vision of the way I wanted it to play out. In other words, the vision is that I felt like that at the University of Florida we played for championships. They wanted to play for a championship. That was the standard that Coach Spurrier had. So I took that piece of it with me. And Coach Groh, he wanted to do this and he even had the sketch of the championship ring. You know, you don't get a ring for going to a bowl game. You get a ring for winning the championship. We created expectations. So that feeling, that aura about that, I felt like we could use that, encompass that and use that as motivation at Marshall to win games. And I think we needed something. I felt like we needed something to tie the community in and the expectation level is that we're in Division I football and they didn't feel like we could even compete, I mean, our people came away from the West Virginia game elated that we were able to scare them that much. And the fear that I had as a football coach, and I remember thinking of this, was the Wake Forest-Tulane syndrome, that they were very content and happy with playing close and settling for that. I didn't want our players, our coaches and our fans to be content."

Mercer said the team took Pruett's words to heart.

"Ever since then that has been the motto of the team—'We play for championships,'" Mercer said. "I think that slogan has always driven the team to perform well under pressure no matter what the circumstances. All during the particular seasons, we were going to try and find a way to get ourselves into championship games. Playing in the Mid American Conference if you're not playing for championships then you're just another of the 117 Division I-A programs. He wanted to set the program apart from that. And at least be able to say even if we weren't going to be able to play for a national title, we would at least be able to say we're one of a number of teams going to a bowl game."

Pennington felt as though Pruett was letting the team know they had set a standard.

"And the standard was that we play for championships and we want to win championships," Pennington said. "Getting close is not good enough for us. You see a lot of times with mid-major schools they take moral victories with losses. And at Marshall, we didn't accept that. So, from that point on after the Ole Miss game, we settled for nothing but a win and nothing but the best. And it didn't matter who we were playing, where we were playing, we expected to win. Coach Pruett did a great job of setting that mindset and really setting the tone as far as how we approached the games and how we approached every opponent."

On January 8, 1998, Randy Moss made the less than surprise announcement expected by all Marshall fans: he was heading to the NFL.

"It's been great playing for the Herd these past two years," said Moss when he made his announcement. "Ever since I was a young boy, I've dreamed of playing in the NFL. Part of my dream is to give back to the person who's done everything for me—my mom."

Suffice it to say, the Randy Moss experiment at Marshall had run its course and it had worked.

"Coaching Randy may have looked tough to the media, it may have looked tough to the fans," Chapman said. "Because the guy came in with so much press. But Randy never gave Coach Pruett one drop of crap. I think it's because he respected him.

**BECOMING A LEADER —** With Randy Moss departing, the Herd forged a new identity under Chad Pennington. *Courtesy Marshall University; photograph by Marilyn Testerman-Haye.*

10

# JOURNEY TO

GREATNESS

"I played with Randy on two different levels. I played with him a couple of years at Marshall and four years at Minnesota and I can just tell you he's the kind of guy if he doesn't respect you, you'll know it. I've seen him play for coaches he doesn't respect. Pruett was absolutely a coach he respected. Yeah, he may have had his Randy moments. But for the most part, he never got completely out of line and just backlashed against the coach and the coaching staff. He was never like that. Coach Pruett would tell you the same thing, that he never had that much of a problem with Randy. It wasn't that type of a deal. Randy was one of the hardest working guys on the team. He trained the hardest. He always was in the best shape. You see a guy with that much athletic ability doing that and it makes everybody better. And Coach Pruett brought that out in him too."

Moss left a legacy Marshall fans and Moss' teammates alike held in awe.

"Regardless of the competition, how many guys could honestly say that they have scored in every collegiate football game that they have ever played in?" Giradie Mercer said. "I don't care who you're playing against. Besides that, this is Randy Moss, so wherever he went on the field for two seasons he was accounted for. They don't care if they leave the other receiver running down the field wide open. You have got to account for Randy Moss. Sometimes one, sometimes two, sometimes a third guy would come in underneath the coverage. And he was still able to get it done. And not only one year, but two years in college. That's totally phenomenal."

Pruett can't say enough nice things about Moss.

"He is an awesome athlete and he is a leader," Pruett said. "I'm not around him anymore, but I was around him as he was growing up and I'll tell you what, he's an awesome person. If he was sitting here right there, I'd hug him. He's welcome in my home and with our grandkids. He's wonderful around kids and I think that he's a little outspoken, but there are a whole lot of folks in the NFL who are outspoken.

"I think one of the reasons we had such a good fit was that I genuinely liked Randy. I've never asked Randy Moss for anything. And I think if I did, he'd give me the shirt off his back. I truly like him and admire him for the effort he gave, what he did for our program and everything about it. And I think if Randy needed me, I'd hitchhike to get to him if I had to. That is the way I feel about him. And I think he would do the same for me, and I think his teammates feel the same way. I just think he's misunderstood. He wants to win and he's so competitive that sometimes he gets frustrated if he's not winning championships because he's won championships in high school. He won two at Marshall, and he wants to win in the National Football League and he never really got that chance."

At the turn of the calendar each year, coaching staffs of the many college football teams are working feverishly to find the players they need to take the program forward. Pruett and his staff were doing the things necessary to ensure they would keep up their excellence by recruiting high-quality players. Among the players Pruett recruited during the 1997 season was a quarterback by the name of Byron Leftwich from Capitol Heights, Maryland.

"We saw him, he was out in Washington, D.C.," Pruett said. "Kevin Kelly, who was the recruiting coach brought the film in. He was playing on a field that didn't even have grass and this big, tall quarterback could really sling the ball. And our staff, we were amazed at his ability. But for some reason he wasn't really highly recruited. Some people were trying to recruit him as a tight end."

Pruett and his staff liked the idea of having the big guy behind center. That helped seal the deal when it came to Leftwich deciding on a school, as did other factors.

"I think our reputation after having quarterbacks like Eric Kresser and Chad, really made a big difference," Pruett said. "The other thing was, during those years—those early years—all of our games were on television up in the D.C. area on a public television station, Channel 56. And I think that having had Randy, and then Chad Pennington on top of that, those things led to his interest in us. In other words, our success really played a huge part in getting him interested in us. You could say signing Byron was the byproduct of the success we had already had."

Contrary to opinions about why he was interested in Marshall, Leftwich said the main reason was Pruett.

"I think it was just the type of person that I thought he was when I first met him," Leftwich said. "I knew he was the type of guy that I wanted to play for. Other places would have let me play quarterback. It was just who Coach Pruett was. I just felt real good and real comfortable about where Marshall was heading—and about the type of person he was. So I wanted to go play for that kind of person.

"Coach Pruett is a people person. He's a guy that can communicate with anybody. He can communicate with you if you're black, white, Chinese, from Hawaii, from California, from New York, from anywhere. He can communicate with any type of person, any type of player and that's what makes a guy like him so special."

Leftwich was attracted to Pruett the first time the two met.

"The first time I met him he came to my house," Leftwich said. "And there was just something about the way he was talking. He was talking just like I can talk. He was talking as if he grew up in D.C. himself."

Giradie Mercer had gone to Leftwich's high school, which led to some familiarity with Marshall as well.

Inking Leftwich prior to the signing deadline in early 1998 meant Marshall would have a successor to Chad Pennington in the ranks.

Meanwhile, Pennington continued to show marked improvement, which would go a long way toward offsetting the loss of a Randy Moss, a player who could not be replaced.

"Chad had more assets than his physical assets," Pruett said. "He gave us fantastic leadership on and off the field, inspiring people in the weight room, the classroom and on the field. And that cut down on a lot of the other problems that you have. You know, the leadership in bringing a team together and having guys rally around him and those type things.

"Offensively, he was getting bigger and stronger and was able to throw the ball down the field more. As he grew and got stronger, his arm strength really grew. With the added zip you're able to push the ball down the field more. You see, with Randy he could out jump anybody, so Randy would tell Chad, 'Throw the ball to the six-yard line.' And Chad might say, 'Well, that's too far.' And Randy would say, 'No, don't worry about that. I'll go get it. You just get the ball where I tell you.' So he had that luxury of Randy the first year. I don't want to minimize Chad's ability, I'm just saying from the jump in ability from the '97 season to the '98 season made all the difference and offset some of losing Randy."

An added benefit to the team's overall improvement was its closeness. In Pruett's first two seasons his team had grown together to form quite a bond. The bond allowed the group to feel close to each other while also giving them an extra sense on the field where they always knew what their teammates were doing.

"The best thing was you could look to the left and you could look to the right of you and you realize this guy you're playing with is with you for the long haul. You realize, 'Hey, we're all in this together and we're going to leave together,'" Mercer said. "That made it all special. A lot of times when you're recruiting for colleges, you recruit what you need. Typically what happens is that you become tight friends and tight teammates with the guys you come in with. At Marshall, that group that became seniors in '99 were all guys that came in together. And we were able to play together, so you had a great tight unit, in terms of teammates who hung together off the field, offense, defense, white, black, whatever you want to call it. We all stayed in Huntington during the summers; we would have a cookout every day. I mean, we all stayed together as a team and I think that alone was one of the key factors in that team being as special as it was."

Pruett helped facilitate the closeness and family atmosphere. His door always was open to talk to players about whatever was on their minds, be it problems, gripes or anything else that might arise.

"If I had a problem I'd go in and talk to him," said Mercer with a chuckle. "You'd go in there trying to figure out the answer to your problems. We'd get in there and we'd talk about everything else and before long you'd be out of there and you'd realize, 'Hey, he never answered my question.' By that time he was off to the next guy."

Chapman realized leadership was needed on the 1998 squad.

"Nobody replaces Randy Moss," Chapman said. "The young guys needed to step up. I took responsibility and so did Chad. We were upperclassmen on the offense and we felt like we had a job to do."

Pruett called the 1998 season a "crucial year" for the program.

"After '97 we lost John Wade, who went to the National Football League, we lost Randy Moss," Pruett said. "You know, in two years there we'd lost a lot of good players, so young guys were having to step up."

Marshall opened the 1998 season at Akron on September 5 and received a scare.

After taking a 10-0 lead on Chapman's four-yard run in the second quarter, the Herd couldn't put away the Zips.

Akron cut the lead to 10-7 late in the third quarter and tied the game at 13 with 13:28 to play in the fourth quarter. Four minutes later the Zips took a 16-13 lead.

But the Akron lead was short-lived.

Chapman scored on a five-yard run to put the Herd up 20-16 with 4:39 to play. Daninelle Derricott then intercepted a Butchie Washington pass to give the Herd the ball at the Akron thirty-eight. Five plays later Pennington found Chapman on a fourteen-yard touchdown pass—Chapman's third touch-

**TANDEM —** Bob's style of offense used the pass to set up the run—here Doug Chapman takes the handoff from Chad Pennington. *Courtesy Marshall University; photograph by Rick Haye.*

down of the day—to give Marshall a 27-16 win.

Marshall looked more like Marshall the next week in the home opener in Huntington, September 12. But once again, the offense had a tough time getting on track.

Troy State took a 12-7 second quarter lead.

But Pennington did what leaders are supposed to do and connected for a twenty-seven yard touchdown to LaVorn Colclough with just under three minutes to play in the first half to take a 14-12 lead.

Division I-AA Troy State didn't find the scoreboard again and Pennington finished with a career high 437 yards passing and five touchdowns in a 42-12 Marshall victory.

Next came Marshall's biggest early-season test at Columbia, South Carolina, on September 19 against South Carolina of the Southeastern Conference. The crowd of 78,717 at Williams-Brice Stadium was the largest a Marshall University football team had ever played in front of in a history that dated back to 1895.

If the size of the crowd was perceived as a big advantage for the home team—particularly when Pennington called time out on the first play—such thoughts were quickly dismissed in the wake of the Herd's ensuing drive that culminated when Pennington connected with Lanier Washington on a thirteen-yard touchdown strike.

Marshall did not score again in the first half, but the defense limited the Gamecocks to one touchdown in three trips inside the Herd's ten and South Carolina led 10-7 at the half instead of 21-7.

Maurice Hines intercepted a pass by South Carolina quarterback Anthony Wright on the first play of the second half to give the Herd the ball at the Gamecocks' twenty-three. Three plays later Pennington threw to Brad Hammon for a touchdown from sixteen yards out to give the Herd a 14-10 lead.

The next time Marshall had the football they rode Chapman's back to the end zone. He gained fifty yards on the drive including a unique seven-yard touchdown run that left the South Carolina defense wondering what had happened.

Pennington took the snap from center before reaching through his legs to hand Chapman the football. Pennington then went right feigning a rollout pass play while the rest of the offense briefly remained stationary. Chapman took off to the left and went into the end zone without having so much as a hand put on him. That gave the Herd a 21-10 lead.

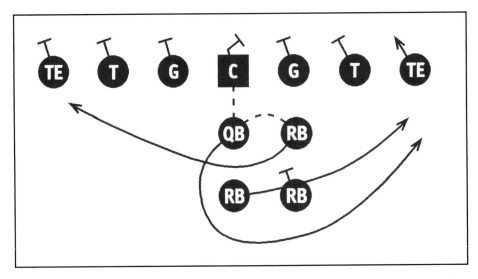

**FUMBLEROOSKIE —** Pruett was audacious enough to try a rarely-used trick play against South Carolina. It worked. *Diagrammed by Tim Stephens.*

"When you play in those big ballgames, usually you struggle to run the ball," Pruett said. "Especially down on the goal line. We got down there and we called that play just to see if it would work. I can visualize it just as it was, everybody stood still and then one of their players came charging across the line and almost disrupted it. But Chapman went around left end for the touchdown.

"The other reason I wanted to do it, it's their home crowd and it makes them look bad. It gets them grumbling. It gets the crowd on them. If you can pull something like that off on them, the psychological effect is invaluable. It gives your team a big lift, too. You're laughing and carrying on. Gives you a lot of confidence."

South Carolina came back late in the fourth quarter to tie the score on a touchdown with the two-point conversion and a field goal to make it 21-21 with just under four minutes left on the clock.

The Gamecocks' defense held and got the ball back to start what might have been a drive for the winning points had cornerback Danny Derricott not stepped in front of a Wright pass and returned it thirty yards into field goal range. "Danny just seemed to be one of those guys who always found himself around the football," Pruett said. "He was in the wrong defense, playing the wrong coverage but he intercepted the key pass at the end of the ballgame. One of our coaches ended up giving him a box of Lucky Charms cereal because he was so lucky."

Two plays after the interception, Billy Malashevich kicked a thirty-seven yard field goal to give the Herd a 24-21 victory. Marshall's sideline emptied onto the field while an eerie silence fell over the shocked crowd at Williams-Brice Stadium, except for 3,000 MU fans in one corner chanting "WE ARE MARSHALL!" A MAC team had beaten an SEC team. This was blasphemy in the church of Southern football.

Everybody was shocked but Marshall.

Mercer told reporters afterward: "Who is South Carolina? Our winning tradition is better than theirs. They haven't won anything since Sterling Sharpe was here probably."

And Mercer made a good case since the Gamecocks had completed only three winning seasons in the '90s til then and had won just one bowl game in its 105-year history. Meanwhile, Marshall had ninety-two wins in the decade to that point.

"We didn't feel that much like we had upset them," Pruett said. "And I felt like the more times we came away with wins like we did at South Carolina and the teams from our conference put together some wins like that, the respect for Marshall and the MAC would grow. But that win was huge because it sort of kicked the season off and it was real exciting for all of us and it sort of gave us the mindset that we could go anywhere and win."

Marshall could not afford a letdown the next week when they moved back to MAC action to play Eastern Michigan at Ypsilanti, Michigan, on September 26.

In the first half Pennington threw a seven-yard touchdown pass to Lanier Washington and a thirty-three yard scoring pass to Jerrald Long before David Foye returned a blocked punt sixteen yards with 8:05 remaining in the second quarter for a 23-7 Herd lead.

"Without Randy, it had to be more of a team effort in '98," Pennington said. "But even without Randy, our receiving corps remained one of our strengths. I felt like I was making better decisions and spreading the ball around more. That gets everybody into the game more, so they enjoy playing more. I had a goal of being more consistent, which meant cutting down on interceptions. In two of our three losses during the 1997 season I had eight interceptions."

Eastern Michigan came back, scoring two touchdowns and successfully converting for two points after each to tie the score at 23.

That's when the Herd's heroes from the previous week against South Carolina took it upon themselves to mount an encore performance.

Derricott intercepted a pass with just under four minutes on the clock to give the ball back to the Herd in Eastern Michigan territory. Pennington then drove the offense thirty-eight yards in nine plays to put Malaschevich in field goal range. And like the previous week, Malaschevich hit from twenty-two yards out with seventy seconds remaining and Marshall had a 26-23 win.

Marshall hosted Miami of Ohio the following weekend on October 3 at Marshall Stadium. Of concern to the Herd was Chapman's slightly separated shoulder and Miami running back Travis Prentice. Not only was Prentice the nation's second-leading rusher, he had blistered the Herd for 203 yards and four touchdowns in the previous year's 45-21 loss to Miami.

The Red Hawks took a 7-3 lead in the first quarter before Pennington threw a sixteen-yard touchdown pass to tight end John White. And Chapman followed with a fourteen-yard touchdown run to put the Herd up 18-7.

Marshall led 21-10 at the half and knew the offense would have its hands full in the second half as the Red Hawks' defense had not surrendered any second half points during its first three games of the season.

For the third consecutive week, Derricott came up with a big play. "Lucky Charms" intercepted a pass and returned it to the Miami twenty. Pennington then connected with Nathan Poole for a sixteen-yard touchdown to put the Herd up 28-10.

Pennington looked flawless in passing for 307 yards. The only blemish on his performance came when Miami's Jay Baker returned an interception fifty-eight yards for a touchdown. But the Herd's defense held Prentice to eighty-four yards rushing, which was 100 yards below his average, while Chapman gained 112 yards on thirty-two carries en route to a 31-17 win to avenge their loss in 1997.

Marshall strong safety Larry Davis addressed why their defense was so formidable.

"We played an attacking defense built on speed," Davis said. "We went after people. We manned down and we blitzed. But we had a lot of different schemes on our defenses. We camouflaged our defenses the majority of the time. We'd show one coverage, but at the snap of the ball we'd go to another coverage."

**SECONDARY TO NONE —** The Herd relied fairly often on Danny Derricott to step up and make plays when they were needed. *Courtesy* The Huntington Herald-Dispatch.

Davis credited Pruett for preparing the defense to best stop the other team's offense.

"We got well prepared, man," Davis said. "The majority of our time was doing mental things, like preparing for the games. Studying the other players, watching game film, watching practice film. Going over their plays in practice until it was just repetitive, until we knew it like clockwork. That's why we were so good. Whatever formation the other team tried to get into we'd already studied. If a certain player came into the game, we already knew a play they were going to run.

"Coach Pruett was real big on study because you could be the best athlete, but it could save you a lot of time, energy and strength if you knew what the other team was doing."

Davis said Pruett had a way of keeping it simple.

"He'd say, 'Well guys, if you want to win, you'll do the things it takes to win. If you want to lose, you'll do the things to lose,'" Davis said. "So it was very simple. All the guys on the team wanted to win. It was like, 'If you want to win, follow me. If you want to lose, then you can pack up your stuff and go home.' He never got rah-rah, like, 'Come on you guys, we've got to get out there and win!' He was like, 'Well guys, you know what you've got to do. It's on you. I did my part as a coach, now you've got to go out there and play and pull together.' He used that simple strategy throughout his whole career. He treated us like adults."

Davis complimented Pruett's no tolerance attitude.

"He stressed being as good off the field as on the field," Davis said. "In school, with our grades, out in the community, in the public, he said it carried over."

Pruett monitored his team's classroom attendance and had the players take around sheets to be signed by professors checking their progress in the classroom.

"We wanted to know if they'd been to class and how they were doing," Pruett said. "And then we, as coaches and graduate assistants, would actually go and look in the classroom to see if they were there. If they weren't, we'd go get them up."

If they didn't go to class Pruett would make them run at 5 a.m.

Pruett also tried to curb his players' nightlife the best he could. Knowing that Thursday night was the big party night at Marshall, Pruett had all different kinds of methods to make his players think before getting into trouble.

Among them was running on Friday mornings or scrubbing the locker room floor.

"That would screw up their whole week," Pruett said. "Pretty soon they realized their big party night just wasn't worth it."

Pruett said the punitive effect had a double benefit.

"It got them to go to class, and it got the players to respect you," Pruett said. "Because it showed you cared about something other than football."

Teaching provided the backbone of Pruett's coaching and he believed there were many ways to teach people.

"We just tried to maximize our strengths, whether on the football field, in the classroom or out in the community. One way you do that is by managing your weaknesses and understanding what your weaknesses are."

Pruett credits a lot of his beliefs for coaching and managing people to his experiences as a teacher.

"One of the things that prepared me more than anything else for being a coach was being a teacher," Pruett said. "A coach is a teacher. In high school I was a wrestling coach, a golf coach and a football coach. And I'm not a very good golfer, so I learned if there's something you can't do or don't know, turn it over to somebody that can. I watched a high school wrestling coach named Billy Martin, who won like twenty-three straight state championships, had a lot of NCAA champions. My sons were wrestlers, so I sent them to his camps and watched him teach. After teaching young kids I learned to keep it simple. Keep it very fundamental and it doesn't make any difference how much the coach knows, it's what the player knows and what he's able to execute. Through this teaching process, I felt if you wanted your players to do well, you wanted to make sure they understood the concepts of the game. That they under-stood how the different parts of it fit together. So they know what someone besides them is doing. I wouldn't ask a player to do something he couldn't do. For example, I wouldn't ask a defensive back to cover Randy Moss one-on-one. It's not going to work. You can't do it. Or, if you're asking them to do something hard, tell them it's hard so if it doesn't work out, they're not crushed and they don't feel like a failure."

When teaching players a concept, Pruett had a tried and true method that worked for him.

"You walk them through it half speed, then three-quarter speed, then full speed," Pruett said. "If you go out and start running plays and they're run-ning it wrong, you're just running something wrong full speed. So it's harder to un-teach than it is to teach it. It's harder to change your golf swing than it is to teach a correct swing to begin with, you know, the correct mechanics. So that was the method we always used in practice. Everything in practice was a progression from the classroom all the way up and, before the players would come in, we would have our coaches get up and present to everybody else on the staff how they organized their meetings, what their teaching progression was, how they were going to do this, and how they were going to teach these particular techniques. We prepared ourselves to coach before we went onto the field. Preparing your coaches is as important as preparing your players. You want your players to be taught within the system that you want. In other words, I didn't want to be cloned when it came to the teaching system, but I wanted the principles of good teaching in our system."

Once on the field, Pruett let his coaches coach by observing during practices.

"That originated from the standpoint that if you're doing something at work and your boss is sitting over there and every now and then he jumps in, well, that pisses you off and takes away your creativity," Pruett said. "And it undermines you. So, we tried to get everything done prior to me going on the practice field. I felt like I had enough confidence, I wasn't worried about the players knowing who the boss was."

Another major facet of coaching college football is to make sure you have as many vine ripe players playing as possible. Leftwich personified Pruett's knack for seasoning players just the right amount of time before giving them wings to fly—and at the most critical of all the positions, quarterback.

"I think I learned that the best plan with all these quarterbacks was play them as a freshman as the backup, then red-shirt them the next year," said Pruett, explaining that getting the initial exposure helped them see things they might not have otherwise noticed the next year when they were red-shirted.

"That was the way we were doing things and it worked," Pruett said. "Because that gave them a chance to learn the system, which was fairly in-volved given what we asked our quarterbacks to do."

Pennington had been helped by Kresser and tried his best to help Leftwich.

"With Byron and me, I just tried to do my best to set the example for Byron on how to study, how to be a student of the game and how to be really cerebral and always be a step ahead of your competition and a step ahead of the defense," Pennington said. "Because that has to be my edge when I play. And that's the example I tried to set for Byron."

**TUTOR IN ACTION** — Chad Pennington used his experience to mentor a new arrival to Marshall football: Byron Leftwich. *Courtesy Marshall University; photograph by Marilyn Testerman-Haye.*

Marshall took a 5-0 record and a 3-0 mark in the MAC when they traveled to Athens, Ohio, to play Ohio on October 10, 1998.

After trailing 16-7, the Herd scored the next twenty-three points to take a 30-16 lead.

LaVorn Colclough hauled in three touchdowns from Pennington, who completed twenty-nine of forty-three passes for 329 yards to lead a hard-fought 30-23 win that Davis sealed with an interception near midfield toward the end of the game.

The Herd returned home October 17, 1998, to play Kent.

Marshall looked lethargic to start the game, missing two field goals in the first quarter and leading winless Kent just 6-0 at the half. But in the second half, Pruett turned to smash-mouth football and watched his offensive line do the job for a running attack that piled up 333 yards. Chapman had 127 yards on the ground, including two touchdowns, as the Herd took a 42-7 win to move to 7-0 on the season and 5-0 in the MAC.

If the running game was there, Pruett employed his troops to run the football, which they did the following week when Ball State visited Marshall Stadium on October 24, 1998.

Chapman ran the football twelve times for ninety-six yards, including touchdown runs of four, thirty-eight, four, and one yards. A quality running game always complements the passing game and Pennington took advantage of the team's ground success by completing thirty of thirty-five passes for 349 yards and a touchdown to lead a 42-10 victory.

Finishing undefeated began to look like a reasonable possibility for the Herd at this point of the 1998 season—even though they remained the nation's only undefeated team not to be ranked. And Pennington was having a special season having completed 170 of 266 passes for 2,010 yards and seventeen touchdowns for the season while throwing just three interceptions.

The week following the Ball State game, officials from the Downtown Athletic Club sent a letter to Marshall President Wade Gilley. According to information from the Marshall Sports Information Department, Pennington was cited in the letter as one of twelve preliminary candidates for the award. The letter went on to state:

"Since there are not nominees for the award, the Heisman committee attempts to guess the most likely contenders and invites them to be part of the live television special.

"At this early stage of the 1998 season, your player Chad Pennington is undoubtedly attracting elector attention. Therefore, it is possible that we will invite him to be present for the announcement."

The notification made it official: Marshall had a legitimate Heisman hopeful for the second time in as many years.

Pennington handled the attention in typical Pennington fashion as he told reporters: "Nothing has changed around here. I'm still the same person. I'm still the same quarterback. I'm not better than anyone else. Being recognized as a contender for the Heisman Trophy shows our team is good and shows I have good athletes surrounding me."

Feeling good about having a Heisman candidate at quarterback and their chances of completing their second undefeated season in three years, Marshall traveled to Bowling Green, Ohio, on October 31, 1998, to play Bowling Green.

But the Herd came out flat. And their first drive was a precursor for what they could expect of their fortunes for the day.

After taking the opening kickoff, Marshall drove to the Bowling Green nine, where the Falcons stopped Chapman on fourth and one to end the drive.

Meanwhile, Bowling Green quarterback Bob Niemet played beautifully, riddling the Marshall defense for 233 yards and two touchdowns through the air to lead the 34-13 upset that snapped the Herd's ten-game winning streak in the MAC.

Marshall never led in the game and managed only to tie the game at 7 when Pennington completed a ten-yard touchdown pass to Long midway through the second quarter. Bowling Green kicked a field goal before the half and the Falcons led for the remainder of the game.

"We ended up beating six teams that beat them," Pruett said. "It was just one of those days. We went up to Bowling Green and it was a cold, dreary, rainy day. We turned the ball over about five times and our kids played with no enthusiasm. Bowling Green Stadium maybe seats 25,000 and of that 25,000 there were probably 22,000 people dressed as empty seats. There wasn't anybody there. We just played bad. We were really flat. For whatever reason, Marshall had a history of playing poorly at Bowling Green. And we fulfilled the prophecy."

Marshall opened November with a chip on their shoulder and Central Michigan appeared to be the ideal whipping boy when they visited Huntington November 7, 1998.

Led by the defense, which recorded its first shutout since back-to-back blankings of Bowling Green and Ohio during the 1997 season, the Herd got back into the win column with a 28-0 victory over Central Michigan.

Chapman scored three touchdowns and Pennington threw two in a business-like effort that righted the ship.

Wofford was next in a game played in Huntington and the Division I-AA school put a scare into the Herd.

Marshall led 29-7 at the half. Chapman rushed for 161 yards and two touchdowns—to become the first Marshall player to rush for 1,000 yards in each of his first three seasons—and Pennington threw for two touchdowns and 322 yards—to become Marshall's all-time career passing leader. Even with all that the game hung in the balance when Wofford lined up for what could have been a go-ahead field goal with just over three minutes remaining in the game.

Enter "Lucky Charms."

Derricott blocked the twenty-nine yard attempt.

"Danny came off the corner to block the field goal," Pruett said. "We had about 600 yards offense in that game, but we'd try to go in for a touchdown and fumble—we just couldn't punch it in. And credit Wofford, they took advantage of everything we gave them.

"Thing about Danny, he wasn't even supposed to be rushing the kick. He was supposed to be protecting against the fake. But that's the stuff he would do. That's why he was 'Lucky Charms.'"

Derricott's block saved the Herd the embarrassment of losing to a Division I-AA school and Marshall escaped with a 29-27 win.

WITH A 10-1 RECORD, MARSHALL EARNED A SPOT in the the Mid-American Conference championship game for the second consecutive season against 7-4 Toledo, the first opportunity to play for a championship since Pruett told his team, "We play for championships."

The team received a little extra motivation from Toledo.

"They had a middle linebacker there, I forget his name," Pruett said. "He sort of challenged us and that really helped us. He said something about how he had a target and he was zeroed in on the Herd. Our guys felt like they were the intimidators, they weren't the ones who were going to be intimidated. So they rose to the occasion that night."

On December 4, 1998, Toledo and Marshall met in a rematch of the previous season's MAC championship game at Marshall Stadium with the winner earning a spot in the Motor City Bowl against Louisville.

Marshall trailed 7-6 in the second quarter when the collective heart of the Marshall faithful missed a beat after Pennington got hit by Toledo defenders and suffered a groin injury.

Leftwich, who had thrown only twelve passes during the season, came on for Pennington and threw an interception.

"Byron went in and we were going to throw the long ball—go for a touchdown," Pruett said. "But our running back went out for a pass instead of staying in and blocking like he was supposed to and Byron was hit right as he threw the ball and he was intercepted. That's what everybody remembered about Byron that season, because he really didn't play much. So everybody was worried about Byron not being a very good quarterback because they remembered that one play and it really wasn't even Byron's fault."

Pennington came back into the game sporting a severe limp, casting doubt on whether the Herd could take Toledo's best punch and remain standing.

Toledo added a field goal early in the fourth quarter to take a 10-6 lead while Marshall continued to struggle. Pennington's return behind center, however, had fired up the team.

Refusing to give in to his injury Pennington and the Herd trumped the Rockets' field goal with a sixty-one yard touchdown drive capped by a nineteen-yard touchdown pass to Poole for a 13-10 Marshall lead.

"That was a game when I just felt like I needed to be out there," Pennington said. "Our defense was playing really well and our offense just kept playing hard and pressing forward. I wanted to be a part of it."

Derricott once again chipped in when he picked up a fumble and returned the ball twenty yards for a touchdown and a 20-10 Marshall lead.

Malashevich added a field goal to push the lead to 23-10 before Toledo scored a touchdown with just over a minute to play. But Marshall recovered the ensuing onside kick then killed the clock to earn a 23-17 victory and a trip to the Motor City Bowl for their second consecutive season.

Afterward, Pruett's mantra rang through the Marshall locker room as personified when Pennington said, "We're not going there [Motor City Bowl] just to give a good showing for the MAC, we're going there to win it for Marshall and the MAC."

Marshall played for championships.

## Chapter eleven

Bob Pruett prided himself on being a teacher, but the teacher in him also understood he needed to be a student as well—there was always room to learn something new. Pruett learned a lesson in the 1997 Motor City Bowl and because of what he learned, he implemented a change.

What Pruett learned from the Motor City Bowl was that the heat would be a factor in the game. In order to prepare for the heat, Pruett created conditions inside the Turf Room in Marshall University's Facilities Building that would simulate the inside of the Silverdome.

"That was my worst experience ever," Larry Davis said. "We were in the Turf Room; they had all the heaters on, so it was about 100 degrees in there. You've got players sweating real bad, like they just came from a car wash or something

**PREPARATION** — Bob Pruett, in getting ready for a return to the Motor City Bowl, turned up the heat on his team—literally. *Courtesy Marshall University.*

*11*

CHAMPIONS

PONTIAC

with no towel. You had players falling down on the ground because of the heat. But when it came to the bowl game, the heat there wasn't anything because we were prepared. We'd gotten used to it. We did that every day for the whole week.

Giradie Mercer said the air inside the Silverdome was different and working inside at Marshall did a nice job of simulating the conditions they would be playing in during the Motor City Bowl.

"There's a different kind of air you breathe inside that dome," Mercer said. "The fact you're getting this warm air into your lungs when you're used to breathing the coldest Arctic air you can breathe. They did a really good job of translating our practice conditions to what we could look for in the game situations, so I think that definitely helped out as well. Because when you try to make that transition from the outside cold to all of a sudden playing in an atmosphere where it's about eighty degrees, and the heat is wearing on you and you're dehydrating, well, it's an awful feeling."

Had a passerby taken a look at the Marshall practices taking place indoors that week, the reaction might have been shock. Like Pruett had flipped out by the way he worked his team in such drastic conditions. A lot of coaches would not have had the support of their team for training in such conditions, but Pruett's troops bought into what their coach was trying to accomplish.

"Coach Pruett didn't really have to do a lot of selling because everybody on the team was so motivated to win," Davis said. "We understood we were the new team in the MAC and the only way we were going to get our name out there was to win a bowl game. We had to win games that were televised. That was great motivation."

The team well remembered what had happened the year before against Ole Miss.

"We understood one thing that something needed to be done to address that potential heat problem," Mercer said. "And obviously, contrary to popular belief, no one likes working out. Nobody likes working outside of their comfort zone, but it was obvious it was a pretty decent Ole Miss team that we had an opportunity to beat the year before and we let the opportunity slip through our hands. So as a team we knew we needed to address that conditioning factor in terms of the offensive and defensive lines. We knew we needed to do something and we were looking to Coach Pruett to find out what the answer was and he came up with the idea of doing some of these drills indoors and doing conditioning indoors. We knew we didn't practice like that all

**FIRST BOWL WIN—EVER —** Preparation paid dividends for Marshall, as they faced off against the University of Louisville. *Courtesy Marshall University; photograph by Brett Hall.*

year; we knew it was only a week, a week where conditioning was the focus. Because you're not only preparing for this opponent, you're preparing for the twelfth man, which is that conditioning factor and the heat factor that's going on in that dome."

At the conclusion of their conditioning regimen, Pruett told his team, "Fellas, if we get to halftime and the game is close, it's our football game."

"And whether that was true or not, our guys had experienced the other side of it," Pruett said.

In addition to having a team better physically prepared than the year before, Pruett had a team more mentally prepared.

"When we went into that game, we knew two things: we were going to be

**HOISTING THE HARDWARE** — John Grace, along with his Marshall defensive team-mates, took exception to the Cardinals' pre-game comments on their abilities. *Courtesy Marshall University; photograph by Brett Hall.*

better conditioned than we were the previous year, and we knew we were going to play more players," Mercer said. "So we went to that game not having that mindset of, 'Oh, I hope I don't wear down,' or, 'What happens if I wear down?'"

In addition to going into the game with a physical and mental advantage from their conditioning drills, Marshall got some motivational fodder from Louisville.

For starters, Louisville Coach John L. Smith made the comment: "This game might go seven hours, the first team to 49 wins." Saying the game was going to be a shootout was something the Marshall defensive players took as a slap in the face.

"Because what he was saying was their defense wasn't that good, but then, when he said it would be a shootout, he was saying our defense wasn't that good," Mercer said. "He said the game was going to be determined by who scored the most points. So our defense didn't like that at all. John Smith was a different kind of guy, so it wasn't just his comments, but some of the comments his players made. One of their players said, 'You guys are from the MAC, you guys actually think you're going to win this game?' It was the most arrogant group of guys that I had ever seen.

"They had all these little comments. At that particular time, Louisville was No. 1 in the nation in terms of scoring offense. And they were just jawing the whole time we were there and they had all these comments like, 'We'll have you guys 60-0 by halftime.'"

Louisville did know how to put points on the scoreboard. Twice they scored 63 points during the 1998 season and they put up 52 in another game. Entering the Motor City Bowl, the Cardinals were averaging 40.4 points a game.

"They were in Conference USA and we got a really strong sense of how superior they felt they were to us in their program," Pruett said. "We sort of used that to motivate our guys. And what Coach Smith said about the first team to forty-nine is going to win, well, that really got our defense going. John Grace and those guys had a lot of pride on the defense....Oh yeah, we thanked Coach Smith for that remark."

Some coaches prefer their teams to play when they are on an even keel instead of jacked up on emotion. Pruett said he didn't look for motivational fodder to use before a game.

"It's just something that if it's there, you use it," Pruett said. "You know, it

**A TIGHT GRIP** — Bob Pruett uses two hands to hang on to the Motor City Bowl trophy, the first of what would be many. *Courtesy Marshall University; photograph by Rick Haye.*

was there and we felt that even though we were still the new team on the block and still trying to establish our identity, we felt like we deserved a little more respect."

Marshall and Louisville played to a 21-21 tie at the half, with all of Marshall's touchdowns coming on Pennington strikes of twenty-nine, twenty-six, and fourteen yards.

A year earlier the Thundering Herd had no thunder when it returned to the artificial surface at the Silverdome to play the second half. Would a year make a difference for Marshall? Particularly given the preparation and conditioning the team had endured leading up to the game.

Pennington and Jerrald Long answered the question less than three minutes into the third quarter. Long grabbed a short pass and turned the catch into a fifty-yard touchdown to put the Herd up 28-21. Marshall quickly added two more touchdowns and a field goal to put away Louisville in a 48-29 victory, the first bowl victory in Marshall history.

"No doubt the heat had been a factor the year before," Pruett said. "We were ahead at the half and just came out dead in the second half. You really can't believe how hot it got down on that field. Particularly when it was not hot outside."

The two teams combined for 1,012 yards of total offense—613 by Marshall. The Thundering Herd had taken another large step toward advancing their program and their national image.

Like a mad scientist, Bob Pruett had calculated a plan for everything to come together chemistry- and talent-wise in 1999.

"By 1999 it had gotten to the point where we pretty much felt like we were going to win every time we stepped out on the field," Rogers Beckett said. "You know, there was never a doubt. You've got to give Coach Pruett the credit for that because he knew what he was doing. He had a good feel for his team. And he knew what we were capable of doing. And the way he went about doing things, the way he taught the players. It was almost like a Step Program the way he brought that team along."

Chad Pennington was the senior leader of a close-knit group of experienced Marshall football players.

**1999 —** Anticipation ran high for Bob and his players— and they did not disappoint. *Courtesy Marshall University; photograph by Marilyn Testerman-Haye.*

12

READY FOR

PERFECTION

Heading into his senior season, Pennington, who now stood six-four, 220 pounds, had passed for 10,102 yards and eighty touchdowns during his career at Marshall and was a legitimate Heisman Trophy candidate after falling short of getting invited to the 1998 Heisman ceremony.

"Our senior class knew after we won the Motor City Bowl that we had a chance to be really special in '99," Pennington said. "And we talked about it. Our senior class is really close. We always talked about it. We worked hard at it and we were fans of each other. I mean, we went out and competed against each other as hard as we could in practice, but, on game days, we were one. And that's why we became a championship undefeated football team, because we just had one mind and one focus. And everybody was focused on it and everybody enjoyed playing with each other. We knew after the '98 season that we had a chance to do something special."

The Marshall players had bought into what Pruett was selling.

"We had confidence in Coach Pruett because he displayed confidence in us," Pennington said. "The schemes that we ran offensively and defensively proved to us that Coach Pruett trusted us as players, trusted our decision-making, trusted what we did on the field. And every game, no matter if we were playing Clemson or if we were playing a Division I-AA school that we were supposed to beat, every game was approached the same. And Coach Pruett always came into the locker room on game day with a relaxed attitude and he made everybody around him, all of us as players, feel confident. And we were relaxed, but we were alert and we were focused."

Pennington was just part of why Pruett felt such confidence in the team he had built. Nineteen starters returned from the 1998 squad that had a 12-1 mark to give Marshall 101 wins during the 1990s—which led all Division I-A schools. Pruett had T-shirts printed for his team with "114" on them, a number representing the number of wins Marshall would have if it managed to mount an 11-0 season combined with wins in the MAC championship game and a bowl game.

While the Marshall passing game was the sexiest part of their team, the meat and potatoes came in the ground game led by Doug Chapman—who had accrued over 1,000 yards in each of his first three season—and a defense that finished ranked sixteenth nationally in 1998 for fewest points allowed at 17.3 points per game.

Leading the defense were tackle Giradie Mercer, who had sixteen tackles for loss and four sacks the previous season; linebacker John Grace, who had

153 tackles in 1998; and Danny Derricott, who had six interceptions and countless big plays the previous year.

"The 1998 season, as good as it was, was really the prelude for '99," Pruett said.

"Our team in 1996 was a really good team, and I think we could have done some special things with that team if we had been in Division I-A. In 1997 we were gaining confidence, you know, we didn't really know how good we could be; same thing in 1998. Then in 1999 we had all that confidence and you had the great senior leadership, like Chad, Doug Chapman, John Grace, Giradie Mercer, Rogers Beckett; they had talent and they were leaders."

If anything personified how far the Marshall football program had advanced in the three years Pruett had been on the job, it was opening up the 1999 season against Clemson at Death Valley.

Understanding that they had a special team, Marshall players, coaches and fans had the feeling that if they could knock off the Atlantic Coast Conference powerhouse in the first game of the season, running the table was a real possibility.

"We definitely had that feeling because we just knew what we had," Beckett said. "You knew what the personal weaknesses of your different teammates and different players were and the coaches did a great job of preparing us. When you have a team that wins like we did—we'd only lost four games in three years—you gain so much confidence. And that's what's really needed out there, where you believe you can overcome any obstacle that may come your way. Whether it's this down, next down, or whatever, the feeling is somebody will make the play to make a difference in the game. I think that set the tone for us. And that's the confidence. That's just what we had. We had a team full of confident players. We trusted in each other and it was a tight-knit group. You know, that's pretty much how I always saw it."

Clemson had a new coach in Tommy Bowden, legendary FSU Coach Bobby Bowden's son, who had taken Tulane to an undefeated season the previous year. Marshall appeared to be the first item on the menu for the hungry Tigers.

Pruett knew Bowden had a unique type of offense, so he and the rest of the Marshall coaches took a road trip down to Tulane to spend four days studying Tulane film from Bowden's previous season.

"It was almost like a David and Goliath game," Pruett said. "Seemed like every time Marshall left the MAC conference, the game was always projected as the small guy going up against a big guy. We saw the game as a time for us to rise to the occasion and make Marshall University recognized and known for being a good football team. It was definitely a big stepping stone for the program just to be playing Clemson."

Anticipating an 80,000-plus crowd at Death Valley, Pruett ran practices with loud speakers blaring full blast.

"We practiced that week with the music up, which was always fun because it seemed to make practice go by a lot faster," Mercer said. "That was one of the things that Coach Pruett did. He was preparing us for that situation. If we had a bunch of new guys, that would have been one of those situations where having 80,000 would be a factor. But because you had guys like Chad Pennington, Nate Poole, James Williams, John Cooper, Doug Chapman, Jason Starkey, Mike Guilliams, all those guys up front, you know the communication factor wasn't that big of a thing because those guys had played together four years. So when Chad Pennington looks over and he gives them a certain look, those guys are going to know what route to run…. It's just a matter of eye contact."

On September 4, 1999, the Marshall bus arrived at Death Valley hours before the Herd would meet the Tigers.

"I'll never forget getting off the bus before the game," Pruett said. "They had crowded a bunch of people around the bus and were yelling and screaming at our players and trying to intimidate them. And I walked by one of them and I said, 'We're going to be a lot better than you people think we are.' We didn't want to be cocky, but we wanted our players to be confident and feel like we had a chance to win every game we played."

Pennington credited Pruett for the team not being uptight in big games, such as the Clemson game.

"Because of the confidence he displayed in us we knew we could get the job done if we just believed in ourselves and just did what we were coached to do," Pennington said.

The team wasn't uptight, but Mercer called the Clemson game emotional.

"You had guys in the locker room before the game who were crying they were so anxious to get out there and show what we could do," Mercer said. "Obviously if you had read all the press clippings prior to the game, you probably would have thought we were going to play against Tommy Bowden

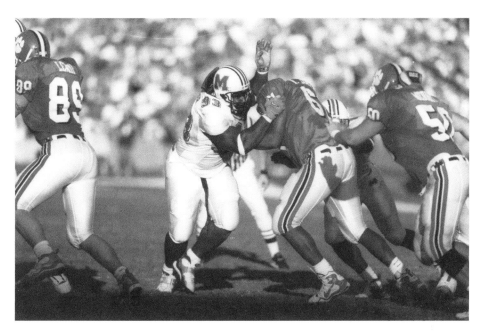

**DEATH VALLEY** — Giradie Mercer (93) in action against Clemson. *Courtesy Marshall University; photograph by Rick Haye.*

and the whole Bowden family, like they were going to play out there for their guys. His family name obviously carried a lot of weight. A lot of people still never gave us a chance. Of course, their players had no idea what they were getting into. They were thinking, 'This is a MAC team,' that sort of thing. We went in there with the mindset that we could pull that game out and that we could do some special things that year."

Chapman said the feeling in the locker room wasn't "whether we were going to win, it was how we were going to win."

"Was it going to be a tight game?" Chapman said. "Was I going to run for a hundred yards? Will Chad throw for 400 yards? Coach Pruett pretty much had everybody in that locker room believing, 'If you play up to your potential, no one can beat you today,'" Chapman said. "That's how we went, we were going into the game in front of 80,000 people. I was actually more nervous when we played Montana in the Division I-AA championship game than I was when we played Clemson. Because we were so well prepared by film work, physically, training staff, and Coach Pruett. He did a great job motivating the guys. He didn't over do it with the rah-rah, corny stuff. He downplayed it to where we didn't know where our coach's head was. He was always on an even keel with us. And as players, we wanted to win it for him because he's so emotional as a coach. He gets into it. He comes out there. He's fired up. You see a coach act like he wants to put the pads on and that gets you fired up. You want to hit somebody harder. We never had any doubts in our minds. I can speak for the offense, I didn't play defense, we never had a doubt in our minds we could move the ball and score on people."

Pruett always had a way of calming down the players right before the game according to Beckett.

"Calming them down and getting them focused," Beckett said. "And I wish I could remember verbatim what he said. But he would always say something like, 'Just imagine yourself,' you know, he's like, 'Close your eyes. Imagine yourself making the big plays.' Whether it's a touchdown or an interception. It was just the little inspirational message that he gave before we took the field. You know, he was a coach that really put trust in his players to make the right decisions on and off the field. But that's one thing, he always gave that sense of hope that things can and will be accomplished. It's just a matter of us executing and just staying together. You know, no matter what goes on during the game, there's no one losing their focus. We're staying together and we're going to come out whether we win or lose together. You know, it was just coming together like a fist. It was that type of stuff that, after a while, you hear it so many times that, you sense what he's saying. And that's what I think and reflect and remember the most about Coach Pruett."

Marshall wasn't through showing they weren't intimidated just yet.

Clemson's tradition is to run down a hill prior to the game, touching "the rock" on the way toward the playing surface—a tactic that can be intimidating to any visiting team standing on the field watching the ceremony.

Pruett had his own ideas on how to combat the grand entrance by the home team in front of the record-setting crowd of 80,250.

"I timed our coming out of the locker room pretty close to the time that they ran down the hill so we'd get more people cheering than booing," Pruett said. "And what we did was run out there just about the 40-yard line to challenge them to come down the hill. We jumped up and challenged them to come on down the hill, waved them down then went to our sideline."

Pennington and his teammates enjoyed the atmosphere.

"I mean, when you're a mid-major and you get a chance to play in front of eighty some-odd thousand and play in a loud place such as Death Valley and a place that has such history and watch Clemson run down the hill after they've rubbed Howard's Rock, the only response that we had was that our center was out on the fifty-yard line saying, "Come on!" So there was no intimidation at all," Pennington said. "We thrived in those type atmospheres, because it was a chance for us to showcase our talent, showcase how good of a team we were. We always had a chip on our shoulders because we knew that people didn't respect us as much as we thought they should."

Clemson didn't appreciate Marshall's lack of fear. They expressed their displeasure when they ran by the Herd's sideline after storming down the hill and made some obscene gestures. Clemson was assessed a fifteen-yard penalty to start the game.

Marshall seized the opportunity and drove the ball to the Clemson seven on their opening drive but came away with just a twenty-four yard field goal by Billy Malashevich.

Marshall's second possession saw the same result as their first drive as they drove the ball inside the Clemson ten before stalling out at the two and settling for a twenty-two-yard Malashevich field goal to go up 6-0.

"We weren't happy about not being able to score touchdowns on those two drives," Pruett said. "When you get chances like that you've got to get it done or it will come back to bite you."

Pennington led another drive in the first half when they reached the Clemson thirty-two before getting stopped. This time the Herd came away empty-handed when Jason Witczak missed a forty-eight yard field goal with 12:04 left in the second quarter.

Marshall's offense pushed Clemson all over the field in the first half taking 205 yards of total offense to the locker room at halftime compared to the Tigers' 105 yards. Despite the advantage, Marshall led just 6-3 at the half.

"That was a hard-fought game," Mercer said. "I think the defense went out there and played some of the best ball we'd ever played."

Marshall's missed opportunities in the first half appeared as though they might haunt them after Clemson's defense toughened up in the second half by using the safeties and linebackers to fill in the gaps left open in the Tigers' line. Random blitzes added to Clemson's improved effort in the second half.

The game turned into a physical standoff between two proud teams.

Hoping to generate some offense, Bowden sat down starting quarterback Brandon Streeter in favor of Woodrow Dantzler. When Dantzler proved ineffective, Streeter went back into the game to lead a ten-play, sixty-seven yard drive that ended when Javis Austin ran the ball in for a three-yard touchdown. That put Clemson ahead 10-6 with just over seven minutes to play..

A lot of teams would have folded at this juncture. After all, Marshall had outperformed Clemson all afternoon and then suddenly found themselves down 10-6 with time running out.

"That's when we reached out to our senior leadership," Chapman said.

Marshall got the ball at their own twenty-seven and began a drive they hoped would put them ahead. Pennington was at his best on the drive, employing all of the savvy he'd acquired during his previous three years as a starting quarterback for Marshall.

Overcoming three penalties, Pennington looked like a legitimate Heisman Trophy candidate while hitting six of six passes on the drive that featured masterful throws like the twenty-five yard pass he threw to Williams, who hauled in the ball and fell out of bounds at the Clemson twenty-one. On the eleventh play of the drive, Chapman went around left end on a sweep, getting key blocks from tackle Mike Guilliams and tight end Gregg Kellett, for a seven-yard touchdown run that put Marshall ahead 13-10 with 1:10 remaining on the clock.

"We were on the verge of getting ripped off in that game," said offensive tackle Steve Sciullo. "The referees called a bunch of penalties on the last drive. Fortunately, they actually missed one. I jumped offsides on the play Doug Chapman scored on. I was happy they didn't catch me."

But the game was hardly over. Clemson's offense, which had been stagnant most of the game, now had life. Streeter completed passes of seventeen and thirty-three yards to drive to the Herd's fifteen with ten seconds left.

Clemson brought in kicker Chris Campbell to attempt the game-tying thirty-four yard field goal. Campbell shanked the attempt and the ball sailed wide left to give Marshall a 13-10 victory.

"We went there expecting to win," Pruett said. "When you win as many games as we had, you come to expect a win even when you're supposedly the underdog against a team like Clemson."

Pruett cited the defensive effort in the game, and the effort of his coaches for the extra work they'd put in getting to know Bowden's offense.

"We really played a great defensive game because we understood the concepts of what they were trying to do," Pruett said. "They were using an up-tempo offense that not a lot of people knew much about. And we really frustrated them during the game. We understood what they were trying to do with tempo. We understood that they would come to the line and look at our defense, then make a call according to the way we lined up. What we did was muddle around and not get lined up until it was too late for them to check and change the play."

Bowden still runs an up-tempo offense at Clemson today, which Pruett said he likely refined after the Marshall game.

"I think he probably learned a lot from that game from the standpoint that he does some things now that counter that," Pruett said. "Because when you get stung a little bit you change your tempo and you try to do some different stuff. But in that particular ball game, we had them confused pretty good."

Playing Clemson first also helped Marshall.

"Playing them in the first game of the season really paid big dividends for us because we had all that extra time to prepare for them," Pruett said. "Looking at our schedule, I knew if we could beat them, we had a chance to win all our games."

Pruett couldn't resist having a little fun with reporters after the game when referencing the success his team had enjoyed in the state of South Carolina during his four years as coach of Marshall.

"I jokingly said we had beaten Wofford, Furman, South Carolina, and Clemson and I said, 'We now have the South Carolina state championship,'" Pruett said. "And I don't know how well that went over, but I told some of their fans that Wofford had been the toughest of the South Carolina teams we'd played."

Pennington appeared to be a much more viable contender for the Heisman Trophy in 1999. Just one problem: Marshall didn't have much of a budget for promoting a Heisman candidate.

"Because we didn't have any money I had to go out and raise the money," Pruett said. "We were on a shoestring budget. I started pushing Chad for the Heisman in '98 so he'd have a chance in '99. I'd say we had less than $30,000 to spend on the promotion, which isn't a lot considering what some of the other schools were spending on their players. One thing that helped us was being on television a bunch and we won.

"When you're the underdog and you win, that always draws attention. Marshall was the Cinderella story."

In the aftermath of big victories, letdowns are inevitable for any team in any sport; Liberty came next on Marshall's schedule September 11 in the home opener at Marshall Stadium with a crowd of 27,374 watching.

**COMING HOME** — After Clemson, Marshall opened its home slate against Liberty, which saw the Herd use extensive substitutions in the second half. *Courtesy Marshall University; photograph by Rick Haye.*

Liberty did not find Marshall in a letdown mode.

Pennington led the first-string offense to six touchdowns and 398 yards of total offense. Pennington accounted for 279 yards through the air while completing twenty-three of thirty-one passes for four touchdowns; Chapman rushed for sixty-eight yards on thirteen carries.

With the game in hand, Pruett turned loose the reserves.

Byron Leftwich entered the game with five minutes left in the third quarter and completed six of eight passes for two touchdowns in the Herd's 63-3 win. Pruett was pleased afterward with the way his team played and the way the reserves had played as well, noting they were the future of the program and they needed to gain some game-day experience. Leftwich ended up being red-shirted after suffering a high ankle sprain and tonsillitis.

Next up on the Marshall schedule was a visit from Bowling Green on September 18. Revenge loomed large in the minds of the senior-laden Marshall squad; Bowling Green had been the team that had served up the Herd's only defeat the previous season—and they had done it in dominant fashion.

Marshall entered the game as the No. 21 ranked team in The Associated Press media poll and No. 22 in the USA Today/ESPN coaches poll. The seventh-largest crowd in Marshall Stadium history—29,741—showed up in anticipation of the Herd exacting revenge.

And the Herd did not disappoint the home crowd. Their coach was the only one they disappointed.

Marshall put four touchdowns on the scoreboard in the first half while rolling up 258 yards of total offense, but just one touchdown on 203 yards in the second half thanks in large part to costly penalties. By game's end the Herd had been penalized nine times for 104 yards, including three personal fouls. Senior center Jason Starkey's personal foul nullified an eighteen-yard scoring pass from Pennington to Williams. Despite the negative vibes from the penalties, Marshall avenged their previous year's loss to the Falcons with a 35-16 victory.

Afterward Pruett noted that his team would not be able to achieve its season's goals if they did not fix their penchant for getting penalized. After three games the Herd had accrued thirty-two penalties for 299 yards.

Penalties aside, it was obvious to players on the team that they had evolved into a special group by the 1999 season.

"There was never a time where we felt like we were going to lose in any game," Pennington said. "We always felt like, as long as there was time on the clock, we had a chance to win. And everybody talks about our offense during that time period, but we had a stellar defense, too. Our defense was tops in the nation in a lot of categories and our offense was very explosive. We had a well-rounded football team and we complemented each other really well on the field. When the defense needed some help, our offense would always step up. When our offense was struggling, our defense would always step up with a big play. That's kind of how we played. We played off of each other, fed off of each other."

Pennington's quarterback education at Marshall was close to complete by his senior season. Pruett and company had spoon fed the leader of their team, challenging him from time to time with more pieces of the offensive puzzle, but never overloading him to where he couldn't run the offense.

"Each year, Coach Pruett and the offensive staff would give me a little bit more to handle," Pennington said. "And by my senior year, I basically called seventy percent of the plays on the line of scrimmage. By then we were doing a lot of no-huddle and I had a lot of freedom to do some things. But it started off slowly, and we just kept building and making the progression throughout my last three years at Marshall."

On offense, Marshall basically used a one-back, multiple formation scheme.

"People knew us mostly for our passing game," Pennington said. "But our running game stayed strong. We had 1,000-yard rushers every year. And if we didn't have a 1,000-yard rusher, our two backs would combine for about 1,500, so we were very strong in the running game and that's why we were also good in the passing game."

Along the way the team acquired its own personality and Pruett was smart enough to monitor that personality without hindering it.

"We were the inmates running the asylum," Mercer said with a laugh. "Coach Pruett really knew how to let that team be. When it came time to focus on the game, that team knew what to do. When it came time for the game, we had some characters out there. And we were just whacky and totally off the wall. Coach Pruett allowed us to be that way and we all appreciated that. He really didn't try to put the hammer down on us too much to where it took the fun out of it."

Chapman said he couldn't put into words how close the 1999 Marshall team had grown.

"We had chemistry," Chapman said. "Everyone was so different on that team as individuals, but everyone respected everybody's individuality. Coach Pruett helped enhance that. He would point out a guy in front of the team, like you would in a family—you've got to be able to joke with your own family, and we did that.

"We were like the two brothers who picked on each other all day long. But when somebody tried to come and fight one of us, we'd both beat the hell out of him. Like Chad and me, we'd talk trash all day, right up until game day. That was my brother and I was his brother. Coach Pruett did a great job of getting all the different characters we had together on that team, keeping us all on one page."

Larry Davis remembered what he was told when he made his recruiting visit to Marshall.

"One of the guys came up to me and said, 'Man, you don't know what you walked into, you're going to win every year you're here,'" Davis said. "I was like 'We'll have to see about that.' And his promise came through.

"My first year playing we won twelve games and I was like, 'Man, I'm glad I did come here and I'm part of something that's going to go down into history.' From that year on it was like we've got something going on."

Mercer recalled Coach Bill Wilt coming to Marshall from Western Illinois.

**LEADING BY EXAMPLE** — With outstanding senior leadership, Marshall was unstoppable with Chad Pennington at the helm. *Courtesy Marshall University*.

"He'd never been around a team like our team in '99," Mercer said. "He'd be like, 'You guys have got to quit joking around, you've got to quit being silly, We're going to get our butts handed to us.' We'd be like totally dying when he started on us that way. We would sing on the way to every game on the bus going to the games. We were always loud, telling all these crazy jokes. We had a team full of guys who were crazy and fun. But once we got off that bus and started getting ourselves ready for the game, it was like a light switch got turned on and we were ready."

Mercer found it amusing how Marshall fans and the media perceived Pruett as a guy who jumped on his team at halftime when they had played poorly in the first half.

"Fact of the matter was, Coach Pruett really didn't say a whole lot at all," Mercer said. "He did one of the best jobs of letting the coaches coach. And he would allow those guys to go make their adjustments. At halftime players would be conversing with other players like, 'What are you getting on this or that?' And we would just make our adjustments instead of wasting time for us getting out butts chewed out."

Marshall, now holding a No. 21 ranking, shored up their game on both sides of the ball the week after the Bowling Green game to play their most complete game of the season against Temple in front of a crowd of 30,194, the sixth-largest crowd to watch a game at Marshall Stadium.

Due to a sore thigh muscle from the Bowling Green game, Pennington had practiced just once during the week, but he showed no signs of rust while throwing for 406 yards—the fourth 400-yard game of his career—and three touchdowns en route to a 34-0 win in Huntington, the team's twenty-seventh consecutive home win.

Nate Poole thrived against the Owls, establishing career highs in catches with ten and receiving yards with 179.

Marshall's defense looked every bit as intimidating as their offense, forcing nine Owls punts while allowing just 185 yards of total offense; Marshall gained 593 yards of total offense.

AROUND THE COUNTRY THAT DAY losses by Arkansas, UCLA, and Wisconsin—all teams ranked higher than Marshall—orchestrated the Herd's jump to No. 17 in both The Associated Press media poll and the USA Today/ESPN coaches poll.

Pennington said talk about the polls rarely spilled from the lips of his teammates.

"There really wasn't any talking about the rankings in our locker room," Pennington said. "Maybe when the rankings came out on a Monday you'd hear the news, but that was about it. We knew that being from a small school in a small conference that we'd only get one chance at a Top 25 ranking. One loss and we were out of there. Our respect lasted only as long as we were winning. So we tuned out the rankings and did our talking in our pads."

However, Pruett's squad knew where they wanted to be at the end of the season. A Top 10 finish would be a tangible indication that Marshall had broken into college football's upper echelon.

"All of our players knew it was out there," Pruett said. "Our seniors had done some special things so they knew it was out there. They believed they could get there. They believed the sky was the limit."

Wearing their improved ranking, Marshall had a MAC showdown awaiting them in Oxford, Ohio, home of Miami of Ohio.

In addition to pitting arguably the best two teams in the MAC against one another—with the winner likely sealing up the East division with a victory, the game featured an added twist. Never, in the history of the MAC, had two Heisman Trophy candidates faced off in a MAC contest—Pennington for Marshall and Miami running back Travis Prentice.

Since Marshall had joined the MAC they had split their two games against Miami, each of them winning at home, but the rivalry dated back to when Marshall originally played in the MAC, so there was no love lost between the two schools when they met. Even after they left the MAC and continued to play there were some memorable games. Marshall fans able to recall the 1970s, well remembered the 1971 game in Oxford, which came a year after the plane crash. In that game the Redskins were attempting to increase their 66-6 lead when time ran out. Five years later the Herd upset Miami 21-16 at Fairfield Stadium, which is remembered as one of the Herd's better victories during the 1970s.

Marshall was motivated to avoid the hiccup during the 1999 season like they had at Oxford in 1997 and like they had against Bowling Green in 1998.

"We went into that game remembering what had happened two years earlier when we played at their place," Pennington said. "We knew it was a tough place to play and that we would have to play our best game to get away from there with a win."

**FIELD DAY IN OXFORD —** By manhandling the Miami (Ohio) Redhawks, Marshall put to rest the bad taste from the 1971 game between the schools. *Courtesy Marshall University; photograph by Rick Haye.*

If that wasn't enough motivation for Marshall, Miami's new head coach, Terry Hoeppner, had served up some bulletin board material when he was quoted in a newspaper article as saying Miami would win the MAC.

"Sure, you're going to say things to fire up your team," Mercer said. "We understood that. Still, it was a pretty good motivating force for us."

Miami had lost at West Virginia at the start of the season but had looked formidable thereafter, particularly Prentice, who entered the Marshall game with over 500 yards and eight touchdowns in four games.

All signs pointed to a highly competitive contest, but Marshall dominated from the opening kickoff and stormed to a 32-0 lead over their rival before surrendering two late touchdowns.

Pennington threw for 294 yards and three touchdowns, moving his numbers for the season to 1,569 yards and fourteen touchdowns. On the other side of the ball, Marshall's defense stuffed Prentice, holding him to eighteen yards on thirteen carries in the first half. Prentice finished with 131 yards on the day after gaining eighty-three in the fourth quarter once the game's outcome had been decided.

Derricott, who had played all season with a cast on his arm, did not wear the cast against Miami and intercepted two passes.

Derricott had a way of tickling Pruett's funny bone, which he did after the Miami game when somebody relayed a Derricott story to Pruett.

"The Miami home crowd sits directly behind the visiting team's bench," Pruett said. "And Danny intercepted a ball and they were really on him because he had this gold tooth. They rode him and rode him—they rode us. All of a sudden we punt and he turns to the crowd—Danny talked in this real high-pitched voice—and he tells them, 'Hold on, just a minute, I've got to go over there and get me a ball. I'll be right back.' Then he went out and did it. When he returned to the sideline he started yelling back at them in that high-pitched voice, 'I told you, I told you, I told you I was going to do it.'"

Marshall recorded an incredible eighteen tackles for losses with Grace leading the way with six tackles and two for losses.

"That had to be one of the most physical games we ever played while I was at Marshall," Pruett said. "Both teams were physical. There was some hitting going on out there."

Marshall's easy way with Miami might have affected a younger team differently than it did the Herd, a squad composed of nineteen seniors.

"We'd been through a lot," Mercer said. "Mostly highs, but the lows, we remembered the lows, the losses. We knew we could not let up and we knew we had to play with emotion."

Toledo from the MAC's West division followed and Marshall caught a scheduling break on this one as they had a week off before playing in a Thursday night game shown on ESPN. The nationally televised contest was the first MAC contest to be aired to the whole country since 1988.

"Those were big games for us," Pruett said. "Anytime you can showcase your program like that it helps a program like Marshall. All of a sudden people see the team that they've heard a little bit about and they're like, 'Hey, that's a good program.' For recruiting it's invaluable. They see you play well and they start thinking about playing where the Randy Mosses and the Chad Penningtons played. We wanted recognition. When somebody saw the 'M' on the side of our helmets we wanted them to know where Marshall was and

**EXCUSE ME, SIR** — Pruett politely questions the line judge regarding the specifics of a call. *Courtesy Marshall University; photographs by Rick Haye.*

to know everything about Marshall. That it's a school located in Huntington, West Virginia, and not only do they have a good football team, but it's a place where you can get a quality education."

Toledo coach Gary Pinkel didn't make the Herd's bulletin board for his comments. Heading into the contest Pinkel called Pennington an "NFL quarterback" and he called Marshall "the best team I've seen in this league this decade, maybe the best ever team" in the MAC.

Marshall carried a No. 15 ranking into the game against Toledo. The Herd, which owned the longest Division I-A home winning streak at twenty-seven games, dating back to a 1995 loss to Appalachian State, also owned the longest overall winning streak with nine, making them a 22-point favorite over the Rockets. Pennington, who continued his run for the Heisman, entered the game ranked second behind Georgia Tech's Joe Hamilton in Division I-A passing efficiency.

Chapman, who hoped to become the first player in Marshall history to gain 1,000 yards in four consecutive seasons, had just 296 yards on the season thanks to a dislocated right thumb. The senior running back had played three games with a soft cast, but had the cast removed for the Toledo game. He also made a fashion statement for the game when he dyed his hair blond.

The Herd took an early 21-3 lead but had trouble putting away the Rockets, who finished with more total yards—481 yards to 477—than the Herd. But Pennington threw for 393 yards with three touchdowns before ultimately pulling away to a 38-13 win.

Marshall had showcased its program on national television. However, there were still non-believers in the program. ESPN analyst Mike Gottfried predicted the Herd would lose when they played Western Michigan. But Western Michigan would be another day. Three games stood between Marshall and their date with Western Michigan in Kalamazoo.

Marshall traveled to Amherst, New York, to play Buffalo on a chilly, windy day. A crowd of just 13,120 showed at the 31,000-seat UB Stadium to see the home team get routed by the Thundering Herd 59-3. Pennington looked like a man playing against boys. The out-manned Bulls saw Pennington complete twenty of twenty-five passes for 339 yards and five touchdowns.

Marshall moved up to a No. 13 ranking prior to Northern Illinois' arrival at Marshall Stadium October 30, 1999. Though Pennington completed twenty-six of thirty-three passes and four touchdowns, he didn't feel sharp and likened the game afterward to the previous year's loss at Bowling Green.

Comparisons aside, Marshall took a 41-9 win to move to 8-0 and 5-0 in the MAC. The Herd suffered a casualty, too, when Chapman hyperextended his knee on the first play of the game.

Perhaps looking ahead on the calendar to their meeting with Western Michigan, No. 12 Marshall went to Kent, Ohio, November 6 and escaped with a 28-16 victory over Kent State.

"We played with no emotion in that game," Pruett said. "We played bad. Nobody was talking about Western Michigan, but I think Western Michigan was on our players' minds. We were lucky we didn't get upset. We were lucky that didn't end our run."

Despite having to escape Kent to remain undefeated, Marshall moved up one spot in the rankings, to No. 11, prior to the Western Michigan game.

On a sunny afternoon in Kalamazoo, a raucous crowd of 30,472 at Waldo Stadium greeted the Herd. The crowd drew silent with just under twelve minutes remaining in the first quarter when the Herd's defensive line powered in to put pressure on Tim Lester. Mercer nearly had the standout Broncos quarterback in his grasp, when Lester let go with a floater. Marshall linebacker Andre O'Neal picked off the pass to register the first interception of his four-year college career and give the ball to the Herd at the Broncos' thirty-two.

Pruett then called Chapman's number.

Making his first start since hyperextending his knee, Chapman ran the ball four straight times before scoring on a three-yard sweep around right end.

The Broncos blocked a field goal before Western Michigan kicker Brad Salent drilled a fifty-three yard field goal to cut the Marshall lead to 7-3. When tailback Robert Sanford ran one in from four yards out late in the second quarter, the Broncos took a 10-7 lead and Gottfried was looking prophetic.

Sanford's touchdown was the first touchdown on the ground against the Herd in thirty-three quarters and it marked the second time all season the Herd had trailed. Pruett didn't panic, offering simple advice to his offense prior to their next possession.

"I just told them, 'Let's go score,'" Pruett said.

Western Michigan's lead was fleeting. Pennington drove the team sixty-nine yards in a minute and forty seconds—capped by a one-yard Chapman touchdown—to give the Herd a 14-10 lead that they took to the locker room at halftime.

**SUNNY KALAMAZOO** — A beautiful fall day saw Chad and the Herd square off against Tim Lester and the Broncos of Western Michigan. *Courtesy Marshall University; photograph by Rick Haye.*

The Broncos felt good to be trailing by the slim margin at halftime and smelled upset. But when Marshall's defense forced Western Michigan to punt three plays into the third quarter, the afterglow from the first half dimmed for the Broncos.

"Our defense made a big stand there," Mercer said. "We took it kind of personal when they ran that touchdown in on us in the first half. The stop [at the start of the third quarter] changed the game. It changed everything about how they approached the game."

Marshall got the ball at their own forty-three and five plays later Pennington hooked up with Williams on a nineteen-yard touchdown and a 21-10 lead.

When Western Michigan got the ball back, the Herd again stopped them, this time on a Yancey Satterwhite interception at the Broncos' thirty-nine, leading to a J.R. Jenkins field goal from twenty-six yards out to push the lead to 24-10.

Feeling like they needed to make something happen, Western Michigan went for it on fourth and four at the Marshall thirty-one with almost six minutes remaining in the third quarter and once again the Herd defense stopped the Broncos.

Pennington then finished off the Broncos by leading a six-play, sixty-nine yard drive capped by a nineteen-yard touchdown pass to Lanier Washington. The clock said 3:42 remained in the third quarter, but the scoreboard, which read Marshall 31, Western Michigan 10, essentially said the game was over.

Lester threw a touchdown pass with 6:08 remaining in the game to equal the final margin before the Marshall offense ran out the clock to clinch their third consecutive MAC East title and a rematch against West champion Western Michigan in the MAC Championship Game.

Chapman finished with 108 yards on twenty-nine carries and Pennington completed twenty-seven of forty passes to eight receivers for 339 yards. Pruett was most complimentary about the play of his offensive and defensive lines noting both had controlled the line of scrimmage.

THE DAY AFTER RUNNING THEIR RECORD to 10-0 for the season, Marshall's football team joined others from the University and Huntington to gather for the annual ceremony at the Memorial Student Center fountain to commemorate the seventy-five Marshall football players, coaches, fans and crew members who perished when the Southern Airways DC-9 jet crashed into a hillside, producing the worst aviation disaster in American sports history.

A thirteen-foot high Memorial Fountain was built in 1972. Seventy-five prongs on the fountain represent the exact number of players, coaches and Marshall supporters who died in the crash. Every year a ceremony is held on November 14 to commemorate the anniversary of the tragedy, at which time the water in the fountain is turned off for the winter and not turned on again until the start of the next school year.

At no time in the history of the ceremony did the event feel more uplifting and triumphant than in 1999. The loss of loved ones still was mourned, but like the phoenix, the program had risen from the ashes to glory.

Pruett was among the speakers addressing the large crowd telling those who lost loved ones that nobody could ever comprehend their sadness and loss from that fateful day. But he added that he knew the victims were looking down and smiling about the way Marshall University picked itself up from the tragedy and built itself into the program it had become.

**BATTLE FOR THE BELL** — Bob and longtime friend Jim Grobe, then coach of the Ohio Bobcats, meet in the middle at the historic Lowe Hotel in Point Pleasant, West Virginia. *Courtesy The Huntington Herald-Dispatch.*

"I know they're saying, 'Way to go, Chad! Way to go Mike! Way to go John! Way to go Doug! Way to go Starkey! Way to go Giradie! Way to go Rogers! Way to go you seniors! We're proud of you.'" Pruett told the crowd. "From the ashes of the plane crash to where we are today is a miracle."

Toward the end of the ceremony, Pruett, Pennington and Beckett unveiled a new plaque at the foot of the fountain that described the accident and listed the names of the victims. A touching rendition of "Amazing Grace" sung by Marshall defensive end Bobby Addison followed when the water was shut off.

Pennington didn't understand the significance of the ceremony when he first arrived at Marshall.

"But after awhile I understood," Pennington said. "And every time we went out on the field, we weren't playing for just ourselves. We were doing it for the community and for all of those who died on the plane."

Marshall finished off its regular season at home against Ohio in the annual "Battle for the Bell."

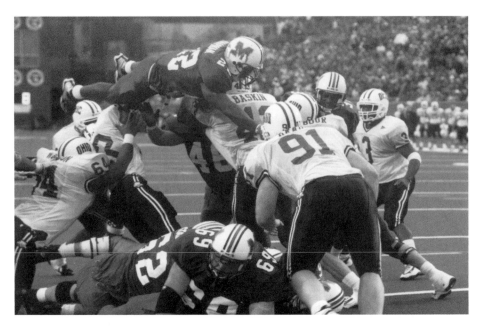

**DREARY DAY** — A lethargic Herd took its time in putting away the Ohio Bobcats on a cold, rainy day in Huntington. *Courtesy Marshall University; photograph by Rick Haye.*

Pruett signed a new seven-year contract during the week leading up to the game that guaranteed him a job as the Marshall coach through 2007.

A Marshall Stadium crowd of 26,053 braved wet weather to watch the 11:30 a.m. kickoff on November 26, 1999.

Whether it was the early-morning start or a letdown after the Western Michigan game, Marshall looked lethargic at the start when Ohio held a 3-0 lead in the second quarter. The Herd finally woke up when Pennington threw a twenty-nine yard touchdown to David Foye. Then he led the team on a seventeen-play, eighty-three yard drive capped by Chapman's one-yard dive for a 13-3 lead.

The Bobcats entered the game averaging a conference-leading 277.6 yards rushing per game. Marshall's defense stuffed the run, holding Ohio to 112 yards rushing and allowed just 106 yards passing en route to a regular-season ending 34-3 win.

Pennington, who had been invited by the Downtown Athletic Club to attend the Heisman ceremony December 11, finished off the regular season with a convincing performance by completing twenty-five of thirty-seven passes for 378 yards and three touchdowns. Before attending the Heisman ceremony, Pennington and the Herd had a date with Western Michigan December 3 in Huntington when Marshall Stadium hosted the MAC Championship game; a national television audience would be tuned in to watch the contest on ESPN2 with the winner advancing to the Motor City Bowl to play Brigham Young.

"We knew it was hard to beat a team twice in the same season," Chapman said. "And we knew they would have revenge on their mind and that it wasn't going to be an easy game."

Marshall expected a tough game, and they got what they bargained for and more.

"In the first half Western Michigan did a great job," Mercer said. "They were a team that spread it out lot and threw the football. That's what they did when we played them a few weeks earlier. In the MAC Championship game they had changed their complete package. They went with two tight ends, a fullback and a short yardage attack in that game. Something we hadn't practiced for."

And Western Michigan built a 20-0 halftime lead, shocking the crowd of 28,069 at Marshall Stadium.

"We beat Western Michigan at Kalamazoo pretty good," Pruett said. "And then we got there at Marshall and we just made a lot of mistakes and didn't play very well in the first half. So we got our players' attention at halftime and came back the second half and really had a big rally and played extremely well."

Mercer recalled what transpired at halftime.

"People thought Coach Pruett must have gone in there and laid us out," Mercer said. "Coach Pruett didn't do that at all. He had more of a business-like approach. He was like, 'Hey guys, we're not that far off. Hey, defense, we'll get lined up, we'll get it right. And offense, we're going to have to score every drive of the second half.' He said that then everybody got with their coaches and made the adjustments that needed to be made."

Chapman remembered Pruett's reaction differently.

"I'll never forget, Coach Pruett, we went into halftime and he pretty much cussed us out," Chapman said. "And he wasn't cussing us out because of what we'd done. He said, 'How can you guys come in here knowing that you didn't do anything that you are capable of doing?' He said, 'If you guys were playing your butts off and they were whopping us, that's different. But not one of you guys on either side of the ball has done what I've seen you do all year.' And when he said it, nobody put down their head. Everybody looked at each other like, 'You know what, he's absolutely right.'

"If you watched the first half and the second half of that game you saw an entirely different team. He didn't have to fuss at certain guys. He just had to say certain things. He wasn't one of those coaches who had to yell and grab facemasks.

"We all were like one big family. Pruett was like the dad. And when Dad wasn't happy we had to do whatever it took to get Dad happy again. So when we went into that locker room at halftime we looked at ourselves and did a self-check, a self-evaluation. No one played well in the first half. We admitted it. I asked the defense, 'What are you going to do in the second half?' They said, 'We're going to stop 'em.' They said, 'What are you going to do?' And we said, 'We're going to score some points.'"

Pruett and his staff believed a comeback was entirely possible.

"I thought we could come back from the standpoint of us doing a combination of things," Pruett said. "Getting after them at halftime and doing some business adjustments. We needed to adjust and get after them a little bit. Just because they were a little different on offense, it doesn't keep you from scoring."

Obviously Pruett had concerns, too.

"They were playing good on defense and we weren't," Pruett said. "We weren't playing. And they had a good team with some good players and they had a good game plan. We knew we had to win the game on defense because we were down 20-0. So if we don't play great defense, I don't think we can score enough points to win."

But things got worse before they got better.

Western Michigan began the third quarter where they'd left off in the first half with a fourteen-play drive that took over six minutes off the clock and culminated with a thirty-six yard field goal to go up 23-0.

Marshall finally got busy on its first drive of the third quarter that saw Pennington cap a five-play, seventy-three yard drive with a thirty-eight yard touchdown pass to Nate Poole. The defense forced a punt and the Herd's offense took the ball up the field again before Chapman took off on a twenty-four yard touchdown jaunt with just over three minutes remaining in the third quarter.

Once again, the Herd defense rose to the occasion with Maurice Hines making an interception at the Marshall forty-eight and returning it to the

**CHEERING SECTION** — Maurice Hines and Marshall mascot Marco are pumped up for the big rematch against Western Michigan. *Courtesy Marshall University.*

Western Michigan seventeen. Pennington followed with his second touchdown pass of the game; this time he went to James Williams for the score that cut the Broncos' lead to 23-20.

Marshall continued to dominate both sides of the ball and took the lead at 27-23 on a two-yard touchdown run by Chapman with 12:36 remaining. Despite their prolonged slumber through most of the second half, Western Michigan responded to Marshall by going up the field and scoring on a four-yard touchdown with 7:20 left to take a 30-27 lead.

"I'll never forget, we came back and we actually went ahead, and then they came back," Pruett said. "We relaxed a little bit and they came back and scored. Then we had to go down on the last drive and score if we were going to win."

Marshall's magical season was on the line when they got the ball back at their own twenty-five with just over three minutes remaining, setting up a vintage slice of Chad Pennington and a lot of drama.

Pennington got sacked for a seven-yard loss on the first play before finding Poole for a twelve-yard gain. On third down the call was for a shovel pass to Chapman, a play that had been successful throughout the game; Chapman had gained forty-nine yards on three shovel passes. This time it didn't work.

Marshall faced a fourth-and-six from their own twenty-nine and had no choice, they had to go for it. The clock read 1:10, if the Herd did not get the first down, the game would be over and Western Michigan would be advancing to the Motor City Bowl.

Pennington and his teammates would have none of it, gunning a nine-yard completion to Williams to give the Herd a first down at the thirty-nine.

Pennington scrambled on the next play, finding the left sideline for a thirty-three yard gain before getting an additional fifteen yards added when Western Michigan was called for a late hit. That put the ball at the Broncos' fourteen with fifty-one ticks remaining on the clock.

Chapman runs of three and five yards moved the ball to the six before Pennington hit Williams at the one. Pennington stopped the clock with fifteen seconds remaining by spiking the football. He then tried to sneak the ball in but went nowhere. Marshall called their last timeout with seven seconds remaining.

"We're third and goal from the one-yard line so we called time out," Pruett said. "We told Chad, 'We're going to run a play-action pass where you fake the ball off a power play off tackle with the fullback leaking to the flat and the tight end out in the flat. And if it's covered, just throw the ball away, don't take a sack.' If he got sacked the game was over. If you run the ball and don't score, the game's over. We had six seconds, so if he rolls out and nothing is there, he could throw the ball away and we'd still have a second or two to kick a field goal and send the game into overtime. We were rolling the dice. But Chad was so smart, you felt like he could do it."

Pennington ran back to the huddle and called the play. If the play didn't work, all of the ashes to glory would be nice talk, but it would not have carried the same weight. Marshall Stadium had one heart beat and it was beating faster every second that passed while waiting for the Herd to break the huddle.

Western Michigan coach Gary Darnell sized up the Herd's physical advantage and figured Marshall would call a run. On the average, the Herd's line outweighed the Broncos' by sixty pounds per man.

**DEFINING MOMENT** — The final drive of the 1999 MAC Championship stands as the most memorable in Marshall football history. *Courtesy Marshall University; photograph by Rick Haye.*

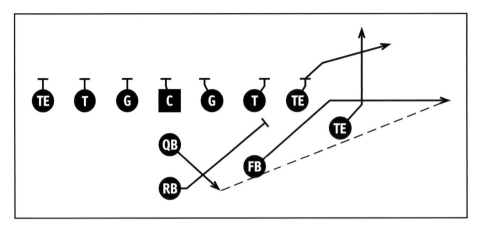

**WOLF —** Against Western Michigan in the 1999 MAC Championship, a pass play disguised as a run decided the game. *Diagrammed by Tim Stephens.*

Pennington took the snap then rolled right and spotted Eric Pinkerton, a converted linebacker and first-baseman on the Herd baseball team who Pruett had enlisted as a blocker for short-yardage situations. He was standing alone in the end zone.

Pennington threw the ball to Pinkerton, who hauled in the second career reception of his college career and his first touchdown; for Pennington the touchdown pass was the 100th of his college career.

Grace intercepted a pass on the game's final play to seal the Herd's unbelievable 34-30 win—the team's sixteenth consecutive victory.

"In our minds we just knew we would come back and win the game," Pennington said. "That's the kind of mindset that team had. Great championship teams find a way to win. Doesn't matter if it comes ugly—a win is a win."

Afterward, Pruett took time to compliment his quarterback—as well as doing a little Heisman lobbying.

"If that's not a Heisman candidate, I don't know what is," Pruett told *The Huntington Herald-Dispatch*. "That's what Heisman candidates do. We were behind at Clemson in our first game and he brought us back. We were behind tonight in our last game and he brought us back."

Fans stormed the field, tearing down the goal posts to celebrate the Thundering Herd's twelfth victory on the season against no defeats and the team's third consecutive MAC championship as well as their third consecutive trip to the Motor City Bowl.

**COMING DOWN —** Bob begins to relax during his postgame interview. *Courtesy Marshall University; photograph by Marilyn Testerman-Haye.*

**HATS OFF —** A jubilant Chad Pennington accepts a Motor City Bowl cap from Coach Pruett. *Courtesy Marshall University; photograph by Marilyn Testerman-Haye.*

**FOLLOWING PAGES —** *Courtesy Marshall University; photograph by Marilyn Testerman-Haye.*

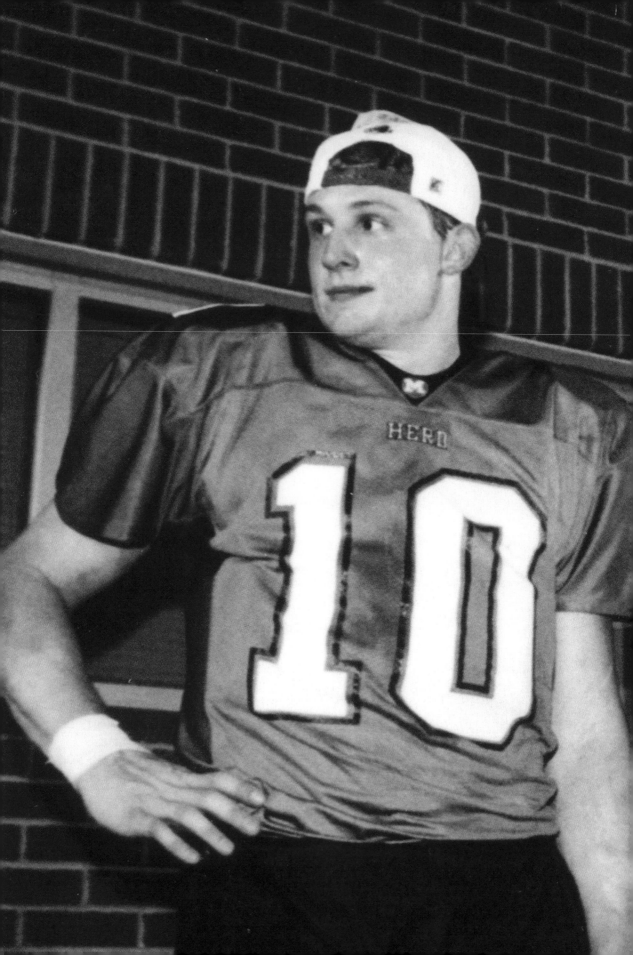

## *Chapter thirteen*

Having gone through the regular season and Mid-American Championship Game undefeated the Marshall faithful were experiencing the ultimate high while their beloved Thundering Herd prepared to meet Brigham Young in the Motor City Bowl. Added joy came in Chad Pennington's consideration for the Heisman, giving the program its second player to be invited to the prestigious Heisman ceremony.

Typical of life, just when everything seems to be rolling along something comes along to upset the calm.

Bob Pruett had enjoyed an incredible four years at Marshall, losing just four games. Success draws attention and Pruett had become a hot commodity. Pruett got the call on a Sunday afternoon while he prepared to go to a late afternoon "get together" at a friend's house. He answered the telephone to

**NOT DONE YET** — Pruett's flirtation with the University of Houston was another contributor to emotions surrounding the Marshall football program. *Courtesy Marshall University; photograph by Marilyn Testerman-Haye.*

*13*

# HEISMAN, HOUST

, & UNDEFEATED

find Houston athletic director Chet Gladchuck on the other end of the line. Two weeks prior to the call the Cougars had fired their head football coach, Kim Helton. Now they were looking for his replacement, prompting them to ask Pruett if he was interested in the position.

"I told him that I wasn't really particularly interested and he started throwing some staggering figures at me money-wise," Pruett said. "So I said, 'Well, let me think about it.' And I asked him to call me back later that night. Then Elsie and I went on to the party and I thought about it. Here at Marshall, we had just agreed to some things in the contract earlier in the season and then they were telling me they weren't going to be able to fund them, so that sort of ticked me off a little bit. There were some things, like we had a deferred compensation plan and they were going to put some money in and help pay off my home, stuff like that. Even though they had agreed to do it, they were having trouble funding it or didn't have anybody working on funding it at that time. There wasn't much progress being made and this is something that had been going on for two or three years. Well, it just got my attention. I've always been someone who believed that you say what you do and you do what you say. But really, at that time we weren't looking to move."

Gladchuck called back and Pruett was invited to visit the campus and talk about the position.

"And I told them I couldn't make the trip because I had a plane to catch for New York," Pruett said.

Pruett's schedule for the week revolved around awards that were being bestowed upon Pennington. Monday evening was a National Football Foundation Hall of Fame dinner where Pennington was to receive an academic award. Pruett had to be in Orlando where Pennington was a finalist for the Davey O'Brien Award, honoring the nation's best quarterback. And, finally, Pruett had to be back in New York over the weekend for the Heisman Trophy festivities.

"So I had a pretty full week and I told them I wanted to think about it," Pruett said.

Houston wouldn't take no for an answer.

"They called and they said they could get my plane ticket changed to where we flew to Houston Monday morning and they could have me back up in New York by Monday night if I'd just come down there and meet the president and look around a little bit and talk to them," Pruett said.

Pruett and Elsie flew to Houston and visited for approximately six hours.

"And they offered me the job," Pruett said. "I met the president and sort of toured the facilities, and they made a very lucrative offer. And I told them I'd think about it. So they agreed to meet me in Orlando Thursday night."

Pruett and Elsie thought about the job during the week while Gladchuck continued to call.

"It was a big decision, so I talked to some people about it," Pruett said. "And [Gladchuck] came down to Orlando Thursday night and made me a really nice offer. I mean, they were going to purchase a very expensive home for us and they were going to give me a good-sized signing bonus. When you added all of it up, it came down to about a $3,000 a day raise. So you can do the math on what the deal was worth."

Pruett told Gladchuck everything about the deal looked good, but he didn't want to do anything until after the weekend.

"I wanted that weekend to be Chad's and Marshall University's and not mine or anything like that," Pruett said. "And we would sort of put it on hold until after that event. But I told him it really looked good and we were leaning toward coming."

Jim and Verna Kaye Gibson, friends of the Pruetts and Marshall boosters, were invited by the Pruetts to attend the ceremony in Orlando and drove up north from their second home in Sarasota to do so.

"We told Bob and Elsie, if they had time, we'd go out to dinner," Jim Gibson said. "Little did we know what that dinner was going to be like."

When they drove into the parking lot of the hotel where Pruett was staying, Gladchuck was saying goodbye to Pruett.

"Verna Kaye said she wanted to yell, 'We are the sons of Marshall,' out the door," Jim said. "And I said, 'We've got to be quiet here, just let him get out of the parking lot.'"

Shortly thereafter Gibson, Tim Haymaker and others began to work behind the scenes to try and get Pruett to stay at Marshall.

"Bob and Elsie were nervous wrecks, I don't think I'd ever seen either one of them that nervous," Gibson said. "Because a financial opportunity had just been dropped in their laps of a magnitude I don't think either one of them ever thought would come to them. And they were having to think about leaving what they were comfortable with the most: of all, their state and their university."

The Pruetts and Gibsons went to the awards ceremony where Pennington lost out to Georgia Tech's Joe Hamilton for the Davey O'Brien Award. The couples then went to dinner at a Morton's in Orlando.

"We talked about the opportunity, we talked about what could be done at Marshall," Gibson said. "And at that time we had been working on getting his million dollar endowment and taking care of it. But Marshall had never had that kind of success. We'd had good seasons and we'd had good coaches, but now that we had success we had a little thing called notoriety, which we'd never had before and we were just getting to where we could handle that sort of thing. So raising money of this magnitude is not an easy thing to do around here. So we knew we only had a short time frame."

After dinner on their drive back to Sarasota, the Gibsons called Haymaker to fill him in on the news.

"It was probably about 1 a.m. Friday morning when we called Tim on our way back to Sarasota," Gibson said. "Verna had the cell phone and I was driving. We were extremely afraid that we were going to lose him. The amount of money he was talking about we knew we couldn't match. But he wasn't asking us to. He never did ask us to match that money. He wanted us to do A) what we promised to do. And B) what he'd asked us to do."

Pennington and his father visited Pruett's room late in the night.

"And, of course, Chad didn't want me to go," Pruett said. "But Chad's a very mature kid, or man for his age; he understood things. But we stayed up until about 1:30 or 2 o'clock."

Pennington tried to be convincing.

"I can remember sitting in his hotel room talking to him about it and what to do," Pennington said. "I was giving my two cents and his wife, Elsie, was there and we were all just talking right then and there about how much love he had for the university, and the passion that he had for our football program."

Before Pruett went to bed that night he was receiving calls about his taking the Houston job. The Associated Press moved a story in which they interviewed Pruett that night and Pruett had told them he had not talked to the Marshall administration, his football team, or his coaches and would not address the rumors of his taking the Houston job until after the Heisman Trophy ceremony that Saturday.

Houston's KRIV-TV went on the air with the story Pruett would be hired while *The Charleston Daily Mail* ran a story quoting unidentified sources that Houston would be paying Pruett a base salary of $650,000 per year, with incentives taking the deal to $1 million annually over six seasons. In addition, Houston would buy Pruett a house and two cars as well as paying off a $350,000 buyout clause in Pruett's Marshall contract.

Pruett wasn't happy with the way the story moved.

Gladchuck "was really a nice guy and was going to do a lot of things for me," Pruett said. "And I think after he left that night, he must have called some of his boosters or something, because the next day it was in the paper that I was going to Houston—and we hadn't signed anything. We had just tentatively talked about it and I was thinking about it. The next day, everything broke loose."

Haymaker, a real estate developer in Lexington, Kentucky, called Pruett and was told that their talks had gone far enough for Houston to make him a serious offer. Haymaker told Pruett to give him a chance to raise some money.

"I don't think you can raise that kind of money," Pruett told Haymaker. "But if you can, there's nothing I'd rather do than stay at Marshall."

Haymaker began making calls to Marshall supporters everywhere.

"It was like Grand Central Station in my office," Haymaker said. "My assistant was bringing in my cell phone, 'Well so and so's on the line from Atlanta, they need to tell you what they can do.' I'm sitting there with a legal pad scratching down 'John Doe is going to give us this. Bob Johnson's going to give us that.' So I'm starting to get some money, so I call Bobby back and I say, 'Look, I think we can pull this off.'"

Pruett told Haymaker Houston had offered him a house.

"Okay, we'll try to get your house paid for," Haymaker told him.

"We found out what his mortgage was and we're going to give him all this money and part of it's going into a deferred annuity," Haymaker said. "One of these deferred compensation packages. But we're going to get him some cash to pay off his house.

"Everybody is exuberant about the football program and how interested he is in people. So everybody wanted to help in any way they could. Calls are just flying in here. Faxes are coming in. And I get no work done for two days. Finally, I call him back and I say, You're not going to believe this, but we've done it."

Dr. Ken Wolfe, a Huntington ear, nose and throat specialist at Veterans Hospital and a close friend of Pruett, was instrumental in putting together the money to raise a $1 million annuity for the coach's retirement.

Meanwhile, Mike Perry, the interim president at Marshall, was off in meetings in St. Louis with a company where he was on the board. And the athletic director was in meetings at an athletic directors meeting. So Haymaker was flying by the seat of his pants to get something done without waiting to have the plan authorized.

Haymaker recalled:

"Bob calls and I tell him I got his coaches raises, 'I've got your contract changed—with some incentives based on attendance we've got your rollover provisions in there, got several things. We up you every time you win a bowl game and every time you win the conference. Got the cash to buy your house. Got the annuity, some of it's in pledges, but it should be there in the next three years, but I think we've got it pulled off.'"

The only thing the deal lacked was Mike Perry's approval.

"So he was OK with that," Haymaker said. "But there was a little more to the story that he hadn't told me about. Friday morning Bob calls me when I'm in the shower and I'm dripping wet and I'm talking to him and I can tell that he's nervous and I can tell something's going on but I'm not sure what it is. And he's like, 'I've got to know. Am I staying? I have to know.'"

"Listen Bobby," Haymaker said. "Let me get my shower so I can get to my office and make my calls and finalize this deal."

"Okay," Pruett said.

They hung up and three minutes later Pruett called again.

"I'm scared to death," Pruett said.

Pruett began to cry, prompting Haymaker to start crying.

"You've got to get over this," Haymaker said. "Just give me a little more time."

"I'm just nervous," Pruett said. "I don't want to hurt anybody."

Haymaker described Pruett as being "so uptight it's not funny."

Pruett then called him from the airport before flying to New York for the Heisman Trophy festivities. Haymaker told Pruett he still needed to talk to Perry before he could do anything.

Pruett then called Haymaker again while boarding the plane.

By then Haymaker had talked to Perry.

"I've got everything finalized," Haymaker told Pruett. "I have to put together a little brief about all the things we have done. But it's done. There's not going to be any backing out, there aren't any changes. We've got the money. Got the package. We've got your house paid. Everything is worked out. But I've got one last thing Bobby, as soon as you get off the airplane, call me."

Pruett did not wait until the plane landed and called Haymaker from the plane.

"I need to ask you a question," Pruett said. "Houston has presented me with a contract."

"They presented you with the written document?" Haymaker asked.

"Actually, I have told them I would take this job," Pruett said.

Because of the nature of the real estate business, Haymaker had a pretty good working knowledge of contracts.

"Have you signed it?" Haymaker asked.

"I signed it, but I haven't given it to them," said Pruett, telling Haymaker that Gladchuck was supposed to be at the airport in New York when the plane landed and he was expecting to receive the signed contract.

Haymaker told Pruett he'd get back to him after talking to several of his lawyer friends about contract law regarding offers and acceptances and deliveries of acceptances—or the things that are generally elements of a contract. One thing Pruett had going for him was he'd never told Gladchuck he accepted the contract.

After conferring with several lawyers, Haymaker talked to Pruett again while the coach was in flight to impart the legal advice he'd received.

"When you get off the plane, when you walk down the concourse, do not say hello," Haymaker told Pruett. "Don't shake hands. Don't look the guy in the eye. The first thing you say is 'I reject this contract.' And I think you're okay."

Pruett couldn't get comfortable and continued to be antsy, making more calls to Haymaker.

"Well, what do you think is going to happen?" Pruett said. "I think Gladchuck is okay. I believe he's going to be all right. You know I've gone a little bit further with this than I anticipated. And I didn't know that Marshall could match all this stuff, so what am I going to do?"

"Go in there and tell him that you're staying at Marshall," Haymaker said. "The last thing they want is a coach who's not committed."

In addition to Pruett's truly wanting to stay at Marshall, the leak had played a big part in his decision.

"That was a big factor in all that," Pruett said. "If everything had proceeded like it looked like it was going to, they were going to have a private jet in Huntington to pick me up when I returned from New York to fly me to Houston and make whatever announcement they were going to have. So I felt I had that amount of time to think about it. I wanted to just leave it the way it was until Sunday and didn't want to disrupt Chad's weekend.

"The thing that got me is that [Gladchuck] left my room on Thursday evening around 10 o'clock and at 1:00 o'clock that night I was getting calls.

You know, we hadn't even got to the next morning and I was getting calls about me taking the job at Houston. And that was one of the things we'd asked them not to do and I don't believe it was Chet's fault. I believe that he had people he had to talk to. You can't keep things like that secret, I guess. But that upset me."

After turning down the job, Pruett's response to the media was simple: "I think it's best for everybody that we leave it that Houston is a great school and a great opportunity. And I wish them well."

Two days later, Sunday December 12, Houston named Wyoming coach Dana Dimel to head up their program.

Pruett had come a long way from the summers when he spent his days spraying weeds for the railroad to be offered a contract worth millions of dollars—and then to turn it down!

"For a guy that never had any money, it was sort of a hard decision," Pruett said. "But, then again, it wasn't hard. I talked with our minister, R.F. Smith, at Fifth Avenue Baptist Church about it, prayed about it. In the end, yes, money is important, it's very important, especially if you don't have it. I know some of the things it can do, but really, basically, we didn't want to leave Huntington or West Virginia. I spent thirty-one years trying to get back to West Virginia and I didn't want to leave."

Once Marshall figured out a way to fulfill the things they already had said they were going to do, Pruett was a happy camper.

"I felt like I had made a commitment to Marshall University and to the state of West Virginia," Pruett said. "And I decided that I didn't want to do anything just for money, because if I did it just for the money, I wouldn't be able to do a good job. And I wasn't real excited about going to Houston."

Pennington said of his old coach:

"I don't know if a lot of people realize the love that Coach Pruett has for Marshall University. Houston came knocking on the door and offered him a multimillion dollar package that most coaches would not turn down. And he turned it down to stay at Marshall and to watch this program move on into the twenty-first century."

ON SATURDAY, DECEMBER 11, Wisconsin running back Ron Dayne was named the winner of the 1999 Heisman Trophy.

**HEISMAN, ACT II** — From left, Drew Brees, Joe Hamilton, Ron Dayne, Michael Vick, and Marshall's own Chad Pennington surround the 1999 Heisman Trophy. *Courtesy The Huntington Herald-Dispatch.*

Dayne had run for nineteen touchdowns and 1,834 yards—for a Big Ten school.

Joe Hamilton finished second with Virginia Tech freshman Michael Vick at third, Purdue quarterback Drew Brees came in fourth and Pennington fifth.

Dayne had 586 first-place votes and 2,042 points, Hamilton had ninety-six first-place votes and 994 points, Vick twenty-five first-place votes and 319 points, Brees had three first-place votes and 308 points, and Pennington had twenty-one first-place votes and 247 points.

"In our book, Chad was the Heisman Trophy winner," Pruett said. "I think his numbers and performance stood up against any of the other guys; he just didn't play in one of the BCS conferences. The MAC and Marshall University just didn't have the national recognition that the other schools had."

Pruett would be staying at Marshall and any distractions concerning the Heisman Trophy were finished. The only thing left on the horizon was a date with Brigham Young University in Pontiac, Michigan, at the Motor City Bowl.

"Our focus was to finish what we started," Pruett said.

Finishing what they started would mean closing out the season undefeated.

FOR PENNINGTON AND HIS MARSHALL TEAMMATES, playing in the Silverdome at the Motor City Bowl now felt like home. And rightly so since they had grown used to spending Christmas in Pontiac for the annual bowl game that they had played in the two previous seasons.

Brigham Young, which compiled an 8-3 record, brought challenges to the Thundering Herd, particularly for the defense, which had to find a way to stop Kevin Feterik, who had passed for 3,554 yards and twenty-five touchdowns during the 1999 season.

Virginia had defeated BYU and the Cougars had lost their final two Mountain West Conference games to Wyoming and Utah, but they still had earned a share of the conference's championship.

"Our senior class felt like losing that game would have been a major setback for us and the program," Pennington said. "We wanted to finish off our careers at Marshall with an undefeated season. Anything less than that would have been a disappointment and would have meant we did not accomplish the goals we set at the beginning of the season. Our senior class wanted to be Marshall's first undefeated team in Division I-A."

Once again, the Marshall coaching staff pulled out the space heaters and made practicing for the Motor City Bowl an exercise in survival. But the players handled the routine even better prior to the 1999 game after seeing how well conditioned they had been the previous year against Louisville.

Pruett held his conditioning secret close to the vest and even managed to employ a little gamesmanship prior to facing BYU. Four days before the game, Cougars coach LaVell Edwards and Pruett were talking when Edwards mentioned the temperature inside the Silverdome.

"We're chit-chatting and he tells me, 'It's a little chilly down there in the dome,'" said Pruett with a smile. "He goes on, telling me he had to wear a sweatshirt during practice and stuff like that. I said, 'It really gets cold. That's a cold place.'

"So they came out during the game, all their coaches had sweatshirts on. And about the middle of the first quarter, their sweats just got peeled off and their guys were dying. We just sort of had our way with them."

Pruett had prepared his team far more than simply by conditioning them.

"Defensively, we found a flaw in their pass protection," Pruett said. "And they're a throwing football team. We hit their quarterback so many times in the game he yelled at the offensive line in the huddle. We must have knocked the quarterback down thirty times. I think we ended up with eight sacks in the game."

**SQUARING OFF** — Brigham Young University's Cougars and quarterback Kevin Feterik, under center, fell to Marshall's running game, led by Doug Chapman. *Courtesy Marshall University.*

Though Marshall allegedly was stepping up a level in competition by playing BYU, which had been National Champions in 1984 and was a perennial bowl participant, Marshall's players didn't experience a case of the nerves. Pennington credited Pruett for being able to soothe the team.

"There are a lot of times I can remember going into big games, when we played Clemson, when we went to Western Michigan when they had a really good team and it was supposed to be the MAC game of the year, when we played BYU, people were really surprised about how relaxed we were out on the field the day," Pennington said. "Before those games we were having fun and we felt confident in what we were doing. Coach Pruett had a way of getting us into that frame of mind."

While Marshall's defense would dominate, they did allow the Cougars to march fifty-seven yards in ten plays on their second possession, which led to a field goal and a 3-0 BYU lead.

Marshall looked snakebit when Billy Malashevich missed a field goal early in second quarter—the first of three misses on the day—and shortly thereafter Jared Lee picked off a Pennington pass at the Cougars thirty. Fortunately for the Herd, Nate Poole forced Lee to fumble. Lanier Washington fell on the ball and Pennington made the Cougars pay on the next snap of the football when he found Chapman at the twenty-five and the Herd tailback headed up field. After juking a defender at the ten, Chapman angled his way into the end zone for the thirty-yard touchdown to give the Herd a 7-3 lead with just over eight minutes left in the half.

Marshall couldn't get anything going and clung to a 7-3 lead late in the third quarter when Pennington stepped to the line and read the Cougars' defense. What the Marshall signal caller saw was a BYU defense that was slanting inside, so he called Chapman's number with the hope of getting something outside.

Chapman took the handoff from Pennington and found an opening created by left tackle Mike Guilliams' block. After shaking free from a tackle, he broke toward the Marshall sideline with his teammates cheering him on. About the time Chapman reached the fifteen he began to battle cramping in his legs, but he managed to cross the goal line to complete the eighty-seven yard touchdown run that gave Marshall a 14-3 lead. The way the defense was playing it looked like a solid advantage.

Feterik could not get on track thanks to the Marshall rush and was knocked out of the game in the third quarter with a shoulder bruise after completing just six passes in eleven attempts for 125 yards.

Feterik's replacements fared no better as the Marshall defense held BYU to 204 yards of total offense, which included the telling figure of minus sixteen yards rushing.

Chapman added a one-yard touchdown dive in the fourth quarter to give the Herd a 21-3 lead, which is how the game ended. The senior running back was named the game's Most Valuable Player after chalking up three touchdowns and 133 yards on the ground.

The game marked the first time BYU had been held without a touchdown since 1974.

The magic never ran out and the Herd finished the 1999 season with a 13-0 record.

"For the seniors, that game was the exclamation point on our four-year run at Marshall University," Chapman said. "The whole season, the final game, all of it was a dream come true for the whole team."

Pruett remembered Chapman as a player who always stepped up for the Herd.

**MOST VALUABLE PLAYER** — Doug Chapman proved to be a threat in both rushing and receiving. *Courtesy Marshall University; photograph by Marilyn Testerman-Haye.*

**A LINEMAN'S DREAM** — Giradie Mercer scrambles for a loose ball. *Courtesy Marshall University; photograph by Marilyn Testerman-Haye.*

"Doug gave us a great effort the entire time he played for Marshall," Pruett said. "And it seemed like in every big ballgame we played, you could always expect Doug Chapman to be there to step up and do some great running for us."

By winning, Marshall moved to a record of 35-4 since stepping up to Division I-A and 50-4 since Pruett took over as the Herd's head coach in 1996.

When the job was done, Pennington took a moment to smell the roses.

"I'll always have great memories of all of us seniors walking off the field at the Motor City Bowl after the game," Pennington said. "We kind of all walked off together and it was really neat and it was really cool. That was a special group of players, a special team. We really had something."

Pruett carries a picture in his mind from a poignant moment following the trophy presentation.

"Suddenly it was all over and a bunch of seniors got together at the middle of the field and held hands as they walked off the field," Pruett said. "That's what a close-knit group they were. They were a real special group of players. That just was another way for them to illustrate the closeness and the bond they had with each other."

Though Marshall would have liked consideration for a higher stature than the Motor City Bowl during the bowl season, Pennington took solace in the fact the team had done all it could.

"Well, you always want a chance to prove how good you really are, but at the same time, no one can ever take away that undefeated season from us," Pennington said. "And it doesn't matter what level you're on, to go undefeated is one of the hardest things to do. And to do it in Division I-A, and in just our third year at that level and to beat some quality competition—like Clemson and BYU—we felt really good about what we were doing. So we really didn't worry about it—not getting into a better bowl." We talked about it a little bit, but at the same time, we knew we couldn't control that, so we didn't worry about it."

Marshall's senior class had done the heavy lifting for the future of the program, a future Pruett called so bright that he needed to wear shades.

"I don't care what anybody says, anybody can say whatever they want, but I feel like that team—our '99 team—we could have put that team and that '96 team against any team in the nation," Rogers Beckett said. "I'd have put that eleven—from '96 or '99—on either side of the ball, because I felt man for man, we could have matched up with anybody.

**UNDEFEATED** — Bob savors the moment. *Courtesy Marshall University; photograph by Rick Haye.*

"We finished ranked in the Top 10, that's great. That's not our decision. But we took a lot of pride in being undefeated. We had a great season. We capped our career off with an undefeated season. I had four losses my whole college career. So you can say what would've, could've or should have been, you look at it from the polls and stuff."

Beckett said the proof of how good a team Marshall really was came at the NFL combine when Beckett said Marshall had more players in attendance than Notre Dame or FSU. The following April Marshall had players selected in each of the first four rounds of the NFL draft.

On the Thundering Herd's horizon was a season opening game at Michigan State and a game at North Carolina. Schedules would follow that included trips to Virginia Tech and Georgia, while Pruett and Marshall fans continued to bang the drum for a home-and-home series with in-state rival West Virginia.

Marshall's Thundering Herd had risen from the ashes to where they reigned as the No. 10 ranked team in the country.

"There's no doubt that what happened at Marshall was a miracle," Pennington said. "To reach the heights Marshall reached from where the school was, there's no other explanation."

**OUTGOING SENIORS** — Rogers Beckett (42), Chad Pennington, and Mike Guilliams (63) walk off the field—together. *Courtesy Marshall University*.

**THE FINAL STATEMENT —** With a final ranking of 10th in the nation and an undefeated season of 13-0, the senior teammates left nothing to prove, and walked off the field and into sports history together. *Courtesy Marshall University; photograph by Rick Haye*.

Bob Pruett had spent much of his coaching career at the "have not" schools—or the places everybody wanted to schedule for homecoming games.

Marshall had been one of those schools, particularly during the 1970s in the years following the tragedy of the team plane crashing. Under Pruett, Marshall became one of the schools a coach did not want to see on his schedule.

"It's just like Kentucky refused to play us, 'We ain't playing you,' you know," Pruett said. "A lot of people believe that on any given day Marshall is going to beat you—and we did—which made it tougher to schedule some of the big-name teams. But that's what you want. That kind of respect is the reason why you're pushing your program."

Raising the bar can be a double-edged sword, as any

**PLENTY IN THE CUPBOARD** — After graduating nineteen seniors, Bob still had something left to build on. *Courtesy Marshall University.*

14

FOLLOWING U

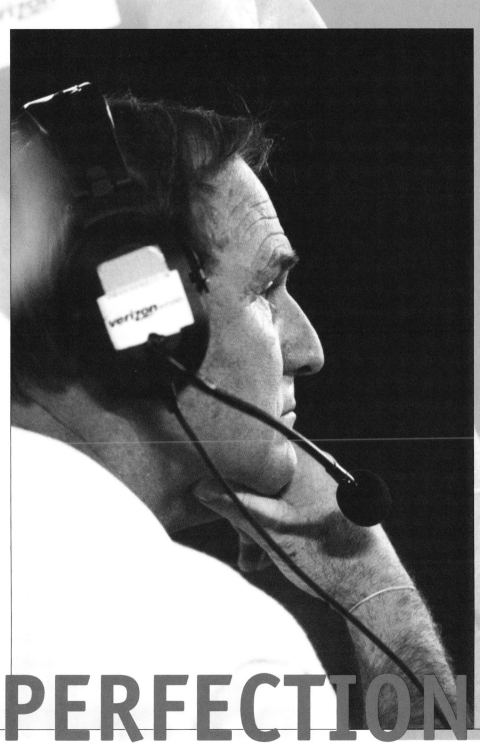

P PERFECTION

successful coach can attest. Expectations grow, which brings more pressure.

"I think that one of the things that you admire about Joe Paterno and Bobby Bowden is their longevity at one university," Pruett said. "I mean you want to create expectations, but then you have to live up to them. You see it everywhere. There's even talk now every now and then about [Tennessee] Coach [Phil] Fulmer. You know, like 'We're going to get rid of him if they don't do this or that.' He's the winningest coach right now. He's done fabulous things and it's his school, but when you raise that bar, get ready.

"Coach Spurrier did it at Florida and there's some rumblings at Florida State and Penn State and all that stuff. It's just the level of expectation that's created. Look at Ron Zook when he took over at Florida when Spurrier left. He took the Gators to bowl games three straight years, but that just didn't meet expectations. It wasn't that it was that bad, it's just perception. What people think and what people want. And you know, there's an old saying that your friends come and go—your enemies accumulate."

Pruett is well known for his wonderful sense of fun. Humor has been one of the vehicles he's used to communicate with players; the man loves a good laugh. And over the years he's been able to enjoy some good laughs provided by his players.

He shared some of the funnier ones.

One of Marshall's defensive linemen had spent the summer at ROTC Camp in Kansas.

"I asked the young man what he'd done this summer and he told me he'd been to ROTC camp," Pruett said.

"I'll bet that was real intense, wasn't it?" Pruett said.

"No sir, Coach, foxholes," the player answered believing Pruett had said "in tents."

Curtis Head, who punted for Marshall and went on to play in the Canadian Football League, walked by prompting one of Pruett's players to nudge the other and say, 'You know who that is, that's Curtis Head, he's playing overseas in Canada.'

One of Pruett's players from Chicago was driving a recruit around the Marshall campus in his car when the recruit asked the player, "Where are you from?" The player answered, "Chicago," to which the recruit said, "No you're not. If you're from Chicago, why do you have those Illinois license plates on your car?"

Another player called Pruett at home and Elsie answered the phone.

The player said his name and asked, "Is Coach there?"

"No, he's not," Elsie said.

"I've got some bills," the player said. "I need some work this weekend. I want him to get me a job."

"Well, he's not here," Elsie said. "Would you like him to call you?"

"Yes," the player said.

"What's your number?" she asked.

The player proceeded to give Elsie his jersey number.

A recruit made a trip to Marshall and he dined with Pruett at the coach's steak restaurant. When they were finished eating, Pruett asks him, "Do you want any dessert?"

"He looks down at the menu and says 'Yeah, give me that apple pie a la mode' and he says, 'and by the way, put a little ice cream on it.'"

Pruett's wit is punctuated with his own little sayings that he comes up with and that have come to be known as "Pruettisms."

Some of the more memorable Pruettisms include:

After a bad loss: "Now I know how Custer felt, except he didn't have to watch the Battle of the Little Big Horn on films the morning after he lost."

When asked what he thought of having the MAC Championship Game at Marshall Stadium: "It doesn't take Willy off the pickle boat to figure out it's an advantage."

At a press conference Pruett's cell phone rang, which he used as an opportunity to tweak West Virginia as he proceeded to act like the call came from the Mountaineers, who wanted to set up a game with Marshall: "OK, I'll call Miss Cleo to see if we can get the stars aligned."

When suggesting that West Virginia was afraid to play Marshall in Huntington: "If you're scared, get a dog."

A favorite: "Don't be pissing on my back and telling me it's raining."

Teasing with one of his players: "Son, if your IQ dropped a point, you'd be a plant."

A lot of coaches like to distance themselves from their players. Not Pruett, he enjoyed the interaction.

"I wanted to be part of them, around them," Pruett said. "I've always enjoyed kids and being around people."

A coach needs to decide what kind of coach he wants to be. Pruett decided he wanted to be involved in his players' lives and to always be accessible.

"I had a policy that my door is never shut unless I was in there talking to a player," Pruett said. "So they didn't need appointments. All they had to do was come in there and we just left it that way."

And if Pruett's phone rang, he answered it.

"I didn't need a secretary to answer the phone and make appointments for me," Pruett said. "I mean, she did make them, but it wasn't necessary to go through her, whether it was players, students, media, faculty or fans. That's just the way I wanted to do it. And with our players, I joked with them. And every now and then, they'd take a shot back and you'd just laugh. If you're going to do that, you've got to be able to take the shot back and not get mad about it. And I think in some respects, the players appreciated that."

PRUETT HAD TURNED DOWN THE HOUSTON JOB in December and was happy to be staying at Marshall. But there was just one last temptation.

Al Groh called Pruett in February of 2000 to offer his old assistant at Wake Forest a job with the New York Jets coaching the secondary.

Moving to the NFL would have been something new for Pruett. But it came just when the NCAA was looking into some things at Marshall.

"The thing about the deal was I really like Al," Pruett said. "He's one of my closest friends. And I thought the prospect of coaching in the NFL was something that I would look at.

"We thought about it and talked about it for a while. It wasn't an open-and-shut case because I was a little intrigued with coaching up there. I thought that would be a pretty nice deal. And it was good money."

The base salary for coaching the Jets' secondary exceeded Pruett's base salary at Marshall.

"I never could get past the NCAA thing," Pruett said. "I felt like I was obligated or I needed to stay there and see Marshall through it. If you want to run, you know the NCAA's coming in on you. I felt like I owed Marshall University that. I just felt like it was a necessity that I stay there and see the school even though if I go to the Jets I'm out of it completely."

Out of loyalty to Marshall Pruett called Groh back and declined the offer.

MARSHALL'S "H.E.L.P. PROGRAM" PROVED INVALUABLE for helping students matriculate.

Many times when athletes came onto the H.E.L.P. roster, it was through this program that learning disabilities were discovered. Instead of simply being happy about getting an athlete into Marshall, they would be routinely tested upon entering the school.

"We would test them for any type of learning disability because it was to their benefit if they did have some problem, some difficulty, to get them into this type of program because it gave them extra tutorial help and extra attention," Pruett said. "The program was one of the biggest reasons we had such a great graduation rate. And the biggest problem we had with our student athletes was in getting them to utilize the thing because of the stigma of special education. In other words, back in time, when kids didn't learn they called them 'special needs' students. Athletes have so much pride they don't want to be identified as a special needs student. And we couldn't get them to take the test or couldn't get them to go use it. Finally, when we were able to sit down with them and work with them and get them to utilize what the H.E.L.P. program offered, they would be a lot better off."

Pruett would try to convince his athletes to get checked out by using an analogy with an automobile.

"I'd tell them, 'It's just like if the brakes go bad on my car, I can't fix them, I need help, I need a tutor to show me how to fix them, I need help,'" Pruett said. "I'd tell them, 'This has nothing to do with you not being smart. It's part of the brake system. Your learning ability needs repair and these are the people who are going to help you repair it.'"

Pruett acknowledged that seeing his players finding their way in the classroom and graduating was very rewarding.

"I think to see guys that people would tell you would never graduate or couldn't do college work, to see them come and succeed by getting their degrees then after graduating having successful careers outside of football, I'm telling you, that just makes you feel great," Pruett said. "After all, getting an education is the point. Some of my ex-players are coaching and teaching, others are doing all sorts of things. Some are attorneys. That was just a really rewarding part of the job. I've often said one of the most gratifying experiences and probably the most rewarding, feel-good part about Marshall is the graduation rate and the success rate of our student athletes. Especially against the odds when people said they couldn't and wouldn't graduate. If you talk to our student athletes—the guys who played for me—they'll tell you that one thing I was tough on was the academics to make sure they went to class and that they were doing fine."

PRUETT AND MARSHALL UNIVERSITY WENT INTO the 2000 season having lost nineteen seniors from a 13-0 team. And while the losses looked devastating, Pruett always believed in "coaching up" the players he had to the best of their abilities. Like death and taxes, losing players to graduation is part of being a college football coach. Pruett combated the inevitable the best he could by the way he coached.

"Over the years, a lot of the games we played were probably closer than they could have been or should have been," Pruett said. "But basically what I did was play the younger guys. And that's how I developed our football team. Because a lot of times in the fourth quarter we'd have the game won. And the other team might score two touchdowns in the fourth quarter that might make it a fairly close football game—but it was worth it to play our reserves."

Pruett cited the 1996 National Championship Game as an example of always thinking ahead.

"A lot of the guys on the '99 team played in the 1996 National Championship game and they felt like they were a part of it all because they got into the game," Pruett said. "They got into the game and they played and it got them excited about working hard in the off-season. You don't really ever get any better not playing. You know, some people say that they get better. But you really get better when you play.

"Because you have a better energy level, you concentrate more. In other words, everything's just at a higher standard. And that's the thing that we did the whole time I was there. I played younger people all the time. You know, maybe some of our stats would have been better if I hadn't done that, but our won-loss record wouldn't have been any different."

Integral to whatever success the 2000 team would find would be the work of Byron Leftwich, who was left with the heady task of replacing the Golden Child, Chad Pennington.

Not only had Pennington been a standout on the football field, he had also been a star student in the classroom and he constantly was out in the community doing the types of things people dream their football heroes will do. In short, Pennington had been the All-American boy.

"You know, going into that 2000 season, I was like, man, Chad has helped me, Chad did all he could do to help me be successful," Leftwich said. "And that's how I was thinking. I was like, 'Now it's my turn.' I was excited about the whole situation, because I was going to get a chance to start. You know, the first year at Marshall, that was the first time I had ever played in anything and wasn't a starter.

"I don't care what it was, you know. So it was brand new to me. I was happy that I was getting an opportunity to go out there and play. But at the same time, I had a lot of friends on the 1999 team. Guys I was cool with like Giradie Mercer. Guys I was pretty tight with in addition to Chad himself. When Chad left, I just looked at it as an opportunity to go out there and do what I knew I could do. I knew it was going to be tough, because I was coming in after a guy who had been one of the best quarterbacks in all of football. And he was way loved in Huntington, West Virginia. And that's the way it should have been. It's not like he was a bad guy. He was a good guy. I liked the guy, you know. I hated to see him go, too. But at the same time, I knew that in order to play I had to wait my turn. And my turn had finally come. I was just really excited about playing. I was ready to roll. The people in Huntington would love me too. It's just, you're going to miss Chad. And most people are probably thinking Coach Pruett is going to turn it over to a sophomore who has played four games. But I knew my job. I needed to work hard and make sure that we continued to win championships."

To a large extent, Pennington had helped ensure that his successor would succeed.

"Chad taught me how to play quarterback," Leftwich said. "When I went to Marshall, I didn't know if I was going to be successful. I don't think I was very well prepared for college. But when I got there, Chad was able to teach me how to become good at playing the quarterback position by studying and all the other things you do and the things you don't do to get better.

"When I got there, he was already one of the best players in college football. And for him to do what he did just shows you what type of person Chad was. He was considered by some the best quarterback in college football and at the same time he was still willing and able to try to teach me what he could so I would have an opportunity to be successful. So that was the great thing about Chad. Me and Chad's been friends ever since."

Would Leftwich be able to pick up where Pennington left off to carry the torch as the Thundering Herd's quarterback? History indicated Leftwich would do just fine.

Dating back to 1984, the Herd had a long line of quality quarterbacks.

In 1984 Carl Foder was All-Southern Conference and went on to play QB for the NFL St. Louis Cardinals. Tony Peterson played quarterback for the Herd and took it to its first Division I-AA Championship Game, then Michael Payton led Marshall to the Division 1-AA championship in 1991 and in 1992 he threw thirty-one touchdowns while leading the Herd to their its first national championship. Payton also won the Walter Payton I-AA Player of the Year Award.

Marshall coach Jim Donnan's son, Todd, took over for Payton in 1993 and the Herd returned to championship game. Then the Donnans took the Herd to the playoffs in 1994, where it bowed out in the semifinals against Boise State.

In 1995, Larry Harris started at quarterback and Mark Zban was the backup before both were lost to injury, paving the way for Pennington to take over. Of course, Pennington led the Herd to the championship game before giving way to Kresser the next season.

Marshall had been spoiled at the quarterback position. So even if Leftwich hadn't played much, fan expectations were high.

While Pruett knew he would be without many of the players who had made the program successful for the previous four seasons, he too continued to have high expectations and set seven goals for his team prior to the start of the 2000 season.

The goals were: to have a winning season, win at home, win the Mid-American Conference East division, win a MAC title, win on the road, and maintain the team's national ranking.

At the Marshall media day, Pruett went to his mantra when he echoed an old favorite: "We play for championships. We expect to play for championships. The media, fans and coaches expect us to play for championships."

Pruett remembered what the team had experienced when Randy Moss left and everybody wondered who would take Moss' place while questioning whether the Herd could reach the same level it had achieved with Moss.

"We weren't asking Byron Leftwich to be Chad Pennington," Pruett said. "We were confident he could do the job and we were confident we could continue to play championship football.

"We felt like that we were really in good shape with Byron. We'd lost a lot

**A NEW GUNSLINGER** — With a cannon for an arm and the body of a lineman, Byron Leftwich stepped into Chad Pennington's shoes. *Courtesy The Huntington Herald-Dispatch.*

of other really good players around him. We'd lost Doug Chapman, James Williams, Rogers Beckett, Giradie Mercer, Jason Starkey—all those guys went on and played in the National Football League. So we lost a lot of good players, but we felt like we had some good players. We just had to retool. But we had an awful tough schedule. We had North Carolina, Michigan State, Western Michigan, Toledo, along with everybody else in our division. And they were all in our first six games."

Leftwich had at least one advantage over Pennington according to Pruett.

"He was a great deep ball thrower and he could really push the ball down the field," Pruett said. "And what he was able to do was hold the ball longer because he had so much zip on it, he could really get it in a small area a lot quicker than Chad could."

Leftwich believes Pruett's knowing him and understanding him allowed him to skip any mental games to try and prepare him for starting.

"He knew that I wasn't a guy that let a lot get to me," Leftwich said. "You know, I can stand tall and take the credit and take the criticism, too. You know, that's just the type of person that I am. And I think he knew that. Still, at the same time, I remember he used to tell people, 'Byron is our starter.' And maybe some people didn't believe that I was capable of going out there and doing it, because we didn't have too many people on that team that had been regulars, who had really played and had shown they had a chance to be successful. So, when I went out there, I'm quite sure I had some doubters to begin with up there.

"But I always knew that I would do anything for my teammates. I would go out there and do whatever I had to do for us to find a way to win the football game. And that's the only way I looked at it. I couldn't look at anything else. I just said, 'Man, I'm going to try my best, work as hard as I can and do what I can for us to win.' And I think that showed throughout my teams, with my coaches and everything and that's what everybody began to believe."

The new Herd would be playing in an expanded Marshall Stadium and would have the toughest opening schedule in the school's history. Three of their first five games were against Michigan State, North Carolina, and Western Michigan.

"What we wanted to do early, in 2000, was try to not make Byron have to win the game," Pruett said. "But he was such a great player and we had so many great young players that it ended up that if we were going to win the games, he was the guy who was basically going to have to do it. Which really wasn't as fair for him as we would have liked for it to have been."

Despite the high expectations placed on any Marshall quarterback, Leftwich felt ready.

"Watching Chad was good for me," Leftwich said. "He taught me that everything I did—on and off the field—would be a reflection on me and all of my teammates, so I needed to set an example on the field, in the community and in the classroom."

MARSHALL OPENED THE BYRON LEFTWICH ERA on August 31, 2000, against Southeast Missouri State, coached by former Marshall assistant Tim Billings, at Marshall Stadium.

Leftwich threw for two touchdowns—completing thirteen of twenty passes for 205 yards before sitting out most of the second half—while Chanston Rodgers, who replaced Doug Chapman and was coming back from a torn knee ligament, ran for three touchdowns and the Thundering Herd looked like they weren't going to miss a beat with their new troops as they rolled over the Indians 63-7.

The Herd knew they could expect a different level of competition the following week at East Lansing, Michigan.

"I remember saying, 'Man, why do we go to Michigan State the year we lose all these great players?'" Leftwich said. "That was what I felt like at first, then I was like, 'Hey let's go do it.'

"I'd watched those guys on film and I felt like we could play with them. And that was just my attitude towards it. I wasn't in awe that we were playing Michigan State. It wasn't like 'Hey man, we're playing Michigan State.' I was like, 'Michigan State is playing Marshall.' I knew the type of players that I had around me and I knew we were capable—if we executed—of finding a way to win the football game."

Marshall and Michigan State played September 9, 2000, and the Herd showed no signs of being intimidated by their Big Ten opponent and its bruising running back, T.J. Duckett.

A crowd of 72,983 showed up to watch the two teams that wore green meet. Pruett used the color scheme to loosen up his team.

"I told them, 'If you get nervous, just look up in the stands, everybody is wearing green—you'll think it's a home game,'" Pruett said.

Pruett also went out on a limb.

"I predicted a team wearing green would win," said Pruett with a chuckle.

While the Herd played the Spartans tight, they lost 34-24 after Leftwich was intercepted twice at critical moments during the game.

Marshall's season didn't get any easier on September 23 when they traveled to Chapel Hill, North Carolina, to play the University of North Carolina.

The Thundering Herd had everything going its way when Leftwich connected with Darius Watts on a twenty-seven yard touchdown to take a 9-6 lead with twenty-two seconds remaining in the first half. In the third quarter, Marshall picked off two passes from North Carolina quarterback Ronald Curry, putting the Herd in position to leave Chapel Hill with the victory.

But Curry recovered from his lackluster third quarter to throw two fourth-quarter touchdown passes to take a 20-9 lead.

Marshall had the ball midway through the fourth quarter when two of the four banks of lights at Kenan Stadium went on the blink causing a fourteen-minute delay. The lighting still wasn't full strength when officials signaled the game to resume. Leftwich was more than happy to exploit the difficult lighting situation by first throwing to Watts for thirty-seven yards to the Tar Heels' twelve. Brandon Carey ran for a Herd touchdown on the next play to make it 20-15 after the Herd failed to make their two-point conversion.

But Curry followed by leading a seven-minute drive; Marshall was out of timeouts and couldn't stop the clock and the game ended.

Pruett got a little prickly afterward when asked about not having any timeouts at the end of the game and delivered a vintage Pruettism: "I'd like to have had them at the end. We didn't have them. It didn't take Kojak to figure out we needed timeouts at the end."

Pruett and the Marshall coaching staff felt slighted in the Michigan State and North Carolina games.

"We felt like we got robbed both places," Pruett said. "They called two touchdowns back in North Carolina."

One was a fumble recovery by Max Yates that was returned for a touchdown and the other was a punt return by Maurice Hines for a touchdown.

"They called us out of bounds, which we were clearly in bounds, you could see it plain as day on the film," Pruett said. "I wrote a letter to the ACC commissioner and cut out the film and sent it to him. He agreed with me that there were some bad calls. He asked me not to publicize the letter."

At Michigan State it was a pass interference call that went against Marshall.

"That was in the fourth quarter and it really hurt us," Pruett said. "We had a chance to go to both of those parks to try and win two big ball games which would have been really good for us, but we weren't quite able to get it done."

Leftwich did what he needed to the following weekend against Buffalo when he completed twenty-five of thirty-six passes for 379 yards in a 47-14 win at Marshall Stadium. That game was looked upon as a tune-up for Western Michigan's arrival in Huntington for a much anticipated MAC contest televised by ESPN on a Thursday night.

Marshall overcame a 23-0 lead in the MAC championship game ten months earlier. Now Western Michigan would return to the scene of the crime.

The Broncos returned a quality team that lost its season opener at Wisconsin 19-7 then won at Iowa before exacting revenge in Huntington.

The closest the Herd got came following a huge break with just under eight minutes in the game with the Broncos leading 24-3. Marshall capitalized on an eleven-yard punt that gave them possession at the Bronco's twenty-six. Nate Poole then hauled in a ten-yard touchdown pass from Leftwich to cut the lead to 24-10. Just over a minute later, Larry Davis recovered a fumble and returned the ball to the Broncos' thirty-eight. A Leftwich pass found Lanier Washington at the goal line, but Washington couldn't hang on to the ball. The Broncos intercepted Leftwich's pass on the next play, which essentially ended any hopes of a comeback and Western Michigan had a 30-10 win.

The loss ended Marshall's thirty-three game home winning streak; the streak dated back to the 1995 Division I-AA championship game against Montana. Even worse, the Herd found themselves with a losing record at 2-3 five games into the season and they would have to travel to Toledo to play the Rockets, who had captured the MAC's Western Division in 1997 and 1998 only to lose to Marshall in the MAC championship game. As if Toledo needed any more incentive to beat Marshall, the Herd's win over the Rockets had kept them out of the MAC championship game in 1999.

The Marshall game was the hottest ticket in Toledo. Bleacher seats were added to the Glass Bowl—which had a seating capacity of 26,248—which allowed another 3,000 fans to watch.

Toledo routed Marshall 42-0 in the worst defeat for Marshall during

Pruett's five-year tenure. The Herd's hopes for a fourth consecutive MAC championship looked to be in jeopardy as did the chances of even making it to the championship game to defend their title.

Sitting at 2-4, Pruett decided to address his team on the concept of being a team.

"We got embarrassed at Toledo," Pruett said. "And after six games in the season we'd already lost as many games as we had the previous four years. So after the Toledo game we got back to Huntington and I gathered all the players in a room and gave each of them a flashlight. And I called the offense up front and darkened the room. Then I had them all turn on their flashlights. So we had eleven flashlights glowing in the dark room. Then I had the running back turn his off and I said, 'See where our hole is? He just fumbled.' Then I had the offensive guard turn his light off and I said, 'All ten of us are doing the right thing and the offensive guard just missed his block.' And I brought the defense up and did the same thing with them. One [of the players] didn't run a stunt—got out of his gaps, whatever would be relative to defense. And I did the same thing with the special teams. And then I had everybody turn their lights on. And I said, 'Now, as a team, we can light up this room.' And then we had a section in the corner, they turned their lights off and I said, 'It doesn't make any difference what these forty people are doing if five or ten of them aren't doing it right, as a team we can't light the room. And the only way we're going to win as a team is for all of us to perform together. We have the talent.' I think that that was a huge turning point in our program."

Pruett followed by giving each player on the team a rubber band.

"I told them all to put the band on their wrist," Pruett said.

Pruett held up a single rubber band and demonstrated how easily he could tear it. Then he grabbed a bunch of the rubber bands from the box he'd passed around the room. He twisted them together and then showed how he couldn't tear them apart. Then he told the team: "If we all band together and unite, we can have a great football team."

Leftwich remembered Pruett's motivational ploy.

"It was the first time that we, as players, had faced something like that because we were so used to winning. Coach Pruett started pulling out these rubber bands all over the place and telling us, 'Band together, we're going to fight through it, we're going to fight through it.'"

After having such great success during his first four seasons, then having a sudden drop, it would have been understandable for Pruett and his staff to reconsider the way they were doing things; to question if they were doing something wrong. But doubt never crept into the equation.

"One of the things that I think was one of our strengths was that we believed in our system and we knew our system worked," Pruett said. "You certainly always need to evaluate your system. But I don't think we really started doubting each other or what we were doing. What we did was gain more resolve in making our system work.

"We felt like that we had good players. You know, I have a saying I like that goes, 'the best players don't always win, but the best team does.' And I told our guys we needed to be the best team. And if we were the best team, everything else would take care of itself. And it did."

Marshall went on a roll after the Toledo game, beating Kent State 34-12, Akron 31-28, Bowling Green 20-13, and Miami of Ohio 51-31. MU's 6-2 mark in the MAC clinched another East Division title as the team headed to Ohio to finish the regular season.

"We went up to Ohio where we never really played extremely well," Pruett said. "That's a big rival for us. And we had already clinched the title at that time, and just for whatever reasons, we didn't play as good as we were capable of playing and they played really good. They had a good football team and they beat us."

Losing to Ohio 38-28 to end the regular season and having to play Western Michigan again didn't exactly bode well for the Herd as they headed back to the MAC championship game.

But some interesting circumstances came forward to serve as motivational fodder for Pruett.

The MAC championship game had been played for three years running at Marshall Stadium, where the 2000 game was scheduled as well. Complaints about having to play Marshall for the championship at Marshall's home field reached a crescendo in 2000, leading to a change.

"The conference commissioner decided to make it even," Pruett said. "And what he came up with was for us to change locker rooms and sides of the field. We had to dress in the visitor's locker room and during the game we were on the opposite side from where we normally were.

"Well, Western Michigan had their choice of going to the visitor's locker room if they wanted to. But they chose to take our locker room. So on the last day of practice before the game, we decided to get the players stirred up a little bit."

In the middle of the Marshall locker room was an area that had "Go Herd" and "Marshall Football" on it and visitors to the locker room were not supposed to stand on either.

"While we were out practicing, I had the managers go in and we covered up that center area with Western Michigan's emblem and then put each one of their player's names on each one of our player's locker with their number," Pruett said. "So when they came in there, they saw a Western Michigan's player on their locker and their emblem on the floor."

The players' reaction got the desired effect.

"And, I mean, it was just like our guys played possessed," Pruett said. "All of them seemed to get up for the game. In other words, it really motivated them."

The 2000 MAC Championship Game was held December 2. The Herd got a pair of first quarter field goals to take a 6-0 lead and Leftwich connected with Watts on a forty-four yard touchdown for a 13-0 halftime lead. But two Jeff Welsh touchdown passes in the third quarter gave Western Michigan a 14-13 lead.

Marshall needed a hero and Lefwich answered the call.

The Marshall quarterback showed great poise in leading an eighty-yard drive culminating with a twenty-nine yard touchdown pass from Leftwich to John Cooper with six minutes left for a 19-14 lead that held. Leftwich finished with 358 yards in the air.

Despite the disappointing way the season had started, Marshall had pulled its act together to claim its fourth consecutive MAC Championship. In the process it became clear that Marshall University had another special quarterback in Leftwich.

"He really grew in his leadership role and in every aspect of his game," Pruett said. "He just started to gain confidence and, you know, that was huge for him and for us, because, as he gained confidence our football team got a lot better."

And despite the wishes of Motor City Bowl officials—who wanted a new team for the annual game played at the Silverdome, Marshall was headed back to the bowl for the fourth consecutive year.

Cincinnati was the Herd's opponent this time around and instead of taking the Motor City Bowl's desires to heart, Pruett sounded like P.T. Barnum as he promised them Marshall would bring a big crowd and the Herd would put on a show.

**ANOTHER CHAMPIONSHIP** — Byron and Bob accepted Marshall's fourth MAC Championship trophy at halftime of a Herd basketball game at the Henderson Center. *Courtesy Marshall University.*

Cincinnati tied for second in Conference USA after winning five of its final six games and had defeated Miami of Ohio 45-15—the team Marshall had defeated 51-31.

Marshall ended the 2000 season on a winning note with a 25-14 win on December 27 over Cincinnati in front of a crowd of 26,018 fans at the Silverdome.

Leftwich starred for the Herd, throwing a seventy-seven yard touchdown pass and running for another to earn the Most Valuable Player award.

"I think that was a big win," Pruett said. "We didn't have Randy Moss or Chad Pennington, which showed we were more than one or two guys. But we'd won almost sixty games in five years and you can't do that with just one or two guys."

Marshall had played Cincinnati with a chip on their shoulder. The Herd players sensed that the Bearcats felt superior to a lowly MAC team such as Marshall.

"Didn't matter how much we had won, most of those guys on Cincinnati looked at the MAC as teams they felt they should beat," Pruett said. "We felt like Cincinnati was really cocky and our guys were working hard to go back to the Silverdome. I kept talking to them about turning setbacks into comebacks. And, you know, I think they really bought into it and that helped us a lot."

Leftwich had grown over the season and he felt like the win against Cincinnati, and the way the team finished the year, would go a long way toward nurturing a championship in 2001.

"You've always got confidence in yourself, but until you are able to go out there and win games on a consistent basis and do certain things, you don't know if you can really do it," Leftwich said. "And by the time we got to that bowl game with Cincinnati, we all had confidence. Not just me, everybody on that team had confidence. We had lost so many guys to the NFL and we all had confidence in ourselves by the end of the year. And sometimes it takes time for you to bond or gel and it just so happened it took us going 2-3 to get us turned around."

**MOST VALUABLE PLAYERS** — Byron Leftwich, left, was named the Motor City Bowl's MVP of 2000, while Michael "Kool-Aid" Owens—who began his Marshall football career as a walk-on from Logan, West Virginia—won the Lineman Award for his outstanding defensive play. *Courtesy Marshall University*.

# *Chapter fifteen*

Bob Pruett had waited to be a college head coach for much of his life, so he never took for granted his position once he attained the job at Marshall University.

Over the years he had learned a lot from all of his coaching stops. He never felt so well fed with football knowledge as to not listen to other coaches about their ideas for stopping certain offenses and defenses. He even managed to employ soliciting opinions from other coaches on strategy as a recruiting tool.

Pruett, as we saw earlier, learned to do his homework on how to stop things other teams were doing successfully. Usually he would accomplish his task like he did while preparing for FSU or Tennessee by picking up a little morsel of information here and a little morsel there. Once he became a head

**TALKING SHOP** — Bob catches up with friends from the Florida Gators' staff prior to the game. *Courtesy Marshall University*.

15

FORTIFYING T

THE PROGRAM

coach he expanded his brain power to include the high school coaches he and his assistants met with while making recruiting trips.

"I think the gathering of information on particular opponents and studying those opponents really paid off and I think that was one of the keys to our success defensively over the years, because we would do various studies on the different programs, Pruett said. "And we even got so where we incorporated it as a recruiting tool. In other words, when our coaches would go out recruiting, we would ask the high school coaches and the other coaches what they'd do on recruiting weekends, what they would tell the recruits and, you know, if we were recruiting against someone, we could talk to our recruits and tell them what it was going to be like when opponents' recruiters called and what they were going to tell them and how they were going to treat them. So we would have a way of countering the things the other programs were selling. In other words, if their university had a School of Law and we didn't have one, which we don't, we'd find a way to work around it."

Pruett perceived himself as the CEO of a company, which in his case was Marshall football. Reigning as the CEO of the Herd, Pruett believed in hiring good people.

"You have to have good coaches," Pruett said. "You have to have good support systems. You have to have good players. You've got to oversee all of those type things. But the key is to hire good people who believe in your system. I had a saying, 'Exploit your strengths and manage your weaknesses.' In other words, understand what your weaknesses are and be able to manage them. If your weakness is you don't have much money, you've got to really utilize your money well. If you have a strength in Randy Moss, get him the ball.

"I wanted my coaches to be an extension of what I believed as far as how to play offense and defense, then turn it over to them. Allow them to have the creativity to run your system the way they saw fit. I was very fortunate in having been able to hire some really good coaches.

"Our coaches came to Marshall, left and went to other programs. They all really got good jobs, but that's the reason we were able to attract good coaches. They knew I would help them go on to bigger and better things and help their career. And while they were with me they were going to have the creativity and freedom to interject some of their things in a football season within our system. Understanding on game day that there was a certain picture we needed to see and we didn't want to get outside of that picture. So they understood that I was going to help them, be with them and do everything I could because we had these systems to run. And if we needed to tweak the system, we'd tweak it in the off-season, but we all went into the season on the same page. And it worked."

Pruett continued to learn on the job, and also kept up his own private battle in trying to make a West Virginia-Marshall series a reality. Pruett understood he was on the right side of the battle in this one. Yes, West Virginia once had nothing to gain by playing Marshall. But beating Marshall had become an accomplishment and it would have been a positive thing for the state of West Virginia.

So Pruett had a field day taking his shots at West Virginia.

T-shirts echoed the Pruettism directed at West Virginia: "If you're scared, get a dog."

And there was the billboard—right outside Morgantown—that touted Marshall and declared, "We play for championships." Pruett's slogan particularly grated on West Virginia fans since Marshall had won four consecutive MAC championships while West Virginia was a middle-of-the-pack team in the Big East.

"They chopped the sign down, tore it right down," Pruett said. "It was right off the interstate."

More on the serious side, Pruett continued to tell the Governor of West Virginia, Bob Wise, that the game would be good for the state and that he thought the Governor should apply some pressure on the powers that be to make the game happen.

"The thing was—to me—playing Marshall wasn't a risk anymore," Pruett said. "Because if you beat Marshall, now that's a feather in your cap. For three straight years after the '97 game, at the end of the year we were ranked higher nationally than West Virginia. It's just a turf battle. But I had lots of fun out there. I mean, I'd goad them all the time, like, 'Let's go ahead and schedule West Virginia, we'll take the BCS [ratings] hit.' Stuff like that. I'm sure it irritated them."

Pruett had felt confident in Byron Leftwich's abilities, but after the 2000 season he felt even more confident going into the 2001 season with an incumbent at quarterback the caliber of Leftwich, who had completed 279 of 457 passes for 3,358 yards and twenty-one touchdowns during the 2000 season.

"Having a quarterback like Byron really gives you great confidence going into the next season, it really does," Pruett said. "Especially when you have one of Byron's ability. It would let you really be creative on offense and let you know that you can do some things offensively like throwing the ball downfield. And we had good receivers. The combination of the two just made us that much better."

Among Leftwich's strengths was an innate ability to see the field.

"Reading the defensive coverage and seeing the field, it was amazing how much knowledge of the game that he had and was able to comprehend," Pruett said. "And we did a lot of things at the line of scrimmage with our quarterback. We were able to let him really control the football game. A lot of people do it from the sidelines, call in the plays and what not. We were able to let the guy on the field get a feel for the game and call some plays himself."

Pruett believed in the feel for the game a quarterback acquires by calling his own plays, similar to the way a pitcher and catcher get into a certain rhythm in baseball when they call their own pitches.

A funny side note about Leftwich calling his own plays was the fact he was the continuous thread in the offense since he had played under four different offensive coordinators.

"All of the guys we had were great coaches, all really, really, outstanding coaches and we felt very fortunate to have each and every one of them, so I'm not saying that as a negative about them," Pruett said. "But it's awful hard on the player to keep adjusting to a different coach because each coach has a little different way of doing things. Even though we were running the same system, they all had their own language."

Pruett's offense would see the coordinator send in a play to the quarterback with four options on each play where he could either run or pass.

"Our quarterback could check in or check out of the play, even do something completely different if he saw something," Pruett said. "Like when we had Randy Moss. If we had a chance to hit the home run or throw for a touchdown and if the defense was giving us something, we'd take it."


PRUETT AND HIS HERD WERE EXCITED about their opening game of the 2001 season. They were scheduled to travel to Pruett's old stompin' grounds in Gainesville, Florida, to play the powerhouse University of Florida Gators.

"Once I went back to Marshall I had the Gators on my mind," Pruett

**DEFENSIVE STRUGGLE** — Max Yates had his work cut out for him between the high-powered Gator offense and a depleted Marshall defense. *Courtesy Marshall University*.

**RALLYING THE TROOPS** — Bob used everything he had to keep the Herd in the game with the Gators. *Courtesy Marshall University.*

said. "I wanted to schedule a game with Florida. I always thought it would be a good measuring stick for our program to see how far we had come and how far we needed to go."

Pruett might have been thinking about Florida being a measuring stick, but his policy was not to talk a lot about the teams they were going to play.

"In other words, we told our guys that everybody was after us," Pruett said. "And basically what we would do is talk about what we had to do to be a good football team, to return to being champions. So what we wanted to really focus on was our football team and what we had to do to maintain the championship level."

Marshall's visit would also coincide with Florida being ranked as the No. 1 team in the country, the first time Marshall had ever played against the No. 1 ranked team in Division I-A. The game would be shown nationally on ESPN2.

Florida was the program Pruett had tried to emulate since arriving to Huntington. And one area in which he had enjoyed great success in shadowing the Gators was getting his players to always believe they were going to win. Marshall had grown used to winning during Pruett's tenure—the team had won 86.6 percent of their games under Pruett—resulting in the belief they could go anywhere and come away with a victory.

"Coach Pruett always told us that the next game was the most important game," Leftwich said. "As a team we knew that was going to be a big game for him. It's too bad what happened."

Playing at Florida's fabled Ben Hill Griffin Stadium, known simply as "The Swamp," Pruett knew his team could expect at least 85,000 screaming Gators fans for the contest. So the drill was the same the team underwent prior to away games against Clemson and South Carolina. Pruett had speakers hauled out to the practice field and played them loud enough to where the people in Morgantown could have heard the Gators' fight songs coming from Huntington.

Most important about the game to Pruett was that it followed in line with his ongoing pursuit of excellence. If Marshall indeed wanted to be considered one of college football's elite teams it would need to be able to play with the big boys, such as Florida— and come away with some wins.

"Going into that game I figured having practiced against that offense [while the Florida defensive coordinator] was an advantage," Pruett said. "But you needed to have pretty close to equal talent for that to become a real advantage. We certainly would have been better off if what happened didn't happen."

Florida went into the week a 30-point favorite over the Herd. But that was before the NCAA stepped in on the Thursday before the game to announce that twelve of Marshall's players would be suspended for the game for receiving extra work benefits. According to the NCAA, two would have to miss one game and ten players were penalized three games.

"We had a misinterpretation of a rule and we thought that it was permissible for these non-qualifiers to work their first year [at Marshall]," Pruett said. "And we had gotten them jobs. Then we find out it wasn't permissible, so the players had to pay the money back. And depending upon how much money they had made, they would be suspended accordingly. If they made a total of over six hundred dollars, they would lose three games and it graduated down from there. In that first ball game, we had a bunch of players suspended. I personally felt like it wasn't the players' fault that we had gotten them their jobs."

Pruett called the 2001 season the toughest season he has ever experienced because of what occurred.

"These kids, they came in there and we found them a job," Pruett said. "I came to Marshall in 1996 and this job program had been going on since 1992, so really I inherited it. That was really frustrating. But, as the NCAA said, it was our responsibility to understand the rule and we had people where that that was their job. All of us had to share in the blame."

Pruett stopped short of making any comments about the NCAA.

"You don't win that war," Pruett said. "That particular problem was very unfortunate. But once it was over you move on to the next problem. And when you're the head coach of a college football team there's always something else."

When Marshall arrived at Gainesville they were minus two starters—running back Franklin Wallace and nose tackle Marlan Hicks—and two often-used reserves in running back Brandon Carey and receiver Denero Marriott.

"[Having the suspensions] was a huge distraction for everybody," Pruett said. "We're playing a great team in Florida, they had a lot of talent and we're playing them at their place. And we had kids in the locker room talking about all the stuff that had happened instead of what they needed to be focusing on to beat Florida."

Leftwich felt like the loss of the suspended players indeed played with the team's heads.

"I mean, that was going to play a part in our having a chance to win this

**FLASHES OF BRILLIANCE —** Byron Leftwich was able to make some headway against an aggressive Florida defense. *Courtesy Marshall University.*

football game, so it was tough," Leftwich said. "You know, it's tough because you begin to wonder, 'Man, can we do it without this guy, without that guy, do we have enough depth to play a team like Florida? And to find out on Thursday, two days before we played them, that was tough to deal with. But once the game started that wasn't the excuse why we lost, because we were still able to go out there and do some good things, but we just fell a little short."

Florida routed Marshall 49-14.

But to say the Herd rebounded would be a huge understatement. After the Florida loss, they won ten in a row while averaging 37.5 points per game. Leftwich led the way by throwing for 3,711 and thirty-four touchdowns to the likes of a talented receiving corps featuring future Denver Bronco standout Darius Watts.

Among Leftwich's accomplishments was his becoming the first quarter-back in the history of the MAC to pass for 400 yards in three consecutive games; he was named the MAC's offensive player of the year.

"Between 2000 and 2001 Byron matured a lot," Pruett said. "He became a great leader."

Among the ten wins was a 42-18 drubbing of Ohio, which served as a nice payback for the previous season's 38-28 loss at Ohio. Marshall lost three times in the MAC during the 2000 regular season and, after the Ohio game, had avenged two of them as they took care of Western Michigan in the 2000 MAC championship game. The only 2000 loss not to be avenged was the 42-0 loss to Toledo.

Leftwich remembered the Toledo loss.

"I had a terrible game," said Leftwich, who threw an interception and fumbled twice; two turnovers were converted into touchdowns by the Rock-ets. "We really wanted to get our revenge [against Toledo]. Winning the MAC championship would have done that."

Even though the Herd had a 10-1 record and held a No. 20 ranking nationally, Pruett knew they had their work cut out for them if they were to win their fifth consecutive MAC championship.

"Toledo had the same team we had played the year before and when they took care of us good," Pruett said. "Making up forty-two points is a lot to ask."

The Herd had compiled a 16-2 mark since the previous season's loss to the Rockets, while Toledo entered the championship game after losing to Bowling Green 56-21 in their final game of the regular season.

One thing had been pre-determined prior to the game: Marshall would not make a return visit to the Motor City Bowl.

Regardless of who won the game, Toledo would head to Pontiac, Michigan, while Marshall would go to the December 19 GMAC Bowl in Mobile, Alabama.

For the first time, Marshall would be competing for the MAC championship at a different venue than Marshall Stadium. This time the Herd would find out how it felt to be the visiting team at the championship game playing the home team.

Marshall didn't appear to be rattled early on when they built a 20-0 lead over Toledo, completely taking the home crowd out of the game.

"Well, we jumped out to a big lead in the game," Pruett said. "We were ahead 20-0 when we drove the ball down to their 1-yard line where we had first and goal. But Byron misread the signal coming in from the sideline and called a play-action pass and it wasn't. We called a sneak, and he got sacked running the play-action. So we ended up kicking a field goal to make it 23-0. I think a touchdown at that point would have put the game away. Then we started fumbling the football. Bad things happen when you fumble the football. In other words, we should have easily won that football game."

The Rockets managed to cut the Herd's lead to 23-10 by the half, which was crucial to Toledo's success since it allowed running back Chester Taylor to get back into the game. Marshall had held the talented Toledo running back to just thirty-six yards in the first half, but he got it going in the second half when the Rockets scored on their first four possessions to take a 35-29 lead. The lead changed three times in the fourth quarter alone.

Leftwich responded to the Rockets going ahead by leading his team on an eighty-seven yard drive that he finished off with an eighteen-yard touchdown to pass to Denero Marriott, Marriott's fourth touchdown catch of the game with almost twelve minutes left on the clock. That gave the Herd a 36-35 lead.

Taylor, who ran for 188 yards, scored his second touchdown of the game on an eight-yard run with just over six minutes remaining in the game to put the Rockets up 41-36.

Leftwich mounted one final drive, but his pass on a fourth down fell incomplete in the Rockets' end zone with two minutes and forty-three seconds remaining. Leftwich finished with 420 yards passing after completing thirty-two of fifty-two with one interception, but the Herd lost 41-36. It was their first-ever loss in the MAC championship game.

"That was a sad feeling," Leftwich said. "Because we were a team that always had found a way to get it done. We weren't used to losing. From the second I stepped on the Marshall campus, no matter what happened, if Marshall was in a close game at the end, our team would always find a way to win. You know, that was our mentality, like 'Ain't nobody going to beat us in these championship games.' That's just the way we thought. And, when it happened, I remember saying we felt human. We felt real human after falling short. It just didn't even seem real. It didn't seem right to see guys like Max Yates and Ralph Street walk off the field without that championship ring in their senior season. That was tough to deal with because I wanted those guys to go out champions. We had played so hard together and it was only right that those guys go out on top with a MAC championship ring . But we fell a little short."

MARSHALL HAD BEEN TRAVELING TO PONTIAC, MICHIGAN for the Motor City Bowl for four years. So spending the holiday season in Mobile, Alabama, brought a new feeling for the Herd.

For starters, Pruett didn't have to go through the familiar conditioning drills that he had used so successfully in preparing the team to play in the sweltering Silverdome since Ladd-Peebles Stadium was open air.

Marshall's opponent was East Carolina and Pruett's troops were having a difficult time mentally coming back from the devastating loss in the MAC championship game. Marshall found itself in a situation where they had to lose to really appreciate what they had, which was having ownership of the MAC championship.

"I think that's one of the sad things about it," Pruett said. "We had dominated that league so much we felt like adversity was the only way to wake up. People rise up to the level of competition. It's that way in anything, business or whatever. If they're competitive they're going to raise their level up to yours. And the league did, you have to give them credit for that. They really did. Some of the schools did. Toledo did. Bowling Green did, Miami of Ohio did. Those schools put in the resources and did the things they had to do to be competitive."

Once the GMAC Bowl started, Marshall resembled a team in new

**CHANGE OF VENUE** — Marshall went south to Mobile, Alabama, in 2001, appearing in the GMAC bowl. *Courtesy Marshall University.*

**I CAN TAKE HIM** — Bob sizes up the GMAC Bowl mascot upon arriving at the airport in Mobile. *Courtesy Marshall University.*

**RUNNING FOR DAYLIGHT** — In a game remembered for his passing skills, Byron also displayed some fine footwork. *Courtesy Marshall University.*

**FOLLOWING PAGES** — *Courtesy Marshall University.*

surroundings, unsure of their abilities, and unable to function.

Leftwich threw behind his receiver in the first minute of the game and East Carolina's Ty Hunt picked the ball off and returned it twelve yards for a touchdown. What followed made Hunt's interception resemble the start of a track meet.

Marshall briefly appeared to regroup before Leftwich couldn't handle a high snap from the shotgun formation and fumbled. The ball bounced around until East Carolina's Jerome Stewart grabbed it and rambled forty-three yards to put the Pirates up 14-0.

East Carolina quarterback David Garrard then led a six-play, sixty-four yard drive, breaking free for a nine-yard touchdown to cap the drive and take a 21-0 lead. The Pirates next added a field goal to make it 24-0.

"If you look at the first quarter of that football game, we were still feeling sorry for ourselves about losing the championship game," Leftwich said. "We were feeling real human."

The Herd finally got on the scoreboard when Leftwich connected with Watts for a thirty-five yard touchdown pass to pull within seventeen points with over six minutes left in the first half. But the Pirates answered with two more touchdowns before halftime to take a seemingly insurmountable 38-8 lead at halftime.

Offensive line coach Mark McHale approached Pruett while the team ran to the locker room at halftime.

"Mark, who is at Florida State now, is a great man and a great coach," Pruett said. "And he comes waltzing up beside me and he says, 'Bob, no matter what, when you get in the locker room I want you to be positive.' So when we got in the locker room I had everybody get out of the locker room, all of the trainers, all the doctors, nothing but coaches. And I had the coaches go back in the where they could talk about the game plan while I talked to the team."

Pruett knew bowl games could get out of hand, so he needed to do something to inspire his team. Thus, the normally business-like Marshall coach tried a different tact once in the locker room.

Pruett's face assumed a bemused expression while discussing his halftime antics at the GMAC Bowl.

"All the players huddled around and they got in their little groups by position," Pruett said. "There was a big table of cups of water and Gatorade, and the offensive line—which had played poorly in the first half—was sitting

right there at the table. And one of them bent down to get a cup of water and I took my hand and just raked all those cups of water over onto the players. I said, 'You want water? You all don't deserve water.' I said, 'Coach McHale told me to be positive no matter what.' So I am going to be positive. I'm positive your ass is going to walk home if you all don't start playing better."

Offense tackle Steve Sciullo got soaked.

"It was just classic Coach Pruett," Sciullo said.

Leftwich laughed at the memory.

"Oh, man, all that Gatorade got all over Sciullo," Leftwich said. "It was the funniest thing because Coach Pruett was so hot he swept off the whole table of Gatorade and it all fell on Sciullo and it took everything in me to not laugh because it was so funny. It was a serious situation, but what just happened was just so funny. And, when that happened, I could not hold my laugh in and we went out and we just looked at each other and said, 'Hey, man, let's come back.'"

Pruett didn't care that the guy he soaked stood six-foot-four, 310 pounds.

"It really didn't make any difference which one I got," Pruett said. "I did it for effect. We were behind in a ballgame and, as the score indicated, playing so very poorly, and I thought that we should be winning. I was so mad, we were just piddling the game away. Oddly enough, even though we'd only scored eight points, we were moving the ball. And I knew if we were going to win the game we had to do it on defense. We had no chance unless our defense played great, because we wouldn't have enough opportunities if they didn't play great."

Pruett had his team's attention.

"And then we went on and started talking about how I'd been in bowl games before and how I'd seen teams show a tendency when they were down that bad to quit because, you know, they're down. The seniors know they don't have to look at the film the next day. They'd go home for Christmas. Especially your seniors, if you don't watch it, they start worrying about getting hurt and wrecking their chances to play in the National Football League. You'll notice there are a lot of lopsided scores in bowl games for that reason, like, 'Well, the season's over, let's get it over with.' So I talked to them about not quitting. And then I started talking to them about how we were going to come back and win the game. And I told them, 'The only way we can come back to win the game is to band together and believe. You've got to have faith.'

**STALWART LINEMAN** — Steve Scuillo was the recipient of a halftime motivational ploy by Coach Pruett. *Courtesy Marshall University.*

**OFF TO THE RACES —** The 2001 GMAC Bowl was the most entertaining—and emotionally draining—in Marshall's history. *Courtesy Marshall University.*

"And I told them, 'You've got to have strong faith. You've got to believe in the guy next to you. You've got to believe in the system. You've got to believe in the coaches. You've got to believe in yourself. You've got to take care of your job first.' I mean, they'd run an option play and we didn't do the right assignments and we're fumbling the ball around. Finally, I said, 'But the biggest thing is you've got to believe and you have to have faith that we can do this. It's like having faith in God. We all know he's in this room. We can't feel him. We can't touch him. But we know he's here. We can feel his presence. He's here in the room. That's the strong type of faith that you have to have in your teammates. Believe in what we can do if we're going to try to win this ball game. That's the type of faith that we've got to have.' Then I told our defense they had to get us back in the game—our offense was moving the ball, we just weren't scoring. So I said defensively they had to get us back in the ball game."

After Pruett's talk the team broke into their individual groups and talked about the adjustments that needed to be made.

"East Carolina was playing well, but it wasn't so much what they were doing to us as what we were doing to ourselves," Pruett said. "And a lot of times, that's the case. But the other thing is that we really readjusted our run defense."

Despite the margin separating the two teams, Leftwich didn't remember having a sense of panic about the Herd's situation.

"You know, we were only down thirty points," Leftwich said. "We were so used to throwing that we knew we could score thirty points in a quarter. But we needed to focus on keep doing what we were supposed to do each play instead of worrying about how much we were down by. You know, one touchdown at a time. I kept telling the guys, 'One play at a time. One play at a time.' We knew they couldn't stop us from getting in the end zone if we just kept at it like that.

"We knew East Carolina wasn't thirty points better than us. No way were they thirty points better. And we knew that we could go out there and score thirty points quick and get the game back. We figured, 'Hey, we're going to win this game 42-38. That's how we looked at it. I mean, just thirty points, all we need is thirty points. That's four touchdowns and a field goal. We were so accustomed to doing that and once we got out there in the second half, that's what started happening. We just started going out and doing the things that we had always done."

Marshall scored first in the second half when Ralph Street stepped in front of a Garrard pass and scored from twenty-five yards.

Two minutes later, Marshall scored on a nine-yard touchdown run to narrow the margin to 38-22. Then came the play that really seemed to break the Pirates' backs.

"They ran a play we had worked on all week that was a quick screen to the wide receiver," Pruett said. "Our coaches on defense had done a great job of scouting them. So they ran this play. Terrence Tarpley, who was a defensive back, saw it coming and stepped in front of the receiver and intercepted the ball and ran it back for a touchdown."

By the time the third quarter finished, Marshall had outscored East Carolina 28-3 to make it 41-36.

"We got back in the ball game and got our heads above water," Pruett said.

Denero Marriot hauled in a thirty-yard touchdown pass from Leftwich to cut the Pirates' lead to 44-42, but the two-point conversion failed. East Carolina scored another touchdown and Marshall added a field goal to set up

**DEFENSIVE POINTS** — Terrence Tarpley (21) and Ralph Street celebrate Tarpley's interception return for a touchdown. *Courtesy Marshall University.*

**SPIDER-MAN** — Darius Watts continued to be Byron Leftwich's go-to receiver the entire game. *Courtesy Marshall University.*

Leftwich's last-minute heroics. With no timeouts to aid his quest, Leftwich drove the Herd eighty yards in the final minute of the game before finding Watts for an eleven-yard touchdown with seven seconds remaining to tie the game at 51. Marshall was a Curtis Head extra point away from completing their unlikely comeback.

"It was funny, because Curtis Head was a punter," Leftwich said. "We forced him to kick—he was our field goal kicker. Curtis Head was an excellent punter—never kicked field goals in his life. But all through the year, he had missed like eight extra points and made every single field goal, but he would miss extra points. I remember walking along the sidelines after the touchdown and everybody was cheering, thinking the game was over. And right before he kicked the ball, I turned around and just looked at Coach Pruett because in my mind I'm thinking about how Curtis had missed all those extra points."

Head's extra point attempt sailed wide right and East Carolina had another shot.

"Coach Pruett just grabbed his face and said, I can't tell you what he said, it was s-h something, two more letters," Leftwich said. "I just looked at him and we just looked at each other. You almost wanted to start laughing because it was like, 'Man, how in the world did he miss that extra point?' Once he missed the point, I went over to Curtis and told him, 'Hey, don't hold your head down, because I promise you we're going to need you at some point later in this game.'"

Franklin Wallace ran one in from two yards out to give Marshall the lead in the first overtime—and Head made the extra point, but East Carolina answered with a twenty-five yard touchdown run to send the game into a second overtime.

The Pirates had the ball first in the second overtime period and got a thirty-seven-yard field goal. But would a three-point lead be enough to hold off the red-hot Leftwich and the Herd?

The answer was no.

Leftwich hit Josh Davis in stride for an eight-yard touchdown pass to give the Herd their remarkable 64-61 victory in the highest-scoring postseason game in college football history. It was also the biggest comeback in bowl history.

Leftwich finished with 576 passing yards and four touchdowns to lead the Herd to their fourth consecutive bowl win.

**FULL HANDS —** Chris Crocker, a standout safety for Marshall, had plenty of work with David Garrard and the East Carolina offense. *Courtesy Marshall University*.

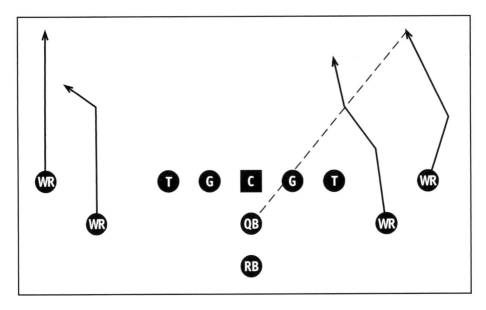

**DOUBLE SLANT / MANBEATER** — A thing of beauty when properly executed; against East Carolina, Leftwich hit Josh Davis to pull off the 64-61 win over East Carolina. *Diagrammed by Tim Stephens.*

A lasting memory for Pruett from the game is the discomfort he endured so as not to disrupt the positive karma in the second half.

"When the game started it was warm," Pruett said. "I was wearing a shirt and a sweater vest. Then the temperature dropped about twenty-five degrees during the game. I was freezing but I wasn't about to change a thing. Of course, after the game they douse me with water—ice water—and I'm really freezing then. And I started cramping. I was about to die. My ribs were hurting, that was something. I usually don't remember little things like that, but I do that because I was freezing. But like I said, we started coming back and I wasn't about to change anything. I was way too superstitious for that."

Despite feeling like he was bordering on hypothermia, Pruett was elated.

"I mean, that was awesome because we had just made the biggest comeback in bowl history," Pruett said. "A lot of our fans left at halftime. And the ones who stayed couldn't believe we won the game. There were a lot of people back in Huntington who didn't know we won until they woke up the next morning. I'm sure they went to bed ready to fire me."

**WATCHING THE CLOCK —** A back-and-forth game left the Marshall faithful wondering how things would turn out. *Courtesy Marshall University.*

**STILL MORE HARDWARE** — Bob hoists the 2001 GMAC Bowl trophy. *Courtesy Marshall University.*

**FINALLY OVER** — The scoreboard says it all. *Courtesy Marshall University.*

**PHOTO (LEFT)** — Bob's look after Marshall missed the extra point that sent the ECU game into overtime. *Courtesy Marshall University.*

## *Chapter sixteen*

Bob Pruett and his Marshall program had come a long way. Entering the 2002 season, the Herd had a No. 19 ranking, putting the team in the preseason Top 25 for the first time in the school's history.

Byron Leftwich became the third Marshall player in six years to become a legitimate Heisman Trophy candidate. Great things were expected of the Thundering Herd's signal caller heading into his senior season.

Leftwich fondly remembered the excitement of the program attaining such a lofty plateau and the Heisman attention.

"All the Heisman stuff was good because it drew attention to the program," Leftwich said. "I didn't look at it like I was this great player or anything, more like I was getting the

**SENIOR LEADER** — Once again, Pruett found his team possessing outstanding leadership. *Courtesy Marshall University.*

16

ANOTHER HEIS

MAN HOPEFUL

attention because I happened to be the quarterback on a good team. Plus, the school had a tradition for developing quarterbacks. I was just the latest.

"The funny thing was, we had always been a Top 25 team. But people were finally realizing we were a Top 25 team. And they were recognizing that before the season."

The Marshall experience had been everything Leftwich expected when he entered the school and Pruett had been the person he thought he would be and more.

"I found out that he was an even better guy, you know," Leftwich said. "Because a guy like Coach Pruett, you can tell that he's a good guy, but you don't really know what type of guy he is until you're able to be around him all the years I was. And I can't speak for any other coaches, but he's one of the guys that really cares about you as a person. A lot of times football is a business, like 'What have you done for me, what have you won, you know.' But he treated everybody the same. Didn't matter if you were a Heisman Trophy candidate or if you were the rookie or freshman that didn't have a chance at playing. He treated everybody with respect and he treated everybody the same."

Leftwich chuckled. "And he could make you laugh."

"He always made you laugh, but he always had your back no matter what," Leftwich said. "And you just knew Coach Pruett loved you. So you loved him back, because, you know, he showed you love. He wanted you to go out there and be a heck of a football player for him, but, at the same, if you worked, he wanted to make sure you graduated from college and, when you got out of college, that you had an opportunity to get a job and be successful in life. That was his whole thing, to be successful in life and to graduate from college. He wasn't just a guy saying it. You can tell when a person's just saying it. If somebody is just saying it, man, you can tell. You know when it's not sincere. But you knew every time he talked to you and everything he said, he was real sincere about it. There haven't been too many people I've met in this world that are like Coach Pruett. You very seldom meet people like Coach Pruett in a lifetime and that's why he's so loved by everybody that leaves Marshall. You can't find one person that says bad things about him. Everybody always has good things to say about Coach Pruett because that's just the type of person he is."

Pruett and Marshall University knew how to handle the attention of having a Heisman Trophy candidate, which allowed Leftwich to enjoy the recognition.

"They'd done it twice before," Pruett said. "So any time you do something before, you know how to do it and how really not to do it. You know what not to do and what to do. I had a schedule where I would talk to about ten or fifteen reporters a day. And then on certain days, I wouldn't talk. We just set up a schedule. Maybe you're going to give two hours this day, two hours that day. And it was the darnedest thing I ever been through. I mean, a lot of people dreaded it. But I had fun with it because it taught me a lot. It taught me a lot about just about everything, about football, about just the way people perceive you, the way people perceive the Heisman, and I was having the time of my life. It was fun. I'm glad I had a chance to go through it."

Leftwich led the Herd to a 50-17 victory over Appalachian State to kick off the season on August 31, 2002. Appalachian State entered the season ranked No. 2 in the Division I-AA rankings and managed to stay in the game into the third quarter when they trailed just 23-17.

But Leftwich was just too much, throwing for 469 yards and four touchdowns.

Two weeks later, Marshall—ranked No. 19—would get their biggest test of the season in a September 12 Thursday night battle against No. 11 Virginia Tech televised from Blacksburg's Lane Stadium on ESPN.

If the Herd managed to take a victory on the road against the tough Hokies they would have been in line to have a special season, perhaps similar to the nature of those the team experienced when Eric Kresser and Chad Pennington were seniors.

"We knew Virginia Tech was tough," Pruett said. "You didn't want to look ahead, you know. But you could see if we win that game we have a chance to move up to a place we'd never been."

Unfortunately for the Herd, they were never in the game.

Virginia Tech's "Untouchables"—Kevin Jones and Lee Suggs—combined for 324 yards, moving the Hokies to a 33-0 lead in front of a crowd of 65,049 before Leftwich finished with three touchdowns in the final period as Marshall absorbed a 47-21 loss.

Leftwich finished with 406 yards passing, completing thirty-one of forty-nine passes, extending his streak of 400-plus yards passing to five.

Despite the sting from losing their first game, the Herd regrouped to put together a string of wins over Central Florida, Kent State, Buffalo, Troy State, and Central Michigan before traveling to Akron November 2, 2002.

Akron's Rubber Bowl would host the contest, but the Zips were not having a good season; they were only 1-7 to that point.

Meanwhile, Marshall was coming off a 23-18 victory over Central Michigan in which Leftwich threw for 374 yards and two touchdowns to surpass the 10,000 yards career mark. And Leftwich had the receivers to spread the ball around in Denero Marriott, Darius Watts and Josh Davis—who all exceeded 100 yards receiving against Central Michigan. The Herd carried a 4-0 MAC record to Akron. The Zips were 2-2 all-time against the Herd at the Rubber Bowl and had lost their last two games at the Rubber Bowl by an average of seven points.

Still, Akron was a team the Herd was supposed to beat. But Marshall was dealt a surprise in the first quarter when Leftwich injured his shin while throwing a pass. After leaving the game for one play, he came back in and led the Herd on a touchdown drive before leaving the game again to have X-rays taken.

"I'll never forget it, man," Leftwich said. "I had thrown a skinny post to Darius Watts and the guy rushing me dove over the top of my running back. I was throwing the ball so my leg was planted. My running back tried to cut him and he jumped over him. So it just so happened that when he landed, he landed directly on my leg. I heard something pop. Once I went on the ground and grabbed my leg, I knew something was wrong. And I tried to get up and walk and I couldn't."

After he got Leftwich to the sidelines, Pruett wouldn't let his star quarterback go back in the game.

"First of all, he never wanted to leave," Pruett said. "I had to force him to go get it X-rayed. He was going to stay there and play and I wouldn't let him go back into the ballgame until he got it X-rayed."

After Leftwich was forced to leave the field, he got into an ambulance and left the park.

Leftwich recalls:

"And, you know, I'm riding to the hospital and I just kind of asked the guys if they can get me back in time to play because I'm thinking I'm going to get back in there before that game was over."

The ambulance driver told Leftwich he wouldn't be able to get him back in time. Given an answer he didn't like, Leftwich had the driver take him back to the field. Leftwich returned to find Terrence Tarpley injured and getting ready to have X-rays taken himself and they found a closer location.

"Terrence and I are good friends, so I'm telling him I broke my leg, and he was like, 'No man, you can't think that way, you've got to stay positive,'" Leftwich said. "But you know when you really hurt yourself, and I knew I'd really hurt myself. So I was sitting there when they took the X-rays and the doctor looked at it and he was like, 'Yep, it's broke.'"

Leftwich believed his college career was over, so he asked the doctor if he could finish out the game.

"I'm thinking this is my last time playing in a Marshall uniform," Leftwich said. "It's the last time I'm going to get a chance to play with my teammates. And the only thing I wanted was to have my last time of being in the huddle with the guys I'd worked with so hard. These were the same guys I put blood, sweat and tears in with for four years and, here it comes your last year, you're kind of letting everybody down by going out there and allowing yourself to get hurt. So I just wanted to experience that one more time, you know. And I remember hopping out of the van. I was in a lot of pain, but when the Marshall fans saw me get out of the van—I still had my uniform on—and when I heard their cheers, somehow my leg didn't hurt as much as it had. I don't know if that was adrenalin or what, but if it wasn't for those fans I don't think I could have gone back out on the field, because I was in too much pain. I couldn't even walk at that point. I was still hopping on one leg. And when they started cheering, I was going for the locker room because I was just determined that the doctors was going to give me something to shoot myself up with so I ddin't feel the pain. But, when I heard the crowd, I started walking and I remember asking them, 'Can you guys give me anything for pain?' And they said, 'No. We can't give you anything for pain because it's a bone.' And I'm like, 'Man, you can't do anything?'"

Leftwich's mother was on the field and she grabbed her son's arm, telling him he wasn't going to play, because he barely showed signs that he could walk.

"I had to grab her and tell her, 'Look, go back up in the stands and just watch the game, I'm okay, I'll be fine,'" Leftwich said. "She let me go and I looked at Coach Pruett and he looked at me."

Leftwich told Pruett everything checked out fine and ran back into the ballgame.

"At this point Coach Pruett still doesn't know anything about my leg because the doctor is sitting in the locker room," Leftwich said. "And that's when Coach Pruett called a time out and I limped out to the huddle. And when I get there, Denero Marriott tells me, 'What in the hell took you so long?' They'd never seen me get hurt. I was a guy who never got hurt. So I'm thinking to myself, 'Man, if they only knew.'"

Leftwich returned to the game in the third quarter with Akron leading 24-10. Even though he would throw for 259 of his 307 yards after the injury, Leftwich clearly was damaged goods and barely able to move around. Nevertheless, he rallied the team to within 27-17 of the Zips.

"I remember telling Sciullo in the second half, 'I'm wearing down,'" Leftwich said. "Because the adrenalin, it was strong, but at the same time, my leg was just giving up. You know, it was getting to the point where I could barely walk. And invariably, we go out there and get the ball back. We throw a long ball to Darius Watts and he lets somebody catch him from the behind sixty yards down the field. There's no way I can get down there."

Leftwich's plight set the stage for one of the more poignant moments in Marshall football history. Leftwich's teammates recognized their leader would have a hard time getting down the field, so Sciullo, Stephen Perretta, and Nate McPeek picked up Leftwich and carried him down the field while the officials moved the chains. Remember this is late in the game when everyone is tired, a point when courage is often the only element that gets players through the next play. Yet Leftwich's linemen thought enough about their quarterback to lug him down the field when they themselves were to the point of running on fumes.

"Nobody said nothing to each other, they just picked me up," Leftwich said. "Sciullo told me, 'Hold your arms up.' Then he picked me up on one side and Perretta picked me up from the other side. McPeek was in the front leading the way and they just carried me down the field. Looking at it now, it was the funniest thing in the world, because you never, ever saw anything like that before. But we didn't think about anything, we were just trying to win that football game. We were trying to do whatever we could to win and I couldn't get down there, so they lifted me up right into the shotgun. I called the play and we went again."

Pruett still gets choked up thinking about what happened that night against Akron.

"When the doctor got back and told me what was going on and Byron had a hairline fracture and he finished the rest of that ballgame, whew," Pruett shook his head in disbelief. "Then when the guys picked him up, it was awesome. The players loved him. He's got such an infectious personality and he's such a likeable guy and such a team guy."

Despite the heroic gesture, Marshall could not overcome the turnovers. Nine times the Herd fumbled and they lost five of them as the Zips took the unlikely 34-20 victory.

Leftwich had a broken tibia.

The injury cost Leftwich any chance he had at the Heisman Trophy—he would finish sixth in the vote.

"It wasn't one of those deals where they told me I couldn't do any more damage if I played," Leftwich said. "It was a thing where, 'You're going to be in a whole lot of pain and, if somebody hits this thing, it can go any time.' You know, it wasn't cracked all the way through. It was cracked halfway. I mean, it was painful when I went out there and I knew all these guys were seniors and I knew all these guys I came and worked with. There was no way I was going to let these guys down if I could walk and deal with the pain. There was no way I was going to let the fans or the Herd down. So I knew that I was going to do anything possible to get back out there and play."

Doctors cleared Leftwich to play and he ended up missing just one game—against Miami.

Stan Hill, in substitution for Leftwich, threw four touchdown passes to lead a 36-34 Wednesday night victory in a game played in Huntington. The game came down to a final play that had Hill pump faking on a rollout, then vaulting his body into the endzone for the winning score.

"Byron was like a coach during that game he missed," Pruett said. "He helped out Stan, who was the quarterback who took his place, kept him confident. He'd see things in the game and talk to Stan about it. He was exactly what you'd want in a great leader, which is what he was."

When Leftwich returned, the team rallied around their leader.

"Our offensive line didn't give up a sack the rest of the year when he came back," Pruett said. "And he played with that broken leg. At times you admired the kid so much. He had such joy. You cry. It brings tears to your eyes, to have someone who's the ultimate team player, who wants to give his all for his team. Compete and do that. He's just a tough guy who can endure pain."

Following the Akron loss, Marshall finished out the regular season with wins over Miami, Ohio, and Ball State to once again win the MAC's Eastern division and earn a date in the championship game against Toledo.

And Leftwich was doing just fine lining up in the shotgun formation. Against Ball State, Leftwich completed thirty-five of forty-two passes for 401

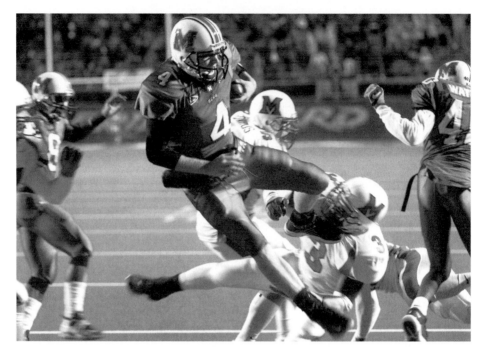

**LEAP OF FAITH** — With Byron sidelined, the Miami (Ohio) game came down to the last play—a quarterback keeper by sophomore back-up Stan Hill. *Courtesy The Huntington Herald-Dispatch.*

yards and two touchdowns.

Like the circumstances from the previous season's MAC championship game, both teams entered knowing their postseason destinations. Toledo would head back to the Motor City Bowl while Marshall was once again destined for the GMAC Bowl. The 2002 championship game returned to Huntington, where Marshall had forty-eight wins and just one loss since Pruett's arrival.

Toledo planned to pin their ears back and pressure Leftwich, who won MAC player of the year honors for the second consecutive season.

"He wasn't completely healed from the broken leg, but going into that game, when they asked me about Toledo's plans, I made the comment that he was so good at reading what was going on at the line of scrimmage that if you blitzed him somebody's band is going to play and it's usually going to be ours," Pruett said. "Byron was going to get rid of the football."

Toledo coach Tom Amstutz did pay the Marshall quarterback a huge compliment when he noted prior to the game: "I don't know whether to try to coach against him or try to get his autograph."

The game boiled down to one drive when the Herd got the football at their own twenty-seven with just over three minutes remaining trailing 45-42. How would Leftwich finish his career in front of the home fans? Patrons of the Thundering Herd clung to their seats waiting for the answer to the question.

A pass interference call gave Marshall the football at the Rockets' forty with fifty-four seconds remaining. Leftwich had a good idea about what the Rockets would do with their pass coverage.

"We were sitting in the huddle and I told Darius Watts to run the deep post and I would make sure that I kept the free safety in the middle of the field," Leftwich said. "I knew what they was going to do in certain situations because we had played them so much. And we had played them in key situations. So I knew they were going to roll with the single high [coverage] and they were going to try to double Watts. I just tried to hold that free safety in the middle of the field."

Leftwich turned to throw the ball to Watts.

"And once Watts is even with somebody, there's nobody on this planet that's catching him," Leftwich said. "I threw it on the right side of the field."

Leftwich's body language held the safety long enough to ruin any hopes the Rockets had for successfully double covering Watts.

Watts caught the ball at the ten and ran into the end zone to make it 49-45 Marshall. The Herd once again ruled the MAC and Leftwich finally had exacted his revenge against Toledo.

LEFTWICH'S SWAN SONG CAME IN THE GMAC BOWL December 18, 2002—this time they didn't need Pruett to sweep the water cups off the table at halftime to get his team in a state of mind to play. Instead, Marshall looked like they'd been there before while taking a 17-0 lead and never looked back en route to a 38-15 victory over Louisville.

Leftwich threw four touchdown passes in his final game wearing the green and white to earn the distinction of being the first player in Division I-A to throw four touchdown passes in two different bowl games.

Marshall finished the season 11-2, giving Pruett a mark of 80-13 after seven seasons.

# TOUGH WINS AND LOSSES
## Chapter seventeen

Coaching is not an easy profession.

Bob Pruett and his Thundering Herd teams had accomplished much by the end of his seventh season, but once again he'd have to retool after losing talented Byron Leftwich.

Meanwhile, the rest of the MAC was catching up and the schedule kept getting tougher.

In 2003, the Herd began the season with two of its first four games against Southeastern Conference powerhouse Tennessee at Knoxville, and against Kansas State at Manhattan, Kansas, to play eventual Big 12 Conference champion Kansas State.

Marshall went to Knoxville on September 12 to face the 12th-ranked Volunteers in front of 106,520 people at Neyland Stadium—the largest crowd to ever watch the Herd play.

**VOLUNTEER NATION —** Prior to the game, Bob chats with Tennessee coach Phil Fulmer. *Courtesy* The Huntington Herald-Dispatch.

17

TOUGH WINS

AND LOSSES

An interesting side note to the game was the fact it pitted Pruett, who had the best winning percentage among active coaches in Division I who had at least five years' experience (Pruett was 81-13 (.862) since 1997 when the Herd moved up to Division I-A), against Tennessee coach Phillip Fulmer, who was second at 104-25 (.806).

Quarterback Stan Hill got the Herd going with a nine-yard touchdown pass to Jason Rader for a 7-0 first quarter lead.

Tennessee answered with a touchdown early in the second quarter before the Herd got a field goal to regain the lead at 10-7. Tennessee got a touchdown with twenty seconds left in the first half to take a 14-7 lead.

Marshall stood toe-to-toe with Tennessee holding the highly-touted Vols to 168 yards of total offense in the first half while the Herd accrued 168.

The Vols seemed to awaken at the start of the second half with a touchdown early in the third quarter for a 21-10 advantage.

Neyland Stadium turned into a raucous party. Tennessee's band played "Rocky Top" to get the vast orange canvas of Tennessee fans worked up into frenzy.

But Marshall wouldn't go away.

Hill connected with Darius Watts for a thirteen-yard touchdown before the Volunteers answered with a three-yard touchdown pass with just under three minutes remaining in the third quarter for a 28-17 lead.

Hill then found Josh Davis for a sixty-five yard touchdown with a minute and nineteen seconds remaining in the third quarter to cut the lead to 28-24. But Hill had to leave the game early in the fourth quarter with a knee injury putting junior college transfer Graham Gochneaur into the Herd's driver seat.

Gochneaur, who had red-shirted the year before, didn't seem flustered— completing seven of ten passes—but the Herd couldn't get anything going. Tennessee added two field goals and escaped with a 34-24 victory.

"Tennessee knew they had been in a game," said Pruett of the loss.

Marshall followed the Tennessee game with a 24-17 loss at home against Toledo for only the second home loss since Pruett became the coach. And the Herd didn't have a patsy to lick their wounds against in their next game as they traveled to Manhattan, Kansas, for a game against tough Kansas State.

Kansas State entered the game with a forty-one game non-conference home winning streak and thoughts of earning a BCS Bowl bit and perhaps a shot at the national-title. Marshall limped in after a physical game against Tennessee that cost them the services of Hill, who continued to nurse his injured knee.

**GRABBING AN UPSET —** Marshall sneaked into Manhattan, Kansas, and held off the sixth-ranked Wildcats, the highest-ranked team ever to fall to the Herd. *Courtesy* The Huntington Herald-Dispatch.

Playing the role of Top 10 bully, the Wildcats took an early 7-0 lead and were perched on the brink of pushing the lead when they drove the ball to the Herd's nine. That's when Johnathan Goddard interrupted the party.

Kansas State quarterback Jeff Schwinn attempted to pitch the ball to standout running back Darren Sproles, but Goddard smelled out the play. The Herd's left end snatched the pitch from the air and returned the ball eighty-four yards for a touchdown to tie the game.

In the second quarter the Herd answered a Kansas State field goal with a Gochneaur to Darius Watts scoring strike from nine yards out; the extra point missed to put the Herd up 13-0. Nick Kelly added a thirty-three yard field goal to give Marshall a 16-10 halftime lead. But the contest was hardly put away.

Both teams traded field goals before the Herd's blown snap on a punt attempt midway through the fourth quarter gave the Wildcats the ball at the Herd forty-four. Nineteen seconds later Sproles eluded Marshall defenders to find his way into the end zone for a 20-19 lead with just over eight minutes remaining in the game.

The feeling in the stands among the sea of purple was that the home team had dodged a major bullet, but they now had the lead and their undefeated season could continue.

But the best-laid plans of mice and men....

Marshall returned the kickoff to their own forty, then used ten plays to drive the ball the remaining sixty yards to take the lead on Gochneaur's rollout three-yard touchdown pass to Jason Rader with three minutes and thirty-four seconds remaining. Then the Herd made the conversion for two points to take a 27-20 lead.

An interception gave the Herd the ball back at the Wildcats' thirty-six with less than three minutes to go to give the game a distinct flavor of a Marshall victory. But the Herd couldn't kill the clock and when they failed to convert on a forty-five yard field goal attempt with a minute and twenty-seven seconds to go, the Wildcats got the ball back.

Marshall would have to withstand one final surge by Kansas State if they were to gain the first win in school history against an Associated Press top twenty-five team and the Wildcats made it clear that stopping them would not come easy.

A huge play for the Wildcats came when Sproles caught a screen pass and took it thirty-three yards to the Herd's three with twenty-five seconds remaining. That's when the Herd defense bowed its collective neck, pushing the Wildcats back.

After an attempted quarterback sneak picked up a yard, Kansas State was penalized for illegal procedure to put the ball back to the seven. The Wildcats managed to spike the ball on the next play, then went back to Sproles on a screen pass; this time the Herd held the Wildcats' star to a one-yard gain setting up a fourth-and-six.

With Donte Williams covering, Schwinn's pass to diving receiver Davin Dennis fell incomplete in the end zone. Marshall had gone into Manhattan and accomplished the improbable with a 27-20 upset victory over the Big 12 powerhouse.

Pruett called the win over the Wildcats one of the biggest in school history.

"If you go back and look at the big wins Marshall football has, that one ranks right up there right behind the Xavier victory after the airplane tragedy that took all those lives," Pruett said.

Splitting with two of college football's heavyweights might have be enough for Marshall years earlier when stepping on to the same field with a Tennessee or Kansas State would have brought great satisfaction. And they finished with an 8-4 mark, which is a good mark for most programs, yet Pruett was disappointed. Their reign as the MAC's East division champions came to an end against Miami of Ohio when Ben Roethlisberger—who would go on to NFL fame as a rookie with the Pittsburgh Steelers—led a 45-6 route of the Herd. Pruett's mission statement was clear and it held true for every season: "We Play for Championships."

And the 2003 Thundering Herd did not play for a championship. Nor did the Herd get a bowl bid, which was one of the reasons they opted to change to Conference USA, effective in the 2005 season. Conference USA has five bowl tie-ins.

"Yeah, to go 8-4 with the schedule we played, that was disappointing not to get a bowl bid," Pruett said. "You would have thought we had enough of a track record at that point to merit bowl consideration somewhere, but there are so many alliances it's tough to get an at-large type of bid."

The next season saw even more frustration.

The Herd's 2004 non-conference schedule once again featured a pair of college football heavyweights in Ohio State and Georgia; both games were played on the road.

After losing to Troy 17-15 in their opener, the Herd had to travel to Columbus, Ohio, to play Ohio State, the seventh-ranked team in the country. And while "three yards and a cloud of dust" was an old Ohio State mantra, the pass gave Marshall fits. Specifically passes thrown to Santonio Holmes, who caught touchdown passes of eighty and forty-seven yards from quarterback Justin Zwick and finished with ten catches for 218 yards.

But Zwick also connected twice with Herd safety Chris Royal. The first interception by Royal gave Hill, who was back at quarterback for the Herd, the opportunity to hit Brad Bates for a nineteen-yard touchdown that tied the game at 21.

The kicking game haunted the Herd against the Buckeyes.

In the aftermath of Royal's second pick the Herd had a chance to take the lead on a thirty-five yard field goal. But Ian O'Connor hooked the kick with just over three minutes remaining in the fourth quarter.

Earlier in the game when Marshall had the ball at the Ohio State eight, O'Connor set up to attempt a twenty-five yard field goal. But instead of taking the three points, Marshall tried to run a fake that failed resulting in dire consequences: no points.

When Marshall got the ball at their own thirty-one with a minute and thirty-six seconds to go, Pruett elected to go the conservative route on the road. Rather than risk a turnover deep in their territory with time running out, he chose to run the football on three consecutive plays. Ohio State called timeout after each play to force a Marshall punt.

O'Connor, who wasn't having the best of days, was also the Herd's punter and managed a punt of only twenty-six yards. Ohio State got the ball at their own forty-five and Zwick hit three passes to put kicker Mike Nugent close enough to kick a game-winning fifty-five yard field goal with two seconds remaining.

While the Buckeye faithful of 104,622 strong celebrated, Marshall could only think about what might have been. Particularly frustrating was the fact Marshall's defense had held Troy and Ohio State to under 100 yards rushing.

The following week Marshall traveled to Athens, Georgia, to play third-ranked Georgia and got smothered by a swarming Bulldog defense in a 13-3 loss after taking an early 3-0 lead.

While the Herd had lost close road games against college football heavyweights, they finished at 6-6 after losing to Cincinnati 25-14 in the Fort Worth Bowl. Expectations for the program had risen and under Pruett's guidance the Marshall program had gained a national reputation as a football powerhouse. Thundering Herd fans were disappointed. To say Pruett did not feel that pressure would be inaccurate, but he wanted to have that kind of pressure, because success raised the bar for how high a program could go. Pruett had raised the bar and challenged the program to get better every year.

"The '04 season, talent-wise, we were as good or better than we've ever been," Pruett said. "We had a bunch of seniors, but we didn't have the chemistry. We just didn't. Without pinpointing anyone's name, we didn't have the team chemistry or the team leadership, which was a drawback. Looking back and analyzing it, it seemed to me when we had a decision to make, the decision was mostly the wrong decision. I'm talking about character decisions and stuff like that. But we had a lot of good individual guys. We just didn't have the team chemistry. There's always a certain amount of individualism, but it just seemed like there was a little bit more that year. As the coach, I was able to pull it together as well as I would have liked too. Because, if I could have pulled it together a little bit better, I think the 2004 team could have been a 10-3 team instead of a 6-6 football team.

"And then our schedules got better. In other words, earlier we were playing the South Carolinas and Clemsons and now we're playing the Tennessees and the Virginia Techs. We're playing Top 10, Top 5 teams. I think some of the injuries played more of a factor in the latter two years. And I think not being able to tie the thread of the closeness of the football team, coming back to the statement: the best players don't always make the best team. We had players who were as good as any other year's, we just weren't as good as a team. Which, in hindsight, probably makes me appreciate the special chemistry we had on some of the other teams we had."

Marshall's NCAA problem put them on probation beginning in 2001, with their punishment being a loss of a total of fifteen scholarships and a five-year probation period. The scholarship losses kept the Herd's number at eighty rather than eighty-five, which eventually took its toll on the team's depth.

"There's a residual effect from losing all those scholarships," Pruett said. "But I never did dwell on that sort of thing, because it's a negative. So the players will always tell you I always talked about positives. We're going to do this. We're going to do that. By not dwelling on that, we had two outstanding recruiting classes that I think we restocked and reloaded. It's young talent, but we restocked and reloaded our program to be a dominant team in Conference USA."

Marshall fans figured Pruett had something up his sleeve heading into the 2005 season. No reason to doubt their beloved coach. Most never saw what happened next coming.

On March 9, 2005, Pruett shocked the Thundering Herd faithful when he announced his retirement at a news conference. Some believe the school's not approving an indoor practice facility for the football team contributed to Pruett's announcement. That wasn't the case, according to Pruett. In fact the day he retired the practice facility actually received administrative approval. His decision was based on timing and he believes he made the right move for the school and for him.

"The problems weren't any more or any less than when I got there," Pruett said. "It was just time for both sides to step back and reevaluate their positions. It was time for the change. I felt like some of the things that were stagnant in the water, like the new turf and the weight room and the academic support system, and the salaries for the coaches, that we'd sort of come to a standstill. So as far as retiring, let's just say it was time. In a lot of ways, I believe it was time. Ultimately, Marshall University is still my school, I'm a big boy, and I made the decision. I will always love Marshall and I hope they'll always love me."

Pruett leaves Marshall with a lasting legacy of having two undefeated seasons and a 12-1 season while compiling a 94-23 mark with five MAC championships. There aren't a lot of coaches who have experienced one undefeated season. Under Pruett Marshall pieced together unprecedented winning streaks, sent players to the NFL, compiled a solid graduation rate, won five bowl games in seven bowl appearances, achieved national rankings, nutured three legitimate Heisman Trophy candidates, and had countless other accomplishments. Pruett's regime established the M Club at Marshall, which is the Lettermen's Club. When he arrived in Huntington he was told such a club had been tried in the past and never worked. Now it's strong and works as a fund-raising arm for the program. When Pruett arrived at Marshall, attendance was approximately 17,000 per game. When he left average attendance was 26,000 a game.

"I've always said a program without jewelry is a program in trouble," said Marshall athletic director Kayo Marcum. "You've got to have the watches and you've got to have the rings. So when you look at what was done in Division I-AA and what was done in the Mid-American Conference, and you look at Bob's coaching record, these things don't just happen. There are people who make them happen. And he's the type of guy who makes things happen.

"You can provide some coaches with all of the resources in the world and they'll coach OK. But can they win championships? Can they be nationally ranked? And coach Pruett was able to do those kinds of things. When you really look at the legacy, it's the people that you've coached and how well they do later. And they all don't have to do it in sports. They leave sports and do other things.... When you look at Pruett's legacy you look at those players and how well they did later on. I have to believe they'll have a connection to Coach Pruett the rest of their lives and vice-versa."

Selby Wellman is a Marshall booster and a close friend of Pruett's and said what Pruett does when people aren't watching is what distinguishes him.

"Probably the hidden thing most people don't know about Bobby is the size of his heart," Wellman said. "I mean, examples I've seen on numerous occasions I've seen him get in his car and drive to visit someone in ill health who was either a former player, or maybe the parent of one of his players, or something like that. Anybody he's had contact with he does those things behind the scenes.

"And second, the other character thing, Bobby is probably the single largest fund raiser for Marshall University, and he does that behind the scenes as well. To say he loves Marshall University, well, that's really an understatement. Marshall University is a part of him. It's part of his DNA for Marshall and the state of West Virginia. His roots are here. It just personifies Bob Pruett. There is no limit to what he'll do to help Marshall University and help the boys he has coached."

A final item to Pruett's Marshall legacy came when West Virginia Governor Joe Manchin announced that the long-awaited West Virginia-Marshall series would begin September 2, 2006 at Morgantown. West Virginia would also host the 2008, 2011 and 2012 games; Marshall would host games in 2007 and 2010 with the 2009 game going to the team who had the best record from the first three games.

Pruett's chirping, lobbying and dogged persistence had finally paid off with the series he felt would be so meaningful to the state of West Virginia.

Where does Pruett go from here?

Since stepping down he's been busy talking up new Marshall coach Mark Snyder, who played free safety at Marshall and graduated in 1988.

Pruett has enjoyed traveling and spending time with Elsie. They have spent time with their three sons—Rodney, Stephen and Kenneth—and four grandsons—Sam, Adam, Bobby and Jacob—and a granddaughter, Savannah.

Pruett's health is excellent and, at least for the 2005 season, he wants to be a Marshall supporter and fan.

Having been a coach since graduating from Marshall, Pruett has kicked back and relaxed, taking time to work on his golf game—though he says while he was taking lessons the golf pro made him the present of a tennis racket.

Pruett's relaxing often includes hours at a time on his lawn mower cutting the grass at his home in Melody Farms or the lawns of some of his neighbors.

"He went down to Sears and bought a lawnmower and they said, 'Do you want it delivered?'" Elsie said. "And he said, 'No, I'll be back a minute. So he went out and got his gas can. He came in and filled the lawnmower up with gas and drove it out and they're all standing there watching him drive it home. They're still talking about it. Then when he would tear up the lawnmower he'd just drive it up the hill and drive it down to the mall, which is just below our property. And one Sunday he did that, I was scared that he was going to get hit, and then when I followed him I followed too close."

Typical of Pruett's wit, he told Elsie: "Get back. You're more dangerous to me than the other cars."

"One of our neighbors was getting a cup of coffee down there and said she looked over and saw this lawnmower coming across the mall parking lot and she said, 'Who's that idiot driving that lawnmower?'" Elsie said. "And then she said, 'Oh, my gosh, it's Coach Pruett.' She got so tickled, but that's just Bob."

Elsie said in some respects she was surprised by her husband's retirement and in other respects she was not.

"My prayer was if it was wrong for the Lord to stop it and he did so many times, so I guess it's what he should have done," Elsie said.

As this book went to press Pruett had not yet decided what the future held for him... Would he coach again? That remained a possibility. But for the present he planned to sit out his first football season since he was a youngster. He had some engagements lined up as a motivational speaker and planned to do some work for ESPN. And on the slow days when Bobby Pruett feels like reflecting, he can glance in the rearview mirror and remember how he did his part to help Marshall University's football team rise from the ashes to unimaginable heights.

**SERIOUS HARDWARE** — The collection was still growing at the time of this publicity photo. *Courtesy* The Huntington Herald-Dispatch.

Bob Pruett has touched many lives during his sixty-plus years of living. Here are the voices of some he's touched.

**Kayo Marcum**, Marshall athletic director:

"In all my years in athletics, I've seen only two coaches who could outcoach their resources—John Calipari and Bobby Pruett. I always thought I would beat Bobby Pruett out of Marshall. I'm surprised that didn't happen."

**David Pancake**, local magistrate and congregation member at Fifth Avenue Baptist Church, where Pruett is a member:

"Every year at Fifth Avenue we have a project such as a Habitat House and invite people to speak. We had some other coaches come and they spoke and left. Bobby Pruett spoke and stayed. We had the money raised by the end of the day."

**TEAM PLAYER** — Bob motivated his players for the good of the team—Trod Buggs, shown here, played at three different positions for the Herd during his career. *Courtesy Marshall University.*

18

TRIBUTES T

O A COACH

**Allen Reasons**, pastor at Fifth Avenue Baptist. He and Pruett often trade barbs:
"I can't believe Pruett's part of writing a book that actually has words in it."

**Chad Pennington**:
"Coach Pruett's greatest strength is his ability to reach the public, to reach out to them. He really created a connection between the public and our team. We became a part of the community because of him. He could really handle the big game. He makes players believe in themselves. He had a lot of confidence in us and we had a lot of confidence in him. … The exposure he brought to Marshall was incredible. People all over were hearing of Marshall. Kids wanted to come play here. … Coach Pruett knew how to adjust. He made us a good second-half team. He's a tough act to follow."

**Joe Feaganes**, Marshall golf coach:
"Bob is a great ambassador for Marshall University. He has a great commitment to the university – not just the football team – the entire university. He's very supportive of the other programs."

**John Sutherland**, Marshall assistant women's basketball coach:
"I've looked up in the crowd and seen Coach Pruett at our games. That's not the case at a lot of places, where the head football coach shows up at other sports."

**Gary Darnell**, former assistant with Pruett at Wake Forest and former head coach at Western Michigan:
"Bobby and I are friends. We talk just about every week and not just about football. He was a dear friend to me at Wake Forest. We went through a lot together there. He's a great football coach and a great human being. … Everyone marvels at the job Bobby did at Marshall. They set the standard for the league. You hear people say that this team is well coached or that team is well coached. Marshall was well coached."

**James Williams**, wide receiver under Pruett and formerly of the Seahawks and Lions:
"I learned a lot from him. We won a lot of games. He knew how to win. Because I came to Marshall and played for him I made it to the NFL. I thank him for that."

**SPEEDSTER —** James Williams was the fastest receiver on the Marshall roster during Chad Pennington's senior season. *Courtesy Marshall University, photograph by Rick Haye.*

**Chris Crocker**, defensive back, the Cleveland Browns:

"He wanted to win and he wanted us to win. He wanted us to be not just the best players we could be, but the best team we could be. He prepared us well. We always thought we could win any game we played."

**Jim Grobe**, coach at Wake Forest and former coach at Ohio. Also was an assistant with Pruett at Marshall in the late 1970s:

"I knew Bobby. When the MAC let Marshall in the league, I knew we were letting the fox in the henhouse."

**Shaine Miles**, Marshall assistant under Pruett and Mark Snyder:

"I feel really close to Coach Pruett. He got me my start in coaching and I owe him so much for that."

**John Grace**, who plays for Calgary of the Canadian Football League::

"I couldn't believe it when I heard he resigned. I was really surprised. He always had us ready to play. He gave us a lot of confidence. We thought we could play with anybody. He always had us ready for big games."

**Lee Owens**, former coach at Akron, now at Ashland College:

"Marshall set the bar high. When they came into the league, we all knew they were good, but we wondered how they would be in November when it was cold and the snow was flying and the wind was blowing. They showed that they were capable of handling that. They were very, very good."

**Rick Minter**, former head coach, University of Cincinnati:

"Bob Pruett did a great job at Marshall. They were the bell-cow program of the Mid-American Conference while he was there. Marshall was to the MAC what Florida State is to the ACC."

**Mark McHale**, offensive line coach at Florida State, former MU offensive coordinator, on the 38-8 halftime deficit at the 2001 GMAC Bowl:

"We were going off the field at halftime and I told him, 'Don't put them down. Whatever you do you can't put them down. If you do, they'll quit on us.' He didn't put them down. He convinced those kids that we still had a chance to win that game and we won it."

**LaVorn Colclough**, wide receiver in 1996 and 1997:

"He inherited a loaded team, but he won with it. We won a lot of games and we had a lot of fun. Those were good times playing back then."

**Robert (Bob) Hardwick**, vice president, First Sentry Bank, Barboursville, West Virginia:

"I consider myself priviledged to have been a witness to greatness. Coach Pruett motivated and inspired young men to excel on and off the field. However, his true greatness resides in his heart. I watched him pay tribute at the funeral of R.F. Smith, pastor at Fifth Avenue Baptist Church. Coach Pruett cried uncontrollably while talking about his love and respect for his friend. Our coach laid open his heart for all to see—'a great man who just happened to be a great friend.'"

**Phil Herrold**, Marshall fan from Barboursville, West Virginia:
"Coach Pruett's going to be missed by all of his. He did a wonderful job and gave us a lot of memories."

**Rebecca Elswick**, Marshall fan from Milton, West Virginia:
"Coach Pruett is the definition of a successful coach, teacher and motivator. He is a role model. He touched the lives of so many young men."

**Dave Elmore**, Marshall fan and member of the congregation of Fifth Avenue Baptist:
"I can't thank Bobby enough for what he did for Marshall, for all of us. He gave us so many thrills on the field and gave the community so much off the field."

**John Pinkerman**, assistant director Boy Scouts of America, Huntington:
"Anytime I'd ask Bob to speak, he'd say yes. He would speak to our Boy Scout fundraisers and he would tell the people there, 'Whatever you're thinking about giving, that's not enough. Add more to it. The young men in Boy Scouts are an investment in your future. They're the people who are going to be working for you in a few years.' People always gave more when he spoke. And Bob gave, too. He always kidded me that when he spoke for Boy Scouts all it cost him was $125."

**Dr. Ken Wolfe**, a Huntington ear, nose and throat specialist at Veterans Hospital and a close friend of Pruett:
"Bobby Pruett's not only a tremendous coach, he's also a remarkable person. I don't think he has any rival for his degree of caring about the Huntington community. He's given hundreds of talks around the community without expecting any compensation, and visited innumerable people in the hospitals."

# A P P E N D I X

## Stats, Awards, & Highlights, the Pruett Years

### Bobby Pruett's Championship Game Records

Nov. 16, 1996 Southern Conference Marshall 42, Furman 17
Dec. 21, 1996 NCAA Division I-AA National Marshall 49, Montana 29
Nov. 15, 1997 Mid-American Conference East Division Marshall 27, Ohio 0
Dec. 5, 1997 Mid-American Conference Marshall 34, Toledo 14
Dec. 26, 1997 Motor City Bowl Mississippi 34, Marshall 31
Nov. 7, 1998 Mid-American Conference East Division Marshall 28, Central Michigan 0
Dec. 4, 1998 Mid-American Conference Marshall 23,Toledo 17
Dec. 23, 1998 Motor City Bowl Marshall 48, Louisville 29
Nov. 13, 1999 Mid-American Conference East Division Marshall 31, Western Michigan 17
Dec. 3, 1999 Mid-American Conference Marshall 34, Western Michigan 31
Dec. 27, 1999 Motor City Bowl Marshall 21, Brigham Young 3
Nov. 11, 2000 Mid-American Conference East Marshall 51, Miami (Ohio) 31
Dec. 2, 2000 Mid-American Conference Marshall 19, Western Michigan 14
Dec. 27, 2000 Motor City Bowl Marshall 25, Cincinnati 14
Nov. 10, 2001 Mid-American Conference East Marshall 27, Miami (Ohio) 21
Nov. 30, 2001 Mid-American Conference Toledo 41, Marshall 36
Dec. 19, 2001 GMAC Bowl Marshall 64, East Carolina 61
Nov. 23, 2002 Mid-American Conference East Marshall 24, Ohio 21
Dec. 7, 2002 Mid-American Conference Marshall 49, Toledo 45
Dec. 19, 2002 GMAC Bowl Marshall 38, Louisville 15
Nov. 12, 2003 Mid-American Conference East Miami (Ohio) 45, Marshall 6
Dec. 23, 2004 Fort Worth Bowl Cincinnati 32, Marshall 14

## Bobby Pruett vs. All-Opponents

Akron 5-2
Appalachian State 2-0
Army 1-0
Ball State 3-0
Bowling Green 4-2
Brigham Young 1-0
Buffalo 6-0
Central Florida 3-0
Central Michigan 4-0
Chattanooga 1-0
Cincinnati 1-1
The Citadel 1-0
Clemson 1-0
Delaware 1-0
East Carolina 1-0
Eastern Michigan 2-0
East Tennessee State 1-0
Florida 0-1
Furman 2-0
Georgia 0-1
Georgia Southern 1-0
Hofstra 1-0
Howard 1-0
Kansas State 1-0
Kent State 8-0
Liberty 1-0
Louisville 2-0
Massachusetts 1-0

Miami (Ohio) 6-2
Michigan State 0-1
Mississippi 0-1
Montana 1-0
North Carolina 0-1
Northern Illinois 2-0
Northern Iowa 1-0
Ohio 7-1
Ohio State 0-1
South Carolina 1-0
Southeast Missouri State 1-0
Temple 1-0
Tennessee 0-1
Toledo 4-3
Troy State 2-2
VMI 1-0
Virginia Tech 0-1
Western Carolina 1-0
Western Illinois 1-0
Western Kentucky 1-0
Western Michigan 5-1
West Virginia 0-1
West Virginia State 1-0
Wofford 1-0
Youngstown State 1-0

**Total 94-23**

## Marshall Football Coaches By Number of Victories

| | | | |
|---|---|---|---|
| **1.** | **Bobby Pruett** | **94-23** | **.803** |
| 2. | Cam Henderson | 68-46-5 | .592 |
| 3. | Jim Donnan | 64-21 | .753 |
| 4. | George Chaump | 33-16-1 | .670 |
| 5. | Boyd Chambers | 32-27-4 | .539 |
| 6. | Charlie Snyder | 28-58-3 | .331 |
| 7. | Charles Tallman | 22-9-7 | .671 |
| 8. | Herb Royer | 21-31-2 | .407 |
| 9. | Tom Dandelet | 18-16-2 | .528 |
| 10. | Stan Parrish | 13-8-1 | .614 |

## Bobby Pruett Profile

**Age:** 62

**Hometown:** Beckley, West Virginia

**Family:** Wife, Elsie; Sons Rodney, Stephen, Kenneth; Grandsons, Sam, Adam, Bobby, Jacob.

**Education:** Beckley High School, 1961; Marshall University, B.A., social studies and physical education, 1965; Virginia Tech, M.A., administration and physical education, 1972.

**Academic Honors:** Marshall University Distinguished Alumni Award, 2003

**Athletic Career:** Beckley High School: football, wrestling, basketball, track. Marshall University, football, wrestling. Virginia Sailors semi-pro football.

**Coaching Career:** Marshall assistant 1979-1982; Wake Forest assistant 1983-1989; Mississippi assistant 1990-1991; Tulane assistant 1992-1993; Florida assistant 1994-1995; Marshall head coach 1996-2004.

**Coaching Highlights:** NCAA Division I-AA national champion: 1996; Southern Conference champion: 1996; Mid-American Conference champion: 1997, 1998, 1999, 2000, 2002; Motor City Bowl: 1997, 1998, 1999, 2000; GMAC Bowl: 2001, 2002; Fort Worth Bowl: 2004.

**Coaching Record:** 94-23.


## Bobby Pruett's Coaching Record Through the Years

1979 Marshall Defensive backs coach 1-10
1980 Marshall Defensive backs coach 2-8-1
1981 Marshall Defensive coordinator 2-9
1982 Marshall Defensive coordinator 3-8
1983 Wake Forest Defensive backs coach 4-7
1984 Wake Forest Defensive backs coach 6-5
1985 Wake Forest Defensive coordinator 4-7
1986 Wake Forest Defensive coordinator 5-6
1987 Wake Forest Defensive backs coach 7-4
1988 Wake Forest Defensive coordinator 6-4-1
1989 Wake Forest Defensive backs coach 2-8-1
1990 Mississippi Defensive backs coach 9-3 Gator Bowl
1991 Mississippi Defensive backs coach 5-6
1992 Tulane Defensive coordinator 2-9
1993 Tulane Defensive coordinator 4-8
1994 Florida Defensive coordinator 10-2-1 Sugar Bowl
1995 Florida Defensive coordinator 12-1 Fiesta Bowl
1996 Marshall Head coach 15-0 I-AA title game
1997 Marshall Head coach 10-3 Motor City Bowl
1998 Marshall Head coach 12-1 Motor City Bowl
1999 Marshall Head coach 13-0 Motor City Bowl
2000 Marshall Head coach 8-5 Motor City Bowl
2001 Marshall Head coach 11-2 GMAC Bowl
2002 Marshall Head coach 11-2 GMAC Bowl
2003 Marshall Head coach 8-4
2004 Marshall Head coach 6-6 Fort Worth Bowl

## Bobby Pruett Game-By-Game

### 1996

**Regular Season**
Marshall 55, Howard 27
Marshall 42, West Virginia State 7
Marshall 29, Georgia Southern 13
Marshall 37, Western Kentucky 3
Marshall 45, Chattanooga 0
Marshall 45, VMI 20
Marshall 56, Western Carolina 21
Marshall 24, Appalachian State 10
Marshall 56, The Citadel 25
Marshall 34, East Tennessee State 10
Marshall 42, Furman 17

**NCAA I-AA Playoffs**
Marshall 59, Delaware 14
Marshall 54, Furman 0
Marshall 31, Northern Iowa 14

**NCAA Championship Game**
Marshall 49, Montana 29

### 1997

**Regular Season**
West Virginia 42, Marshall 31
Marshall 35, Army 25
Marshall 42, Kent State 17
Marshall 48, Western Illinois 7
Marshall 42, Ball State 16
Marshall 52, Akron 17
Miami (Ohio) 45, Marshall 21
Marshall 48, Eastern Michigan 25
Marshall 45, Central Michigan 17
Marshall 28, Bowling Green 0
Marshall 27, Ohio 0

**Mid-American Conference Championship**
Marshall 34, Toledo 14

**Motor City Bowl**
Mississippi 34, Marshall 31

### 1998

**Regular Season**
Marshall 27, Akron 16
Marshall 42, Tory State 12
Marshall 24, South Carolina 21
Marshall 26, Eastern Michigan 23
Marshall 31, Miami (Ohio) 17
Marshall 30, Ohio 23
Marshall 42, Kent State 7
Marshall 42, Ball State 10
Bowling Green 34, Marshall 13
Marshall 28, Central Michigan 0
Marshall 29, Wofford 27

**Mid-American Conference Championship**
Marshall 23, Toledo 17

**Motor City Bowl**
Marshall 48, Louisville 29

### 1999

**Regular Season**
Marshall 13, Clemson 10
Marshall 63, Liberty 3
Marshall 35, Bowling Green 15
Marshall 34, Temple 0
Marshall 32, Miami (Ohio) 14
Marshall 38, Toledo 13
Marshall 59, Buffalo 3
Marshall 41, Northern Illinois 9
Marshall 28, Kent State 16
Marshall 31, Western Michigan 17
Marshall 34, Ohio 3

**Mid-American Conference Championship**
Marshall 34, Western Michigan 30

**Motor City Bowl**
Marshall 21, Brigham Young 3

## 2000

**Regular Season**
Marshall 63, Southeast Missouri State 7
Michigan State 34, Marshall 24
North Carolina 20, Marshall 15
Marshall 47, Buffalo 14
Western Michigan 30, Marshall 10
Toledo 42, Marshall 0
Marshall 34, Kent State 12
Marshall 31, Akron 28
Marshall 20, Bowling Green 13
Marshall 51, Miami (Ohio) 31
Ohio 38, Marshall 28

**Mid-American Conference Championship**
Marshall 19, Western Michigan 14

**Motor City Bowl**
Marshall 25, Cincinnati 14

## 2001

**Regular Season**
Florida 49, Marshall 14
Marshall 49, Massachusetts 20
Marshall 37, Bowling Green 31
Marshall 37, Northern Illinois 15
Marshall 34, Buffalo 14
Marshall 42, Central Michigan 21
Marshall 50, Akron 33
Marshall 42, Kent State 21
Marshall 27, Miami (Ohio) 21
Marshall 42, Ohio 18
Marshall 38, Youngstown State 24

**Mid-American Conference Championship**
Toledo 41, Marshall 36

**GMAC Bowl**
Marshall 64, East Carolina 61

## 2002

**Regular Season**
Marshall 50, Applachian State 17
Virginia Tech 47, Marshall 21
Marshall 26, Central Florida 21
Marshall 42, Kent State 21
Marshall 66, Buffalo 21
Marshall 24, Troy State 7
Marshall 23, Central Michigan 18
Akron 34, Marshall 20
Marshall 36, Miami (Ohio) 34
Marshall 24, Ohio 21
Marshall 38, Ball State 14

**Mid-American Conference Championship**
Marshall 49, Toledo 45

**GMAC Bowl**
Marshall 38, Louisville 15

## 2003

**Regular Season**
Marshall 45, Hofstra 21
Tennessee 34, Marshall 24
Toledo 24, Marshall 17
Marshall 27, Kansas State 20
Troy State 33, Marshall 24
Marshall 49, Kent State 33
Marshall 26, Buffalo 16
Marshall 41, Western Michigan 21
Marshall 42, Akron 24
Miami (Ohio) 45, Marshall 6
Marshall 21, Central Florida 7
Marshall 28, Ohio 0

## 2004

### Regular Season
Troy State 17, Marshall 15
Ohio State 24, Marshall 21
Georgia 13, Marshall 3
Marshall 33, Miami (Ohio) 25
Marshall 16, Ohio 13
Marshall 27, Kent State 17
Marshall 48, Buffalo 14
Marshall 20, Central Florida 3
Akron 31, Marshall 28
Bowling Green 56, Marshall 35
Marshall 31, Western Michigan 21

### Fort Worth Bowl
Cincinnati 32, Marshall 14

---

## *Bobby Pruett Marshall players drafted by the NFL*

- Rogers Beckett, safety, second round, 2000, San Diego Chargers
- Doug Chapman, running back, third round, 2000, Minnesota Vikings
- Chris Crocker, safety, third round, 2003, Cleveland Browns
- Johnathan Goddard, defensive end, sixth round, 2005, Detroit Lions
- Byron Leftwich, quarterback, first round, 2003, Jacksonville Jaguars
- Chris Massey, long snapper, seventh round, 2002, St. Louis Rams
- Randy Moss, wide receiver, first round, 1998, Minnesota Vikings
- Chad Pennington, quarterback, first round, 2000, New York Jets
- Steve Sciullo, tackle, fourth round, 2003, Indianapolis Colts
- Paul Toviessi, defensive end, 2001, second round, Denver Broncos
- John Wade, center, 1998, fifth round, Jacksonville Jaguars
- Darius Watts, wide receiver, second round, 2004, Denver Broncos
- James Williams, wide receiver, sixth round, 2000, Seattle Seahawks

## *Bobby Pruett Marshall players signed as free agents by the NFL*

- Rogers Beckett, safety, 2000, San Diego Chargers
- Rogers Beckett, safety, 2003, Cincinnati Bengals
- Doug Chapman, running back, 2004, San Francisco 49ers
- Earl Charles, running back, 2004, New England Patriots

- Earl Charles, running back, 2005, New England Patriots
- B.J. Cohen, defensive end, 1999, Oakland Raiders
- Melvin Cunningham, cornerback, 1997, Miami Dolphins
- Josh Davis, wide receiver, 2004, Miami Dolphins
- David Foye, wide receiver, 2000, Philadelphia Eagles
- David Foye, wide receiver, 2001, Miami Dolphins
- John Grace, linebacker, 2000, Tampa Bay Buccaneers
- Mike Guilliams, tackle, 2000, Cleveland Browns
- Chris Hanson, punter, 1999, Cleveland Browns
- Chris Hanson, punter, 2001, Miami Dolphins
- Chris Hanson, punter, 2001, Jacksonville Jaguars
- Scott Harper, guard, 2001, Baltimore Ravens
- Scott Harper, guard, 2004, Washington Redskins
- Stan Hill, quarterback, 2005, New Orleans Saints
- J.R. Jenkins, kicker, 2002, Baltimore Ravens
- Gregg Kellett, tight end, 2002, Chicago Bears
- Gregg Kellett, tight end, 2002, Indianapolis Colts
- Eric Kresser, quarterback, 1997, Cincinnati Bengals
- Billy Lyon, defensive tackle, 1998, Green Bay Packers
- Billy Lyon, defensive tackle, 2003, Minnesota Vikings
- Denero Marriott, wide receiver, 2003, Philadelphia Eagles
- Nate McPeek, tackle, 2004, Green Bay Packers
- Giradie Mercer, defensive tackle, 2000, Philadelphia Eagles
- Giradie Mercer, defensive tackle, 2001, New York Jets
- Giradie Mercer, defensive tackle, 2002, Carolina Panthers
- Andre O'Neal, linebacker, 2000, Kansas City Chiefs
- Andre O'Neal, linebacker, 2001, Minnesota Vikings
- Steven Perretta, guard, 2004, Indianapolis Colts
- Nate Poole, wide receiver, 2001, Arizona Cardinals
- Jason Rader, tight end, 2004, Atlanta Falcons
- Yancey Satterwhite, cornerback, 2003, Cleveland Browns
- Jason Starkey, center, 2000, Arizona Cardinals
- Erik Thomas, running back, 1997, Arizona Cardinals
- Llow Turner, running back, 2000, Tampa Bay Buccaneers
- John Wade, center, 1998, Tampa Bay Buccaneers
- Butchie Wallace, running back, 2004, Minnesota Vikings
- Butchie Wallace, running back, 2005, New Orleans Saints
- James Williams, wide receiver, 2003, Detroit Lions
- Jamie Wilson, tackle, 1997, Carolina Panthers
- Jamie Wilson, tackle, 1999, Indianapolis Colts
- Max Yates, linebacker, 2002, Minnesota Vikings
- Max Yates, linebacker, 2003, San Francisco 49ers

## *Players who set Marshall records under Bobby Pruett*

### Postseason records
- Passing efficiency: Eric Kresser, 1996, 169.08 rating

- Receiving yardage: Randy Moss, 1996-97, 979 yards
- Interceptions: Melvin Cunningham, 1993-96, 6 interceptions
- Punting yardage: Chris Hanson, 1995-98, 1,978 yards
- Punt return yardage: Tim Martin, 1993-96, 392 yards

## Team records
- Rushing yards in a season: 1996, 3,395 yards
- Yards per rush: 1996, 5.8 yards per rush
- Most completions: 2001 vs. East Carolina, 41 completions
- Most completions in a season: 2002, 383 completions
- Most net yards in a game: 2001 vs. Akron, 726 yards
- Most touchdown passes in a game: 1997 vs. Ball State, 6; 2001 vs. Ohio, 6
- Highest single-game completion percentage: 1996 vs. The Citadel, 100 percent (11-for-11)
- Highest season completion percentage: 2003, 67.6 percent
- Most net yards in a season: 1996, 7,287 yards
- Most net yards per play in a season: 1999, 7.86 yards
- Highest average total offense yards in a season: 2001, 505 yards per game
- Most receptions in a game: 2002 vs. Ball State, 44 receptions
- Most receptions in a season: 2002, 383 receptions
- Most touchdown receptions in a game: 1997 vs. Ball State, 6 touchdowns; 2001 vs. Ohio, 6 touchdowns
- Most touchdown receptions in a season: 1997, 44 touchdown receptions
- Most total points in a season: 1996, 658 points
- Most touchdowns in a season: 1996, 87 touchdowns
- Most conversion kicks made in a season: 1996, 82 kicks
- Most field goals made: 1999 vs. Miami (Ohio), 4 field goals
- Highest average per punt in a game: 2001 at Toledo, 63 yards
- Most fumbles in a game: 2002 at Akron, 9 fumbles
- Fewest fumbles lost in a season: 1999, 6 fumbles
- Most victories in a season: 1996, 15 victories
- Most consecutive victories: 1998-2000, 18 victories
- Most points allowed in a victory, 2001 vs. East Carolina, 61 points
- Consecutive victories at Joan C. Edwards Stadium: 1996-2000, 36 victories
- Single-season attendance: 1996, 227,712 in attendance

## Individual records
- Most yards per rush in a career: Erik Thomas, 1993-1996, 6.5 yards per rush
- Most all-purpose yards in a game: Randy Moss, 1996 vs. Delaware, 348 yards
- Most passing attempts in a game: Byron Leftwich, 2001 vs. East Carolina, 70 attempts
- Most passing attempts in a career: Chad Pennington, 1995-1999, 1,619 attempts
- Most completions in a game: Byron Leftwich, 2001 vs. East Carolina, 41
- Most completions in a career: Chad Pennington, 1,026 completions
- Most net passing yards in a game: Byron Leftwich, 2001 vs. East Carolina, 566
- Most net passing yards in a career: Chad Pennington, 1995-1999, 13,143
- Most touchdown passes in a game: Chad Pennington, 1997 vs. Ball State, 6; Byron Leftwich, 2001 vs. Ohio, 6

- Most touchdown passes in a season: Chad Pennington, 1997, 42 touchdown passes
- Most touchdown passes in a career: Chad Pennington, 1995-1999, 115 touchdown passes
- Highest completion percentage in a game: Eric Kresser, 1996 vs. The Citadel, 100 percent (11-for-11)
- Highest completion percentage in a season: Stan Hill, 2003, 69.6 percent
- Highest completion percentage in a career: Byron Leftwich, 1998-2002, 65.1 percent
- Most net plays in a game: Byron Leftiwich, 2001 vs. East Carolina, 82 plays
- Most net plays in a career: Chad Pennington, 1995-1999, 1,855 plays
- Most net yards in a game: Byron Leftwich, 2001 vs. East Carolina, 566 yards
- Most net yards in a career: Chad Pennington, 1995-1999, 13,091
- Most receptions in a game: Josh Davis, 2004 vs. Akron, 15; David Foye, 2000 vs. Kent State, 15; Denero Marriott, 2001 vs. East Carolina, 15 receptions
- Most receptions in a career: Josh Davis, 2001-2004, 306 receptions
- Most net receiving yards in a game: Randy Moss, 1996 vs. Delaware, 208 yards
- Most net receiving yards in a season, Randy Moss, 1997, 1,820 yards
- Most touchdown receptions in a game: Randy Moss, 1997 vs. Ball State, 5 touchdowns
- Most touchdown receptions in a season: Randy Moss, 1998, 28 touchdown receptions
- Most touchdown receptions in a career: Randy Moss, 1996-1997, 54 touchdown receptions
- Most points scored in a season: Randy Moss, 1996, 174 points
- Most touchdowns in a season: Randy Moss, 1996, 29 touchdowns
- Most conversion kicks made in a season: Tim Openlander, 1996, 82 kicks
- Most conversion kicks made in a career: Tim Openlander, 1994-1996, 211 kicks
- Most tackles for loss in a game: Johnathan Goddard, 2004 vs. Miami (Ohio), 4 TFLs; Johnathan Goddard, 2004 vs. Akron, 4 TFLs; Johnathan Goddard, 2004 vs. Western Michigan, 4 TFLs; Johnathan Goddard, 2003 vs. Kent State, 4 TFLs; Jamus Martin, 2003 vs. Kent State, 4 TFLs
- Most tackles for loss in a career: Johnathan Goddard, 2001-2004, 63.5 TFLs
- Most sacks in a game: Johnathan Goddard, 2004 vs. Miami (Ohio), 4 sacks
- Most sacks in a career: B.J. Cohen, 1994-1997, 51 sacks
- Highest punting average in a game: Curtis Head, 2001 vs. Toledo, 63.0
- Longest punt: Curtis Head, 2001 vs. Toledo, 75 yards
- Most punt returns in a season: Tim Martin, 1996, 49 returns
- Most punt returns in a career: Tim Martin, 1993-1996,150 returns
- Most net return yards in a game: Damone Williams, 1998 vs. Ohio, 140 yards
- Most net return yards in a season: Tim Martin, 1995, 515 yards
- Most net return yards in a career: Tim Martin, 1993-1996, 1,458 yards
- Most touchdown passes in a season: Chad Pennington, 1997, 39 touchdown passes
- Most touchdown receptions in a season: Randy Moss, 1996, 28 touchdown receptions
- Most touchdown passes in a career: Chad Pennington, 1995-1999, 115 touchdown passes
- Most all-purpose yards per game: Randy Moss,1996-1997, 167.7 yards per game

**Players who set NCAA Division I-A records under Bobby Pruett**
- Most games catching a touchdown pass in a season: Randy Moss, 1997, 12 games
- Most consecutive games with a touchdown reception: Randy Moss, 1997, 12 games

- Most touchdown passes in a season by a sophomore: Chad Pennington, 1997, 37 touchdown passes

### Players who set NCAA Division I-AA records under Bobby Pruett
- Most games catching a touchdown pass in a season: Randy Moss,1996, 11 games
- Most receiving yards gained by a freshman: Randy Moss, 1996, 1,073 yards
- Most touchdown passes caught by a freshman: Randy Moss, 1996, 19 touchdown passes (record for all divisions)
- Most touchdown passes in a single game: Randy Moss, 1996 vs. Montana, 4 touchdown passes
- Postseason net yards receiving: Randy Moss, 1996, 636 yards
- Postseason touchdown passes caught: Randy Moss, 1996, 9 touchdown catches
- Net yards receiving in a game: Randy Moss, 1996 vs. Delaware, 288 yards

### Mid-American Conference records set under Bobby Pruett
- Most passing yards in a season: 2002, 4,804 yards
- Most penalties in a season: 1999, 105 penalties
- Most touchdown passes in a season, 1997, 41 touchdown passes
- Attendance at home games: 1998, 173,516 in attendance
- Attendance at a bowl game: 1999 Motor City Bowl, 52,449 in attendance
- Most touchdown receptions in a game: Randy Moss vs. Ball State, 1997, 5 touchdown receptions
- Most points scored in a game: Randy Moss vs. Ball State, 1997, 32 points
- Most touchdown passes in a career: Chad Pennington, 1997-1999, 100 touchdown passes
- Most touchdown passes scored or passed for in a season: Chad Pennington, 1997, 40 touchdown passes
- Most touchdown passes in a season: Chad Pennington, 1997, 39 touchdown passes
- Most receiving yards in a season: Randy Moss, 1997, 1,647 yards
- Most touchdown passes caught in a season: Randy Moss, 1997, 25 passes
- Most points scored in a season, Randy Moss, 1997, 152 points
- Most touchdowns scored in a season: Randy Moss, 1997, 25 touchdowns

### Southern Conference records set under Bobby Pruett
- Most points in a season: 1996, 658 points
- Most touchdowns passing in a season: 1996, 41 touchdown passes
- Completion percentage in a game: Eric Kresser, 1996 vs. The Citadel, 100 percent (11-for-11)
- Most touchdowns in a season: Randy Moss, 1996, 19 touchdowns
- Most games catching a touchdown pass: Randy Moss, 1996, 11 games
- Most extra points: Tim Openlander, 1996, 82 points
- Most extra points in a career: Tim Openlander, 1994-1996, 164 points
- Most punt returns for a touchdown: Tim Martin, 1993-1996, 4 touchdown returns

## Honors and Awards

### Coach Pruett
- 1996 All-American Football Foundation Frank Leahy National Coach of the Year
- 1999 All-American Football Foundation Johnny Vaught Lifetime Achievement Award
- 2003 Blue-Gray Game head coach
- 1996 Chevrolet National Coach of the Year
- 1998 The Herald-Dispatch Citizen of the Year
- 1998 Mid-American Conference Coach of the Year
- 1997 National Coach of the Year by "Coach of the Year Clinics"
- 1996 West Virginia Sports Writers Association Coach of the Year
- 1997 West Virginia Sports Writers Association Coach of the Year
- 1998 West Virginia Sports Writers Association Coach of the Year
- 1999 West Virginia Sports Writers Association Coach of the Year
- 1999 Marshall University Hall of Fame
- Winningest football coach in Marshall history by victories (94)
- Winningest football coach in Marshall history by percentage (.803) * more than one season

### Assistant coaches
### Larry Kueck
  2003 Blue-Gray Game

### Players

### ABC Television All-American Team
- Darius Watts, wide receiver, 2001, second team

### ABC Sports All-Time All-American Team
- Randy Moss, wide receiver, 2003

### American Football Quarterly All-American Team
- Melvin Cunningham, cornerback, 1996
- Eric Kresser, quarterback, 1996
- Billy Lyon, defensive tackle, 1996
- Randy Moss, wide receiver, 1996

### Anson Mount Scholar-Athlete Award
- Chad Pennington, quarterback, 1999

### Associated Press All-America First Team
- Billy Lyon, defensive tackle, 1996
- Randy Moss, wide receiver, 1996
- Randy Moss, wide receiver, 1997

### Associated Press All-America Second Team
- B.J. Cohen, defensive end, 1996
- Melvin Cunningham, cornerback, 1996
- Aaron Ferguson, guard, 1996
- Eric Kresser, quarterback, 1996
- Tim Openlander, kicker, 1996
- Johnathan Goddard, defensive end, 2004

### AT&T Long Distance Award
- Chad Pennington, quarterback, Sept. 7, 1997
- Randy Moss, wide receiver, Sept. 7, 1997
- Chad Pennington, quarterback, Sept. 13, 1997
- LaVorn Colclough, wide receiver, Sept. 13, 1997
- Chad Pennington, quarterback, Sept. 20, 1997
- Llow Turner, running back,, Sept. 20, 1997

## Sammy Baugh Award
• Chad Pennington, quarterback, 1999

## Fred Biletnikoff Award
• Randy Moss, wide receiver,1997

## Fred Biletnikoff Award Semifinalist
• Darius Watts, wide receiver, 2001

## Red Blaik Leadership Award
• Billy Lyon, defensive tackle, 1996

## Blue-Gray Game
• Nate McPeek, tackle, 2003
• Luke Salmons, guard, 2003
• Butchie Wallace, running back, 2003 (MVP)

## Bronco Nagurski Award Finalist
• Johnathan Goddard, defensive end, 2004

## Buck Harless Student-Athlete Award
• Chad Pennington, quarterback, 1998-1999
• Chad Pennington, quarterback, 1998-1999

## Burger King Scholar-Athlete of the Week
• Chad Pennington, quarterback, Sept. 25, 1999

## Lowell Cade Sports Person of the Year
• Chad Pennington, quarterback, 1999

## CNN/SI College Football Player of the Week
• Randy Moss, wide receiver, Sept. 27, 1997

## J.D. Coffman Scout Team Player of the Year
• Doug Hodges, safety, 1996
• Jason Redman, wide receiver, 1997
• Andrew Cowen, quarterback, 1998
• Eddie Smolder, tight end, 1999
• Ben Poe, defensive back, 1999
• Judd Tabor, linebacker, 1999
• Brad Bates, wide receiver, 2000
• Jesse Wisnewski, offensive lineman, 2000
• Jeff Mullins, tight end, 2001
• Curtis Keyes, safety, 2002
• Nathan Kiskis, defensive end, 2002

• Steven Bobrowski, lineman, 2002
• Will Albin,fullback, 2003
• Nathan Kiskis, defensive end, 2003
• Jimmy Skinner, quarterback, 2004

## CBS Sportsline.com All-American Team
• Johnathan Goddard, defensive end, 2004

## *College Football News* All-American Team
• Darius Watts, wide receiver, 2001
• Byron Leftwich, quarterback, 2001

## Compaq Plays of the Week
• Bobby Addison, defensive end, Sept. 11, 1999
• Doug Chapman, running back, Dec. 27, 1999
• James Williams, wide receiver, Sept. 11, 1999

## CoSIDA Academic All-America
• Jimmy Parker, defensive tackle, 2000
• Chad Pennington, quarterback, 1998
• Chad Pennington, quarterback, 1999

## CoSIDA Academic All-District First Team
• Jeff Mullins, tight end, 2004
• Jimmy Parker, defensive tackle, 2000
• Chad Pennington, quarterback, 1998
• Chad Pennington, quarterback, 1999

## CoSIDA Academic All-District Second Team
• Chris Massey, long snapper, 1999
• Jimmy Parker, defensive tackle, 1999
• Scott Pettit, tight end, 2000

## Draddy Scholar Athlete of the Year Award
• Chad Pennington, quarterback, 1999

## East-West Shrine Game
• Rogers Beckett, safety, 1999
• Josh Davis, wide receiver, 2004
• Max Yates, linebacker, 2001
• Darius Watts, wide receiver, 2003

## Florida vs. USA All-Star Game
• James Williams, wide receiver, 1999

*Football Gazette* **All-America First Team**
• Randy Moss, kick returner, 1996

*Football Gazaette* **All-America Second Team**
• Randy Moss, wide receiver, 1996
• Jamie Wilson, tackle, 1996

*Football Gazette* **All-America Third Team**
• B.J. Cohen, defensive end, 1996

*Football Gazette* **Offensive Player of the Week**
• Randy Moss, wide receiver, Nov. 30, 1996

*Football Gazette* **Defensive Player of the Week**
• B.J. Cohen, defensive end, Nov. 30, 1996

*Football News* **Preseason All-America**
• Randy Moss, wide receiver, 1997
• Byron Leftwich, quarterback, 2002
• Darius Watts, wide receiver, 2002

**Football Writers Association All-America**
• Randy Moss, wide receiver, 1997
• Johnathan Goddard, defensive end, 2004

**Football Writers Association National Team of the Week**
• Marshall, following victory over Kansas State, Sept. 22, 2003

**GMAC Bowl MVP**
• Byron Leftwich, quarterback, 2001
• Byron Leftwich, quarterback, 2002

**GMAC Bowl Offensive MVP**
• Denero Marriott, wide receiver, 2002

**GMAC Bowl Defensive MVP**
• Yancey Satterwhite, cornerback, 2002
Gridiron Classic
• Kevin Atkins, linebacker, 2004
• Johnathan Goddard, defensive end, 2004
• Nate Griffin, tackle, 2004
• Jason Rader, tight end, 2003

**Hardman Award as West Virginia Amateur Athlete of the Year**
• Randy Moss, wide receiver, 1996
• Chad Pennington, quarterback, 1999
• Byron Leftwich, quarterback, 2001
• Byron Leftwich, quarterback, 2002

**Heisman Trophy Finalists**
• Randy Moss, wide receiver, fourth place, 1997
• Chad Pennington, quarterback, fifth place, 1999
• Byron Leftwich, quarterback, sixth place, 2002

**Hula Bowl**
• Doug Chapman, running back, 2000
• Johnathan Goddard, defensive end, 2004
• Paul Toviessi, defensive end, 2001

**Jacobs Blocking Trophy**
• Aaron Ferguson, guard, 1996

**Las Vegas Classic**
• Stan Hill, quarterback, 2004

**Mid-American Conference Championship Game MVP**
• Randy Moss, wide receiver, 1997
• Chad Pennington, quarterback, 1998
• Chad Pennington, quarterback, 1999
• Byron Leftwich, quarterback, 2000
• Byron Leftwich, quarterback, 2002

**Mid-American Conference Defensive Player of the Week**
• John Grace, linebacker, Sept. 19, 1998
• John Grace, linebacker, Oct. 3, 1998
• John Grace, linebacker, Sept. 4, 1999
• Danny Derricott, cornerback, Oct. 2, 1999
• Ralph Street, defensive end, Oct. 23, 2000
• Max Yates, linebacker, Oct. 6, 2001
• Duran Smith, linebacker, Oct. 21, 2002
• Roberto Terrell, cornerback, Sept. 9, 2003
• Entire team, Sept. 22, 2003
• Gladstone Coke, linebacker, Nov. 11, 2003
• Jamus Martin, defensive end, Nov. 24, 2003

- Johnathan Goddard, defensive end, Dec. 1, 2003
- Johnathan Goddard, defensive end, Sept. 11, 2004
- Johnathan Goddard, defensive end, Oct. 4, 2004
- Johnathan Goddard, defensive end, Oct. 11, 2004
- Johnathan Goddard, defensive end, Oct. 23, 2004
- Chrys Royal, safety, Oct. 30, 2004

**Mid-American Conference Offensive Player of the Week**
- Randy Moss, wide receiver, Sept. 6, 1997
- Chad Pennington, quarterback, Sept. 12,1998
- Chad Pennington, quarterback, Oct. 3, 1998
- Chad Pennington, quarterback, Oct. 19, 1999
- Chad Pennington, quarterback, Nov. 16, 1999
- Byron Leftwich, quarterback, Oct. 30, 2000
- Trod Buggs, running back, Sept. 8, 2001
- Byron Leftwich, quarterback, Sept. 29, 2001
- Byron Leftwich, quarterback, Oct. 20, 2001
- Denero Marriott, wide receiver, Nov. 10, 2001
- Brandon Carey, running back, Sept. 23, 2002
- Butchie Wallace, running back, Oct. 7, 2002
- Byron Leftwich, quarterback, Oct. 14, 2002
- Byron Leftwich, quarterback, Oct. 28, 2002
- Stan Hill, quarterback, Nov. 18, 2002
- Byron Leftwich, quarterback, Dec. 2, 2002
- Stan Hill, quarterback, Sept. 9, 2003
- Entire team, Sept. 22, 2003
- Darius Watts, wide receiver, Oct. 27, 2003
- Butchie Wallace, running back, Nov. 3, 2003

**Mid-American Conference Special Teams Player of the Week**
- Curtis Jones, kick returner, Oct. 30, 2000

- Maurice Hines, punt returner, Nov. 6, 2000
- Roberto Terrell, kick returner, Sept. 29, 2001
- Curtis Head, kicker-punter, Nov. 3, 2001
- Curtis Head, kicker-punter, Sept. 23, 2002
- Curtis Head, kicker-punter, Oct. 21, 2002
- Jeff Mullins, long snapper, Dec. 2, 2002
- Entire team, Sept. 22, 2003
- Ben Lewis, punter, Nov. 17, 2003
- Ian O'Connor, kicker, Sept. 4, 2004
- Ian O'Connor, kicker, Oct. 11, 2004
- Emanuel Spann, wide receiver, Oct. 18, 2004
- Ivan Clark, kick returner, Oct. 23, 2004
- Ian O'Connor, kicker, Oct. 30, 2004

**Mid-American Scholar Athlete of the Week**
- Chad Pennington, quarterback, Sept. 4, 1999
- Curtis Head, kicker-punter, Sept. 24, 2002

**Mid-American Conference First Team**
- Rogers Beckett, safety, 1998
- Rogers Beckett, safety, 1999
- Jimmy Cabellos, guard, 1998
- Jimmy Cabellos, guard, 1999
- Doug Chapman, running back, 1998
- Doug Chapman, running back, 1999
- B.J. Cohen, defensive end, 1997
- LaVorn Colclough, wide receiver, 1997
- LaVorn Colclough, wide receiver, 1998
- Chris Crocker, safety, 2001
- Josh Davis, wide receiver, 2001
- Danny Derricott, cornerback, 1998
- Danny Derricott, cornerback, 1999
- Danny Derricott, cornerback, 2000
- Johnathan Goddard, defensive end, 2004
- John Grace, linebacker, 1999
- Mike Guilliams, guard, 1998
- Mike Guilliams, guard, 1999
- Ricky Hall, defensive tackle, 1998
- Curtis Head, kicker-punter, 2002
- Maurice Hines, cornerback, 2000
- Gregg Kellett, tight end, 2001
- Byron Leftwich, quarterback, 2001
- Byron Leftwich, quarterback, 2002
- Jamus Martin, defensive end, 2003

- Larry McCloud, linebacker, 1997
- Nate McPeek, tackle, 2001
- Nate McPeek, tackle, 2002
- Giradie Mercer, defensive tackle, 1998
- Giradie Mercer, defensive tackle, 1999
- Randy Moss, wide receiver, 1997
- Jimmy Parker, defensive tackle, 2000
- Chad Pennington, quarterback, 1997
- Chad Pennington, quarterback,1998
- Chad Pennington, quarterback, 1999
- Nate Poole, wide receiver, 1999
- Nate Poole, wide receiver, 2000
- Steve Sciullo, tackle, 2001
- Steve Sciullo, tackle, 2002
- Jason Starkey, center, 1999
- Ralph Street, defensive end, 2001
- Paul Toviessi, defensive end, 1999
- Paul Toviessi, defensive end, 2000
- John Wade, center, 1997
- Darius Watts, wide reciver, 2001
- Darius Watts, wide receiver, 2002
- Darius Watts, wide receiver, 2003
- James Williams, wide receiver, 1999
- Max Yates, linebacker, 2000
- Max Yates, linebacker, 2001

## Mid-American Conference Second Team
- Rogers Beckett, safety, 1997
- Toriano Brown, defensive tackle, 2002
- Toriano Brown, defensive tackle, 2003
- Jimmy Cabellos, guard, 1999
- Doug Chapman, running back, 1997
- Earl Charles, running back, 2003
- Chris Crocker, safety, 2002
- Josh Davis, wide receiver, 2002
- Josh Davis, wide receiver, 2004
- Sam Goines, linebacker, 2001
- John Grace, linebacker, 1998
- Curtis Head, kicker-punter, 1999
- Curtis Head, kicker-punter, 2001
- Curtis Keyes, safety, 2004
- Jamus Martin, defensive end, 2002
- Jamus Martin, defensive end, 2004
- Denero Marriott, wide receiver, 2001
- Larry Moore, cornerback, 1997
- Andre O'Neal, linebacker, 1999
- Jimmy Parker, defensive tackle, 1999

- Steve Perretta, guard, 2001
- Steve Perretta, guard, 2002
- Ron Puggi, defensive end, 1998
- Ron Puggi, defensive end, 1999
- Jason Rader, tight end, 2003
- Brian Reed, guard, 1997
- Jamie Rodgers, tackle, 1998
- Duran Smith, linebacker, 2002
- Jason Starkey, center, 1998
- Charles Tynes, linebacker, 2003
- Butchie Wallace, running back, 2001
- Orlando Washington, defensive tackle, 2001
- Orlando Washington, defensive tackle, 2002
- Max Yates, linebacker, 1999

## Mid-American Conference All-Academic Team
- T.C. Beaver, kicker, 2000
- Rogers Beckett, safety, 1999
- Joe Deifel, tight end, 2001
- Cory Dennison, long snapper, 2000
- Cory Dennison, long snapper, 2001
- Andrew English, quarterback, 2001
- Stephen Galbraith, quarterback, 2000
- John Grace, linebacker, 1999
- Paul Hardy, offensive lineman, 2000
- Scott Harper, guard, 2000
- Curtis Head, kicker-punter, 2000
- Curtis Head, kicker-punter, 2001
- J.R. Jenkins, kicker, 1999
- J.R. Jenkins, kicker, 2000
- Dewayne Lewis, defensive tackle, 1999
- Josh Lohri, wide receiver, 2001
- Chris Massey, long snapper, 1999
- Chris Massey, long snapper, 2000
- Chris Massey, long snapper, 2001
- Nate McPeek, tackle, 2001
- Jeff Mullins, tight end, 2004
- Ian O'Connor, kicker, 2004
- Andre O'Neal, linebacker, 1999
- Jimmy Parker, defensive tackle, 1999
- Jimmy Parker, defensive tackle, 2000
- Chad Pennington, quarterback, 1997
- Chad Pennington, quarterback, 1998
- Chad Pennington, quarterback, 1999

- Scott Pettit, tight end, 1999
- Scott Pettit, tight end, 2000
- Chuck Spearman, quarterback, 2000
- Jimmy Tyson, defensive back, 2001
- Butchie Wallace, running back, 2000

## Mid-American Conference Offensive Player of the Year
- Randy Moss, wide receiver, 1997
- Chad Pennington, quarterback, 1999
- Byron Leftwich, quarterback, 2001
- Byron Leftwich, quarterback, 2002

## Mid-American Conference Defensive Player of the Year
- Max Yates, linebacker, 2001
- Johnathan Goddard, defensive end, 2004

## Motor City Bowl MVP
- Chad Pennington, quarterback, 1998
- Doug Chapman, running back, 1999
- Byron Leftwich, quarterback, 2000

## Motor City Bowl Defensive MVP
- B.J. Cohen, defensive end, 1997
- John Grace, linebacker, 1998
- Giradie Mercer, defensive tackle, 1999
- Michael Owens, linebacker, 2000

## NCAA Top VIII Award
- Chad Pennington, quarterback, 1999

## Nissan Frontier National Player of the Week
- Byron Leftwich, quarterback, Nov. 17, 2001

## Paul Warfield Award
- Randy Moss, wide receiver, 1997

## *Playboy* Preseason All-America
- Randy Moss, wide receiver, 1997
- Steve Sciullo, tackle, 2002

## Davey O'Brien National Quarterback Award Finalist
- Chad Pennington, 1998
- Chad Pennington, 1999

## Senior Bowl
- Chad Pennington, quarterback, 1999 (MVP)
- John Wade, center, 1997

## Vern Smith Mid-American Conference MVP Award
- Randy Moss, wide receiver, 1997
- Chad Pennington, quarterback, 1999
- Byron Leftwich, quarterback, 2001
- Byron Leftwich, quarterback, 2002

## Sports Network All-America First Team
- B.J. Cohen, defensive end, 1996
- Aaron Ferguson, guard, 1996
- Billy Lyon, defensive tackle, 1996
- Randy Moss, wide receiver, 1996

## Sports Network All-America Second Team
- Eric Kresser, quarterback, 1996
- Chris Hanson, punter, 1996
- Larry McCloud, linebacker, 1996
- Randy Moss, kick returner, 1996

## Sports Network All-America Third Team
- Tim Openlander, kicker, 1996

## All-Southern Conference
- B.J. Cohen, defensive end, 1996
- Melvin Cunningham, cornerback, 1996
- Aaron Ferguson, guard, 1996
- Chris Hanson, punter, 1996
- Eric Kresser, quarterback, 1996
- Billy Lyon, defensive tackle, 1996
- Tim Martin, wide receiver, 1996
- Larry McCloud, linebacker, 1996
- Randy Moss, wide receiver, 1996
- Tim Openlander, kicker, 1996
- Brian Reed, guard, 1996
- Scott Smythe, safety, 1996
- Jermaine Swafford, linebacker, 1996
- Erik Thomas, running back, 1996
- John Wade, center, 1996
- Mike Webb, tackle, 1996
- Jamie Wilson, tackle, 1996

## *Sports Illustrated* All-Bowl Team
- Michael Owens, linebacker, 2000
- Byron Leftwich, quarterback, 2001

### *The Sporting News* Freshman All-America
- Randy Moss, wide receiver, 1996
- Josh Davis, wide receiver, 2001

### Thorpe Award Finalist
- Rogers Beckett, safety, 1999

### Johnny Unitas Golden Arm Award Finalist
- Chad Pennington, quarterback, 1999

### Walter Camp All-America
- B.J. Cohen, defensive end, 1996
- Melvin Cunningham, cornerback, 1996
- Aaron Ferguson, guard, 1996
- Billy Lyon, defensive tackle, 1996
- Randy Moss, wide receiver, 1996
- Jermaine Swafford, linebacker, 1996
- Randy Moss, wide receiver, 1997
- Johnathan Goddard, defensive end, 2004

### Woodson Award Finalist
- Randy Moss, wide receiver, 1997

Bob and Elsie Pruett, children and grandchildren. *Photo courtesy Elsie Pruett.*

# I N D E X

Courtesy Marshall University; photograph by Rick Haye.

**Bill Chastain** was a sportswriter and columnist for *The Tampa Tribune* for over twelve years. He currently works for MLB.com covering the Tampa Bay Devil Rays baseball team. He is the author of *The Steve Spurrier Story: From Heisman to Head Ballcoach, Payne at Pinehurst: The Greatest U.S. Open Ever,* and *Steel Dynasty: The Team that Changed the NFL.* He lives in Tampa with his wife Patti and their two children, Carly and Kel.

## SPONSORS

*The publishers and the family of Coach Bobby Pruett here express their deep gratitude to the following sponsors who helped make this book possible.*

### Coaches circle
(Gifts of $3,000 or more)

*Buck Harless, International Industries, Inc.; Jim and Verna Gibson, Sarasota, Florida; First Sentry Bank, Huntington and Barboursville; Tim Haymaker, Lexington, Kentucky; Selby Wellman, Raleigh, North Carolina.*

### Captains Circle
(Gifts of $1.000-$2000)

*Sim Fryson; Frank Gaddy and Alex Vence and the Huntington Arcade; Grace Associates, LLC, Editors & Publishers;* The Huntington Herald-Dispatch; *Friends of Coal.*

### Fans Circle
(Gifts of $500-$900)

*James C. Hamer, Kenova; Richard Lewis, Charleston; an anonymous fan from Barboursville.*